PR   Lewis
6023   The witch and the
E955   priest
W5

~~Evelyn Oronos~~   AUG 4 71
~~549-94-7429~~

NOV 3 '71   ~~Martha Sammon~~
~~481-62-94~~

NOV 8 '72 ~~M. Hamlin 570-64-8647~~

PR   Lewis, Hilda Winifred, 1896-
6023   The witch and the priest [by] Hilda
E955   Lewis.   New York, McKay [1970]
W5   304 p. 21cm.

        Includes bibliography.

        1. Flower, Margaret, d. 1618--Fiction.
2. Flower, Philippa, d. 1618--Fiction. I.
Title.

The Witch and the Priest

HILDA LEWIS

The Witch and the Priest

DAVID McKAY COMPANY, INC.

New York

THE WITCH AND THE PRIEST

First American edition, 1970

For

ALFRED T. G. BLACKMORE

FOREWORD

In 1618, Margaret and Philippa Flower were tried at Lincoln for witchcraft. On their own confession they were found guilty and hanged. The Witchcraft Tomb in the church of St. Mary, at Bottesford in Leicestershire, still bears witness to their deeds.

An account of their trial is to be found in a pamphlet entitled:

The wonderful Discoverie of the Witchcrafts of MARGARET and PHILIP FLOWER, Daughters of JOAN FLOWER, neere BEVER CASTLE; executed at Lincolne, March XI, 1618; who were specially arraigned and condemned before Sir HENRY HOBART and Sir EDWARD BROMLEY, Judges of Assize, for confessing themselves Actors in the Destruction of HENRY lord ROSSE with their damnable Practices against others the children of the Right Honourable FRANCIS earle of RUTLAND. Together with the severall Examinations and Confessions of ANNE BAKER, JOAN WILLIMOTT, and ELLEN GREENE, Witches in Leicestershire.

Printed at London by G. Eld and J. Barnes, dwelling in the Longe Walke, neere Christ Church. 1619.

The casting of the spells as described in this book follows their confessions; and the celebrations of the Witches' Sabbath are described in the confessions of witches throughout Christendom. Whether the casting of these spells actually brought about the desired end; whether the witches actually flew or drugs lent them the illusion of flying, does not matter. What matters is that the witches themselves believed in their supernatural powers.

And so the dark tale unfolds according to its own dark laws.

7

The law against witches does not prove that there be any: but it punishes the malice of those people that use such means to take away men's lives. If one should profess that by turning his hat thrice and crying out *buz* he could take away a man's life, though in truth he could do no such thing, yet this were a just law made by the State that, whoever should turn his hat thrice and cry *buz* with the intention to take away a man's life, shall be put to death.

John Selden. 1584–1654.
The Table-Talk.

The land is full of witches. I have hanged five and twenty of them. . . . They have on their bodies divers strange marks at which, as some of them have confessed, the Devil sucks their blood, for they have foresworn God, renounced their baptism and vowed their services to the Devil.

Sir Edmund Anderson.
Lord Chief Justice.
1530–1605.

Chapter One

> . . . to my beloved sister, Hester Davenport, widow of
> this parish; and, upon her death, the sum aforesaid, to be
> used for the building and maintaining of a hospice for four
> poor women of this parish . . .

THE Reverend Samuel Fleming put down his pen.

Now why had he done that? There were bequests more
worthy of his charity—a sum to maintain some poor scholar
at Cambridge, his own university; a legacy to some poor
parson, heaven knew they were hard put to it, some of them,
to keep body and soul together. Learning, piety—were not
these more important than the comfort of old women who
could always beg a crust or scrape a few vegetables from the
ground or find an armful of kindling in the woods?

He moved restless, knowing his answer and not relishing it.

No. There was nothing so pitiful, so utterly helpless as
old women—if they were ugly enough or poor enough;
nobody in such need of succour. Children threw stones after
them; and parents, far from checking their brats, called
names after them harder than stones, more death-dealing than
stones; calling . . . witch.

Witch. The word had haunted him this twelvemonth, a
burden upon his heart, ever since the women had gone to
their death. . . .

Hand still upon the paper, he heard the tapping of Hester's
heels along the flagged passage; even before her knock fell
upon the door he had thrust the writing into a drawer—Hester
fretted sufficiently about his altered looks without a reminder
in the shape of a will.

Her head still dark beneath the muslin cap came round the
door; brother and sister looked at each other. It was hard to
believe there was but a few years between them. But, though
his hair had whitened completely this last year, the likeness
between them was clear—the good forehead, the eyes kindly
yet shrewd repeating the promise of mouth and chin.

"Samuel," she said, sharp yet tender, too, "your thoughts run on the matter again! Why must you torment yourself? It makes an old man of you before your time."

"I have passed my threescore years and ten . . ." he reminded her, rueful.

"What of it?" she asked stoutly, pitying his frail looks. "Last year your hair was dark as my own—or almost. And you carried yourself upright as any man. And now . . . now . . . Samuel, they were witches." She nodded vigorously, "They were witches all three!"

"Joan Flower never confessed," he reminded her, sombre. "With her dying breath she protested her innocence."

"What did you expect? She denied. But God spoke." She saw how he looked about the pleasant room as though, even now, the quiet air held some imprint of that dreadful day. "As for the daughters," she said, very firm, "nothing could be clearer; they confessed—who should know that better than you? They confessed everything."

He sighed, remembering Margaret all tears and terror; remembering Philippa all brag and bravado. Yes, it was true. Joan Flower had been a witch; and she had brought them—the two young girls—to the Devil. She would have gone to the gallows with them, had she not been lucky enough to die first.

What was it, he asked himself for the hundredth time, that brought men and women to the Devil? They lived poor and wretched, blind and diseased often as not; and in the end they died on the gallows.

He raised his troubled head. "What is this power the Devil has so that men and women willingly renounce their part in God? Is it that God's servants are not so zealous as the Devil's? It is a question I should ask—indeed, *must* ask. I am a priest and the women were of my flock. I knew Joan Flower when her goodman was alive and there were no tales either of whoring or of witchcraft. Yes, and I baptized her daughters. A decent woman, so I thought; not-over devout; but coming now and then to church and bringing her girls with her."

"Yes, she made some show of virtue," Hester told him. "Whether to shield her daughters from her ugly ways, or to shield herself from their eyes, who can say? When the girls left home she was not ashamed to show herself in her true colours. She came to church when it pleased her—which was seldom enough! It was then the tales began to go about. Oh no, not of witchcraft but of the shocking life she led—of the men she welcomed at all hours; Peate and the others."

"I rebuked her," Samuel Fleming said. "I preached against her from the pulpit. But—" and he sighed, "much good that did, seeing she was not there to hear."

"The village heard; and it turned its back on her," Hester reminded him. "But much she cared, snug in her cottage carousing with her men."

"I was not zealous enough. I should have gone into her house. I should have wrestled with her soul."

"You did go."

"Once. Once only." And he sighed, remembering how he had allowed himself to be driven away. Oh, she had been polite enough, dusting a stool that he might sit. But hostility had streamed from her, pushing him out. He had felt not a priest but an intruder. He had not gone there again.

Even when the tales began to change their character—that was after the girls came home—still he had done little enough . . . until it was too late. He had barely listened; it was all too fantastic. The Flower women were whores; but they were not witches.

"You know," he told Hester now, "I smiled—actually smiled, God forgive me—at the notion of this quiet and peaceful parish of mine suddenly producing a crop of witches. I forgot there were other peaceful parishes where people went quietly about their business; and then, suddenly——"

"—the witches about their ugly work!" Hester finished. "Pendle and Chelmsford, St. Oses, and Warboys, and Derby—" she counted on her fingers, "oh and more than I can remember. Do not trouble your heart, Samuel. The hangings of last year are justified. The confessions fitted into each other like a neat piece of dovetailing. They were guilty; all of them guilty; beyond any doubt, guilty."

But for all that he was troubled still. He looked about him; the fine calf bindings of his books, the good rugs upon the polished floor, the rich smell of his tobacco, could not reassure him. This room, he thought, would never be free of the women. Always they would be here, coming between him and his work, between him and his prayers, tormenting him with their accusations.

"They were brought to justice. Their own tongues proclaimed it!" Hester cried out, passionate at the care in his face.

"But . . . were they?" he asked, insistent. "Suppose they believed they were able to do mischief by witchcraft but were unable to do mischief? After all, the King himself, that mighty witch-hunter, even he has his doubts—and says so. Once he exhorted all men—and in particular such of us as are priests and justices—to be zealous against witches. Now he exhorts us to caution. Fear and malice on the part of the accusers, too-hasty decision on the part of the judges—these King James thinks have been too long a canker in the body of the State."

"That comes well from him!" She went over and took from a shelf a copy of *De Demonologia* and put it down, open, before him.

Samuel turned the pages. "It is, I suppose," he said, "the most damning tract against witchcraft. And yet—how long before the King declares there's no such thing as witches at all? He's honest. If he thinks fit to alter his mind, he'll say so."

"One can hardly quarrel with that . . . I suppose," she said thoughtfully.

'All very well for the King! But how about those that obey his command? In particular, how about priests and magistrates and judges? And how about those poor souls who have already suffered under the King's justice?"

And it was at him again—a dog at his throat—the old question.

'Hester," he said; and again, "Hester. There is a question I ask myself and go on asking . . . and can find no answer. How if the poor hanged creatures were nothing but desperately unhappy; a little crazy, maybe with their miseries? Or—how if they were poor, merely; and ugly and ignorant and uncouth? That—and nothing more?"

Hester seated herself at the table, spreading the skirts of her silk gown.

"They were guilty," she said. "Why else would they confess to crimes they never did? They knew well enough confession would bring them to the gallows."

"It is not hard," he told her sadly, "to think of a reason—to think of any number of reasons. Fear of the gallows to begin with; and a most desperate hope to escape it by a show of penitence. Or pride; inordinate pride driving them to confess to crimes they never committed. Or belief, perhaps; belief that they can, indeed, alter the laws of Nature. Or else hopelessness; knowing that truth in one, cannot stand against the lies of the many. How many, many times has evidence been found to be false? More than one witch—so-called—has been hanged by the lying tongue of a spiteful child that knew not what it did.

Oh Hester! Magistrates and judges alike are godfearing men . . . yet innocent folk have hanged. Once we accept the fact of witchcraft, we must accept, also, the confession. I, myself, would have gone on believing in both to the end of my days had I not had a hand in the death of those women. Was I a righteous judge or a credulous old man? It is a question I ask . . . and go on asking."

"The responsibility was not yours." She put out a hand to comfort him. "You did not judge the women. You were one of the magistrates—and only one of them. You examined; you did not judge. You found there was a case to answer and you sent them forward to the Assize. The judge that hanged them was the Chief Justice himself!"

"That should comfort me," he said, "but . . . it does not, it does not. Try as I may I cannot shift responsibility from where it belongs—my own shoulders. Others may acquit me; my own heart—never. For the plain truth is this. The trouble began long before they were brought before me as a magistrate. And I should have known it. I should have dealt with them as a priest. Before everything I am a servant of God. If I had gone again to Joan Flower; if I had striven again and again—might not everything have been different? But, having rebuked her, I was content to forget her, yes, even when the tales named her not only whore, but witch.

"Hester, there is a question I ask myself, ask and cannot

leave asking. Have I been a bad shepherd, not loving all men equally, nor reckoning their souls of equal worth?"

"You are no angel," she told him, drily, "to love all men equally, nor are all souls of equal worth! No, do not argue the point! Can you pretend that the soul of any one of those wicked women is worth the soul of—let us say—Francis?" And she looked at him very straight.

She had hit her nail shrewdly upon the head; he was forced to admit it. For he loved Francis Manners above all men.

"Francis!" he said softly. The lines of his face relaxed and she was glad, knowing him released, for a little while, of his burden, as chin on hand, his thoughts went back to other days, more innocent days.

'I remember so well the day he was born and the joybells pealing. I baptized him; I carried him in my arms when he was sick, played with him when he was well. I loved him as a man loves his own son. And now Francis is the sixth earl. Four earls I have seen . . . four earls. But then . . . forty years. It's a long, long time."

His thoughts went back remembering Edward, the uncle of Francis, who had first brought him to Belvoir. Students at Cambridge together—King's men both and good friends— though one had been heir to a great earldom and the other a simple scholar. When Edward succeeded to the title he'd invited his friend—already a fellow of King's and beginning to be known as a subtle disputant—to be his own chaplain.

Life was good those days to the two young men; up at the Castle, down at the Rectory—for Edward had given him the living of Bottesford—each busy about his duties; and plenty of time for riding and hunting and talking.

And then Edward died—young, like so many of his family; and his brother had taken the title. But John had not long enjoyed his dignities. By the end of that same year he, too, was dead, leaving his two young sons Roger eleven and Francis eight.

Delightful lads; good to look upon, upright and forthright like all the Manners. But even then there had been a difference between them. Roger weighted with his new dignities—eleven years old and an earl!—had shown a clear, hard pride. But

Francis, ah Francis. There had always been a simplicity about him; the simplicity that comes not from a great name but from a great soul. And that simplicity had been his undoing.

Samuel Fleming sighed deeply.

How much of that candour, that trust in men had come from his own fostering? He had himself strengthened the boy's innate gentleness and trustingness, holding before the child the greatest of all Models. Had he made Francis too vulnerable?

"Francis," he told Hester now. "From the very first so sweet, so trusting a nature. And I—God forgive me if I was wrong—strove to keep him so. I should have remembered his great position and the jealousies of men. I should have striven to make him hard; hard and shrewd. Instead I have made him vulnerable."

"Francis is not vulnerable. He is strong. How many men could suffer what he has suffered and kindness not turn to poison within him?"

"Yet he is changed," Samuel said, sadly. "So old and cold and shut within himself. Only forty and no more joy in life!"

"He will come back to his own nature," Hester promised. "And joy will come with it."

"A little time ago goodwill to all men shone from him like a light."

"It was like warming your hands at a good fire." Hester nodded.

They fell to silence both of them, remembering how the young life that had begun so fair grew overcast—and overcast indeed. Yet Francis had borne it all with a perfect patience.

He had married young and death had robbed him of his bride. And though he had married again to raise up sons, and though Cecilia was loving and kind to his motherless little girl, the death of his first love had all-but overthrown him.

And then, a few years later, brother followed wife into the grave; and not the earldom with all its honours, all its riches could comfort him. Yet, this, too, he had taken with courage, carrying his grief in silence, bearing himself kindly and showing himself serviceable to all—rich and poor alike.

And then came two little sons to bring light and

laughter to his sad house. But the new life he had built with such courage he had not been let to enjoy. He had been made to suffer as few men suffer. Still he had borne it with a most sweet courage, comforting Cecilia and hiding his own heart's pain; scanting none of the duties of his great calling and taking all from the hand of God, not knowing it had come from the hand of the Devil.

It had all begun over six years ago—the winter of sixteen twelve. Henry, the elder boy, had peaked a little. "It is nothing," Cecilia said. "A childish ailment. With the spring it will pass."

But neither with spring nor summer had it passed. Instead, the first of the fits had fallen upon the four-year old. And then fit following fit, coming quicker, coming stronger, lasting longer . . . and the frightened child growing daily weaker, and the physicians unable to find cause or cure.

Through the long summer days the child had wasted to his death. Little Henry with his sturdy limbs and his rosy cheeks —what had he to do with the wasted shell they had lowered into the grave?

Samuel Fleming sighed deeply. He had been glad, almost, to see the tormented child quiet at last. He had thought, God has taken him. Now there is neither hope nor fear. Now there is peace for us at last.

Well, he had been wrong!

Quite suddenly the sickness had struck again—struck Catharine, beloved child of her father's first marriage; struck the baby Francis, doubly treasured because he was the only son now—Lord Roos, heir to the earldom.

Catharine had thrown off her sickness, the wild, headstrong little girl. But the baby had followed his brother into the grave.

Still Francis had borne himself patiently, not complaining against God nor blaming any man. He had gone to London as usual to attend the King at Newmarket and Whitehall. Everything according to custom . . . except that a little coffin had gone with him for burial at Westminster.

No-one at court—even those who knew him well—had guessed at the depths of his sorrow, except the King, perhaps.

James, for all his foolishness, had an understanding heart; sometimes his foolishness was lit by gleams a wise man might envy.

But fate had not done with Francis yet. On his return home the sickness struck again—the strange, dire sickness, sparing his wife as little as himself; as though God had meant to put an end to him and his family altogether.

It was then that the whispering changed its tone. Now it was no longer satisfied to call the Flower women *whore*; it called them *witch*. And it was then he should have listened, he their pastor; and listened all the more since Francis refused. Francis, in those days, believed well of all men. That any of his people—his own people to whom heart and purse were ever open—should wish him evil, was a thing not to be considered. So he had continued steadfast in his sickness, bearing all with patience and trusting in God.

Samuel Fleming rose and paced restless; catching Hester's worried look he said sadly, "It was that—being brought face-to-face with the wickedness of his own people—broke Francis at the last."

"Men like Francis are not broken; they are stronger for their grief. He will come back. You will see."

"God grant it!" he said. Francis may return, he thought, but I shall not see it, not with these mortal eyes.

Hester went over and stood by him. "Francis will come home and you will see him. Certainly he will come home to his own place and to those that love him."

He turned his head that she might not see his grief and stared out over the bright garden. Francis will not come; not yet; not for a long while yet . . . if ever. He has fled from the great house bereft of the children. . . . *Yet come home, come home, Francis. You have wandered enough. You have turned your back on Christian lands, your only companions black savages, unbaptized* . . .

And, standing there, sending his heart out to Francis, he fancied he knew what the reply would be. *Black savages are more white, more Christian than my own baptized people of Bottesford.*

But still he went on beseeching. *We are lonely without you, castle and village. Come home, Francis, and beget yourself an heir.*

"It is time Francis came home and begot himself an heir!"

Hester said suddenly with the trick she had of speaking his thoughts.

"I pray for it night and day." He fetched a deep sigh, thinking, how, in the good days before the trouble there had always been visitors up at the Castle; not only the King and his friends but wits and scholars and poets. Now the great house seemed empty as a tomb. "A man needs to rub up his wits," he told Hester sadly. "Mine are more than a little dusty."

How lonely he is, she thought, watching the restless play of the fingers. Loneliness makes a man restless. . . .

"Dear Samuel, will you not walk abroad a little this fine day?" she asked, knowing that, as always, his sad heart must lead him to his church; and God would, for a little, take away his loneliness.

"Why yes!" he said and picked up his hat and cloak. He stepped into the wide flagged passage and through the kitchens; it was the quicker way; and besides, he loved the wide cool rooms with the great ovens and the scrubbed tables and the bright pans.

Jennet, the young maid, lifted a face all rosy from the fire and smiled. "Are you wanting the Mistress?" she asked bobbing to her curtsey. He shook his head returning her smile and stepped out-of-doors.

Spring was warm in the rectory garden; he could feel life stirring in the black, moist earth, and in the bare espaliers on the old yellow walls. He crossed the planks that led from the garden across the little river and into the churchyard. The smell of violets went with him all the way.

It was quiet within the church of St. Mary the Virgin; chilly, too, after the springtime garden. Cold struck upward from the stone floor, through to the bones of the old man. He knelt, a little clumsy, to thank God, as he always did, that his work had fallen in so fair a spot. He rose and looked about him, loving this church of his.

Gold candlelight upon gold alabaster; and men and women lying here in the dignity of their last sleep. Even that frail countess, who fearing childbirth, had chosen to die instead, lay there, the fruit ungathered from the womb. Yes, even she,

20

with her sick childish face and her thin body—save for the rounded belly—partook of that same high dignity of death.

The candles threw a warm light upon the altar and upon the rough-hewn figure of Robert de Roos, watching over his buried heart. His body lay elsewhere, but his heart rested in this beloved place.

He turned to consider the empty space on the south side of the chancel. Here the child Henry lay. "It is very lonely for a little boy," Catharine had said with one of her rare flashes of imagination. "Why did my father take Francis to lie in Westminster? Now it is lonely for them both."

"They are not lonely any more," he had said to comfort this curious child already half-woman. "They are God's lambs and they lie in his bosom."

"Lambs like better to frisk and play," she had said and had turned abruptly and left him lest he should see tears in the large, dark eyes. A proud girl hiding her wild heart.

Francis, too, would sleep here one day; already the mason had made his drawings for the tomb. Samuel did not like them very much—a great stone canopy arched high above the figure of Francis lying between his two wives; the great folds of their skirts overflowed on each side, engulfing him like the waves of the sea. The little boys knelt at their father's feet, and, at his head, Catharine.

It was all too large, too pretentious; and it was too ugly, too sad—each little boy carried a skull—this dwelling upon death.

But though it was best for Francis to turn his back upon the past, Samuel himself could not forget it. He never entered this church of his where the child lay and where the Flower women had once knelt, without asking himself how he had failed? How much was his own fault? And lately, and more insistent than ever, Were the women truly witches?

It was at him again, the question that had haunted him this twelvemonth; and, again he answered it.

They had been witches if ever witches existed. And that witches did exist was beyond doubt. *Thou shalt not suffer a witch to live.* The Scriptures had it plain.

But he could not comfort himself that way.

These were the ancient scriptures of the Jews. Men had learnt mercy since then . . . or had they?

He turned from the altar and paced the stone flags of the aisle; empty pews stretched to left and right.

If there were no witches, how was it that cattle had been curiously slain; and men, women and children died unnaturally and horribly? If these things had not been brought about by witchcraft, then they had happened through human wickedness. Witchcraft or poison—the evil-doer deserved to die. Murder was still murder.

And what of those who willed evil; who employed no means but an evil spirit—not the familiar spirit, but their own wicked will? The will to slay. Then such a man deserved to die also whether he had actually brought his wickedness about or not. Surely he who has murdered in his heart is as guilty as he who has done the deed!

He turned again to face the altar.

Spite and evil; these things are never harmless. They are essences set free to work destruction. And yet, if for ill-wishing alone, a man deserved to die, there wouldn't be enough gallows in England to hold them all! Besides, though the will to slay is evil, it is still not so evil as the deed. For before the deed is done a man may be drawn to repent; but the victim dead, God Himself cannot undo it.

The deed is done. A little child goes down in fear and pain into the grave. . . . Henry would be eleven now; a comely boy; a steady eye; his father's noble spirit. That had been clear in him, young as he was. And the other child, an infant; scarce more than a babe at the breast when the trouble began. Six years old when he had died. He would be eight now or thereabouts.

So much beauty, so much promise lost! If the children had died by human wickedness—whether by witchcraft or any other means—then one need not lament unduly upon what charge the murderers had died.

He shook his head at that piece of sophistry. When the law takes away a man's life, then everyone must be clear about the reason.

Yet he went on arguing with himself.

If the witches had not died when they did, maybe Francis and Cecilia, yes and Catharine, too, would be lying here beside this child.

But even that could not quiet his conscience.

The only ones that could speak as to their innocence were the women themselves. And they had spoken—the mother denying; the daughters confessing. What had led Margaret and Philippa to embrace a shameful death? Had it been the Devil betraying his own? Or God in his infinite mercy condemning the flesh that the soul might live?

But . . . suppose they had been innocent?

His heart began to race again so that he was forced to lean more heavily upon the altar rail.

Had their tongues been loosed by the cruelty of man to man? Had they said anything—anything at all—for a little sleep, a little respite from the continual questions? He had heard of such things . . .

. . . In other places, perhaps. But not here; not here in Bottesford where he sat on the Bench with Eresby and Manners and Pelham—good Christians all.

Not that, oh God, not that!

He went carefully upon his knees. A year ago he had been certain of the justice they had received; now he was no longer sure. Innocent people had been hanged before! Dear Christ, show him the truth; the truth about the women in whose death he had played his part.

He rose stiffly and, on his way out, paused for a moment at the place where his brother lay buried—Abraham, scholar and wit dying unexpectedly, dying peacefully here, before all the trouble began. Would to God he himself had died then! God grant, at least, that he also lay his tired bones in this dear place! He shut the heavy door behind him. His feet took him without his knowing through the churchyard and over the little stone bridge he himself had built—a nearer way for people to come into church—and through the marketplace and along the lane where, the track disappearing into a copse, the witches' cottage still stood.

Its windows were broken now, where the villagers had thrust their billhooks, and weeds were growing high as the

23

low chimney; there was grass springing in the thatch. No-one came near it now, not even in broad daylight. Evil clung about it, they said. You would never know when you mightn't turn to face a wicked ghost. That was all nonsense of course. And yet, even in this bright spring morning there was something forbidding about the place.

His feet went stumbling upon the trailing bushes and he put out a hand to steady himself. He found himself staring into the red eyes of a cat—a white and spiteful cat that seemed in two minds whether it should fly at his throat or run back into the bushes.

He all-but crossed himself.

Chapter Two

He all-but crossed himself; then, remembering the King's changing views on the subject of witches and that a priest must lead his flock against superstition, in secret as well as in public, his arm fell. But all the same, *Rutterkin*, he challenged, with the name of Joan Flower's familiar. The cat was no longer there. Had it slunk away so quickly that his old eyes had not been good enough to follow it? Or had it disappeared—by magic?

And, suddenly, he found himself calling Joan Flower's name in the deserted place. And now the question that had tormented him this twelvemonth burst forth. *Did we wrong you bitterly, you and your two daughters? Or were you rightly judged? Tell me. Tell me, Joan Flower.*

There was no answer. He called again, more urgently. *Were you a witch, Joan Flower? Were you a witch?*

And now he heard a sound like the sighing of a long-dead voice . . . or perhaps it was the sighing of his own heart.

You judged me.

And suddenly she was there—Joan Flower as he had seen her last—dark hair streaked with grey, falling ragged about her face; and that face twisted to one side in a dreadful grin as she lay dying of the fit that had stricken her down.

And now he remembered the first time he had seen her— thirty years ago; and how he had stared to find so exotic a creature in his remote village. A tall young woman with a high bosom and a fine carriage. Sixteen—though she'd looked older —when she came limping into Bottesford on her blistered feet. Come from beyond Derby; and before that from London. Brought up in a gentleman's house she'd said when he questioned her fine speech. Her father? She didn't know—never set eyes on him. A foreign gentleman her mother said; Italian or Spanish or Scots. Her mother? A servant; a good servant; clever with her needle. So they'd kept the child; spoiled her above a little. She'd been let to play, at times, with the little lady of the house—an only child and lonely. When she was old enough, the young lady had taken her to be her maid—that was where she'd picked up her fine speech. They'd turned her away at the last and she not yet fifteen. Why? Her mother was dead and the young visiting gentlemen too free with their glances. . . .

That was *her* tale, the Bottesford gossips said, resenting from the first *that foreigner* with her fine looks and her fine ways and her fine speech.

John Flower, honest fellow, had seen her and fancied her; married her, too. Paid for what he might have had for nothing—so the gossip went. A bad woman, a bad wife, a foreigner.

Well, as to the truth of all that he didn't know. Gossip had held its tongue while her husband lived; John Flower had a strong arm—and knew how to use it. But certainly she'd looked foreign enough with her great dark eyes, and the proud shoulders, and the black hair that streamed backwards beneath its scarlet riband. What decent married woman of Bottesford would go about capless and all tied about with scarlet ribands? As for John Flower, maybe he had made a bad bargain. A silent sad man—when the drink was not in him—he'd said nothing. But for all her brave looks there'd been no sweetness in her face, not even when she'd sent him, the rector, one of her sidling, sidelong glances. Yes, she'd tried that game upon him, too, taking him for one of those lustful parsons, of which God knew, there were enough and to spare; not shepherds but wolves, ready to destroy the lambs entrusted to their care. She'd been all invitation and no kindness; men should beware of her he had thought, his own heart-beat a little quickened. For others had found a sweetness in her; even in little Bottesford she'd had her fill of lovers.

And now again she was fixing him with those same eyes; but they were mournful eyes, holding all the sorrow of the world. But even as he looked, they were beginning to change; the look he knew was coming back to them; the wanton look. And . . . yes, she was growing younger; but for all that not so very young; a gap where a tooth was missing.

So she had looked when she went up to Belvoir more than

ten years ago, to ask work for her daughters. How old had she been? Thirtytwo? Thirtyfive? Her elder daughter Margaret was close on fifteen.

"That day," he said, "was the beginning of everything."

"It began before that," she said and put a finger to her forehead as though to smooth, still further, time's marks. "It began the day I understood my daughters were growing up . . . and I growing old. But," she said, and there was a sweetness in her now, so that he began to understand, a little, why men had loved her, "you are not so young yourself, priest; and it blows cold. Come within doors."

The door gave at her touch and he followed her in.

There was a fire in the deserted cottage, the hearth swept. He had not expected that. The white cat lay stretched along the warm hearth. Now it sprang up and spat; she quieted it in an unknown tongue.

It was not uncomfortable in the dark little room. For all its musty smell, it was clean enough, with fresh rushes strewn upon the earth floor. Some rogue or beggar not knowing the tale, he thought, had sheltered for the night.

"No," she said, "such gentry would not leave all clean, let alone make it so. It is the wandering spirit returning to its earthly home." She smiled into his startled eyes. "The eyes of a ghost see clear through flesh and blood to the thoughts within." She stooped to the hearth, holding her fingers to the blaze; he could see clean through them to the glowing wood. "The old and the young may see us sometimes; with them the veil between this world and the next is thin." And again he glimpsed the sweetness in her.

There was a stool each side of the hearth; she took one and motioned him to the other. Between them the white cat stretched and stared at him with spiteful eyes.

"It is strange," she said. "A priest of God and the ghost of a witch. Yet here we sit together like old friends—we that were never friends in the flesh. But why should we not be friends?" Her hand went out as though to touch him, but stayed short. Yet for all that his flesh crept with the cold. "Though you helped to hang me, who shall say you were wrong? But oh priest, priest, the cruelty of men!"

"And women?" he asked remembering the bitter evil she had done. "What of women?"

She sighed; on the breath of her sighing he felt again the coldness of her presence and drew a little nearer to the fire.

"The cruelty of men and the vanity of women. Between those points, priest, the sun spins. The vanity of women—" she said again, "it brought me to the Master. Growing old—it was a thing I could not endure."

"There is nothing to fear in age."

"Not for you, priest. But for me."

"It could bring its own beauty."

"To you," she said, gently. "But not to me; not to my sort of woman."

He sighed, knowing it to be true. And yet, that day she had gone up to the castle she had looked young enough; younger than most women of her class that toiled in the fields and in the kitchen. "Yet you were comely," he said. "And what is a wrinkle here and there?"

"That is a man's question; and his own eyes answer him. As for me—the day I saw those wrinkles, it was the beginning of the end. I had to keep my looks, priest; they were my livelihood; my only livelihood when John Flower died."

"And before he died?" Samuel Fleming asked.

"Honest John had a heavy hand and I walked carefully though not always righteously, for I was sick of supping always at the one dish; and that dish lacking salt or savour. And then he died, good John, honest John and left me without a penny piece and my two girls to fend for. So I was glad enough to take to my trade. And why not? I loved men and they loved me."

He made a little movement of recoil and she laughed.

"We are in duty bound to love all men," she said and there was a look of mischief about her; he could easily believe her to be of the Devil.

"I loved men—but not women. Nor did any woman love me. They could not forgive me my face—such as it was."

That was true; it was her looks that had started all the trouble. Women would come to him with their tales; and every tale ending with complaints about her looks . . . A man's woman and foreign with it, her good looks a gift from the Devil—how else did she keep them? A woman's a hag at thirtyfive; but she? Certainly her look of youth came from the Devil!

"And yet," she said, "I did love women, too . . . once. I'd nurse them. I was good at simples; it was a knowledge I had of my mother. But I'd get no thanks. They'd drink my possets and all the time they'd watch me out of the corners of their eyes. Or while I'd sweep the room, the good wife in her bed would stare as though any minute I'd fly away on her broomstick. Oh yes! They'd enjoy the fruits of my labour—and call me witch for my pains. But I was no witch then; no more than you, yourself!

I'd never so much as thought of a pact with the Master, why should I? I had all I wanted—men; and food; and wine; a new kerchief or buckles for my shoes. Not much perhaps by a lady's reckoning, but enough.

And then, one day, quite suddenly, I understood these good things must come to an end—and the time not far-distant." Her rueful smile showed the gap where she had lost a tooth. "Soon no man would want me. That was the day I took the Devil for my Master.

A hot summer day it was; and I in this very room. There was a hollyhock tapping against the window and a thrush singing *Be quick, be quick*. Or maybe it was my own heart singing because I was waiting for my lover. No, priest, never look at me like that! I've had men; but when I say I loved them, I meant in the way of trade. I've never had but one love."

"Peate!" he said, remembering the scandal. Peate's wife had stirred up the trouble, poor, stupid Ann Peate, pitting herself against this quick, bright creature. Yet—as in the old fable—the quick, bright thing had lost; the slow stupid creature had won.

She nodded. "He was my true love. At least *I* was true. A woman needs the comfort of a man's body and Flower had been dead above five year. And what was he at the best of times? A clod, scarce warmer living than dead! Often I'd thought of helping him where he belonged—clod among clods. But I never harmed him."

"To wish him dead—was that no harm? I think he knew. I think he was glad not to get well again."

She shrugged. "You think it was wicked of me to take Peate; to take all the men who'd come—and there were plenty, I'll own. But what harm? I'd give them happiness, adventure, excitement . . . all the things their wives couldn't give."

"And what did you take from their wives?" he asked, grave.

"Nothing. Or their men wouldn't have come to me. Those women! They had their homes; they had their men and the work of their hands. They had a safety I hadn't got . . . *a safety I hadn't got.*" She laughed a little. At least he could not be sure whether she laughed or cried—there was a wailing note to the sound.

"Well!" and she was brisk again. "There I was waiting for Peate. And then I heard his feet come along the path.

The steps went round the house. And then I heard a voice; a woman's voice; Margaret's voice. A child I'd thought her. I should have known better. No woman's a child at fifteen. Her voice was high as a fiddlestring; a woman's voice when the flesh is stirred. *No!* she cried out. *No!* But it was clear that she meant *Yes*.

Peate laughed. I knew that laugh. Tender; enough to melt the marrow in your bones. I was listening, all soft and silly with love. I don't know how long it was before I understood that he was playing me false with another woman; and that woman my daughter. Perhaps it was a minute; perhaps an hour. The bitter heart has no truck with time.

I started up then; I went to the door. But I didn't open it. No need to look through any door to know where those two were going; no need to guess, neither, what they were going to do together in the darkness of the wood.

I came back to my place and I sat there among the ashes and I held my head in my two hands. And my heart was broken. And I never once thought of Margaret—not as Margaret my daughter, my child to be protected. I thought only of the woman who'd taken my lover.

I'd lost my lover to a younger woman.

I sat there rocking myself backwards and forwards trying to think my way out of it. But nothing would come into my head save that I was growing old and she was young; and she must go away. But where, and how? I hadn't any money and I hadn't any friends. But go she must. She must go.

And then there was Philippa—Philip we called her. If I'd thought of her as a child who could blame me? Going on for thirteen and thin as a rat. If I hadn't been so taken up with Peate I'd have known before this, it was Philip would be the danger. Quick where Meg was slow; dark and a high colour where Meg was pale; warm where Meg was cold. Meg took after her father—a true-bred Flower. They used to joke about it. A real flower they'd say. Remember? And it was true in a way. She was a pretty thing—if you like them pale and slow; but her face, to my mind, was a little stupid.

But Philip. The Devil knows who fathered her. Not Flower. Her eyes were narrow and dark, slanting a little, with a squint to them. She could do more with that squint than another woman with eyes like stars. There was a man going with her then. It was Tom Simpson took her maidenhead. Twelve years and no virgin . . . and I didn't know; didn't even think about it. That day it was Meg troubled me. And sitting there all hopeless, I thought, Let her stay, let her go—it's all one. Lose your looks—lose your man.

Old. I was growing old. An old woman. What would there be for me in the long days to come—the longer nights?

I remember sitting there and fighting myself not to look at my face in the fine mirror Peate had brought me from Lincoln Fair; I did not dare to look. But all the time my fingers kept straying . . . a wrinkle or two; not many. But enough, enough. My hand went creeping alongside my mouth. And then—it's strange—I haven't a body any longer; and I know the vanity of vanity. But still it's hard to tell you what I found . . ."

She paused, he could see she was driving herself to speak.

". . . In the corner of my mouth, the left corner—a hair. So soft, so small, my finger couldn't be sure. I tried it with my tongue. My tongue could feel it; my tongue was sure. A hair, so soft, so small. Innocent. But it wouldn't stop that way. I would pull it out; but it would grow again. And more of them; more.

I forgot about Margaret! I forgot about Peate. I forgot everything but that little soft hair. It was stupid of me. One hair; one little hair. But I remembered women I'd seen . . . old women . . . beards. And *witch* the children would call after them. *Witch*.

I'd been handsome enough; still was. But I'd lost my first tooth, seen my first wrinkle; and now, my first hair. Soon the children would be calling after me; after me, too.

I went on sitting there. The room got dark; and then more dark. Margaret hadn't come in yet and I didn't know where Philip was. Up to the same tricks as her sister if I'd only known. I was glad they were both away. I didn't want to see either of them. And especially I didn't want to see Meg.

It got very dark in the room; and still I went on sitting there with my poor face hidden in my hands; as though I wanted to shield it even from the dark. And then, suddenly, I was shivering; bitterly cold for all it was midsummer.

A man was in the room with me. I knew it without looking up. He must have slipped in quiet and forgotten to latch the door. I looked up to scold him for his carelessness but the words froze on my lips.

I could just see him, a shadow in the red of the fire. He was all in black and his head higher than this ceiling; he was forced to carry it bent a little to one side. And I knew it wasn't a man at all. Not a human man. I knew it by the terrible cold that came from him; I knew it by the fear in my heart.

He began to speak. A deep voice he had. He said he knew my troubles; and, if I chose, there'd be no more sorrow for me ever. I'd live like a queen, doing as I pleased and no man nor woman to say me nay.

I wouldn't listen at first. Live like a queen—I shouldn't know how. I'd been poor all my life and I'd got along pretty well. I'd done much as I pleased; and, if there was little in my pocket, there was always a hare for my pot or a piece of fat bacon. I had my men!

He told me there was nothing in this world I couldn't have. I'd never grow old, he said. And that's how he caught me—

by a hair, a little, little hair. And so for the sake of keeping my looks and taking my pleasure, I sold my soul."

Samuel Fleming's voice came out on a sigh. "So you did sell your soul?"

She nodded. "But you know that very well. You judged me, priest. But I did not sell it then; not that first time. For though he promised everything heart could desire, the payment was heavy. I should have to vow to serve him alone; forswearing God and his Son; my baptism and all part in Him. And this pact I must seal with my blood, the pact there's no undoing. For, priest, what they say is true. When you seal that pact with your blood the place will never heal. See!" She held out her arm and showed him the angry place scarring its smoothness. "When the Master puts his mark upon you, you carry it to your death. And to your death, indeed! How many of his servants has the mark not brought to the grave! And how many innocents, too! For between the Master's mark and the marks of nature, it is not always easy to tell, such is his cunning. And so they swing alike—the witch and the innocent."

"Not alike." Samuel Fleming shook his head. "The innocent fly straight to the bosom of God."

"And does that comfort them as they dangle, the breath choking in their lungs and the eyeballs starting from their head? If your god is all-powerful, priest, and if he hates wickedness, why then does he allow it? It seems to me a very great nonsense."

"God wills us to choose. God has no delight in the bird that is snared but in the bird that is free. He wills us to be free that we may choose."

"How are poor souls to judge, all ignorant as we are? But I stray from my tale. The Master said he would send a spirit to serve me though I had signed no pact. It should serve me for a little while that I might see how well he cared for those upon whom he had set his love . . . even though they had not, as yet, set their love upon him.

We stood there facing each other, and I saw the man that was no man begin to melt upon the darkness; you could see the firelight through him before he vanished altogether. A

33

little warmth began to creep back into the room; and while I knelt by the hearth to warm my starved fingers, a cat jumped upon my shoulder. A white cat. It put down its head, weaving from side to side. Suddenly it leaped and there was a sharp pain beneath my breast.

Darkness came up at me and into the darkness I went down. When I came to myself the fire was out and the room bitter-cold. My first thought was that I'd been dreaming. I rubbed my eyes and looked about me.

There on the hearth a white cat glared at me with red eyes. There was blood about its mouth; there was blood above my heart."

Samuel Fleming bowed his head in sorrow though it was an old tale, finished and done with. How could he help but grieve, he that had helped her to her death? And his grief was the greater that he had failed to bring her to the loving kindness of God.

"Priest," she said, "it grows chill and you are old. You should be gone from this place. But come again. It is not given to every man to see into a woman's heart—and that woman a witch."

He said, very grave, "I shall not come here again."

"Should you not try to understand why it all happened, and how it happened . . . to the end, the end in which you played your part?"

"I shall not come here," he said again. "It is forbidden to consort with spirits."

"But spirits are not forbidden to consort with men; nor is it forbidden to men to dream. And, indeed, they cannot escape their dreams."

There was something sly about her.

"Why do you haunt me?" he asked sharply.

"Because you call me back, you with your unceasing thought of me and your everlasting questioning. Since I died denying my Master, the gates of Hell are shut against me; since I died unshriven, the gates of Heaven are shut against me also. I come because you will not let me rest. While I was yet alive you did not with a full heart wrestle for my soul. But because you grieve for my sake, one more chance is given

34

you to win my soul for your god. If you fail, your soul is in peril also, because you failed to do that which your god set you to do. But it is all in vain, the toil and the anguish. I am not to be won. Are you not afraid, priest?"

"Yes. I am an old man and I am afraid. I will not meddle with ghosts." He crossed himself.

He shivered violently and put his hands to his eyes.

It was twilight in the copse and he had fallen asleep. There was a light wind blowing, rustling the leaves and rustling the grass. And in the rustle he thought a voice whispered, *Men cannot escape their dreams.*

He rose stiff and, with his old man's walk, moved slowly towards home. And he did not notice that the white cat followed him all the way.

Chapter Three

HESTER DAVENPORT cried aloud when she saw the cat and tried to drive it away; but it would not be driven. "A witch's cat if ever I saw one!" she said.

"Think no ill of it because it is white," he said, remembering with shame how he himself had challenged the little creature. "This is nothing but a starveling kitten." And then, as still she stared with dislike, added gently, "We are told to be circumspect when we talk of witches."

"Who tells us?" she asked sharper than one should speak to a priest, even though that priest be one's brother.

"Our sovereign lord King James. Have you forgotten?"

"That man!" she cried. "A foreigner that does not know his mind from one year's end to the next. First we are told to hunt out witches; then we are told to walk delicately in the matter; and soon, God help us, we shall hear there's no such thing as witches at all! But it is the Scriptures that have the last word; not the King."

"But . . . if there *are* no witches?" he asked, speaking his own fear.

"Holy Script makes no mistakes nor does it lie. And, if there are no witches why does Christendom frame laws against them; yes and burn them, too?"

"You are too wise for me," Samuel said and she could not know whether he jested or not. He had always a dry way with him; yet he was a humble man, too.

The cat would not be driven away; and because Hester was a kindly woman, and because it seemed little and harmless, against her better judgment she set out a dish of milk and so ended her hope of being rid of it.

.   .   .   .   .

The Reverend Samuel Fleming wore a frail look. He was slow and quiet as he went about the house. He tired when he went the little distance to his church which was no more than the length of his own garden. He did not walk save when he must; and he never went near the deserted cottage.

Hester, he could not but think, was right. Men chopped and changed but the word of God stood firm. As for this dream of his, it was of no account—born of his own distress. He could do nothing for Joan Flower now. He was a shepherd of souls while they could yet be saved. She was dead and damned.

Dead and damned, priest? If your god is all-merciful as you say, do we not come at last into his hands, good and bad alike?

He looked up sharply. Who had echoed the voice of his own heart?

She was standing there as she had stood that time he had sent for her; the first time she had set foot in his house.

There had been fresh complaints about her behaviour. Not only did they say she was in league with the Devil, they gave chapter and verse. Let anyone vex her, though it be but a babe in arms, and her curse would surely fall.

He had not believed it. About her scandalous living he was prepared to rebuke her afresh, warn her that it gave rise to darker tales, threaten her with the stocks if she did not mend her ways, or with the pillory. That she had sold herself to the Devil, that she worked unholy spells, was a thing he could not believe. A witch might be anyone—he'd known that very well. It might be the foreign and the feared; it might be a man's mother or his sister or his wife or his child. But still he had not believed Joan Flower to be a witch . . . not then.

He had begun on the old, safe ground, rebuking her dissolute living—her idleness, her drinking, her men. She had stood there, not quite smiling beneath dropped lids. He had told her how such conduct must give rise to rumours; he mentioned some of the ugly things she was said to have done. She had overlooked Peate's child so that it had sickened and all-but died; she had blighted the corn in Simpson's field. She was able to do these things, they said, because she had sold herself to the Devil.

She had stood there, dark head thrown back denying, denying everything. He had not believed the tales—he saw now—because he had not wanted to believe them. He had been glad of her passionate denials.

"But of course," she said, scornful and smiling, her ghost's head high as that of the living woman, "did you expect me to put my head into the noose? Yes, it was true by then, all the things they said against me. But it was not true at first when they began to whisper. I was no witch. I had signed no pact, accepted no Master. Yet, in spite of that, from the day Rutterkin came to dwell with me, everything went as I wanted it to go. I had not to speak; I had to think, to think only, and the wish was granted."

"You had not yet signed yourself in your blood; but you had already accepted the Devil in your soul. Were you not afraid of the danger to your soul?"

"I was too happy to think of my soul."

"So it is with all men," he said and bowed his head. "When all goes well with the belly, then they forget the belly; when all goes according to their desire, they forget the soul. But let belly ache or desire go awry—then they remember."

"It is the way of all men, as you have said," she told him, "and you cannot quarrel with me for that! When the Master helps you, it all happens so simply, that, at first, you do not understand it is brought about by his will. So it was when I rid myself of Margaret, and of Philip, too; by that time I knew of Philip's tricks, the Master had sharpened my wits.

It all came about so homely, so natural, no-one would have thought the Devil had a finger in it. I did not think so myself . . . until afterwards. That is the cleverness of the Master.

I went up to the Castle, to ask the steward if he would take Meg on in the kitchens. I did not think he would; he was a proud fellow. Servants are prouder than their master; have you found that?"

He nodded. "Men are God's servants, but there's many a man thinks he knows better than God."

She made a little gesture of impatience at this excursion into philosophy. "I meant to coax him if I could—the steward, not God. I'd always got pretty much what I wanted out of men though I'd never much luck with God—your god.

As I walked, I gathered, idly, as one does a posy—cow-
38

parsley and meadowsweet and daisies; and sorrel for colour with my white blossoms. It was a lovely day, the sun yellow and hot as I liked it. It could never be too hot for my foreign blood. The trees were dark with full leaf and the grass each side of the road all white with dust. And I was singing as I went because the world was lovely; and, if I chose, I need never grow old.

I pushed open a gate—the gates were always open then."

He nodded. In those days, no-one had ever found the gates locked, more's the pity!

"I was making for the steward's office when suddenly—there was my lady herself, coming out of the walled garden. There was a basket of apricots on her arm; and her gown was the colour of the fruit, all gold and glowing and very rich. Now that was the Devil's own luck. How else did it come about I should meet the lady alone and no-one to hinder me?

She was a pretty creature, I had to own—though it angered me to have to admit it. *She* hadn't a wrinkle . . . that was to come.

We stood there, she with her eyes on my country bunch, me forgetting my curtsey all agoggle as I was at her apricots.

'Oh,' she said, 'how pretty!' And she put out a hand to my wild posy. And, as she took my flowers, I noticed her hand, how white and soft, how long and fine. That hand of hers said all the difference between us. . . . She was fine and I was common; dirt."

"I doubt she thinks in such a way, or ever did," Samuel Fleming said. "She has a humble soul."

"Humble?" she laughed. "Oh priest, you are simple! So grand she is, so sure, she can afford to play humble—a pretty game. But scratch her in her high humility and she'll scratch back."

"You must pardon a countess for being human, too," he said, drily.

Joan Flower laughed again. "That day, at least, she was sweetness itself—a honeypot. There she stood, holding my wild posy and nodding and smiling. Oh, she took my posy but she gave me nothing in return—she with her basket full of apricots."

"She didn't think of it," he said. "That's all."

"That's all!" she echoed, mocking. "She never thought of it because I wasn't the sort of creature to eat apricots. Oh, she'd send down a blanket or a pillow if you needed it, or a gown or shawl, maybe; but if she'd given me never a thing but just one apricot when we stood face to face that day, maybe the whole story would be different. I don't know.

Well there she stood, sniffing at my flowers, and she asked my name—she'd forgotten, if she ever knew. So I told her; but I was not best pleased. And I told her how my girls were growing up ignorant and wild and how they needed the training only a great house could give.

'Why then,' she said, 'they shall come here, if you are willing!'

If I were willing! 'Bless your ladyship,' I said; but I did not take the name of God upon my tongue, though afterwards I was more bold; and died for it.

'Go now,' she said and made no bones about getting rid of me. 'And I will tell Master Screvens what I have arranged.' And she smiled at me over the posy. 'And you can tell your girls to come.'

'But my lady,' I said, 'he will want to see my girls—he or your housekeeper; whether they be fair spoken and clean in their habits and know the difference between *mine* and *thine*!'

'If they are like their mother they will pass,' she said. 'And if they are not—well, they can learn I suppose.'

'The rector will speak as to their character,' I said.

'No need. I remember your husband,' she told me. 'A good man in the garden, diligent and honest, too. Let your girls come when they are ready. If they are good and work well, then they shall stay. If not, why then they must go. Now that's a bargain!'

She lifted the skirts of her satin gown and smiling she walked across the grass. And still she held my posy. And it was only afterwards I remembered I had plucked parsley and cinquefoil—devil's plants both. I stood there and I watched her go; she was like a creature from another world with her lovely gown and the lovely walk she had; and head and shoulders enough to melt your heart . . ."

"And yet," he said, "she didn't melt yours."

"No," Joan Flower said, "no! She turned when she'd gone a step or two and came back to me. 'Good woman,' she said, and again she'd forgotten my name, though afterwards she remembered it—as she'll remember it to her dying day—'I like you well. If you yourself should need work at any time, you will find it here.'

It was then I began to hate her—the sweetness, the innocence. No woman of full age should be so innocent. She sets herself up, a mark for the wicked."

"So short a time for the Devil to take hold!" he sighed.

"I was never one of your good ones," she reminded him. "I was fertile soil. I hated her because she was good; and because she made herself defenceless against evil. And most of all I hated her because she had not thought to offer me an apricot." She was silent; then she said, soft and bitter, "My lady the Countess of Rutland, with her white hands and the jewels on her long fingers, and the richness of her gown, and the safety all about her so that she could admit whom she wished into her house and have no fear."

"Yet, she had cause to fear," he reminded her.

"That came afterwards. Still one may say, in the common way of speaking, she could do the thing she willed whatever it might be, and no tongue wag against her, no hand punish. Madam the Countess. There she stood as much above me as an angel from heaven and I the dirt at her feet. Surely the Devil entered into me so that I hated her goodness.

I watched her go with that lovely walk of hers and I turned about for home. As I went, I forgot for a while my anger and remembered only that my wish had come about; and come about so simply. Everything would always be simple for me now . . . until Judgment Day; and that was a long way off.

Margaret was not pleased when I told her she was for service up at the Castle; she had set her heart upon Peate and meetings would be hard to come by under the watchful eye of Madam Housekeeper. She was a heavy girl, sullen and resentful, but you would not notice it until you came to know her. That white skin of hers, those blue eyes, that light hair drew the eye. Yes, she had a proud and sullen spirit, prouder

41

than my own. And that is strange, seeing I have good blood in my veins; the man that fathered me was a fine gentleman, my mother said. But Margaret was the child of John Flower that was a clod, a turd, a cake of dung."

"A good man," Samuel Fleming said, severe. He looked at her, suddenly sharp. "You were not sorry when he died."

She shrugged. "I missed him the way you'd miss a dog or cat of which you were tired. Oh I wished him out of my way, often enough! But," she said quickly, "I never did him any harm."

"To wish him dead, was that not harm?"

"Who knows what lies in the secret heart?" she shrugged again.

"He knew. And he had no mind to get well. Nor did you grieve for him overlong. He was not cold before you found your comfort."

"I was too hot to grieve for a cold man. But we talk not of me but of Margaret. She would not go to slave in the Castle, not she! She swore it. But Philip skipped like a little sheep, a little black sheep. It was fine in the Castle, she said; warm and food in plenty; plenty of men, too. Meg tried to prick her with thoughts of Tom Simpson—any wench would get him and Philip away! But Philip twirled about and laughed. She had but to crook her little finger she said, to bring him running.

I remember the day we set out. Meg and Philip carried their bundles on their shoulders; such small bundles—we were very poor."

"You soon learned to increase your possessions—all of you," he said.

"Why not?" She pretended she did not take his meaning. "They were to earn good money up at the Castle. Well, there we were, trudging along, kicking up the dust of the road when William Berry came along in his cart. He was going up to Belvoir with a dozen of hare and he gave us a lift. So there we were riding high above the dirt of the road; and again I found myself thinking how these days everything turned out so easy and so fine. And then I wondered how things would go with me if, after all, I refused the pact. It was like a cold wind blowing at my back, so I put it out of my mind. I thought instead how, when I got home again, the house would be mine . . . mine as it had never been; empty—a quiet and blessed peace; and how I need not look this way and that to see did Peate come lusting after Meg, nor where my little black sheep went frisking. The day would be never too long. I could lie abed when I chose; and for company there was Rutterkin that was a child to me—a better child, more obedient than either of my girls. He was like a baby to me."

"You . . . suckled him?" And again his face was drawn with his disgust.

"Not then. He was not my familiar; I had not made the pact. I fed him with buttermilk; and with cream when I could come by it."

"Cats have large appetites for such small creatures," he smiled, remembering how Hester had complained more than once, lately, that the cream had dwindled.

"I had enough and to spare! Oh but they were good days. In the daytime the quiet and the peace; and at night . . . at night . . ."

At the lust in her eyes he covered his own.

"It was then the tales began to go about, the new tales, the dark tales," he said.

She nodded. "Nothing too bad for them to lay tongue to. And yet I had done no evil; not then. Had I wanted to I had no power. But I did not want to. I was happy. I did good . . . until I learned sense. Brownlow's brat fell sick; the brat that's alive and well now, that pelted me with stones, that cried filthy names after me—that was the child I saved. And not by witchcraft, neither; but by the use of simples—a wisdom I had of my mother. I put the right charms about his neck, gathered in the right place and at the right time—precious herbs some of them, hard to come by. Night after night I sat with him. I cleaned his eyes and his ears. I drove the sickness away with my own strength. But it was Nan Brownlow began the muttering about me; the muttering that brought me to my death."

"Those that leave the common path of men are hated."

"I had not left it yet."

"You left it when you accepted Rutterkin; when you fed him—though it was with buttermilk and not with blood. It

43

was then the pact was made, though not yet signed. It is the way of the Devil to undo human foolishness with the cunning of the serpent. You had left the common path and so you were feared. And where there is fear, there is the desire to punish."

"Yes, there was the desire to punish!" she sighed. "And yet I had done no ill. I had taken no maid's sweetheart nor any woman's true husband." She stopped his protest. "Peate had long been faithless—before ever he met me. It was his nature. Believe me, priest, I had injured no woman nor harmed any child; nor any cattle nor crops. Indeed, I helped where I might; and when I might not, sat within my house, my cat for company."

"Was that all you had for company? There were tales of strange creatures—toads that were not toads, weasels that were not weasels, dogs that were not dogs."

"I always loved creatures. They had no fear of me. Rutter-kin was a spirit; the others, common creatures and my pensioners. But the stories went about . . . they went about. One by one my men forsook me with lying words, false excuses, smooth promises—lest the witch be angered. But soon I didn't care. What were they, after all, but common dung, even Peate? *Give me the name, I'll play the game!* It's an old saying. They'd given me the name *witch*; and soon I had but to choose from such delights as you, priest, cannot begin to imagine."

"God forbid I should!" He crossed himself. "And soon you did choose?"

"And soon I did choose. Quiet by day; but at night . . . at night there were lights in my house; and you could hear the singing and the stamping of feet and the clapping of hands."

"We could hear it," he assured her, drily, remembering how this one and that had come to him with complaints; and how, in the dark of the morning, he had often enough lifted his head from his books, seduced by that faint lewd singing and the troubling rhythm of their hands and feet.

"If the men I had known no longer came," Joan Flower said, "I had better company—witches foregathering. And though all Bottesford and beyond hated me . . ."

"With good reason," he said.

"With no reason . . . at the first; I have told you, priest.

Still, I was content. What did I want with country clods? Bread without salt. And so I lived content and harmed no-one. I had what I wanted."

"What you wanted was evil. That was harm enough."

"I wanted it only for myself."

"It could not rest there. Evil calls to evil."

"Should not good call to good? I had not spared myself to help my neighbours. I'd physicked their cattle and delivered their lambs when the ewes could not drop them. Yet in the end they stoned me from their doors."

"Good can never come from out of evil," he said. "You cannot run both with God and the Devil."

"A sick child cured? A beast eased of its pain? Good grows side by side with evil, priest. And, given a chance, it may conquer evil. You should know that."

"It is true," he said. "Does Satan lend you his serpent's wisdom?"

"It is God's wisdom," she said, grave.

He lifted startled eyes; and even while he stared, saw her outline soften and blur; and then her whole body tremble and disperse and be lost upon the air.

Chapter Four

SHE was waiting for him when he came out of Goody Mayhew's cottage. He had not set eyes upon her since she had said the name of God, and, saying it, had vanished. That was all of two weeks ago. He had been glad to be troubled no more; yet he'd been a little sorry, too. Let her be a ghost, let her be some fancy of his troubled mind, he might have fitted the story together, come at last to the truth.

He could no longer comfort himself with assurance of her guilt; no longer wholly believe she had cried upon God to witness her innocence and He had struck her down so that like a dumb beast she had died. Might he not have misread God's answer? The thought had troubled him incessantly these last two weeks. Instead of a punishment might it not have been a grace? Had not God saved her from fear and shame and the last agony of the rope? Had He not taken her from the cruelty of men? But, could it be called a grace to die without making one's peace with God? And, if indeed she wandered now in endless space, she had answered that question herself.

As he battled against the wind—for the mild spring had turned bitter—he could feel the cold pierce through the good wool of his cloak and strike to the very bone. Or perhaps it was the cold that streamed from her as she stood against the gate regarding him. For all the windblown curls and the gay scarlet ribbon, there was little gaiety about her. She wore a bitter look.

"The old woman's gone!" she said and there was satisfaction in her eyes.

He nodded. "God rest her soul. She made a hard end."

"I saw to that!" Joan Flower said. "I stood by her bed."

"Could you not let her die in peace? She cried out your name as she gave up the ghost."

"She had need. She was one who tormented me."

"I had thought it was t'other way about. You had tormented her bones with pains; you had bewitched her cow . . ."

46

"Old woman's bones! They are always full of aches and pains. As for the cow!" She laughed outright. "No need to waste good spells on such rubbish. The cow came to its natural end—old and dry and fit for nothing but the pot. Not but what she didn't deserve it!" She nodded towards the cottage where the dead woman lay. "She was one of the first to name me witch, she and Nan Brownlow together, before ever I'd set eyes on the Master. But I never harmed her. I never harmed anyone . . . until my first Sabbath."

He shivered less with the cold than at the look in her eyes, the voluptuous look.

"Priest," she said, as once before, "you should be within doors. You are frail beyond your years; and if you should die this week or next, how shall you save my soul?"

It was true, though she had spoken, mocking. Without a word he turned his face towards home . . . and all the time she followed him.

They had come now to the Rectory and he went within, she following. Hester came to meet him, shivering in the gust from the open door.

"It is colder than ever," she said. "I am chilled to the bone. I would say it will turn to snow except . . ." she looked, a little puzzled, at the high, crystalline sky. "And you, brother, look cold as death. Come into the study; Jennet has built you a good fire and I will bring you a posset. Yes," and she nodded to the white cat that brushed against her skirts, "and for you a pannikin of milk, if you are a good little cat." She put out a hand to take up the little creature but it shrank, spitting. "So small and so fierce," Hester said fondly. And he smiled seeing how quickly she had forgotten her rancour against the cat; so do we cherish those things to which we have shown a kindness. "Yet it is a good little cat," she said, "the best I have had. He keeps the house free of vermin, yes, of rats bigger than himself. And for that he shall have both thanks and milk."

But still the cat backed, eyes red as the Rector's pipe when he drew upon it. Behind him he heard Joan Flower whisper, "Make do with the sweet milk; you will get nothing else from that one. There will be no pact with the Master in this house."

Hester turned sharply and went out. Joan Flower said, and

her laughter had a wicked sound, "What would she say, good mistress Davenport, the white sheep, the silly sheep, if she knew I was here again in this room; this room where you questioned me doing your bitter duty and where I came to my death?"

Hester came in brisk, tutting still against the cold. She bent to stir the logs, set the mug with its pointed foot in the red of the fire and laid a clean cloth by him so that he might handle his posset when he thought fit. "Do not leave it too long," she warned, sweeping the hearth neat. And when he thanked her for her care of him, answered with that loving scolding of hers, "How can a body care for you that will not care for yourself." She shook her head and went softly from the room.

Joan Flower moved across to the window; he could see clean through her to the high spring sky, water-green through the leaded panes. "Sometimes," she said, her back to him, "I could wish . . . almost, I had made no pact. But when I remember the Sabbath I am shaken." There was an ecstasy about her, a wild and dreadful longing.

Weary he sat down in his chair. He would listen no longer; he would exorcize this unclean spirit. Why should he risk his own soul? Because he might save hers. He had his answer even before the question was asked; her poor soul that wandered homeless. As for his own—it was a risk a priest must take.

"The Sabbath!" she said. "I would tremble all day waiting for the night. I would bathe myself and comb my hair; and I would put paint upon my cheeks and on my lips . . ."

He said nothing, remembering how there had been days when she had gone about hair and eyes wild; and her red lips smiling so that he had thought her a little crazed. Had those been the days when she had trembled waiting for the night?

"The days of the Sabbaths," she said all soft with longing. "Candlemas and Roodmas and All Hallows' Eve; Lammas Day and Christmas tide . . ."

"You were not afraid," he interrupted, stern, "to take our holy festivals, to degrade them?"

"You were not afraid, priest, to take *our* festivals—festivals of the Old Religion, older by far than your Christ. For what is Lammas but Beltane; and Christmas but Yule? and Roodmas is Mayday—the wickedest day in all the year. One might say, priest, that you keep our heathen festivals!" And she laughed. "Ah the Sabbath! How slowly daylight passes till the sun goes down at last and the stars prick in the sky. And within the house the darkness is pricked by rushlight. And it is time. And your fingers shake holding the pot . . . the precious ointment, the flying ointment——"

"Come now," and he was smiling a little. "None can fly but birds and angels."

"Priest, being dead, I can speak no other than truth. I flew. I flew. Oh the wild, free flying. Washed and clean and naked to the skin—the clean, white skin. Anoint yourself with ointment, lie upon your bed. Say the words of power, say them, say them, say them . . . till your eyes begin to close and you feel yourself falling . . . falling.

And then you rise; and you look down upon the houses, the little stinking houses, and you know within them men and women lie together like animals. But you are free . . . flying above the church steeple, higher than the hilltops, higher than the Castle even on its high, high hill . . . higher, higher, until you feel the stars pricking with chill fire and the cold face of the moon.

And the air is full of movement, full of sound—rushing of wings and sound of flights; witches hastening to the Sabbath; witches carried by spirits, by familiars, by lovers; witches on bespelled humans, on bespelled animals, witches on broomsticks, on wisps of straw; or, flying as a bird flies, wild and free in the dark air.

And it is all a sweetness and a wildness, so that you forget to breathe until there is a pain like a knife thrust through your ribs and you must stop to take in air again. And all the time you are coming nearer to the Sabbath, nearer to the worship, nearer to the dancing and the feasting and the wild, wild love-making."

"Stop!" he cried out, and thrust a finger into each ear.

She smiled at him. "How shall you help me—or any other—if you will not listen?" And when still his fingers were at his ears, she added, sly, "Without your understanding I cannot be forgiven."

"It is for God to forgive you," he reminded her.

"Only if I truly repent; and repentance waits on you. You were my priest. So, if you would condemn my soul which God would save, you will shut your ears."

The fingers came from his ears.

"That first Sabbath of all, Rutterkin carried me; Rutterkin swollen to the size of some great beast from foreign lands, a lion or a tiger, such as you may see, so they say, in the Tower of London. He was great and fierce and wild, roaring through the sky, high as the moon. I was frightened; I felt too near to God. I thought he must stretch out his hand and crack me like a flea between his finger and thumb.

That was the only time I was afraid. Your god made no move towards me and I forgot my fears.

So there I was, crouched upon Rutterkin, half-fainting with my fear, until the earth swung up to meet me and I stood for the first time in the place of the Sabbath."

"And where was that?" he asked, stern.

"I may not tell you. I may confess for myself; I must not betray others. It was a bleak meadow, high up in the hills; the moon shone stark from black and tumbling clouds. There was a great flat stone in the middle, very high—as it might be a throne; and it was empty. And, facing it sat the witches, men and women, in the pattern of a young moon."

Samuel Fleming would have asked his question but she stayed him with a movement of her hand.

"I may not name them; but this I will say. The servants of the Master are everywhere—castle as well as cottage; and in your monasteries and in your churches, likewise. Yes, there they stand, serving even at your high altar."

She saw disbelief in his face and said gently enough, "It is true and you may believe it." He groaned at that and her hand went out towards him; without touching him, dropped again.

"It is a hard thing for you to believe that servants of the Devil may be found at your high altars. But so it is; and why your god allows it I do not know! Perhaps he is not so strong as the Master."

"He is stronger; and that could be the reason," Samuel Fleming said, and smiled again.

"He that was Captain of the coven made a movement

where I should sit and I went tip-toe to the lowest place and there I sat, hands clasped, eyes downcast, like the rest.

And, as I sat, I felt cold come upon me and my whole body tightened, as a player tightens the strings of his viol; and I felt my neighbour tighten likewise. It was as if we were bound each one of us by the same cord.

The great stone was no longer empty. Seated thereon like a king, but more glorious than any king—my new Lord."

"The Devil?" Samuel Fleming's voice came out in a whisper.

She nodded. "He wore the likeness of a man; but he was greater and taller and more comely than any earthly man. He was all in black and a black mask over his eyes. Two great horns went curving above his head; and, between them, was a flaming light.

And so we sat unmoving—we looking upon the Master and He looking upon us. Then, very slowly, he stood upright upon the great stone and we rose and prostrated ourselves on our knees all naked as we were; and my hair fell over my breast and over my belly to cover my nakedness.

Then the others rose and moved in procession to greet the Master with the kiss of homage; but me the Captain signalled to stay where I was. I was not a witch and might not share in the sacred rites and I remained kneeling. And when the rite was done the witches came again each to his place and sat down cross-legged but I remained kneeling.

And, so kneeling, I heard his voice. 'Where is she my new servant?' And still I knelt and I was very much afraid. Yet, priest, had you offered to take me hence and crown me with salvation, I could not have moved.

Then He raised his head, that head terrible beneath the branching horns and the great light burning between them. And He beckoned and I rose and went towards Him and knelt again; and all the time my heart fainted with its fear. He bent to me and I felt his breath cold; it was cold . . . frost cold, snow cold . . . and colder yet. For such a coldness, priest, there is no word.

'Come you of your own free will?' He asked.

'Yes, Lord,' I said.

'No-one has threatened you nor tormented you that you should come?'

'No, Lord."

'Do you acknowledge Me to be your sole and only God; to obey every order and to spread my darkness?'

'Lord, I do.'

'Do you give me your soul now and for evermore?'

'Yes, Lord.'

'Do you abjure God the Father, God the Son, God the Spirit?'

And again I said, 'Yes, Lord.'

'Do you cast off Mary and all the hosts of saints, repudiating your baptism and all promise of Paradise?'

'Lord, I do.'

'Then here I make my pact with you in the presence of the congregation, sealing you to my service. I will give you victory over your enemies. And I will give you happiness. Be you my good servant and I will be your good Master. How say you?'

'Lord, I say Yes.'

Then the Captain stepped forward holding a knife all of stone and very sharp; he bade me hold out my arm. Then he drew the knife across my flesh and the blood came out slow and dark. And that place never healed. It is a mark I bore to my death and after." And as once before, she held out her arm that he might see the angry scar.

"Then the Horned One spoke in a great voice. 'You have renounced your Christian baptism; now I baptize you in the name I shall give you; and by that name you shall be known in the coven but in no place else.' Then He cried out the name; and the congregation cried it after Him."

"And the name?" Samuel Fleming asked.

"I may not say it. Then He drew a parchment from his breast—so sure He was of me and rightly. And He dipped his finger in my blood and wrote my new name and set it above the other. And He took my finger and He smeared it also with my blood and I made my mark . . . and, priest, it was a cross."

"Did you not think then of the cross?" he asked, pale. "And of Him Who died upon it."

"The cross is older than Christ, priest. I went back to my place and we sat at his feet and we learned of Him. He told us what He would have us do and how we might do it."

"Were you not afraid?"

"How should I be afraid? Your god had no more power. The Old God protected me."

"But—" Samuel Fleming spread his hands. "The wickedness. The wickedness you had just done; the wickedness you were to do!"

"When you have done a good thing, priest, you are glad. It is a gentle gladness and it grows upon what it feeds. So with evil; but it is not a gentle gladness, it is a strong, wild joy. And that, too, grows upon what it feeds, so that you can never do too much of evil and you are mad with the joy of it.

Then, one after another, each man and woman stood up in his place and told of the wickedness he had done. Little things they were, very small evils. And I sat there listening, and despising such small evils, and thinking of this thing I might do, or that, to be outstanding in his eyes so that He would love me best.

And so we came to the end of our telling and it was time for the feasting. I saw tables spread with a fair cloth laden with smoking meats. Such food, priest! The Devil knows how to lure souls."

"Through the belly—both food and lust."

"Since men are what they are, the Devil is wiser than God."

"But God wins in the end. He will win even you in the end."

"Perhaps my Master will win *you*. You smile; but you may smile too soon!

So we sat down and we said Grace as is seemly. *We bless this food in the Devil's name*—that is our Grace; and then began the feasting. Three great tables set together in the shape of a horseshoe; and every witch sitting in order. Those that had done great wickedness next to the Master; those that had done least, at the bottom of the two tables. As for me, though I had as yet done nothing, my seat was by the Master."

"Because you purposed great evil?"

"Because of that. And because I was new received. And

because I was not uncomely—the Master likes a pretty face; a pretty face and a pretty tune. So there I sat; and Rutterkin leaped from nowhere to sit upon my shoulder and I fed him with fat bits. And I drank the wine, the sweet wine from hell; and I ate the fat flesh, the fat flesh from hell. And every now and again the Master would bend and kiss me upon the lips; and I was no longer afraid.

When we had eaten and drunk and thanked the Master from Whom all good things come, He rose in his place; and, leaning upon our arms, we listened to his commands.

First and foremost we must bring new souls to his service. That is the chief thing. It is our first duty; but it is not our last. He spoke to us one by one laying his commands upon us. This one to bewitch a certain man; another to kill this child; a third to go grave-robbing for bones to make our powders; a fourth to steal infants as yet unbaptized . . ."

Samuel Fleming lifted a white, sick face.

"Yes." And she nodded. "It is well that mothers and nurses keep good watch. What we do with these infants I will not tell now. Everything in its place! To some He gave poisons; to others receipts to make their own poisons. . . ."

"And to you?"

"No command. He said I had wit to seek my own evil. And, priest . . . I had.

When the Master had made an end of speaking, the Captain blew upon his horn and the Master cried out in a great voice, 'Do ye my commands or die the death!' And we answered him, crying out, 'Har, Har!'

Then the Captain cried out bidding us take our places for the dancing. We stood up in two rings, the women in the inner ring, the men in the outer, back to back; and the Master sat on his high stone in the middle and the Captain played upon the flute. It was a wild, sweet tune to keep your feet itching. And forwards we would go; and then backwards, knocking our buttocks against those of the men in the outer circle, and nodding our heads and crying out loud. What the words were, I will not tell; but they give one strength and joy; and you leap and leap, higher and still more high, until you leap, so it seems, higher than the moon.

Then, at the command, the Captain put down the flute and the rings broke. We moved, then, into a long line, the Master at the head and the Captain at the foot.

The Master began to move—a hand here, a foot there, twisting and turning and leaping; nodding and laughing; mewing like a cat or barking like a dog or roaring like a beast of the forest. And what the Master did, that we copied; and the Captain watched that not one witch missed one move. Faster and faster, twisting and turning and leaping widdershins; and the Master whose hand held mine turning now and again to kiss me . . . upon the mouth and upon the breast, so that all did likewise with their partners; all except the Captain who danced with his whip for partner; and this long whip he brandished to catch those that were slow in the dance.

Then the Master let go my hand and every man did so by his partner; and we stole, one by one, into the dark of the bushes. And there—never hide your eyes, priest, for this is a thing you must know—we lay and a spirit with us to be our lover; to each man and each woman, a spirit. As for me I lay with the Master."

"Woman," Samuel Fleming groaned, "are you so lost to shame? Is there no lesson for you here? Do you worship a god that couples with a woman?"

"Do you not worship the Son of God that was conceived of a woman? And why not? Gods have done so since the beginning of time. Such a lover I have never known; or did know, ever again. For the Devil when he lies with you is cold as well water. And it is a cold that makes you faint with desire so that you pray the moments not to pass and you swoon with the joy of it. Nor is the desire ever satisfied; for it is a net to keep you snared until the next Sabbath."

"Had you no moments, however fleeting, when you came to your right mind?"

"My mind was my Master's mind; my body, his body. It ached for his caresses; and ached indeed. For after the Sabbath it is as though you have been beaten and bruised from head to foot. You long to sleep until the Sabbath comes again." Her arms went out in a yawn. "It wearies me even now to think upon it, so that I long to seek the grave again."

"Your unquiet grave," Samuel Fleming said thoughtful. "Do you not *see* you had done better to die the death. Then you would have risen again in Our Lord."

"Dying is never pleasant, priest, as you will find out. And, if your god is merciful as you say—which I take leave to doubt —why then, even I, damned as I am, may come at last to his mercy."

"Yes," he said, "you will come."

"You will come," he said and lifted his eyes and found himself talking aloud in the empty room. It was a habit that had grown upon him this last year. He looked about him in the gathering dusk. Was she a creature born of his imaginings or had she truly stood with him in this room? He did not know. The things she had said—the flight through the air, the Sabbaths and their orgies—he had known of them before. Others had testified and good men written them down.

He sighed deeply.

He did not know. If what he had heard was born of his own knowledge, he would pray for her soul; if spoken by her dead lips, then he would wrestle for it, wrestle until he had won her again for God.

He rose to his feet; and facing the window where she had stood, went slowly to his knees.

Chapter Five

"ARE you afraid, priest, that you pray so long in your church; and shun the empty cottage by the dark wood, and shun the comfort of your own room?"

He was sitting in Hester's parlour, holding the skein of her wool, for she was knitting him warm stockings against the winter. From the floor the little cat raised a paw and scrabbled at the wool. "Down, naughty one!" Hester said and tapped it lightly. She did not see how the cat glowered at her with red eyes.

Presently Hester said, shivering a little, "Such a house for draughts I never knew. Here we are almost into June and I must get me a shawl."

It was when the door had closed behind her that he heard Joan Flower's voice, saw her eyes openly mocking.

"Are you afraid, priest?" she asked again.

"Yes," he said, "I am afraid. Not of you, but for you. I pray for your soul."

"Then it is for me to be afraid," she said quickly. "I had rather be with the Master than with God."

Hester came back hurrying, the shawl awry about her shoulders. "Jennet, the silly creature, has lost one of our grandfather's spoons; and I must find it at once," she told him. "What a pother!"

"Find it tomorrow." He put out a hand to keep her; he was in no mood for the witch.

"Tomorrow is too late," Hester said and was gone.

He heard Joan Flower laugh again and knew that the loss of the spoon was a magpie trick to get Hester out of the way. She walked across to the spinning wheel and stood flicking at it with her finger so that the wheel turned lazily and stopped.

"I was never a housewife," she said. "When I see this thing I am content to be a ghost!" She struck the treadle a violent blow with her foot so that the wheel whirled viciously.

"Have a care!" he cried out, but the damage was already done.

He came over to the wheel and taking the snapped ends began to splice them. When he had joined the wool to his satisfaction he said, "Living and dying are part of the same thread."

"I have snapped my thread," she told him.

"It may be mended again."

"How shall it be mended? One joins white to white, or red to red; or—as you have done—grey to grey. Colour to colour. You cannot join white to red."

"Though your sins be scarlet . . ." he reminded her and said no more.

In the silence there was nothing but the ticking of the clock, and the crackling of the fire, and the little sound of the cat dragging her claws over the wool of Hester's rug.

"There is a thing I cannot understand," he said, breaking the silence at last. "You sold your soul that you might be forever young. But if you did not grow old it was because you died first; died horribly."

"That I died as I did was my own fault. I broke my pact and denied my Master."

"He had promised you all good things, besides; beauty and power."

"The things He promised, He gave. Beauty; I knew it at the Sabbath. Power; I held it in my hands to make or mar; to kill or cure."

"Such power is from God alone," he said.

"You know better than that, priest! As for your god, he, too, promises all that heart can hope. Yet there is misery and yet there is sin; and men and women hate each other; innocent creatures come to the rope and little children die in torment. And you; what do you say? *The ways of God are passing strange.* And, strange indeed they are! Or you will say *God's ways are not our ways*; and certainly they are not the Devil's ways. For the Master's ways are clear to be seen and his promises easy to understand."

"Then tell me this," he said very quick, "when he promised you wealth, why were you so poor; so poor that you must hire yourself out for work; so poor that when there was no work, you must steal or starve?"

58

"Heaven helps those that help themselves!" She laughed. "So it is with us. When I asked for meat and wine and fine white bread, the Master said, It is yours for the taking. Take it then."

"Meat and wine stolen from your master," he said.

"Meat and wine given me by the Master! It was a good life while it lasted!"

"A good life." And he remembered again the sound of drunken laughter curdling the peace of the quiet night. "Your house was a scandal, an open sewer."

"You Christians find it hard to be merry! They scandalized my name and spat when I passed. But I had worked no harm . . . as yet; and I had done them some good."

"You purposed evil. You were at the unholy Sabbath; you adored the Devil blaspheming the sacred rites of our religion."

"They were the sacred rites of *my* religion."

"You drank human blood, ate human flesh."

"You should not believe all you hear! We drank good wine —Malmsey as I remember. Good beef and mutton, too; and pork besides,—such as you eat, but better. For we stole it and took our choice. But—" she sent him a sly, sidelong look, "it is not of those small sins you wish to hear. It is about my lord earl and his lady; and about the children, how they came by their death. But that is a story you have heard. Was not the confession made, the punishment given? And is not that enough . . . enough?"

"No," he said. "*You* have made no confession. As for me I need that understanding which is the beginning of charity. I looked from the outside and it was all wickedness. But, if you will help me to look within the heart . . ."

". . . then the black thing may not be so black after all? We talk of murder—two young children."

She sat down on the stool at his feet and settled her skirts; the room, seen clear through her transparency, made the homely movement strange.

"We begin then with the earl and his lady," she said. "Good Christian souls."

"Surely you should have spared them for that."

"Priest, use your wits. The better the soul the more merit

to destroy it. And yet I think I should never have done what I did, had it not been for Margaret. It is a strange thing. Meg had a mean soul, good neither to God nor Devil, one might think. Yet in the end God chose her for pardon."

"The stone that the builders rejected has become the head-stone of the corner," he reminded her.

"If such as Meg be the cornerstone, then your heaven is likely to fall about your ears. Surely it is folk like my lord earl and his lady that are the cornerstones of God. Fine folk; serviceable to rich and poor alike; to all the same gentleness, to all the same kindness. Such goodness is hard for a witch to stomach. And yet there were times when I forgot my witch's heart . . ."

"And yet you murdered her children; and yet . . ."

"My witch's heart remembered again; remembered that though she was great yet I was greater; for she served the new, pale god, but I served the dark God, the old God. And, if when I asked she gave freely—or without asking, gave—I did not count it to her for righteousness seeing that all she had was mine if I chose to take it.

Sometimes I would go to the Castle only to be near my lady; for goodness draws the wicked with a thread, and we cannot keep away. I would pretend that I went only to work; I would polish a little, or scrub, or I would give a hand in the washhouse. But, indoors or out, I did not work overmuch. And if there was a thing I fancied I would slip it in my pocket; and, if I did not fancy it, I would take it also. For one must do one's evil where one can.

But whatever was lost in the Castle, there was no complaint made—that was my lady's will; and all was quiet and pleasant, which did not suit me at all. Sometimes I would say to my lady, *It is such a one has stolen your riband, or your fan.* But always she would blame her own carelessness or say one of the children had taken it in play.

But it is easy, maybe, to be kind in such a house with its high rooms and its great hearths that send out warmth in winter—and no soot to choke up your breath, and its wide kitchens and its full larders; and its rich hangings and its soft beds and the presses full of fine clothes . . . and its pictures.

60

I would stand, if I were let, cloth in hand, staring at them as though I could never be done looking. For that was always a marvel to me and a mystery how, with a few strokes upon a piece of linen, a man may bring forth angels and devils and men and women; yes, and trees and flowers and rivers, too and whatever the eye sees. You have but to stretch out your hand, so it seems, to touch flesh or leaves or clear water. St. Peter weeps. Once, indeed, I did put out a hand and brought it back again and was surprised to find it still dry.

And there was a great picture; it was, as you might say, a patchwork, seeing it was made of many little ones; and with a little saying for each. I would stand and I would look at it, one little bit at a time. That picture was like a great book in which one might learn."

He nodded. "I like it, too. It is from Holland and we call it the proverb picture. A proverb, you know, is a wise saying."

"It is strange, priest. I am a ghost and all the sorrows of this world and the next upon me; yet I cannot forget that picture. For it taught in a merry way." And she laughed now, thinking of it. "And one could remember its sayings—if one were wise enough." And she stopped laughing.

"There is one," he told her, gentle, "and it is called *Labour in vain*. Did you never look at it?"

She nodded. "My lady told me the words. Two old women try to wind flax from the same spindle; but they pull in opposite directions. Such a piece of nonsense."

"Or a piece of wisdom," he said, grave. "Are you not, perhaps, that flax?"

"Then neither God nor Devil pulled hard enough." He heard her sigh. "There is another picture, and underneath it says—I remember my lady's words—*If you're born to be hanged then you'll never be drowned*. There is a man struggling in the deep river yet he need not struggle so hard; he will not drown—the gallows await him on the other side. That is not a merry picture; it cuts too near the bone. For so it is with witches. You swim us but you cannot drown us; and we hang instead. I did not think then that Meg and Philip would come to the gallows."

"It is a warning picture," he said, "but you would not be

warned. There is another that might have warned you, too. It is called *Holding a Candle to the Devil?*"

She nodded. "That I would look at often. *Holding a candle to the Devil*—that is a thing we witches do; though not in the way the picture shows. I could never pass the picture but I would remember our own candles burning blue in the black night; and the Master standing before us, the flame between his horns. And I would remember the feasting and the dancing and the singing . . . and the way we made love under the bushes until, for longing, I could barely contain myself beneath the noontide sun."

Again she saw distaste in his face. She said urgent but not ungentle, "Until you can understand that, priest—the joy and the laughter—you can understand nothing. For our lives here are hard and narrow; and there is little laughter. But how should such as you understand—you who live well in a warm house with good clothes upon your back and fine food within your belly? All the wood we gather cannot keep us warm within our houses, for there is no place to store nor to dry it; and the little heat there is runs away through the holes in our roof and the room is bitter with smoke . . . if rain does not put the fire out altogether; and our backs go bare and our bellies empty. But at the Sabbath . . . at the Sabbath we are kings and queens.

You are not a poor man, priest, you live well enough; but neither we at our feasts nor you here in this house, eat as they eat up at the Castle. Were you in the kitchens you would stare until your eyes grew upon stalks."

"I have dined there," he reminded her.

"That is not at all the same thing as seeing it all laid out in the pantries and in the kitchens—shelf upon shelf, table upon table. The pork, the beef, the lamb, the mutton; the capon, the duckling, the teal, the bittern. But poor folk must make do with an ancient hen—if they are lucky—or a piece of pickled mutton. And up there you will see also barbel and bream, and porpoise, oysters and trout. But for us there are herrings and maybe now and again a handful of sprat. And you will find fruits there, and spices—dates and figs and cinnamon and ginger; and in the gardens there are peaches and apricots and melons and sparrowgrass. But what have poor folk save sour apples and turnips maybe?"

"You did not satisfy yourself with herrings nor with pickled mutton, no, nor with hard apples and turnips, neither," he reminded her.

"I was lucky. I had the Master's nod. But there are poor folk who do not serve the Master and they must go hungry."

"Not a sparrow falls to the ground——" he began.

"But still they fall," she said quickly. "And still they lie frozen upon the ground. And, if the eye of your god is upon them, does that make the bitter dying easier? And is it not a shame to him and a disgrace?"

"These matters are beyond your wits."

"And maybe beyond yours also, priest. Well, I was no sparrow to fall to the ground. I would look into the kitchens and I would whisper to Meg or to Philip, Bring me this or that hidden beneath your petticoat. And wine. Bring me wine. And so they would do."

"The other servants did not like your daughters," he said.
"Well, it was no wonder!"

"They did not like my girls before ever they suspected light fingers. For my girls were not easy to like. Margaret was sullen and sly; and though she kept her eyes cast down, men knew that she followed them with lewd thoughts. And those that had sweethearts or wives kept their distance; and those that had none kept their distance, too; for she was one of these still women that drain away a man's strength. And so, for the most part, they shunned her; all except one—and that one we shall come to later. For he was the spark that touched the whole thing and sent it up in flames.

And Philip. Her eyes, too, sought out men. But with her it was different; not downcast nor secret. A bold look that cried *Come take me*. And she, too, as you know, had her man and kept him faithful; a man other women desired, a fine, upstanding man . . . until she was done with him.

If Meg was disliked, Philip was feared. That she, ugly as a rat, should have her man—and keep him—was the top and bottom of the trouble. There were comely girls both at the Castle and down in the village who wanted Tom Simpson and his fine farm; but he would not look at them. The thing reeked of witchcraft they said, not understanding that some women, ugly though they be, have yet the wit to win a man and keep him.

And so the servants would go with their tales to the housekeeper or to the steward or even to my lady herself. But, since nothing could be proved, my lady would not listen. Margaret is a good girl, she would say. And, if you mislike Philippa then you are unchristian; there is nothing against her but her looks and those she cannot help. Pray for a better heart. And she would make it up to my girls with a gift so they should not feel slighted.

So there they were snug at the Castle. Meg in the poultry house would bring me many a fat bird; Philip in the laundry would bring me a fine shift or a sheet; and both were nimble-fingered in the kitchen! And there was my lady, of her Christian charity, allowing no word against either of them. It is well said that the Devil helps his own! Without lifting a finger there was nothing I desired but I might have it.

And so it went on—my girls snug at the Castle and I welcome to lend a hand—all three of us living like fighting-cocks.

How sweet it was up at Belvoir. In the summer I would go trudging the dusty road until it began to mount and I felt the fresh wind upon my face. For, though down in the village, we might stifle with the heat, there was always, even on the sultriest day, a wind stirring up there on the hill. And though the cabbages in my plot might wilt and my onions straggle, thin and dry, the gardens at Belvoir were fit for the Master Himself—so green, so soft; the flowers blooming and the great trees in full, dark leaf.

Sometimes I would catch sight of my lady trailing her silks across the grass. She would beckon, perhaps, and pluck me a rose; a rose I might have but never an apricot—that did not befit my station. Or she would tell me to ask in the kitchen for a mug of ale; ale I might have or cider but never wine—that also did not befit my station. And, Thank you, I would say, dropping my curtsey; and Bless you my lady. But my thanks were grudging, fitting, as I thought, her gifts.

And sometimes the children would come running . . ."

"The little boys?" he asked, his face all drawn with pain.

"One little boy," she corrected him, brightly. "The other was a babe in the nurse's arms. And there was the girl, the girl, too."

She paused; she said softly, "The little boys. I could never look at them without thinking, *If I could offer them to the Master!* And I would picture it—the five-year-old on his knees, acknowledging the Master. But even then I knew it could not be. That child, reared in a Christian home, would make no willing convert. And unless a convert be willing—big or little —the Master will have none of him. And so I would look on the child with longing and I would look on the child with hate. But I would have worked him no harm had not the occasion risen to drive me.

And the baby. I would look at the child at his mother's breast and I would think, Here is one for the sacrifice. Here is the child to offer that our harvests be heavy and our women fertile. And this child, too, I looked upon with longing and I looked upon with hate. But him, too, I would not have harmed had not occasion risen and driven me.

But most of all I hated the mother; I hated her sitting there and suckling the child. She was not one of those too fine to suckle, being simple in her way as any woman. And I would think, Fool to suckle a human child when you might suckle a child of Satan. But that was envy and I knew it even then. For to any woman, witch or saint, it is joy to suckle her child; but to suckle a familiar is bitter pain—and it is a pain that, in the end, brings you to your death.

And so it came about that I hated the mother and the pretty boys; but I did not hate the girl. And that is a strange thing; for the little boys liked me well, the elder running to shew me his ball or with a flower in his hand; and the younger crowing and jumping to come at me. But the little lady could not abide me and kept her distance though my lady chided her, which did not make her any sweeter. And yet I would not have harmed her . . . then; not by so much as a hair of the dark curls that flowered at her waist. Because she spurned me I admired her the more. Because she was wilful I read in her a willing convert."

"You were wrong there, witch."

She shrugged. "Wilful, finding the lusts of the flesh sweet —as she proved and not in so few years neither—why should she not have made a witch?"

"The principles of good were stronger."

"And so we lost her."

"Praise be to God," Samuel Fleming said. And then, "You say you wished the child no harm; yet when you bewitched the little boys you bewitched her also."

"No, priest, not then, or ever."

"Witch, you lie!" And for the first time he called her that name for which she had died.

"Ghosts cannot lie—must I tell you again? The boys we bewitched to their death. But the girl—for all our trying—we could not do it. We could not do it; she was free of us."

"But—" and still he was not convinced, "the same fits that killed her brothers, the same convulsions!"

"Priest, there are those—and especially it is so with children—who must draw upon themselves all eyes. So it was with her. The eyes of all, high and low, must turn upon her. And so at one time they had—the only child and her mother dead.

But then my lord married again and the little boys were born. He loved his girl; but he loved his boys better—and especially he loved his heir. It was natural and the little lady knew it. Do you think she enjoyed that, the proud and pretty child? She was the eldest; child of the first wife. She could never forget that.

And when her brothers fell sick, why then the matter was worse. She would play second fiddle to none, well or sick— hence the convulsions, hence the fits. So much poppycock! Like all children she played her part well; and, in the end—who knows?—she may have come to believe in them herself.

You can easily understand that, priest, you who are wise in the ways of men!" And was she, he wondered, mocking at him? But her face was grave enough. "And have you not heard of a child here and there who has played just such tricks and brought more than one poor soul to the gallows; and afterwards they have confessed their lies? Of course you have heard! Had the little lady been some common child to be brought before the judge, she must have confessed. That her fits were feigned you may believe.

I have told you we bewitched the little boys; but I have not said why. Yet the cause was good; or so it seemed.

Margaret. Margaret once more. She came down from the Castle all white with her anger and her spite. She looked wild that day and bitter with her shame.

At last my lady had heeded the tales, and my lady had sent her away. Shut the gates of paradise against my girl! Never look at me like that, priest. Is it so hard to understand what the fleshpots of Belvoir are to us poor folk? And there is more to it than that. Those that work up at the Castle are well thought of; to be turned away means disgrace.

That day my girl was shut out from heaven more ways than one. For, certain it is, had my lady not driven her away, Meg would never have become a witch. It was not her true nature. She would have married—her sweetheart maybe or another—and lived out the full span of her days.

'But why?' I asked the girl. 'What have you done?'

'Nothing but what you bade me. And what that is,' she said, 'you know well enough! I brought you the food and the clothing as you told me.'

'And is that all?' " I asked.

"And was that not enough?" Samuel Fleming said.

"My lady has plenty!" Joan Flower tossed a careless head.

"Your girl was a thief—and you had made her one!" He was angered by her lightness. "It is not only for a witchcraft a man may hang!"

"Then she hanged for the sheep and not for the tail, which is some comfort," Joan Flower said. "But I knew well that the lady would not send a poor girl away for helping herself to a pretty thing here and there. That is why I asked if that were all.

Margaret said, straight and hard, 'It is not all. I have taken my pleasure here in your house, mother, with Peate and with others; and you knew it well.'

'Life is short,' I told her, 'and we must take our pleasures as we may; that is no sin. But to be found out—there is your sin; and you cannot expect our virtuous lady to be pleased.'

'For my lady's pleasure I care not—that!' She snapped her fingers and there was a wicked look in her pale eyes. It made me think that here, after all, might be substance for a witch. 'But I have lost my sweetheart—and better than him I could not hope to find. For he is one of the upper servants—my lord's own man—and he is a gentleman, almost, and they call him Master Vavasour. He had his will of me; but he thought he was the only one. And, indeed, he was the only one I fancied. But lying with a man—it is a thing like eating bread. Had he been always at hand I would have taken no bread save him. But he is often away—in London or elsewhere with my lord; and now he complains because being hungry I ate.'

'So it is with men,' I told her. 'If *they* go hungry, why then they must eat. But if *we* go hungry—we must starve. As for you—have you not wit to lie to your sweetheart? This almost-gentleman has had his will of you and who is to say different?'

'Peate's wife. She has been up to tell her tale; and she has told it not only in the kitchens but to my lady herself. And they are at Master Vavasour day and night—the women who would have him for themselves; and the dirty louts that would have had me, but I would not suffer them to touch me. One may be hungry, mother; but no bread is better than foul bread.'

'You have made yourself many enemies,' I said. 'I have known it this long while; I have felt ill-will blow upon us three like a cold wind. But for all that I will go to my lady. Maybe I can coax her again.'

Margaret's heavy face did not lighten. 'Were she to ask me to go back—which she never would—I could not show my face up there again.'

'Let us jump that hurdle when we get to it,' I told her. But I was not cheerful; in my lady kindness is strong, but virtue stronger. 'What did she say when she sent you packing?'

'Little. But it was enough. Oh she was quiet! You would have sworn it broke her heart to put me out. For all her softness she's hard as stone. These virtuous women!'

'With the virtuous you must pretend to virtue; you must take your pleasures in secret. You have not done either. Well,

68

it is useless weeping when the milk is spilt. Did my lady send you away emptyhanded?'

'I had forty shilling of her.'

'Your twelvemonth wage! She has not behaved so ill after all. You may live well enough till you have time to look about.'

'Wherever I look,' Meg said, her head hanging, 'I see nothing but disgrace.' And that was true enough so I held my peace.

Presently Meg said, 'She gave me a gift, also; she sent it with me in the cart. The mattress and pillows from her own bed.'

'From her own bed?' It was a thing I could not believe. But even the most nimble thief cannot carry away a mattress unseen. I turned the matter in my mind but could make no sense of it. 'At least you will lie soft,' I said at last.

'Lie soft!' Meg's mouth was bitter. 'Much my fine lady cares about that! Her virtue—or her pride I know not which—cannot endure to use what my body has touched, not though the mattress be cleansed with soap and water and by wind and sun.'

Here was new matter. I looked at her. I could not believe what I saw in her eyes. A fool she was; but surely not such a fool.

She nodded. 'They caught us in my lady's bed.'

'Were you stark crazy?' I asked when I could speak. 'If you were in such haste, you and your friend, were not the fields soft enough for such as you?'

'I was minded to lie softer for once,' she said sullen. And then she said, 'I was minded to fancy myself in my lady's place. What is my lady that she should lie by my lord night after night?' she said sudden and spiteful and yet heartbroken, too.

'My lady is his wife,' I said very sharp. 'Have you forgot it? As for my lord, he is chaste.' Meg's hands fell open and she fetched a deep sigh. 'Come,' I told her, 'you are not so ill-favoured that any fine lord might not take his pleasure of you; but not this one, never this one, my girl.'

Meg said—and it was as though she spoke out of some

dream, 'He is finer and cleaner and handsomer than any man. When I lay in my lady's place . . .'

'My lady's bed!' I said again and even now I could scarce believe it. 'There is an old saying about angels and fools; and, truly, only a fool would dare that much!'

'Safe enough,' Meg said, listless. 'Or should have been. My lady was away—over to Haddon, I think. No-one should enter the chamber once it was swept and garnished. But, as ill-luck would have it, a sewing maid came to take away a sheet. And so'—she shrugged. 'And now they have scratched up every tale about me. They talk—and there is no end to their talking. Up at the Castle, down in the village, tongues wagging; wagging . . . and I with no place to hide my shame.'

I looked at her close; and now I must believe the thing I had doubted before.

'When?' I asked.

'Three months or four.'

'Who fathers it?'

She shrugged. 'Vavasour or Peate. Or some other—who knows?'

'Be easy,' I told her, 'for come what may, it is a shame you could not hide much longer. And it is a shame that may bring us good profit.'

'How?' she asked.

'You shall know in good time,' I said."

Samuel Fleming lifted his head from his hands and groaned aloud.

Chapter Six

HE groaned aloud. Why was she permitted to come and torment him with her hateful tale? He knew the answer well enough. Because in that tale he had played his part. And because the Devil had shut her out; and God had not yet taken her in. And, in the end, to one or other she must go. And so she came back to him now in the form of the girl she had once been, with her sweet shape and her dark hair and her scarlet ribands; a girl any man might love . . . even a priest.

He knew the moment's panic.

How if she lied about God's part in this? How if her coming was yet another Devil's wile to catch his simple soul?

"A ghost," she said softly, "cannot lie. There is a compulsion upon the dead to speak the truth. But whether you believe me or not, it is a battle between us two—my soul for God or for the Devil."

He started. He had not spoken; yet she had known his thought.

"The eyes of a ghost pierce through flesh and bone to the mind beneath. And so I have the advantage of you."

"My advantage is greater," he answered quickly. "And must always be greater, seeing God is on my side."

"What advantage that is we have yet to see!" She smiled. "But you hinder my tale with your doubts and your questions.

Now I had Meg back on my hands. If I knew her she would be spying here and there, putting two and two together in her slow way. If she should discover I was a witch—what then? Would she run to betray me in fear? Or would that same fear keep her mouth shut?

I did not know the answer. But this I did know. I must keep her with me until her child was born. And I must take heed what I said and what I did. For three months and more I must deny myself the sweet joys of our meetings and the sight of the Master's face. And after that? I had one other hope—to make her peace with my lady. I had to be free of the girl. It was not that I did not love my daughter; it was that I loved the Master more.

I told Meg I was for the Castle to speak with my lady. Let her take heart and all would be well. And surely, I thought, the Master will help me!

It was mid-January and the road rutted and slippery as glass. I slipped and slid, cursing my lady and her virtue which was as wintry as the weather.

As soon as I set foot within the gate I knew it was all useless. The steward jumped from his office like a spider from its web and ordered me away. There was nothing for it but to obey, seeing he followed me—every step. But as I went, my eyes looking this way and that, I spied my lady. She was on her way to the stables, well wrapped about with furs, and carrying a basket of apples. I did not love her the better for her furs, nor that her dumb beasts fed upon dainties poor folk could not afford. I ran forward before the steward could stop me. She would have refused all speech with me but I had taken her by surprise.

She returned my greeting, very civil; but she would hear no word of Meg. She could not, she said, allow my girl in the house, an infection to the innocent. It was clear to me, for all her civility, that henceforth—surprised or not—she would not speak with me ever again.

I curtseyed my Goodbye, all burnt with my anger."

"You had no cause," Samuel Fleming said. "She was more than just. Margaret—her sins being proven—was sent away. But Philippa—since there was nothing against her but the clatter of tongues—Philippa she kept."

"And for that she paid dear!" Joan Flower said soft and spiteful. "When I reached home again, Meg met me all hope. Now at the sight of my face she fell aweeping.

'Courage, girl,' I said. 'My lady's is not the only door. If she slam hers another will open.' Meg shook her mournful head and would not be comforted.

And so the days passed. If they were long to Meg heavy with her child and cut off from the Castle, they were longer still for me. Since her coming I had been obliged to miss the esbats. I had no friend in Bottesford and nothing to do but stare at my four walls. But now in two weeks or so Candlemas would fall and I must miss the Sabbath; and, unless I could rid myself of Meg, the following Sabbath also. For the sweet delights of our worship and the sight of the Master's face I must wait at least until May Eve . . . and perhaps longer."

"Your esbats and your sabbaths," he interrupted with an old man's fretfulness. "You confuse me. I had thought they were one and the same."

"Oh," she cried, "how shall you judge of witches that are so ignorant in our ways? The Sabbaths are our high festivals and we hold them four times a year. And to them come witches from covens both near and far to practise with us our holy rites and to adore the Master in his very presence. But the esbat is for the coven only and we hold it when and how we will —every week or more if it please us. We eat and we drink and we take our fill of love, not with any spirit as at the Sabbath, but every man with his woman. And, since we hold no worship, the Master is not with us; but the Captain is there and he is masked; and he wears both horn and tail that we may remember the Master from Whom all good comes. And though I longed unspeakably for the Sabbath, without the esbats I should fall into a melancholy and die.

So as the days dragged on it was clear that there were but two ways out. Margaret must come to the Master; or she must die. Longer than Mayday I would not wait.

I had no wish to kill my girl. So, I began to talk to her, leading her step by step to the heart of my matter. I spoke to her of my new God that is the oldest of all the gods but she did not understand; yet the word *witch* she understood well enough and fell atrembling and would hear none of it. I was not surprised; she had a poor spirit. But how soon the thing that has shocked us shocks us no more! And so when I talked of the feasting and the dancing she brightened; and when I spoke of how we lay in the moonlight and gave ourselves to the joys of the flesh, then her pale eyes glowed and she took in her breath short and sharp.

And so it went on, I talking, and she listening and not being able to close her ears for all her misgivings. Candlemas came and went and I wept within myself for the Sabbath lost.

February and March; and the earth fertile and the beasts great with young—and Margaret also. In mid-April her child was born."

"So Margaret Flower had a child after all," Samuel Fleming said slowly. "And I did not know it; I did not baptize it."

He looked at her very stern. "What became of the child?"

"Priest, it died."

"The truth, the whole truth, witch, for the love of God."

"For the love of the Master, priest! I delivered the child and it breathed; an easy birth and a lusty boy. I would not let it suckle lest she hanker after it. I tied up her breasts and I dipped a rag in milk and it throve."

"I did not baptize it," he said again in a heartbroken way.

"No, priest. We offered it—a sacrifice to the Master."

He leaned his head upon his hand and could not speak.

She said, "If your god takes a child unto himself, you say *Thy Will be done*. So we say, also, to our Master."

Still he said nothing; he went on staring before him.

She said, coaxing, "You make too much of the matter. A new-born babe—what does it know, what does it feel? A long, sharp pin and the thing is done."

And when still he wore his dark, sad look, she said, sharp, "You are a great one for mercy, priest. Yet you helped me to my death and my daughters, also; yes, and others too. And what mercy would you have shown this child? Born of the witch's brood—that alone would have brought him to the rope."

"We talk of a little child," he said.

"And have not little ones swung from the rope's end; yes, and poor dumb brutes that have no soul to know right from wrong?"

She was right on both counts and he could say nothing.

"But why," he asked when he had enough recovered from the sickness in his soul to speak again, "why did you murder the new-born child?"

"It was not murder; it was sacrifice. A priest should know the difference."

He spread hopeless hands. "What use a dead child to your Master? What did you hope to gain?"

"A dead child is more use than a living one. And, what did

74

I hope to gain? What you good Christians pray for—the love of my God."

"A god who catches you in a snare to take your soul?"

"Does not your god do likewise? And, once caught, to be his servant is all your glory."

"I cannot understand." He groaned and hid his face in his hands.

"Then, priest, you should try. For us it is easy. Our own eyes see the God; we talk with Him face-to-face; we salute his body with the Kiss. Priest, priest, if you could see it! The dark night; and in our hands the blue lights burning. We make our own heaven; our stars flame together. And our Lord is in the midst of us."

"Blasphemy." His voice came out voiceless; he looked with horror upon her face lifted and blind with ecstasy.

She made a little movement of impatience.

"How should you understand?" she said. "You with your stale wafers and your thin wine . . . and your old man's blood running slow in your veins? It took Meg many a weary week —and she a young woman full of the lust of living.

And even then she was not won. She longed for the joys of the Sabbath; but she was afraid. At last she agreed to offer the child. For, she said, speaking my own words, a child offered to the Master is happier than a child reared in shame and poverty. *Offer*, she kept saying. *Offer*. She never once said sacrifice, though she knew well what was meant. But that was like Meg—a poor creature that could not look facts in the face.

And so it drew on to Mayday. The wind still blew cold but spring was in the air. Meg took all day about her preparations—she who these last weeks had crouched by the fire scarce troubling to draw a comb through her hair. Now, combed and clean—white skin, pale gold hair—she looked comely enough. We took up the child and I wrapped it in Meg's gown and I put my own shawl about it as a shelter against the night."

"Were you not over-careful of the child you were to murder?" he asked heavy with anger.

"Sacrifice, priest; not murder. We wished to offer it alive and the night was cold. Besides we had no grudge against it and why should it suffer without need? And it was well we wrapped it, as you shall see. Then I anointed Meg with the ointment and I put the child in her arms as she lay upon the bed. When she felt herself first falling, she cried out so loud that I clapped my hand upon her to quiet her. And when we began to rise she screamed again and I took the child from her lest it fall.

And so for the first time she set foot on the place of the Sabbath. When the Master stood amongst us, she trembled like an aspen and dared not look. And when we moved in procession to do homage with the Kiss, she hid behind a tree —for though she might feast with us, she must not join our holy rites; she had neither offered herself nor been accepted. I saw her eyes all dark and staring, but whether with joy or with fear, I did not know."

"With tears, maybe," Samuel Fleming said. "Or . . . disgust."

She laughed at that. "Because we salute Him beneath the tail? Every part of the Master is sweet and desirable. Did not Moses see the hinderparts of God, and was there not a light all about him when he came down from the mount?"

"I see I do not preach in vain," he said, very drily.

"When we had paid our homage and were seated again, the Captain cried out, 'Now to the business of this night. Who has been zealous for the Master? Who speaks?'

And I rose up and I cried out, 'I speak. Here is a sacrifice to my Lord!' And I thrust Margaret forward holding her child.

Then the Master bent towards me. 'It is well done,' he said. 'To you, faithful servant, shall fall the honour of the sacrifice.'

So I killed the child. I killed it quick and clean with a long pin of silver; and it made no cry. But still Margaret trembled like a poplar tree that forever shakes. Then the Captain drew his knife and we offered the blood.

When this was done, the Master said to me, 'What gift would you have in return?' And I said, 'Vengeance, Lord.' Then He said, 'What vengeance?' And I said, 'Vengeance upon my lady Countess that brought this girl to shame.' "

Samuel Fleming let his head drop again upon his hands; but Joan Flower continued undisturbed. "Then the Master

looked at Margaret all drooping in the moonlight. Pretty she
looked, white and delicate; but for all that she was a poor
thing. He turned his back upon her. He looked at me instead.
'I am your Master and you are my servant,' he said. 'But I am
not the Master of this girl. It is a request I cannot grant. As for
the sacrifice, I thank her; but, save at the hand of my own
servant, I cannot accept it.'

Margaret began to cry standing there, the dead child held
outwards upon her hands. Then the Master grew angry, and
all the company murmured that her tears would bring ill-luck.
For witches cannot cry, priest, as you know. Since we have
denied baptism, water will have none of us. And that is a thing
you know also—witches have been swum often enough. But
what you do not know is this—the tears of a Christian, however evil, if he has not forsworn baptism, can bring the power
of the Master to naught.

So they muttered louder and louder, crying out to tear her
in pieces and pour out her blood for sacrifice. But the Master
only commanded me to take my fool away. Then the Captain
blew upon his horn and the Master cried out in a great voice,
Do ye my will or die the death. And his voice was so great with
his anger that the earth shook. Thus He broke up the Sabbath
and there was neither fasting nor dancing nor any love-play.
And when I would have risen through the air and carried my
girl with me, the Master's anger lay so heavy upon me that I
could not fly.

So we trudged the long way home. Margaret had her gown
but I had only the shawl to cover my nakedness and beneath
it I carried the child. The coldness that came from it set my
teeth achatter and our feet were cut on the stones. All the way
Meg wept and would not be comforted. The sun came up and
folk began to stir. A thrifty housewife had already set her
washing on a line; and when her back was turned, I helped
myself to a shift and a petticoat. And now the sun was hot and
we walked in the heat of it; but still the dead child lay cold
against my heart. And, as we went, we begged here and there.
Sometimes we got a crust but more often they set the dogs on
us. In the evening we came into our own country and we
knocked upon Ellen Greene's door over at Stathorne. When

she saw us she would have shut the door again but in the end she threw us a piece of dry bread though she would not suffer us indoors, nor yet even to lie within her barn."

Samuel Fleming raised his startled head. "And we thought her of your company! We hanged her." And he beat his breast.

"Leave knocking upon your breast," Joan Flower laughed. "It was not for love of your god she denied us but for love of mine that was also hers. We had offended the Master.

So we set off again, going slowly upon our rubbed feet; and still Meg wept as she went, and always to the same tune. *I have murdered my child. I am a murderer.*

'Yes,' I told her at last. 'The one that does not adore the Master and takes away life, is a murderer. But the one that adores Him and offers a child for sacrifice is no murderer; he is a worshipper of the old faith that is older and truer than their Christianity——' "

"It is better to do murder," Samuel Fleming cut her short. "With tears and with prayers a man may repent. But to abjure God—there is damnation, eternal torment."

"Eternal torment is our delight; for it is not we that shall suffer but the enemies of the Master. For us—eternal Sabbath in the wide fields of hell.

Priest, we walked through the dark night now resting a little, now walking again as well as we could for our blistered feet. It was dawn when we came at last to our own house; a skim-milk dawn, no light to it. I took the dead child from Meg and she made no sound. I think she knew not where she was nor what she did. I hid the child beneath a cloth and we went to our bed.

We went to our bed but we did not sleep. Meg lay staring at the ceiling and wept. At last I said, 'You do well to weep, for the child is uselessly dead. It might have been much profit to you; it could have brought you the love of the Master.' But I think she did not hear, for even while I was speaking, *Dead*, she said, *dead . . . dead . . .*

'Listen!' I told her and I nipped her hard in the fleshy part of the arm to bring back the wandering mind. 'This night you have offended two Masters that between them rule this world and the next. Between angry God and angry Devil how shall you fare? One or other you must choose; and you must choose now. You cannot live one night forsaken by God and Devil alike.'

And still she moaned and wept and had not courage to say one thing or the other. And, suddenly, like a child she was fast asleep; but in her sleep she wept and moaned.

I dragged myself out of bed, all weary as I was, and summoned Rutterkin. He would not so much as open his mouth until I had paid him—a sure sign of the Master's displeasure; else he had not dared to ask his payment first. When he had licked himself clean of blood, he said, 'You did wrong to bring the unbeliever to the Sabbath. One who hovers between good and evil may yet become the pale god's spy to work us all great damage. That is why the Master refused the sacrifice of the child to his glory. But a child's body is still a child's body. . . .' And when I did not understand he said, 'It has fat for unguents, bones for powders.'

I cried out at that. Such a thing I had never done. I had killed quick and clean for the sacrifice; but I had never laid hands upon a body to tear it in pieces.

'It is the Master's wish,' Rutterkin said. 'But you must keep the girl out of it, lest she run mad and betray us all.'

I left Margaret in uneasy sleep and under my shawl I hid the body of the child. And I never once thought *This is the child born of my child; flesh of my flesh, bone of my bone.* I thought only, The child is dead and nothing can restore it to life. Is it worse that its body work the Master's will than rot in the earth?

But for all that I was glad that Margaret still slept.

The sun was up when I came to the house of Joan Willimott over at Goodby . . ."

Again he lifted an anguished face, remembering how for all her denials, all her beseeching, Joan Willimott had hanged —she and one other of whom he did not like to think.

"Leave your soul-searching," Joan Flower said. "Joan Willimott came to a just end. Her house stood low among trees and it was still dark down there in the coppice when I knocked upon her door.

She was not pleased when she thrust her face through the lattice and saw me standing there; at the Sabbath she had been one of those that cried loudest against us.

'Come down!' I called softly. 'Come down in the Devil's name.' But she would not stir until she had consulted with her familiar which was a little tiny woman that stood upon the floor no higher than my hand."

Samuel Fleming nodded, remembering how, at the last, Joan Willimott had confessed that this spirit was breathed into her mouth by William Berry of Langhorne. These Flower women had brought others down with them to the grave.

"I knew she had agreed," Joan Flower said, "for Pretty came flying down to me and her mouth was wet with blood. She lighted upon my arm as it were a bird—the arm that carried the child beneath the shawl.

I heard the bolts dragged backwards and I went inside.

We did our work with no-one to hinder or to frighten us; for she was a widow and childless and there was no-one besides ourselves within the house.

It was not pleasant work . . . but it was the Master's will. We did not stay to eat; nor, indeed, could I have stomached food; but now and again we would stop to quench our thirst or my companion would tear at a piece of bread with bloody hands."

"Bread?" Samuel Fleming said all amazed. "A witch cannot keep it within her body. So they say; and so—as you well know—I have seen for myself."

"That is nonsense, priest. How else should we live? Bread we do eat—when we have blessed it first in the Devil's name. And water we may drink in the same fashion. But bread that has not been so blessed, and water that has not been so blessed, we take at our peril.

And so I trudged homeward sick and weary and, as I went, I plucked a straw from the hedge and I said, unthinking,

> Horse and bridle away we go,
> Horse and Pellatis, ho, ho, ho!

And, before I knew it, there I stood at my own door. I was happy then because I knew the Master had forgiven me."

Samuel Fleming lifted unbelieving eyes. "Do you truly believe so great a nonsense can work so great a miracle?"

"Priest, does your god need help to work his miracles?

Your master and my Master can manage very well without our help. But the saying of those words is a token—the token of believing. Without the token of faith both your god and mine are powerless."

"You are right," he said and bowed his head.

"Priest, I am right in this—and in other matters, as you will come to find. I went into my house and Margaret lay there on the bed as I had left her. She was candlewhite and her hair spread upon the pillow dank and dark with sweat. From his place among the ashes Rutterkin stared with eyes of living coal.

I signed the familiar he should go. I said nothing to my girl but I blew up the fire and heated a pannikin of milk and I broke off a piece of bread and set them down beside her. She would look at neither; and when, at last, hunger drove her, you might have thought that what you Christians say is true. For, indeed, the bread choked her; she could not swallow and put it down again. Then I took a flagon of wine she herself had brought down from the Castle and we drank together. Soon she was a little more cheerful and, while the wine was within her, I spoke.

I said only what I had said before. With such as Meg you cannot say a thing too often. Since her sacrifice had not been accepted, I told her, she was nothing but a common murderer; and, save for the Master, she would hang. But He, in his infinite pity—though she was not his servant—had carried the body to a secret place and so she was safe.

When I talked of the child her tears began once more to flow. I told her then that, a child untimely dead, any mother's heart must burst with grief; but that same heart must lift with joy, knowing that child a blessed sacrifice to our Lord who is the Ancient God.

But still she was not ready to come to the Master; nor did she come for many a night. But in the end I caught her in the same net that had taken me—the vanity of women and the lusts of the body.

It was when she had a little recovered from the death of her child and was coming again to the appetites of women, that I asked her what man would take her now her lover had cast her off and the Castle forever closed against her? 'But,' I said,

81

'at the esbat you may taste again the sweetness of being desired and the fullness of desire satisfied. And at the Sabbath you shall give your body to a spirit who will know how to play upon it better than any mortal man. When you have felt a spirit lie with you, you will never again suffer the touch of any man's flesh—unless he be of our coven; for that is your duty. But you will not endure any other man, be he prince or peasant; be it the earl himself or that clot of dung Vavasour.'

'And there is one more thing,' I said. 'Women grow old. What man, though his own hair be grey and his gums empty, will take a hag to his bed? But the witch is forever young.'

She looked at me then with the cruel eyes of youth. 'You are well enough for your years,' she said. 'But still you have lost a tooth and will lose more. And still you have a wrinkle or two and will have more. As for Joan Willimott and Ellen Greene—their breasts are withered as empty sacks and their hair is grey and thin.'

'So it is by common daylight,' I said. 'But did you not see them at the Sabbath? Their breasts were full and their hair was dark and their bodies eager. The Master keeps his promises and we shall never grow old. As for you, girl, you are scarce eighteen but still tears have done their work upon your face. Were you as virtuous as that Virgin in whom, no doubt, you are childish enough to believe, yet you would no longer get you a man.'

And that was the end of the battle; for Meg was both lonely and lusting."

"You took her in the net of her lust—your own daughter!"

"How do you bring souls to your god but through their desires? Desire is a prettier word; but it means the same!"

He did not answer and she chuckled. "You must be quicker with your arguments, priest, if you would trip me."

"I have no wish to trip you." He looked her full in the face. "I wish only to bring your soul to God."

"I had rather it were brought to the Master. I would it were one way or the other; it is cold where I wander alone."

"Who would trust your Master? To serve him—that was the condition. Yet still he shuts you out."

"Faithfulness was the condition. I was not faithful. But I

forget my tale. I had won my girl's consent but it was a grudging consent. Useless. Unless she came with her whole heart the Master would not accept her. So I set about to win her—heart and soul."

Samuel Fleming stared at her as if, even now, he could not make sense of her words. "Your daughter," he said. "Your own child; flesh of your flesh. To snare her soul that it might go down to the Pit for ever. Do you not grieve for it now?"

"Priest, do you grieve when you have won a soul to your god?"

He rose and walked about the room. Through the window he could see the great forms of trees black against a sky all pricked with stars. But the quiet night did not quiet him. On the contrary. As he stared the great shapes seemed to move nearer, as though they were dark spirits come to mock him; or worse. He crossed himself. And now they were nothing but trees in a quiet garden, familiar trees beneath whose kind branches he had so often walked.

"Do you regret souls won to your god?" she asked her question again.

He turned about. "I am not quick enough to battle with you tonight. I am old; and I am not well. Give me a little space. Leave me now."

She shook her smiling head. "You cannot drive me away since your god permits me to stay."

"Then leave me of your charity. I can bear with wickedness —natural, human wickedness. But you! Your child, your own child! To lure her by her lusts and by her loneliness, to catch her in the snare of her misery! Can you not see I can bear no more?"

And when still smiling, she stood her ground, he said, "If I die too soon, you will wander between heaven and hell for all eternity."

He had touched her there. "You are clever, priest; and I will go. But you are not zealous enough for your master."

He sat there, eyes closed against the sight of her. When he opened them again, she was gone. It was so cold now in the room that he shivered, yet lacked strength to make up the fire, or, indeed, to move at all.

When Hester came in later, all triumphant, the spoon

brandished in her hand, she found him, head fallen sideways, in his chair. He was so white, so cold that, the spoon clattering to the floor, she cried out and fell to shaking him. When she had roused him at last, she went to the fire and raked it, all noisy with her fear, she that was a quiet woman; and went away to fetch him a hot drink.

"We must have a physician," she said. "Yes, I shall ask Cecilia to send Master John Atkins."

"Pish and tush," he said; but for all that he was weary to the bone. But since he must not die yet—for he had still to win a soul—he agreed to see the physician tomorrow. He had been wrong to forbid Joan Flower from further speaking—he saw that now. He was not sufficiently zealous—she was right in that. Her master had sent her as a challenge. And God had allowed it. God had allowed it since she, even she who had thrown away her baptism and the treasure of Christ's spilt blood, had still a soul to save. Saving it, he knocked a nail into the Devil's coffin.

He asked but one question as he sat sipping the hot drink fresh with lemons that Cecilia had sent down from the Castle —she was forever sending down some delicacy he must otherwise go without.

"The cat? The little white cat?" he asked.

"A queer little thing," Hester said. "He drinks the sweet milk I put out for him but he does not enjoy it; and that is odd in a cat. And—what is odder still—I scratched my arm this morning and he came and would have licked the place. I had to drive him away."

"Drive him away altogether," he advised. And then, more strongly, "Hester, drive him away."

She looked at him, surprised at such unkindness in this gentlest of men.

"He would not go," she said. "Nor would I send him. If I put him out he would come back and mew at my door; and mew upon my heart. And every day his mew would grow fainter—but it would sound louder upon my heart—until I found him dead at my door. That is not charity; it is not even commonsense, for he is a grand mouser." She took up the beaker and left him to his thoughts.

Chapter Seven

"ARE you strong enough yet, oh valiant soldier of God, to hear more of my tale?" She mocked at him where he lay high upon the white pillows of his bed; yet he thought he surprised a gentleness in her eyes.

"Yes, I am strong enough." He moved, weary, in the bed. "Tomorrow or the next day I shall be about again."

"I doubt it. It is not your body they should look to, but your spirit—the thing you call conscience. Still, if you must lie abed you are not ill-done by." She looked about at the flower-sprinkled curtains of his tester; at the quilt Hester had stitched from gay pieces; at the bright fire in the grate—though it was summer the room was cold for a sick man. Light came dim through the curtains of the casement; she went across and pulled them apart. Sunlight leaped in like a sword and she smiled into his dazzled eyes. "Your fire looks pale now, and cold. Yet it would burn me had I a body to burn. But it cannot warm me where neither the light of heaven shines nor the flames of hell."

She sat down unasked upon the edge of his bed, her skirts spread about her like a flower. She had a bright, proud look; she was as comely as any woman he had seen. Had this Joan Flower been born to a high place, he thought, she had not come, maybe, to her bitter end.

"In the end," she said with her ghost's trick of reading his thoughts, "the safety of high places is no safety at all. Neither earthly honours nor great possessions can stay your evil-doer; nor is bitter poverty an excuse. For we are what we are; some of us born to evil—and so it was with me. Why else did my love for the lady—and truly I loved her once—turn to hatred? That she had sent Meg away was just; and that she kept Philip by her still was more than just—as you have said; and I knew it well. But still I could not sleep for thinking, She lies snug beneath fine linen and soft wool; she fills her belly with fine fat foods . . . and I lie here and eat what scraps I may."

"Yet you ate well; you ate what the lady ate—you have told me so."

"True. But it was hers by right; I got only what I stole. Besides, when we are angered we are unjust. I was angered against my lady. I knew that of her freewill she would never see me again; but see me she must! Summer was drawing on and we were near to Lammas Day and the Beltane Sabbath. Very soon Meg must choose. She must join us or die . . . unless the third way opened. If my lady forgave her and took her back, then, with Meg at the Castle, I should be safe enough."

"How could that be a way out?" He lifted puzzled eyes.

"Priest, you are not very subtle. The Castle was her paradise—she might coax her almost-gentleman again. Once back she would keep silent about what we had done to her child; she was not one to court a hanging. And for that same reason she would never name me witch. Like mother, like daughter, so they say. If they hanged me for a witch it could be a hanging matter for her also. Once back at the Castle she would keep her distance; and her mouth shut.

But to live alone with me—that was another matter. If she did not join us, then, left to her loneliness and her fears, she might run mad and tell all she knew. No, if my lady would not take her back, Meg must join us or die.

I took my way up to the Castle and, as luck would have it, I came upon my lord himself. He was not glad to see me. Oh, he was quiet enough; never so much as the raising of his voice. But for all that he would not suffer me near his lady and he made it plain. 'If you will tell me your business,' he said, 'I will enquire into it for you.'

So there I stood twisting my hands and hating him because I was thought not fit to stand in the presence of the lady. My spleen rose and bitterness came up in my throat. Yet I answered gentle as he. 'My lord, it is my daughter. It is Margaret.'

'I will hear no more of her,' he said. 'She is a liar and a thief.'

'Sir,' I told him, 'you wrong my girl—and one day you will be sorry for it.'

'Do you threaten?' he asked.

'Lord,' I said, 'how could I? I meant only you will be

sorry if you think her a thief because of the mattress and the pillows. They were a gift; and my lady will tell you so herself.'

His face darkened at that. 'My lady will tell you—could she bring her tongue to the words—that your girl is all itching flesh; she is a stumbling-block to any clean man.'

'She is no different from any other woman—whoever it might be. She had her sweetheart; and through this slander she has lost him.'

'Slander?' he said and his brows went up. 'The girl was with child.'

'She is not the only one to suffer great wrong, walking alone and no help at hand. What is a girl's strength against a man?'

'I have no liking for riddles,' he said. 'If you have an accusation to bring, then bring it; and bring it now.'

'It is the man Peate,' I said, 'and your lordship knows him well.'

'I do know him well,' he said. 'A decent man and lives well with his wife. Yet I will enquire into the matter and if what you say is true you shall have justice. Go now and do not come again. If I want you I will send for you.'

So away I went all bitter with my anger. For who might be the father of Meg's child no man knew—not even the girl herself. If it were not Peate, that was hardly his fault; but all the same he would deny that he had ever come at my girl. And surely Meg needed no further punishment. She had paid the price of her slip, seeing she had lost this Master Vavasour that was a gentleman's servant and above us in the world's reckoning. Such a chance would not come her way again.

Meg came to meet me sad and sullen and all bedewed with tears. When I told her what had passed and how I had named Peate as the one who, against her will, had done her wrong, she said, all pale and spiteful, 'Then you were a fool! Peate is clever enough to play virtuous and no-one will believe you. You had done better to have named another though you lied.' And she turned and left me without a word . . . Margaret was not easy to love.

My lord sent down a message that he would see me. I found him waiting in the courtyard; he would not suffer me further. He would not allow me, so it seemed, to pollute the innocence of his chaste lady. Had he consulted his own wish he would have sent Philip packing also; but the girl had done no harm that any man could prove; and there was always justice in him.

He was an angry man that day, though, as always, quiet with it. He had made diligent enquiries and there was no truth in my tale. 'So,' I said, 'you put your trust in this bad man; and my girl is lost and abandoned.'

'Lost and abandoned, yes!' he said. 'But by her own desire and her own lewdness. See that she learns to repent or she will be a shame and a charge to you all the days of your life.'

I dropped my curtsey but I was muttering beneath my breath *A black pox upon you!* That is a witch's curse; but it was anger merely; even then I meant him no harm.

I found Margaret still in the same black mood—and who could blame her? She had lost her good match; indeed, any match at all. She had rid herself of her child and was enough of a woman to weep for it. She had been humiliated by the Master because she had shamed the Sabbath with her tears; and its joys were refused her because of her own refusal. Poor Meg with her pretty face and her slow brain and her cold heart!

It was a mistake to have brought her to the Sabbath, to have let her spy out our secrets, to have put into her frightened hands the lives of the whole coven. I saw that when it was too late. Philip now. There was your true witch—by nature; by nature only . . . as yet. But already Goody Simpson was naming her *witch*. How did the girl manage to keep Tom Simpson by her as though he were her shadow? It was a question his mother would ask time and time again. And, who could blame her? Never a man so changed! From an upstanding lad to a thin and fretful loon. She would have moved heaven and earth to break off the match—and that was a good match, too; better even than Vavasour; for Tom owned his farm. Yes, both my girls had lost a match beyond their station, seeing my husband had been nothing . . ."

"He was a good man," Samuel Fleming said, leaning back upon his pillow.

"He was a fool!" Joan Flower answered quick and fierce. "And Meg was his true daughter. But Philip—Philip was mine.

Yet if Tom was bewitched by her, it was not by witchcraft—
she had as yet no knowledge to bring it about.

'Where is my sister?' Meg asked cold and spiteful. It had
vexed her this long while that Philip had not shared her
disgrace.

'In her proper place, I hope; I have not set eyes on her,'
I said.

'I had thought you would bring her home,' Meg said.

'Why should I? Is not one wench at home enough?'

'It is better to come of her own will; otherwise they will
put her out as they put me.' And she began to cry again,
remembering the comforts of the Castle—the piled platters
and the great fires and the making of love in dark corners.
'Certainly they will send my sister away,' she said and there
was satisfaction in her voice. 'She and I were one in everything
and they will soon find it out.'

'No,' I said. 'Our Philip is sharp as a needle; she stands
in good odour.'

'So did you!' she reminded me soft and spiteful. 'They had
nothing against you; but for all that they put you out and my
lady will not look upon your face again. And so it must go
with Philip! She deserves disgrace as much as I do.'

Her pleasure in the thought did not last long.

'And how shall we live then?' she asked. 'Save for Philip
and what she lays hands on, there's naught but a bare cupboard
and miserable scraps.' For, priest, I had kept her short that I
might the sooner bring her to her senses. As for myself, I ate
in secret since Rutterkin brought me all I desired. 'How shall
we live?' Meg asked again. 'Who will bring us a fat hen or a
piece of roast pig?' And she shut her eyes and drew in her
breath as though sniffing the savoury smell.

'Girl,' I said, 'I serve a good Master. If we lack from one
source, be sure He will provide from another.'

'And meanwhile,' she said jeering, 'my belly is empty.'

'If you are hungry,' I said, 'I know of a place where you
may eat and drink your fill.'

She looked at me, half-famished, and I said, softly, 'Tonight
is the Sabbath.'

She cried out at that. She was in mortal fear of being left

alone—she had never been one of your brave ones; and now, since the death of her child, she would start at a shadow. Nor had I, for my part, dared to leave her lest she run mad and cry our secrets aloud. To take part in the Sabbath was not only my deep desire—it was my duty. I must be present; and, present or absent, I feared the Master's anger. I had brought my girl to the last Sabbath and she had profaned it with her tears. For that full amends must be made—both by her and by me. If I did not bring her all willing, tonight, they might well kill me with stones. Win her this time I must.

I said no more but left her to her hunger and to sweet thoughts of a dead child in an empty house. And, as I pulled my onions and my radishes, I would come, very quiet, and look in at the window. There she sat and she had not moved. And so she sat the long day through.

It was going on towards twilight when I set the stew-pot on the fire. A fine fat hen; Philip had brought it already cooked and the broth of it in the basin. The smell came up full of savour and Meg had eaten nothing all day. I dipped a mug into the broth and I cut off a leg and I sat down supping my soup and eating my meat. Meg looked up and her nose twitched but she said nothing. She wanted the food; but she sulked still. I took the pot off the fire and set it on a shelf and I could see how the water came up into her mouth. I smiled to myself. Hunger is as good a way as any other to break a stubborn will.

I set a pan of water upon the fire to wash my body all over; I combed my hair, and I anointed myself for the flight.

Her sullenness could stand against hunger but never against fear. Her pale eyes were dark with it.

'The Beltane Sabbath is fine,' I told her. 'For the Master Himself provides the feast. You have but to say *I will have sturgeon or I will have trout; I will have duckling or teal or partridge; I will have blue figs and apricots and almonds.* And there they are before you, as much as you can eat. And there is white wine and red; and green wine, also—green as poison. But it is not poison, no, indeed! It runs through your blood like fire so that dancing you leap high, high, high! And after the dancing comes the making of love. . . .'

'I have had enough from the making of love,' she said slow and surly but I could see how her blood stirred.

'You would get nothing from this save your pleasure,' I said. 'It is man that breeds upon us whether we would or no. But the Master has more kindness for poor women. You will get no child out of him nor out of his spirits, save by your own wish.'

The red came up into her pale face but she said nothing; only her eyes followed wherever I moved. At last she said, 'I would come with you . . . but I am afraid.'

I made as though I did not hear. I went over to the bed.

'I am afraid to go,' she said again. 'And I am afraid to stay. I am afraid of the dark; and I am afraid of the light—for in the rushlight everything moves and I have strange fancies. I am afraid everywhere in the night because of what we did to my poor child.' And she began to weep.

'You are afraid of many things,' I said and stretched myself upon the bed. 'You are no use to man nor beast; not even to yourself!' And she looked so poor a thing, all white and shaking, I could have struck her. I made myself gentle. I said, 'You have heard the priest in church! More than once he has spoken of obedience to God.' I stopped; I said, very slow, 'He told us of a father once—it is in the Scriptures— prepared to slay his child at his god's command.' She nodded. 'There,' I said, 'is your answer.' "

"Oh," Samuel Fleming cried out, "I see again how the Devil cites the Scriptures for his own purpose. You did not think fit to remind her that at the last moment, God stayed the hand of his servant Abraham and the child went free?"

"I am not such a fool, priest. 'Now you must let me be,' I said, and I still watched her beneath my lids. 'I must rest a little.' And she, all undone with her fear and her hunger, cried out, 'Let me come with you.'

'No!' I said. 'You will weep again; and maybe this time the Master will not be patient.'

'Take me,' she wept and stretched out her hands. 'I will not weep.'

'Once you are a witch, sworn and accepted, you will not weep again,' I said; and I cursed myself for the warning but

I could not stop myself. 'Though your heart swell and your eyelids burst, still you can never weep.'

'I know it,' she said. 'And I accept it. My heart is broken. If the Devil can mend it, why then it is his. I will take him for Master.'

I wasted no more words. I whistled up Rutterkin and commanded him to carry the girl; and I cut my finger and let him lick the blood that she might see how the familiar takes his payment. But I did not let him suck in his secret place lest it make her afraid—she was always a timid thing.

Though now I would have fed her with choice bits from the pot she could no longer eat, so I combed the tangles of her hair and washed the stain of weeping from her eyes and we set forth. And, once more, when she felt the wind above and below and all about her, she clung to Rutterkin and pressed upon him so that it seemed they must fall together and break on the earth below.

Margaret lay back upon my cat and her yellow hair streamed downwards till I thought it must become entangled in the treetops. I called out to warn her but she gave no sign. I saw then she had swooned; she was all her father's child; it was hard to believe she was also my own.

It was late when we came at last to the place of the Sabbath. Margaret slid off Rutterkin's back; her eyes were wide and dark with fear and she was deathly pale. I wished, then, with all my heart I had not prevailed upon her. I had hoped to wipe out the shame of that last Sabbath; but now I feared, I feared greatly that at this last moment . . ."

"God would save her?" Samuel Fleming asked.

"I did not think of that. I did not think even your god could use so poor a soul."

"He makes use of us all."

"A pity then he did not make up his mind sooner. Why did he have to bring her to the gallows first?"

"His ways are not our ways."

"Just as well!" she shrugged. "We arrived late, as I have said; and they had come to the end of the business; and the Captain, according to our custom, cried out, *Is there further matter?* I stood up and I cried out, 'I bring a servant to my Lord.'

'Let her stand forward!' the Captain cried.

I touched Margaret on the arm and she rose up beneath my hand and we took three paces forward. Then the Master came down from his high place. 'This is the girl that wept,' He said. And I answered, 'Yes, Lord.' Then He said to Margaret, 'Lift your head.' And she lifted her head and He said, 'Are you a willing servant?' And she said, 'Yes, Lord.' Then He said, 'Speak that all may hear.' So she lifted her voice and said again, 'Yes, Lord.' Then He said, 'In the presence of this my congregation, I seal you mine.' And he leant forward and nipped her in the left shoulder so that the blood came. She cried out at that; she was ever a soft thing and the pain is sharp. I saw her eyes blink . . . but no tear fell.

'Now I baptize you in my own name,' the Master said. Then the Captain brought wine he had stolen from the church —your church, priest—and he hallowed it to our rites. And he signed her upon the forehead with the Devil's sign, which is your cross standing upon its head. And the Master gave her the name of her new baptism; the name that must not be spoken save at the Sabbath.

'Now you are truly mine,' He said. 'Speak your wish and we shall grant it.'

'Vengeance!' she cried out, and I scarce knew her voice that was always quiet and low, so shrill and clear it was.

'It is granted,' He said. 'And we shall consider the manner of it. But first we must hear mass; and you shall be our altar.'

Then I was glad beyond any word. She had been accepted; and she had been given the honour all witches covet. She lay down upon the great stone, so white she was, so shapely and without blemish, that for this one time I had my pride in her.

Then the Captain, who is also our priest, came to the altar and said the prayers. It is the mass you say in your churches but we say it backward. He knew it well, for he is a priest of your god, also, and if I said his name you would know it."

Samuel Fleming groaned and covered his eyes. "Oh that I could die and hear no more."

"My Master could grant you death," Joan Flower said, quick and sly. "A sweet death . . . a falling asleep."

"And when I awake?"

"Eternal peace."

"You are clever, witch," he said, eyes closed. "But you are not clever enough. For there is no peace for me, not even at my Saviour's feet, without I first save your soul."

"Then you cannot escape my tale and must hear it to the end. The priest lifted the cross but he carried it head-to-foot and the wafer was black; and the wine was hallowed with blood. For he had taken a young child—do you listen, priest of God?—a young unbaptized child that had been stolen for the sacrifice. And he had cut its throat with a knife of stone, very sharp. Some of the blood he had poured into the wine when he had baptized my girl; and some of it he used for the sacrifice, sprinkling it now upon her closed eyes and upon her smiling mouth and upon her breasts and upon her loins. And we stood in silence, our eyes upon the white girl all dabbled with blood upon the altar stone.

And, in the holy silence, the Master spoke.

'For the wrong done to my servant that lies here, two infants have died by sacrifice—her own and that one whose blood now hallows the wine. For these two there must be payment. Two other children must die.'

We sat unmoving and there was no sound of our breathing.

'The children that shall die,' He cried out, 'are children you know well—all of you know well!' He bent to Margaret white and still and smeared with the blood of the sacrifice. 'If you have aught to say against it, speak now.'

Then He put out his hand to her and she stood up from the stone and she said, 'The children I know well. And it is a fair exchange. I, and she that bore the babe we have sacrificed this night, have wept. Now let her who bore the two we shall take, weep also!' And the congregation, both men and women, cried out, *It is just*."

Samuel Fleming said, low and bitter, "The wickedness . . . unspeakable! Do you not see? Even now do you not see?"

"You speak without reason, priest. The child of my child —flesh of my flesh, bone of my bone—was dead; dead to serve the Master. How should I grieve over my enemy's child?"

He would have spoken then but no words came through the sickness in his throat. Only his eyes implored the mercy of silence. But there was no mercy in her. "You cannot stay me," she said, as once before, "since your god allows it. Then the Master took Margaret by the hand and looked into her face. 'It is hard to believe,' he told her, 'that you are that girl who wept before us all at our last Sabbath.'

Then we cried aloud and acclaimed the new witch and made her free of the coven. And the Master took her by the hand and with her He led the dance.

First we danced the dances of our holy rites—to make the corn grow high and heavy in the ear . . . and that is a leaping dance; and the dance to make the fruit abundant on the trees . . . and that is a round dance. And last we did the dance to make the cattle heavy with young and such women fertile as desire it . . . and that is a dance not fit for your ears. You may believe me, priest, that we witches do much good."

He lifted his tired head. "It is your own corn you prosper, your own fruits, your own beasts; and the womb you bless is the womb of your own women. But what of those that offend you? Their corn is blighted; their fruit falls rotten and their cattle drop their young untimely. And the women. Their seed you blast before ever it come to birth; and their children you bewitch to a hateful death. That is your good, witch!"

She shrugged. "As to rights and wrongs, we could not expect to agree. When we had performed the dances of our rites, then we performed the dances of our pleasures; and, always we begin with *Follow the Master*. And as we came and went—leaping, skipping, bowing, bending, hopping, frisking, looping, zigzagging, curving—I caught sight of Margaret at the head of the line and I saw her face all flushed and rosy, the lips wet and red and held a little apart. But her eyes I could not see, for she moved as in a dream—and they were fast-shut.

When the dancing came to an end I did not look for my daughter . . . I did not need to look. So white a body the Master would not give up to another. And, knowing how she had lost her lover, and how no man had touched her since she had been put forth in disgrace, I was glad for her.

And when our delights came to their end, I rose up weary and looked about for my girl. I found her lying drowsy and smiling upon the altar stone; and I called up Rutterkin to carry her home."

Chapter Eight

SAMUEL FLEMING opened his eyes. She was standing there, the sunlight streaming through her body; he could see clear through her to the open window and the summer garden beyond.

"You are almost as much a shadow as I, myself!" she said laughing.

"Nonsense!" He spoke with a briskness he did not feel. "I shall be myself soon. A little more of this—and I shall be well again." He held out a frail hand so that it was stained gold with sunshine.

"We must hope so, priest. For the struggle is hard; and whichever way it goes, it must, at last, come to an end."

"There is but one end," he said. "God always wins."

"Say you so?" And she mocked a little. "Priest," and she spoke again with that strange gentleness of hers, "you are frail and old; and until the battle is won there is no peace for you. Why must you torment yourself?"

"You know the answer; you told me yourself, have you forgotten? I played my part in your life; I must play it now you are dead. We are bound to each other, I think, until the end of time."

"Yes, it is true. True and strange. A witch and a priest bound together until the end of time."

"I shall be glad of your companionship," he said. "And God will be glad, since He will bring it to pass."

"You are courteous, priest. But you are wrong. It is not your god but my Master that will rejoice. Are you ready for my tale?"

"I am ready."

"Margaret had changed since the night of the Sabbath. The sullen look had gone. There was an eagerness about her, a wild, lost look, so that as we walked, others would turn away and cross themselves. And no man, though he might lust after her, dared approach.

But she cared nothing for that now. She lived only for the next Sabbath. As for men—even at our esbats she would have had none of them, save that it was her duty. Had my lord Earl himself stooped, she would not have suffered his breath upon her cheek. Once the Master has taken a woman all men are clots of dung.

Her shoulder ached still where He had nipped it; but now the pain was all joy for his sake who had caused it. And when the pain was gone and nothing left but a blue crescent scar, it served to keep her memory sharp for revenge.

Yet she was no true witch, as I have said before; but a hot young woman troubled by the desires of the body. Had things fallen out otherwise any lusty man would have served her turn. For she had no firm principle of evil. And more; who has ever known a witch that did not cherish her familiar and gladly suckle it with her blood? But Meg could not abide hers. It came to her in the shape of a rat; and I have seen her shudder and shake when the thing put up its sharp snout and nuzzled her flesh.

Eager, restless; that was Meg these days. 'The Master promised me my revenge,' she would say over and over again; and each time I would answer, 'Then he will keep his promise.' And once, 'What is the promise?' I asked, trying her.

She said, 'You know well. Two children in place of those . . .' But for all her eagerness she stumbled and could go no further.

'If you are too nice to name the matter, are you not too nice for revenge?' I asked.

She began again. 'Two children in place of those . . . to be sacrificed.' And she was pale as bone.

'And what revenge shall you take upon them?' I asked.

She looked at me, dumb. I saw how she tried to speak but could not speak.

'You shall have your revenge when you are fit. You are not yet fit since you cannot so much as name it. You will learn that the Master helps those that help themselves—and only those. Well, *what* revenge?'

She said then, very low, 'The death of the two little boys.'

'Which little boys?' I asked.

'You know. You know well!' and her voice came out without sound. And, when still I waited, said very low, 'Lord Roos and Francis his brother.'

'Search your heart,' I warned her. 'Even a witch may know tenderness; and they are fair children.'

'I will have their death!' she cried out. 'Lord Roos has lived longer than the child I bore—five years longer. It is five years too long.'

'And the babe?' I said. 'The little Francis?'

She held her white lips stiff. 'Him, too. He has lived longer than the new-born child.' And she turned her head away. Had a witch tears she would have shed them then.

She turned her face again, and it was all white and working. 'I will have them both . . . both! Master, hear me!'

It was suddenly dark in the room. I could barely make out the Master where He stood wrapped about in a great cloak, black against the blackness. But I knew him by the coldness that came forth and I heard Margaret take in her breath.

He wasted no sweet word. 'You have kept me waiting long; and long enough,' he told her. 'It is a thing I will not endure from any servant.'

'Lord, forgive!' she cried, all humble upon her knees and the wind of her trembling stirred the hem of my skirts. I knew that He would never look upon her with favour again. He is not like your pale god, priest. The Master hates a poor and humble spirit."

"A humble spirit is not poor but rich," Samuel Fleming said.

"Be that as it may, the Master has no use for the humble. He looked upon Margaret with dislike but she was too foolish to understand it. 'Before you can work these children harm,' he told her, 'you must possess yourself of something that is theirs.'

'But I have nothing, Lord, nothing at all. And I am forbid the Castle.'

'Is there no-one to help you?' He asked.

At once I took his meaning. It was my other girl he desired —Philippa. Meg was a fair enough piece of white flesh; but Philip was fit to be Queen of hell.

And when she did not understand but went on kneeling dolefully, He said, 'There is your sister!'

'No!' Margaret cried out, sharp enough now and jealous. And that is another sign she was no true witch; for we witches grudge not the Master the lightest of his desires. And though we would die joyfully to lie in the place of that woman in whom He takes delight, yet we would serve her with all our heart, wishing her no ill since she brings joy to Him we worship.

'No!' she cried out again. 'My sister is too young.'

'Your sister is old as evil,' he said, 'and that's as old as time.' He turned his back on Meg and thrust his dark face towards me. 'Woman,' he said, 'bring Me your daughter.'

'Lord,' I said, 'I serve. But the girl is hard of heart; her will is iron.'

'I will soften both.' He turned again to Margaret where she knelt, head upon her knees; I could see the fall of her fair hair in the darkness. 'When your sister comes freely to my service, you shall have your revenge,' He said and so was gone; and the darkness and the cold went with Him; and the room was bright again and warm.

And now I could get no sense at all out of Meg. Wild and jealous, she could do nothing but tremble and rail. Could she have wept, she might have eased her heart, but all turned inward to bitterness; and this bitterness turned outward again and was writ upon her face.

I sent a message to Philip up at the Castle. I was sick, I said, and she must come at once. It was Berry of Langhorne took it. He was not willing—he had heard the tales about us; and, indeed, it was remembered against him at his own trial. I whistled up Rutterkin to follow him every step of the way— Rutterkin with his long, loping tread. It was the familiar that helped betray us, though the fault was not his. But there were those that swore they saw the white cat change into a man; a man leper-white, even to the hair, except where he was bedaubed with blood and his red, red eyes. That was a lie, priest. Rutterkin never took human shape; nor, when he went about my business, was there any blood upon him. For I did not let him suck upon me until the work was done, save twice, and never at this time. But tales go about poor witches and some of them are true; and some of them are half-true; but most of them are lies. And for half-truths and for lies we suffer more than for the truth; and many innocents also that never worked a spell, along with us."

"You must bear those deaths upon your conscience, witch. But for you and your like they had never been condemned."

"It is *your* conscience, priest, since you sat in judgment. It is for judges to find the truth. But this much was true—the little lady Catharine spied him and cried aloud at the pretty thing and would have taken him in her arms; but he reared himself and leaped and would have had her blood had she not fled screaming.

Philip did not trouble herself to come down that day although she believed me sick; and all night long Meg lay weeping and wailing until I feared the Master would put an end to her and her lamenting.

The next day brought Philip all smiles; heartless—a child who had done no wickedness as yet, but with evil all about her.

Margaret got up and went away.

'My sister is jealous,' Philip said and twirled upon her toes. 'And yet she is fair and I am brown; and she is plump as a pigeon and I skinny as a rat; and she is comely and I am plain. But she has lost her man and mine I keep to the end of days. Or . . .' and she twirled again, 'until I tire of him.'

'That one!' I said. 'That lout, that clumsy fool! My girl, my girl, if you must have a sweetheart I can find you a better.'

'What better?' she asked and stopped twirling. 'What better than Tom Simpson with his good lands and his snug house? Perhaps you will give me to Sir George Manners? Or, maybe, to my lord Earl himself? Why not? It is easy enough to be rid of my lady; and I am just the one to take her place!' she said, very wry; her work-soiled hands went up to her skinny breasts, the smile was crooked on her mouth.

'You hold yourself too cheap. You may be greater than my lady,' I told her. 'Greater than any lady in the land, be it the Queen herself!'

She stopped twirling and came close, peering at me out of her narrow eyes.

'I have a sweetheart for you,' I said, 'that will make you the envy of the world. If you would be Queen of the world, you have but to say so.'

'Queen of the world!' she laughed. 'Oh my poor mother! Certainly it is the madhouse and the whip for you!'

'Leave me out of this!' I said. 'Look into your heart. Are you set upon Tom Simpson?'

'When I could be Queen of the world?' she mocked. 'But since that is a thing I cannot be, why then I will take Tom. I know well how to keep him faithful—which I could not do with a King.' And she laughed again. 'Oh,' she cried, suddenly, 'I am weary of my life at the Castle. My lady is turned against me. She says nothing. But I know it; and everyone knows it. There is not one who does not murmur behind my back . . . and sometimes it is not behind my back. Even the littlest, dirtiest scullion looks at me with lewd eyes and thinks his dirty thoughts. What better could I do than marry Tom?'

'And will you marry the goody, too?'

'I can deal with her,' she said, her eyes hard as stone.

'Girl, what is this talk of bedding with a ploughboy? Or . . .' and I chose my words with care, 'setting yourself against that old witch his mother?'

'Witch?' She took me up at once. 'That is a word they use up at the Castle; but it isn't of Goody Simpson they use it.'

'Of me?'

She nodded.

'Then they shall have good cause. It is time. It has long been time. Now listen. You must lay hands upon something that belongs to the little lord—some small thing that will not be missed; a scarf, or a kerchief, or a lock of his hair. Anything. Anything at all, so long as it is his.'

'Why?' she asked, sharp. She was no soft, stupid thing like Meg. 'What is this talk of my little lord? We speak not of him but of a sweetheart. Are you going to catch him for me? Five years—it's over-young.' And she laughed.

'Only a fool laughs too soon,' I told her. 'One thing hangs upon the other. You must wait for your sweetheart till the work is done.'

'Not I!' she said, very quick. 'I have my sweetheart where I want him.' She turned her thumb downward and pressed it upon the table. 'As for the work, you have not told me what it is.'

'To return evil for evil,' I said. 'To pay them well for your sister's disgrace.'

She shrugged. 'Meg is a fool; she deserves all she gets.'

'We cannot be wise all the time,' I said. 'And who knows when your own turn will come?'

'I can look to myself,' she said.

We were silent while I cast about for another way of coming at her.

'You have never seen the casting of a spell,' I said at last. 'It is a fine sight.'

Her eyes began to gleam within their narrow lids.

'I plan to bewitch Lord Roos to his death,' I said. 'It is a spell that will take time to work. Before it is finished you shall see some rare fun.'

'Yes,' she said, 'yes . . .' and her lips smiled. Suddenly she said, very sharp, 'The little lord is a pleasant child. Why should I return Meg's evil upon this child I like?'

'Leave Meg out of it,' I said smooth. 'You have your own slights to avenge . . . and may have more. Why should my lady grow cold towards you? Why should they slander you behind your back and to your very face? What ill have you done anyone . . . as yet?'

'That is a point,' she said, 'and I must think upon it. As for this sweetheart you talk about, this sweetheart that is the envy of the world, he might well take some holding.' She laughed; still she did not believe me. 'But Tom is an honest fool that I can twist about my finger.'

It was no use speaking more of the matter then; so she returned to the Castle and she had promised nothing.

It was not long before she was home again. I was alone when she came in, her face all blotched with rage and her eyes bitter beneath slitted lids.

She said nothing. But from her bosom she brought out a glove; a child's glove; and threw it across the table."

Joan Flower heard the old man groan where he lay white upon the pillow. "You may well groan," she said, "for now the story quickens. It needed no witchcraft to guess that Tom

Simpson had been weighing matters. The fool was not such a fool after all. The scandal that had blackened Meg was now rising against Philip. Two sisters; birds of one feather! His mother, no doubt, had helped his dull wits to that end. He had loved my girl . . . in a way; the way the rabbit loves the weasel. Now he was finished with her. There would be no snug farm for her now; no, nor any other betrothal in the Vale of Belvoir.

'This!' Philip's mouth worked as though she worried the little glove between her teeth. 'Yes, and all you ask . . . sweetheart or none.' And she looked at me out of the corner of her eye.

'Certainly there is one,' I said. 'And He is a prince; nay, He is a King.'

'You talk in riddles,' she said, impatient, and looked about the room. 'Where shall I find me a prince, let alone a king in this place?'

'I will show you!' I said.

I drew the bolt across the door and hung a cloth upon the window; and, in the darkness I had made, I saw her wondering eyes gleam like a rat's. I spoke no word, but with my finger drew a circle about us in the dust of the floor. I pricked my arm and let the blood flow within the circle; and in the blood I wrote the Name. I stood then, eyes closed, hands across my breast and whispered the words I must not tell. Then I stepped outside the circle and looked to see that she, to the last hair, was safe within."

"Safe? That is a strange word, surely. Did you fear so loving a master?"

"Not more than you fear your god. Yet it was not fear for myself; I was his obedient servant but Philip—there was another matter. She had a mind not to be moved and a pride to match it. And, if she angered the Master, He might tear her in pieces. But not while she stood within the circle. There she was safe. It was the first and only time I set my will against Him.

Then I went round and about the circle widdershins; and all the time I cried softly, *Sathan. Sathan. Hail, Lord. Sathan come!*

I could see Philip's face green where the blood had ebbed

beneath the tan. I felt her shiver before anything happened. She was a harp whose strings the light breath stirs.

In the darkness the door swung open for all it was bolted; and the coldness came in. And cold in the heart of the cold—the Master.

I fell upon my knees; but within the circle Philip stood upright.

I raised my head at last and, save for the cold that streamed from Him, it was hard to believe this was the Master, for he stood there smiling—a pretty boy in green.

And his voice was gentle, too, when He spoke to her. 'Will you become my servant to do my commands?' He asked her.

'You are overyoung to take a woman's will,' she said quickly.

He bent his head towards her then. His eyes were old as time; and in them all the wickedness since time began.

She dropped on her knees within the circle. 'Lord, I will be your servant,' she said and held out her arm that he might take her blood.

'Come forth then from the circle,' He commanded.

So she came from the circle and He bent and wounded her arm, not with a knife or with his hand; but He nipped her with his teeth, which is a thing I had never heard before. When the blood streamed out over her thin, brown arm, He brought out the covenant and she made her mark.

Then He said, 'If you have a prayer I will grant it.' And still upon her knees she answered straight, 'Lord, you are comely above all men; but still it is in the fashion of men. And if my lord stoops to his servant, then let it not be in the fashion of a man but in the fashion of the God.'

He asked, 'Do you know what it is you ask?' And she, 'Yes, Lord. At the Castle there is a picture. A woman holds a swan to her breast. He is her lover; that is well-seen. And he is a god; that, too, is well-seen. And the woman desires the strange mating. So it is with me. I have heard that the Master is tall as a tree and black as night; or that He is a great ram or a goat or a bull. Lord, if I find favour in your sight, let me know I am beloved of the God.'

'I hope you are of the same mind when we meet again!' He

said. 'But if I come to you in the likeness of the God, shall you not be afraid?'

'I have not feared for my soul,' she said. 'Why should I fear for my body?'

'Then let us drink to our next meeting,' He said. And I brought out the wine she had taken from the Castle and they drank together. Then He set down the cup and turned to me, and there was no kindness in him. 'Never again set your will against me,' He said. 'This one time I forgive you since this girl was stiff with pride. It would have been a thousand pities to tear such sweet flesh to pieces.' And so he was gone.

Philip stood very still, smiling beneath half-closed eyes while I took the cloth from the window and the daylight came in again. She shook a fretful head as though it disturbed her after the secret darkness. I offered her some food, for she had eaten nothing since she came but she shook her head and turned on her heel and went back to the Castle.

I rubbed out the circle and opened the window and called for Meg. She would not come at first, such was her sullen way; and when she came, at last, she was wearing her spiteful look.

I lifted the little glove from the table and I remember how I stroked it with my finger-tip, it was so fine and soft and worked with gay, bright silks. I was sorry so fine a thing must be destroyed."

When Samuel Fleming spoke she started; for she was back again in the past—she, for whom all earthly things were past —back again in her little room, a child's glove upon her palm and Margaret staring from her to the glove with untrusting eyes.

"You grieved," he said, "for the bright, soft thing you must destroy. But of the other thing—the bright, soft thing, the thing without price you were about to destroy—you did not think."

"Yes," she said, "I thought. And I was glad. Like you, priest, I served my Master.

'The child's glove!' Margaret said. 'So it *was* my sister that left just now.'

I nodded.

'When my sister is here,' she cried out and beat her hands together, 'then the window is hooded, the door is barred.'

'Would you have the whole world spy upon us?' I asked. 'Come now, set a pan upon the fire. And leave fretting at the glove; we need it to work the spell.'

I mended the fire and she set the pan upon it; when the water boiled we let out our blood and we cast it into the water together with the glove. And, as we stirred together, I said the words.

> Glove shall go
> To earth below,
> From out this pot,
> There to rot.
> Little lord,
> Hear the Word,
> Brew thicken,
> Lordling sicken,
> Peak and die,
> In churchyard lie.

I took the glove from the brew and, with a skewer, I pricked it full of holes; and I called upon my familiar, *Go upwards, upwards,* and he flew up the chimney. I knew then that the Master had hallowed the spell. So I took the glove all sodden and ruined and stained and I digged a little hole and I put the glove into its little grave."

"Woman," Samuel Fleming groaned from the bed, "such wickedness—were you not afraid?"

"Priest, that is a thing you must stop asking. For each time I must answer, *Are you afraid when you go about your master's business?*"

"Your soul is firmly lodged with the Devil," he said. "How may I pry it loose for God? But the end is not yet, and I shall win."

Chapter Nine

HE WAS lying in a cushioned chair, his face turned to the summer garden. Because of the fire burning in the grate and because of the sun streaming in through the open window, he was comfortable. But he was weary, so that although Hester had put the tobacco jar and the long pipe on the stool by his side, they stood untouched.

Joan Flower came in from the summer heat and the cold came with her, so that he coughed and pulled the rug higher above his knees.

But all the same he was forced to smile seeing her there, a wild rose thrust through the dark of her curls. But—and he stopped his smiling—for all her sweet shape she was a lost soul . . . unless he could win her for God.

"In the end," he told her, "God will win."

She shook her head so that the dark curls flew. "No, priest, I am for my Master, now and for always."

"In the end you will come to the mercy of God."

"I did what I did; and even now I cannot repent."

"Yet you will repent," he promised her.

"Priest, have you forgotten what it was I did?"

"How could I forget?" And he remembered little Henry beginning to peak and pine, and the way he would push the food from him or let the spoon drop from his hand. But the terrible fits had not begun yet and they were hopeful, all of them —Francis and Cecilia and the physician, and Hester and himself.

But for all that the child had grown worse—fear deepening to terror in the young eyes; sharp, nervous turn of the head this way or that. And even that had not been the worst of it.

When he remembered how the child had suffered—the sickness, the convulsions, the pain—he could hardly endure to look upon Joan Flower, not though she was dead and suffering for her wickedness. Yet, if under God, he was to be a good shepherd, he must be patient, watching his every opportunity . . .

". . . we had done what had to be done to the glory of the Master . . ."

He came back from his thoughts with a start. If he wanted to win her he must listen; listen to every word, watch for every sign.

"Now we were free," Joan Flower said. "Now we were happy. With this deed, so it seemed, Meg had wiped out the memory of her dead child. And we were the more glad since it was drawing near to All Hallows and our autumn meeting. You know—for I have told you—that at each Sabbath we stand up to tell what we have done to enlarge the name of the Master. When a witch has done no evil, or little evil, then she is pelted with stones or beaten with rods and some have died of it. But when she has done much evil then she is acclaimed in full coven; and she is seated near the Master and He loves and caresses her. So you can understand how Margaret and I longed for the meeting and counted the days.

Last day in October; a clear autumn day all gold and glowing; and we longing for the Feast and restless for the Feast. Oh priest, priest, still they dance and they drink and give their bodies to love. And I—I have no body." He was shocked by the naked longing in her eyes.

She sighed deeply, taking up her tale.

"Meg stood combing out the tangles of her hair. She went about like a slut when there was none to see, but for the Sabbath she must be beautiful. Last time the Master had chosen her above all; this time, surely, it would be so again.

Suddenly she stopped, comb in her lifted hand. 'Philip does not go with us?' she said.

'No,' I said. And then, I added, warning, 'Philip is not our concern. The Master will send for her.'

Meg's pale eyes clouded. 'Will she be laid out upon the altar stone?' she asked with the soft silliness of hers. 'And will they say the mass over her body?' She began to giggle. 'A pretty sight, Philip, with her brown skin and her flat chest and the ribs thrusting through her lean sides!'

'The Master looks upon the inward heart——' I began.

'But He likes the body, too!' she interrupted and, with mock modesty, folded her hands between her thighs.

When it was full dark and the stars pricking in the cold, black sky, we went rejoicing to the Sabbath. Meg rode upon her rat and found no pleasure in it. She could not endure the feel of the creature between her legs; yet for cowardice she must clutch at the greasy skin; and, when we came to a bank of cloud and her mount dropped sharply, she cried out and pressed herself still closer to the thing she loathed.

All about us the air shook with the rush of the flight; with the noise of our mounts and with our wild cries as we threw ourselves forward, all impatient for the Sabbath. Joan Willimott urging herself forward upon her straw rushed by me. Ellen Greene steadied herself and we flew on together.

We were flying now over the field of the Sabbath. Below us lay the wild heath; I could make out the clearing where we danced and the great stone that is the Master's seat white in the moonlight. I heard the sound of beasts and human bodies grounding and we stood upon the sacred place.

It was then I saw my younger daughter streaking naked through the air. She did not so much fly as dart. And when she fell, it was straight and sudden as a falling star. It was as though your god himself reached out a hand to cast her away. She stood upright in the moonlight. Her black hair streamed backward beneath the poison berries of her crown—fine glassy beads of briony with heart-shaped leaves and wicked, purple flowers. And about her little neck she had set a necklace of the same and about her brown thighs also; and the nipple of each small breast she had pointed with a green heart.

There was a wildness about her, a wickedness. I thought, If you should prick a vein there would flow not warm, red blood but cold, green poison. It was hard to believe that this was the child I had once clouted and then stuffed with bread and a smear of honey to stop her noise!

We went softly to our places; for until the Kiss is given we have no desire to speak with another but wait in quiet until our sacred rites admit us to the Master's glory.

Philip dropped lightly into her place, and leaning across her neighbour—for remember we sit man by woman—she whispered, 'Will the God keep his word? If He comes in the shape

He has promised, then I will adore Him; I will serve Him with my body.' "

"Spare me," Samuel Fleming said, his face shadowed by his hand.

"If you are to save me, should you not hear all?" she asked, a little sly. He sighed knowing that she dwelt on these things because she lusted still for the unspeakable rites.

"They were sweet and sacred to me," she said. "And still are . . . and still are. When I lifted my head I saw the Master standing upon the stone. And that is a strange thing; we never saw Him come and we never saw Him go. We lifted our eyes and He was there . . . or He was not there. He had kept his promise; He stood there in the likeness of a great black ram.

I looked sideways at Margaret. Did she still desire the God? Her white face swung towards me between the pale gold of her hair; the fear in her eyes gave me the answer. From my other side I caught a deep long sigh of ecstasy—such ecstasy only your true witch knows. 'And is my sister frightened?' Philip whispered, mocking, 'frightened of this great and noble beast, of this magnificent God of ours? Let her not fear; she will not be called upon.' She said no more but sat; eyes unmoving upon the Master.

And now the trumpet sounded; it is a sound to freeze the words on your tongue and the blood in your veins. We rose up in our places and we made a circle about the God that stood in the shape of a great ram upon the high stone. For the first thing at the Sabbath is to pay our reverence. That is a fine sight, priest! We stand in our circle bending outwards straight as a rod; and we lift a foot forward in the air. And we cry out, Hail Lord, Hail Sathan. Hail, hail! And the leaves shiver on the trees with the sound of our crying; and there is a rolling as of thunder between heaven and earth.

Then the Captain sets a great white candle between the horns of the Master and the children go about . . ."

"The children?" he asked as though unbelieving. Yet he believed it, for the sigh that burst upward seemed to break his heart.

"Yes, priest, I have told you. Have you forgotten? If I could have won the little lord to my Master he need never have died. The children went about and gave us each our candle of black. Then once again the circle swung and, as we stood before the Master, we reached up and kindled our black candles from the white candle that flamed between his horns. And when our flames were steady-burning we broke the circle at that point where the most honoured stands by the least honoured—that is where the newest witch stands by the children—for it is always thus we stand, each one in his place. We moved slowly in our line, the most worshipful at the head and the children at the tail, to give the Kiss of homage."

Samuel Fleming lifted his face, grimacing with disgust; she laughed at that. "The God is not like any man nor any beast. For beneath the tail He wears a face; and it is that face we kiss upon the lips.

At last we three stood before the Master, and, one after another, we knelt to give the Kiss. I saluted Him, and Margaret after me. But when Philip knelt He bade her stand; and He turned about so that she kissed Him upon the face between the horns.

The children stopped moving not knowing what to do— until the Captain stepped forward and flicked them on. The Kiss between the horns. Such a thing we had never seen, no, not even the oldest in all the covens, though we had heard that the Master will sometimes so honour the great—the Kings and the Queens and your fine churchmen that are his servants."

"Then your master is not above the vanities of the world?" Samuel Fleming said quickly.

"He is not such a fool!" She was just as quick. "The vanities of the world—that is his winning card. And now the last kiss given we came again to our places, shielding our candles with our hands; we sat upon the ground crescent-wise facing the Master—and each one with his candle burning blue by his side. You should see it, priest! The dark night and the blue flames burning upward towards the stars.

And again the trumpet sounded. And now it was the time; time for the Master to bid us tell how we had enlarged his kingdom upon earth since the last Sabbath.

So we stood up, one after another; and I sat there marvelling at his patience—so small the evils and so mean. Here a cow with dugs bewitched to give no milk; there an ox or a sheep, sick; or a patch of corn blighted or an apple-tree cankered. But I was wrong, priest. I should have remembered; I should have remembered Margaret and the way small evils grow to big.

And so at last I stood up in my place. 'Lord,' I cried out, 'I have brought another soul to your service.'

'Let it stand forth,' He commanded.

So Philip stood up and went forward. She knelt before Him, her head a little bent. 'Raise your head,' He said and she lifted her face. He stared at her with narrow eyes and from narrow eyes she stared back; and there was no fear in her.

'Is this the shape of the God you desired?' he asked. 'And are you satisfied?'

'Yes, Lord.' Her voice rose clear and we all heard it.

'Now we baptize you in my name,' He said. 'Cast away the name of Christian baptism and take the new; be known by it wherever my servants foregather but in no place else.'

So the Captain brought the goblet and baptized her. 'Two souls you have brought to Me,' He said.

'Yes, Lord,' I answered. 'Two daughters. All I have.'

'It shall be remembered to you,' He said. But, priest, it was forgotten; it was forgotten.

Then He cried out, 'Let the two stand together that I may see them.'

So Margaret came forward all trembling and dared not raise her head; but Philip stood upright. And when they stood together I had my pride in them; for Meg, though but a poor creature, was milk and honey in the moonlight; and Philip in her scarlet crown wore wickedness as saints their halo.

He looked at my white girl. 'You have been my servant for full three months,' He said. 'What have you done for my service?'

And while Margaret shook and could not find her tongue, Philip cried out in a clear voice, 'We have bewitched the little lord up at the Castle. He suffers strange agonies and soon—but not too soon—he shall die.'

'It is good,' He said; 'but not so good. The child's body you will destroy. But what of his soul? Can you win Me his soul?' And He turned to Margaret, pressing for his answer.

'Lord,' she said at last, very low, 'that is a hard thing. For he is most truly a Christian child.'

His lips turned backward over the strong white teeth; he looked as though He might tear her to pieces. But Philip spoke still in that clear voice. 'Lord, we will try!'

'See to it then.' He smiled upon her. 'But—' and his smile was spiteful upon Margaret, 'there is more to do. *Is* there not more to do?'

'Yes, Lord,' she faltered and it was hard to catch her words. 'There is the other boy . . . the little lord Francis. Yes,' and she brightened and her voice came more strong, 'there is the girl, the lady Catharine. We could kill them, all three.'

'See to it then!' He said once more; but He was not well-pleased. And, indeed, it needed no god to know her poor quality.

Philip raised herself upon her toes—she was not tall—and whispered in his ear. And now He was pleased and pleased indeed! He tweaked her ear so that the blood ran down her neck among the red poison berries but she gave no sign of pain, standing there proud yet humble before Him.

'This new witch of mine strikes to the womb of the matter. Speak and tell your purpose.'

Philip said softly, but every sound came clear, 'To kill the children is not enough. For revenge we must go deeper; deep as the insult; and deeper still. They shall have no more children —the lord and the lady. The seed must die and the womb be blasted; she shall conceive no more.' "

Samuel Fleming's frail body shook. "I can endure no further."

"Yet the lady endured it," Joan Flower reminded him. "And the lord endured it; and above all the little ones endured it."

"It is harder, sometimes, to endure for those we love, than to endure for ourselves."

"That is a great nonsense, priest. When another hangs, it is *his* neck that is broken; not our own. So, also, when we ourselves come to the gallows, it is *our* soul takes the fear, *our* bodies the agony.

But that was not the end of Philip's planning. She meant

113

the lord and the lady to go childless not only on earth but in heaven, also. She was bent upon winning the souls of these little ones; with fear and with torment to make them cry out against God, to turn them towards the Master, accepting ease from torment at his hands. Two fine and precious souls lost to your god. And the lord and lady childless on earth and in heaven, alike."

His face crumpled into lines of pain, remembering the torment the children had suffered; and no word of complaint from them, tender as they were, nor from their parents.

"Yes, we failed. But that night—the night of the All Hallows' Feast, we did not dream of failure," Joan Flower said and sighed. "And so our business being done, the Master nodded for us to begin the dances; and, as He nodded, the great light upon his head bobbed up and down; the shadow of his horns jigged like curved swords upon the ground.

I remember well the order of the dances. First we did the Leaping Dance; we leaped so high in the air it seemed we must touch the moon with our finger-tips . . . and that year the corn grew higher than ever was known. Next we did the Dance of Fertility of Beasts; we danced it with so good a will that the cattle brought forth in abundance. Then the Master commanded the Captain to sing. It was a hymn to the Master and it has many verses—but not one fit for your ears. It praises his virility and the chorus we sing together."

She began to hum and in the sunlight her body swayed voluptuously; and now he could hear her low sweet voice and the curious senseless words,

> "Har, har, Devil, Devil.
> Come Sathan, Lord of Evil,
> Dance here, dance there,
> Play here, play there,
> Prance and dance
> Sway and play, Sway and play.
> Sabbath sweet Sabbath of our delight,
> Sabbath great Sabbath and holy the night,
> We wait for the nod of our Master the God.
> Har, har, Devil, Devil.
> Come Sathan, Lord of Evil.

And then, priest, we dance and we stamp our feet and we clap our hands until the ground rings and sends the sound of our joy to the sky; and the sky sends it back again. And so between the ringing of heaven and earth we dance; and the ring moves faster, faster; and the song comes louder, and it is all a madness and a delight and sweet poison in the blood.

And so we came to the last dance of all, the Dance of Follow the Master. Philip stood behind Him and no-one between them. And I stood near, for I, too, was honoured that I had brought her soul to Him. Always, priest, in this dance a witch stands by a spirit—male with female, female with male, that we may know delight. But Meg stood at the end among the children; she went to her place sullen enough; but when she saw how she stood between two pretty boys she brightened and soon she was dancing with the same madness as the rest of us.

Suddenly, with no warning—as is the way in this dance—the pipe stopped and the music broke. It was the moment.

Oh priest, there is no human coupling like coupling with a spirit. No, never close your eyes—it is a thing you must know. And it is a right coupling; for it brings fertility to all who desire it and to those alone. And it is a strange thing; when one couples with a spirit, then he is warm as any man. But when one couples with the Devil He is colder than stone; and when He is cold He begets no child."

He lifted a puzzled head. "But the Devil cannot breed; learned men have told us so."

"Then they lie, priest; in this, as in other things. Have you not heard of Devil's spawn? If the Master considers a witch worthy, He asks her if she will bear his child. If she says No, then when he takes her He is cold as well water. But if she says Yes, then he is warm as a man."

"Shameless, shameless," Samuel Fleming said and groaned.

"Leave your groaning, priest," Joan Flower said, "or I shall think you envy us our pleasures. Nor would you be the first priest to do so; no, nor to join us, too, forswearing your own god and bending the knee to mine. I have seen them, and—" she thrust an impudent face close to his so that he was faint with the coldness that came from her, "they become great men with us; they stand next to the God himself."

"Go," he said. "Torment me no longer with your shameless shames."

"Your spirit is weak," she said, mocking. "But mine is strong. You cannot endure the wild, free smell of evil; but I can endure the stifling stench of good."

"So God shall catch you in the end," he said.

Chapter Ten

HE WAS half-lying in his chair beneath the great cedar-tree; his thin fingers touched the warm earth; in the apple-tree a blackbird sang. He could see it—orange beak and fan-spread of plum-black tail. Its whole body quivered as the song lifted, arched and dropped to the last clear note.

At his back a cold wind struck sudden, unexpected. He turned sharply. In the layered depth of the cedar-tree he caught a glimpse of her pale shadow; and, peering again, heard her light laugh.

"Do you come again," he asked, "to spoil so fair a day with so dark a tale?"

"It is a tale that must be told—to the end," Joan Flower said. She came from the darkness of the tree and dropped at his feet, skirts spread.

"Then since it is so—" he sighed and folded his hands beneath the warm rug, "let us lose no time."

She nodded, brisk. "The sooner the better; so we shall both find our rest.

There was ill-will between my daughters now. There had always been jealousy. Philip envied Meg's fairness; Meg envied Philip's quick tongue and her iron will and the power one felt within her. But until that last Sabbath they had behaved like sisters, standing together against all accusers. Now they were enemies—each for herself and herself for the Devil.

We had cast the spell to bewitch the little lord—you will remember that!" And she smiled wickedly. "Now we waited for news. We waited long and long enough. Philip was still at the Castle and could not come down to us—the house was full, the King avisiting; and no-one in the village would speak with us. It was Joan Willimott sent us her spirit to give us the news— she that in the end betrayed us. Little Lord Roos lay sick . . ."

"So fair a child . . . so bright. . . ." It was as though the old man spoke within himself. He turned suddenly, piercing her with the anger of his eyes. "So little a child, so good. You were woman as well as witch, Joan Flower; how could you do it?"

"I had seen sick children before; I had sacrificed my child's child. I was not likely to grieve for the child of my enemy."

"No-one was your enemy—except yourself. No-one had done you any ill."

"All good folk were my enemy. And especially I hated Madam the Countess with her righteousness, her cold, chaste goodness. I was glad of the wickedness we did. And the more my lady prayed for the child and the more my lady wept for the child, the more glad was I. We played with her as a cat with a mouse. We would call a halt; and then, even while she was on her knees thanking her god, we would call down the sickness heavier than before."

"And all the time," he said and his voice came out in a whisper, "we did not know; we did not know."

"You did not know and you did not guess. You were too highminded, too virtuous—you and the lord and the lady. But in the village they were beginning to guess; they whispered in knots by the pump or by the stocks; yes, and in church, too. They would stop their whispering if they saw me or my daughters. And up at the Castle there was whispering, too. Philip, when she could be spared, would come down, now raging, now laughing, to tell us how the servants dropped into silence as she went by; and how, more than once, turning quickly, she had caught them crossing themselves. But no-one told my lord; and no-one told my lady. Useless. Neither he nor she would have listened then, such was their faith in those that served them. And even when the tales came to your ears, priest . . ."

"I did not believe them, either. You were women of my own flock; I had christened your daughters. Three women I knew—or, God forgive me, thought I knew—and two of them so young. How could I believe they had the power, or the will even, to torment a child, a sweet and innocent child?"

"Yet the thing had been done by others before us; and will be done by others after us; done again and again."

"God forbid! That such things happen, one knows; knows but does not quite believe. Not to *this* child, one says; not by *these* women. Why, I had seen you, all three, kneel in my church, pray in my church."

"You were too simple, priest. To *Whom* did we pray? And what words did we use?"

He knocked his hand against his breast. "That such things can happen!"

"Do happen!" she corrected him. "Happen again and again."

"Not to the people one knows; not *by* the people one knows." And in his weakness and his grief, it was as though a child repeated the thing he wants to believe.

"They say, priest, that you are a wise man, subtle in argument; but you are no match for an ignorant woman."

"The Devil lends you his wit," he said. "But take care, the Devil is a deceiver."

"You are right there, at least." She sighed. "Else I should not be wandering now between heaven and hell. But I never thought then of being lost between the cold stars, I thought only of the greatness of the reward, seeing I had brought two souls to the Master; one, it is true, of no great worth . . ."

"To my Master," he interrupted, "all souls are equal."

"My Master is not such a fool. To Him souls are equal only in the counting of heads. But there are some He covets; and Philip was one. And, over and above that, I had brought sickness upon the little lord and the next step would be death. So I was filled with joy, priest; such joy, priest, you might know, saving a soul; or bringing one you love back from the gates of death."

She was silent a little, then she said, "Tell me, priest! If your heaven is so sweet a place, why do you grieve when one you love is called thence? And . . . why did you grieve for the little lord?"

"Because the flesh is weak; and the child's death untimely and the manner cruel."

"Untimely? That is for your god to say—you believe that, surely? Yet you held, I remember, a service that the child might recover. Why did you not leave it to your god?"

He made a little helpless movement with his hands.

"Your god did not listen." She spoke on a small bubble of laughter. "He did not grant your wish as our Master listens, granting us our prayers."

"Yet he deserts you at the end."

"It was I deserted Him—never forget that, priest. As for the end—it is not yet. That service you held. I was there. I and my daughters. All three."

"I saw you and I thought, These are no witches. No witch would dare to set foot in holy Church nor take the blessed Wafer upon her tongue."

"You were wrong. We came into church when it served our purpose; and the Wafer we took upon our tongue . . . but we did not swallow it. We kept it safe. The Wafer, once desecrated, works the blackest magic. Yes, priest, you do well to groan. But you would do better to look at your congregation, not being deceived because a face is known to you. For here an old man, or there a young woman—yes, or even a child—is turning your prayers to mockery . . . and worse. Yes, we prayed, my daughters and I; but behind our hands we laughed to see how you were fooled."

"God is not fooled," he said quite gently. "Maybe you laughed too soon."

She shook her smiling head.

"You say you were woman as well as witch; you say the witch's heart knows tenderness. Yet you sat there knowing the wickedness you had done and were not moved from your purpose, not though you saw men and women weeping and praying."

"Are you moved from your purpose, priest, when we curse or weep; or when we pray to our Master? Well, you held your service and you wept and you prayed; but your god did not listen; and the child grew yet more sick. And all your prayers were no use. They were no use at all."

"Why did you not kill him outright? Why did you play with him, now catching him back a little way towards life, now hurrying him to the grave?"

"You grow forgetful, priest. It was because we had still to win his soul for the Master."

"That was a thing you could not do. It was perhaps God's purpose that the child should die; but not that he should lose his immortal soul."

"No," she agreed, thoughtful. "No. We tried but we could

not pry him loose from God. Philip would creep into his chamber while the nurse slept and she would whisper in his ear. *Would you be well again? You have but to say the word and my Master will cure you. A word . . . a little word; or no word, even; a nod; a nod only and there will be no more pain. You will run free upon the cool grass and you will play and you will laugh for joy.*

But he cried out against her and more than once she was forced to put a hand over his mouth; and each time she was so angered she could have strangled him where he lay. But she desired his soul. The child cried out against her so loud that she dared no longer come into his chamber. So we sent Rutterkin. He would sit upon the pillow . . ."

"I remember," Samuel Fleming groaned. "The child cried out, *The cat! The cat!* We looked and there was no cat; and we thought it was the sickness."

"It was no sickness, priest. And when the child would not listen, the cat lay upon his chest so that he could not breathe; and the cat scratched him, face and hands. You thought it was the frenzy of his sickness."

"God forgive us," Samuel Fleming said.

"Then Joan Willimott tried. She sent her spirit—the little lady all in green and a face fair enough to win a little child."

"But not this child."

"Not this child," she agreed. "And so time wore on and it was spring."

"And still within doors the child lay sick."

"Yes, sick to death. But he did not die; for we could not win his soul. And then it was summer; but still we could not win him. And so it came to September; and the corn standing thick and heavy and yellow; apples ripening; and the plums purple on children's lips and hands. September, sixteen hundred and thirteen, I remember it well."

"We all remember it," he said. "In that late summer the child died." He was silent for a while; then he said, "He died patiently, putting his trust in God."

"But God—your god—did not listen."

"He listened. He saved that most precious soul. For eternal happiness the child endured a little while of pain."

"Spoken like a priest. A Christian priest! *A little while of pain!* There was torment enough to break a strong man. But the child endured it. Not with patience, perhaps, as you would like to think—this was a mortal child and no saint. But, true it is, he never cried out against his god . . . though he cried often for God's help. Philip told me that; Philip stealing by his door to listen; Philip sending out her own shadow to stand by his bed while the nurse slept."

"A true witch to watch over her victim's pain!" Samuel Fleming could hardly speak for anger and for grief.

Joan Flower laughed. "It was her pleasure and her duty. A little more and a little more—and maybe he would blaspheme against his god."

"You do not know God," Samuel Fleming said, "Whose nature is all merciful even to such as you. Let any man cry out against Him, being ignorant and tormented and He will understand. But when a child cries out in pain then there are tears on the face of God."

"If your god is so tender, why did he not wipe away the child's tears, and his own, at the same time?"

"The battle of good and evil is always joined. God gives free choice even to a child."

"Priest, you are a fool! What choice to a suffering child?"

"Yet there *was* a choice," he reminded her. "And the child chose."

"Yes," she said, and sighed. "You are in the right of it there! The Master was wrathful when the child died and his soul safe from us for ever. I remember the funeral . . . the early leaves drifting as we followed the coffin . . . the funeral coach all hung with black; and behind it, all in black, men and women walking, a long, long line. And we walked too, my girls and I. Already the wind was blowing chill; and I remember thinking, Soon it will be winter; and then comes spring again; but the child lies locked for ever in the black earth. He will never be free to run again. And then I thought, But he is free for ever of the wide fields of heaven; and I was sad that we had not taken his soul.

It was a great burying for so little a child, priest. Gentlefolk from great houses both near and far; and servants from the Castle; and all of us in Bottesford and from other villages besides. Your church could not hold us all. Those that could not come within, stood without."

"But not you, witch, not you," Samuel Fleming said, bitter. "There you stood, a decent woman in your black gown . . ."

"My lord earl sent black gowns to all who had served in the Castle, yes, even to Meg, though they had turned her away."

"He made no distinction, more's the pity," Samuel Fleming said. "And I looked about, seeing women, yes, and men, too, all noisy with their tears; and then I saw you, standing there very quiet and your face pale. I thought, They turned her from the Castle not for her own shame but for that of her daughters. Yet she bears no malice, grieving for the death of the child. And this is the one they call *witch!* So I thought to show you some kindness; and I said, 'Joan Flower, there is room for you.'"

"And so I came inside . . ." She smiled.

". . . while good women stood outside and wept."

Joan Flower nodded brightly. "I could not take my eyes off my lady where she sat all hung with black. I could not see her face beneath the veil but I knew it was soiled and spoiled with tears. And I thought, *The Devil shall wipe away your tears.* But He never did. She was obstinate in her faith. I could not take my eyes from her, nor from the little one she carried in her lap. She had tied a black riband about his arm; and I thought, *Soon you shall weep for this one, too.*"

Samuel Fleming held out a hand as though beseeching her to stop. He could not endure, in his weakness, that the dark tale be unfolded step by step.

"But the thing happened!" She nodded brightly. "And we know it happened. It cannot be altered by a hairsbreadth. All your silence cannot undo it.

When I could tear my eyes from the lady I looked upon the lord. There were lines down his face as though you had taken a sharp stone and scored soft clay. But he gave no other sign; his eyes stared straight before him. And the girl, the little lady, sat by him in her black gown and her head very high. For all I saw of tears, c▪ their marks, she might have been a witch. A proud girl; she could have served the Master well.

When you prayed, priest, and when the choir sang, then tears fell like silent rain. Only the lady sat unweeping, and the lord and the girl; and the little one chuckled, not knowing what it was all about. As for myself, I would have wept too, had I been able—for here was a soul lost to my Master and bound instead for your cold heaven. Oh priest, for all you talk of love, your faith is loveless."

"As you understand it." And he looked at her with compassion.

"I see no joy in it; nor music nor dancing nor drinking nor feasting. And there is no marriage nor any delight of the flesh. Can you wonder, priest, that the God men worshipped before your Christ was born wins yet—day by day more souls and still more?"

"The Devil goes about the world seeking whom he may destroy; but it is God that wins in the end He will win you too—though what He will make of you, He alone knows."

"No, priest. My Master will win; he will win me back again. And, take care, priest. He may win you, also. He is stronger than God. And what he will make of you I know very well. You are learned and you are steadfast; He will make you his Captain and his priest in Hell."

"I have no desire for such honours," he said, drily.

"We shall see! Well, the child was buried—that noble piece of flesh rotting like humbler folk; for death treats all alike and life goes its way and nothing can hold it back. Winter—snow and rain and mud; frost and cold winds cutting like a knife. And then the sun again; green buds on trees, primroses in the copses. Philip up at the Castle; Meg in the cottage with me.

It was a fine life we had, we two; though to others it looked poor enough. I would not have changed it, not even to lie in my lady's bed. No . . ." she smiled, wicked and sly, "certainly not to lie in my lady's bed, not with what we had planned for her! They hated us now in the village. I did not care though once I had wept. Now I welcomed it; I was filled with pride that folk feared me and crossed themselves when I went by. As for friends—I had them and to spare! Witches from far and near, from this coven and from that, would come to us to eat and to drink and to take their fill of love."

"You made the night unclean. Your drunken songs, your filthy games! It was then you began to change; and your face showed it, showed it clear. I think the death of the child had left its mark."

"Which child?" she asked, quick and impudent.

"The child at the Castle; the child you had known, perhaps had loved a little. Joan Flower, you began to grow old."

She sent him a wicked look but he went on. "Yes, old. Lines. Not lines that come for a good life, but ugly lines . . . lines of an ugly life. Could you not see, even then, that your Master was a liar? Had he not promised you youth; had he not promised you beauty as long as you lived?"

"Priest, you are told in heaven you shall wear a halo about your head and upon your shoulders great wings. And though you have never seen any man wearing his halo like a hat, nor spreading his wings like a bird, still you believe it is true. Your faith tells you that in heaven it is so.

So with us. My hair was streaked with grey; the lines were in my face; my eyes sunk deep within the bone. That was how you, the unbelievers, saw me. But, priest, what was it the Master saw and those others at the Sabbath? They saw the round cheek, the fresh colour, the sweet shape; they saw the dark curls, the bright eyes, the red mouth. As for this life of ours, what is it but a dream, as you have often said? A dream, a dream, merely. Priest, the Master fulfilled his word."

Samuel Fleming shook his head. "You were taken in the net of his deceit. You were old; and ugly with wickedness. Good people hated you everywhere."

"I desired the hatred of the good."

"It brought you to your death. And now that you wander unhouselled, still you are obstinate not to be saved . . . and I am a frail and foolish old man." He lay back, eyes closed, lips moving in prayer. "Yet," he said and opened his eyes full upon her, "God is strong and He is merciful. And in the end He will see to it that you are saved."

"Say you so, priest?" There came to him the distant sound of light and mocking laughter. The wind had freshened so that he shivered and rose and went within from the emptiness of the summer garden.

Chapter Eleven

"OH, you are not well again!" she cried with sweet compunction, seeing him sunk again in the pillows of his chair; and, though it was high summer, logs crackled in the hearth and firelight shone through his fingers as he held them to the blaze.

"I lingered overlong in the garden yesterday," he said. "But, indeed," and he sighed, "I cannot be well until you are won for God."

"Then you will never be well!" Her face shone white and wicked between the tossed waves of her hair.

He let the taunt go by.

"So many things they said of you," he told her, sadly. "And how to tell false from true I did not know . . . and do not know."

"Yet you judged me," she said as she had said before. "Well, priest, what is it you desire to know?"

"They said you blighted the standing corn; one day golden and thick in the ear, and the next——" he spread empty hands.

"I remember it." Her smile was mocking. "That was the year the little lord died—the first little lord. I had seen the corn as I walked in the funeral."

"Mildewed, useless. We went hungry that winter."

"Priest, did *you* go hungry?"

The red came up into his pale cheeks; the hands spread upon his knees trembled a little. He had eaten less, certainly; but for all that he had not starved.

She said, with that sudden sweetness of hers, "There was many a one fed from your kitchens. Though you did not go hungry, yet you shared."

"I could have shared more." He beat upon his breast. "A hard, hard winter. That was the year the Simpsons were ruined. They had to leave the farm. Tom hired himself out at the Castle . . ."

"Yes," she said, all soft spite, "the lord gave him a house

—not so good as mine; a hovel. But they were glad enough to get it, he and that fine mother of his!"

He looked at her. "Did you bewitch their crops and their orchards and their beasts?"

"Do you think I could?"

He spread his hand. "I know not what to think."

"He had cast off my daughter. I paid him for that. But had his harvests failed and his beasts died and I done nothing, still I should have borne the blame."

"Your will was bad towards them; it is hard to judge the power of a wicked will."

They were silent both of them. He lifted his head at last. "They say you ran about the countryside in the shape of an animal—a hare or a dog or a cat."

"Do you believe I could?"

"I have read in books . . . such things, it seems, can happen. Yet reason rejects it." He lifted a troubled face. "But who am I to pit my poor reason against the wisdom of learned men, both old and new? God forgive me, but I do believe it."

"Then you are right. A small creature has its ear close to the ground. It hears more than the one that stands upright. And, what is more, so little a creature may do much damage— and no-one the wiser. But, make no mistake, priest. It is no easy thing to go inside the skin of a small creature, a creature that is hunted. You are weak then; for you take upon yourself every danger that besets it. You never know if you will come home again."

In the quiet room she began to sing in a low voice, very sweet and thin.

> And I shall go into a hare,
> With sorrow and grief and muckle care.
> And I shall go in the Devil's name
> But . . . when shall I come home again?

There was so haunting a sadness about her, it sent tears pricking in the old man's eyes.

"Priest, priest, never weep for me," she said. "There is always the spell to return us again . . . if we have time to cast it. But there is not always time. There was the winter they pelted me with stones; that was the winter the second child lay sick at the Castle."

"Yes," Samuel Fleming said. "Yes . . ." and was silent remembering the grief and the horror when the sickness that had killed Henry struck at Francis. No comfort now in thinking *Soon he will mend.* The end of this sickness they knew too well. Their hearts had been broken with pity for the child lying there, not knowing anyone, and crying out wild with his fears. All the prescriptions written by the learned Master Atkins had not helped; the three-year old had trembled so that the truckle-bed shook with him; there was no warming him. And he had cried out until his voice cracked and there was no hushing him . . . a baby lying there in mortal terror and crying out that a white beast lay upon his heart.

"The tale was all over the countryside," Samuel Fleming said, "every man, woman and child watching for the white beast."

She nodded. "Cat or hare or so small a thing as a mouse. Black, brown or grey, it was all one. For once the hunt is up any quarry will serve and many an innocent creature comes to its death. Well, they could have spared their pains! There was no white beast . . . then. It was all a sick child's fancy—a picture seen, an old tale heard. I was never in his chamber in my life, though it was not for want of trying. We needed something that was his to cast the spell—a riband, a plaything, a lock of hair—something warm from his own breath, his own life-blood. We were not able to put our hands on such a thing. Philip had done her best; but she was not let out of the kitchens. The others mistrusted her; did she but move to go to the privy, there was always one that followed. From spring to autumn we had tried. How we had tried! The Master had long grown impatient; Philip found him a hard lover. When the first snow came I knew I must go into a hare. . . ."

"The child sickened before the snow."

She nodded. "But it was not our doing. It was fear working upon him and within him—fear in the heart of his father, of his mother, in all those that stood about him; and, most of all, fear in his own heart. He might have got well again; he might have died without our help. We could risk neither. And, over and above his dying, there was the winning of his soul. The first child had slipped from the hand of the Master; this soul we must win. And that was why I went into a hare. . . ."

"Why did you choose a hare; and a white one, seeing that up at the Castle and down in the village, every eye watched for a white beast?"

"I did not know it. Philip had not been down from the Castle and no-one spoke to us. But though I knew nothing, still I did not want to be a hare. I was afraid. Life is a black burden to a small weak creature, blacker still when it feels and thinks like a woman.

I waited for the first snow—white against white is hard to see. I went carefully at first; but when I got beyond the village and there was no-one about, I began to lillip and then to run. And then, because I was in part a hare, the thing I was about to do, seemed, after all, not so very important. That, priest, is part of the risk one takes when one becomes a beast. The risk is not all from outside; some of it comes from within one-self. You lose for the time, some human part; you think, you act in the nature of the beast.

So there I was free of the world; and the snow all about me crisp and clean. There is a smell to the snow wild creatures know. I began to circle for the joy of it, throwing up the snow with strong, hind legs.

But I was only half a hare. I had not the safety of being all animal. And so it was that I forgot the smell of man; and I did not remember it again until the rank odour came strong to my nose.

It was Tom Simpson, all crazy with his wrongs. I froze. It was too late. Already his hands were on a stone. I turned and ran; and he came after, flinging his stones. A clumsy fool. By the Master's grace he missed each time.

I lost what wits I had. I should have made for the woods; instead I doubled back to the village—the hunted creature makes for home. And as we ran, he pressing me hard, he cried out *Witch, witch!* And men and women came running from their houses. And, even then, I had gone free, but his mother, a pox upon her, ran out carrying a knife and she flung it as I ran. It caught me upon the left hind leg so that I limped as I went and there was blood upon the white ground.

A small wound; not much to see, but steady-bleeding. So, twisting and dodging and bleeding, I ran into the thicket behind my house and, as I went, I put together with sorrow and pain and muckle care the spell to borrow me. So when they came to my house there was a little blood upon the snow and no hare; only myself with a stocking about my leg to hide my hurt, busy about my bread. And though they called *Witch, witch, come out!* And though they threw stones against my door, it was fast-shut. There was nothing they could do and they were forced to go home again.

I kept within doors until my wound was healed. But still they would gather about my house calling *Witch, witch, come out!* When I was sick of their baiting, I called upon the Master and he sent a great, black dog and they fled screaming.

And so I was saved; even when I left my house none dared lay a finger upon me—for who knew when the black dog would not spring from the ground? But it was a safety that could not last. I think I knew it that first time they stood about my house and cried out against me. And yet I would not let myself believe it. I had been about the Master's work; he would protect me.

But the work! It was hardly begun; and how to set about it I did not know. For still I lacked the thing—the child's small thing—to cast the spell. That thing I had not got; nor did I see how I was to come by it.

And to make bad worse, Philip was restless up at the Castle. She felt anger and hatred all about her. Oh, she was clever! There was still nothing proved against her; but there was talk aplenty—ugly talk that, day by day, grew yet more ugly. Who knew when she would be sent packing . . . and nothing of the child's in her hand? Something I must have. I must have it.

And to add to my troubles Meg was no longer eager about the work. She had lost, so it seemed, her desire for revenge and I had to keep pricking her on. To tell truth, her life was too comfortable. Poor we might look—and were; but we lacked nothing. We ate and drank well; we had our gossips within the coven; we had our junketings at the esbats and we had our divine Sabbaths. Had Master Vavasour, for whom she had once sighed, come down from the Castle with his frenchified airs and his master's cast-off clouts, though he looked fine enough to pass for a gentleman . . . almost, I doubt she would have looked at him. For at our own merrymakings she did not go short of lovers; and though at the Sabbath her place was among the children, there was ever a pretty boy to serve her pleasure.

She was jealous still of Philip. In spite of his displeasure, the Master delighted in the girl. She was to bear Him a child; but this, I fancy, Meg did not know; certainly she never mentioned it. And, indeed, we saw so little of Philip that Meg, so it seemed, forgot her jealousy for days on end. Only at the Sabbaths and afterwards, did she remember.

Between Meg grown lazy with content and Philip unable to lay hand on anything that belonged to the child, I grew wretched; and I grew frightened. I loved the Master; but I feared Him more.

And then, when I had all-but given myself to despair, Philip came down to the cottage. It was New Year's Day; the snow had melted a little and frozen again. Old folk kept within doors; but the young went sliding and slipping and shouting for joy. I could hear before ever she reached the door, her small tuneless singing; it was a sound to warn her enemies. She put her hand into her pocket and brought it forth again, her long, lean witch's hand; and on her open palm—a child's small glove.

Without a word she flung it across the table.

'A glove!' I said. 'Once more a glove. A good omen.'

'How did you come by it?' Meg asked, slow and sullen.

'Master Vavasour gave it me,' Philip smiled her wicked smile.

Meg's pale face flushed; when the colour died she was paler even than before. However little she desired her almost-gentleman now, she was not minded for her sister to pick him up.

'The man's in love with me,' Philip said, careless. 'I might have taken him once—he's a prettier man than poor Tom. But no man shall touch me now, nor any spirit, neither. I am for the Master.' She stretched her arms above her head and her small breasts lifted. Margaret sent her a glance of hatred but Philip only laughed. 'Let us not trouble our hearts about this

Vavasour who is nothing to either of us. Here is the glove. And here is the time and place. We have waited long enough.'

Meg said very slow, 'The first little lord is dead. There should be . . . pity.' "

"Pity?" Samuel Fleming repeated. "Does a witch know pity?"

"We are human, priest," she told him very drily. "We know pity, yes; and remorse, too. For what is our remorse but a backsliding into goodness? It is as natural as your Christian backsliding into evil. And our compassion, also, is easy to understand. For look, priest; when you see a man tormented of God, though it be for his soul's good, yet you pity the poor flesh. So it is, sometimes, with us. Meg was young; she knew how the first little lord had died—the pain and the fear. It was a child she had known; a dear child, merry and kind. No, it was not strange she should feel compassion—though she must fight against it.

But with Philip there was no compassion as there would be no remorse. 'Come now!' she said. 'We have dallied over-long.' And when still Meg made no move, cried out, 'Will you wait until the next Sabbath . . . and the Master's anger? Or do you expect Him to be patient for ever?'

At that, I brought out the basin and filled it with water and set it upon the fire.

'This is *your* vengeance,' Philip told Meg, spiteful still. 'It must be *your* blood.'

Meg would have refused had she dared. She feared to draw her blood; and, indeed, she could ill afford it, being white and slow; and, besides, as I have said, her desire for vengeance was grown dim.

Philip's lips smiled but her eyes did not smile. 'If you will not—then I will. But be warned; the Master will not take it kindly of you.'

Meg went so pale, it was as though the blood were already drained from her but she reached out for a bodkin and pricked her arm. A drop fell into the basin; and Philip mocked, saying, 'She is tender of herself! Let her pray the Master will be as tender of that white flesh!'

I said nothing; I had no wish to bring upon myself Philip's

ill-will. I took up a knife and stabbed the little glove, the pretty, tender glove; I stabbed it again and again and when I held it before the fire the light came pricking through. Steam was rising from the basin and I flung the glove into the boiling water. It twisted and turned and rolled about like a small thing in pain."

"A small thing in pain . . . a child . . . a little child," Samuel Fleming said low and slow.

Joan Flower nodded, smiling. "Meg stood and trembled. I saw her catch hold of the table; she leaned there, dumb, while together with Philip I said, first the Words of Power, the secret Words, and then the Spell.

> Glove shall go
> To earth below,
> From out this pot
> There to rot.
> Little lord,
> Hear the Word.
> Brew thicken,
> Lordling sicken,
> Peak and die,
> In churchyard lie.

And I called upon the familiar. 'Rutterkin, go upwards.' But he crouched among the cinders and did not stir.

'The spell is hard to cast today,' Philip said and fixed unsmiling eyes upon her sister. She stood, head bent a little as though she listened. 'Hard; but not too hard!'

Suddenly she turned about and stretched her arm towards the basin. Her eyes were closed and her voice came out strong and strange; as though some other—the Master, perhaps—used her as his mouthpiece.

> Glove defiled,
> Destroy the child,
> Choke breath,
> Till death,
> Springtime sleet,
> His winding-sheet.
> I call upon the Devil's Name,
> Master, bring me not to shame.

And when the voice that was not the voice of Philip had done speaking, Rutterkin, with no word from me, flew upwards through the chimney. Philip opened her eyes and looked about her, as though she had come a long way.

'The spell is cast; the time is set,' she said. She looked full at Meg. 'Nothing can alter it—not though you run blabbing. All you can do is bring yourself to the gallows.'

Meg licked her dry lips. 'I?' she said. And again, 'I.' And when she would have gone on speaking, Philip turned her back. Then I took up the shrunk and riddled thing that had been a child's gay glove and we went out together to bury it. And, as I went, I was shaken in spite of myself. It was a tender little child. Priest, it is hard never to backslide into goodness.

Now it was growing towards dusk and time Philip should be moving but she gave no sign; she sat there yawning delicately as though sleep buttoned her eyes. Meg went about restless, touching this and that; at last she said, 'Should you not be going, sister?' Philip's narrow eyes flew open in surprise. 'Did I not tell you? I am not going back.'

'But you must go!' I said at once. 'There is your bond of service. They will send after you. I doubt you will relish the whip!'

'There shall be neither sending nor whipping. My lady has sickened of me this long while; but there is nothing against me save talk. She is a fool, that one! She will never punish without proof. Punish first, say I; let proof come later!'

Meg said nothing. She was staring in such dismay at the thought of her sister's company that Philip's laugh was almost goodnatured. 'Have no fear,' she said, 'your nose shall never be twisted for me! Not here, nor at the Castle, nor yet at the Sabbath do I take any woman's lover—man or spirit. I am for the God!'

Meg's dismayed look turned to anger. Philip had pricked true and deep. Wantoning with a pretty boy might suit Meg well; but her pride bled that she had no choice.

I looked from one to the other. If those two came to open quarrel, there was danger for us all. Philip must go back at once. It could not be for long—soon enough my lady must see her condition; but long enough to give my dull Meg time to understand that things were on the change.

'You must go back at once!' I said again. She looked as though to defy me but I went on, 'Little lord Francis is sturdier than his brother that is dead. That one wasted like a candle; this one, little though he is, will make a fight. The spell we have cast is strong; but the child may be stronger . . . and the Master helps those that help themselves. Take this. He gave it to me to use at need; and need, I fancy, there may be!'

She opened the packet and stirred the green powder with a long, lean finger. 'Pretty!' she said.

'Poison?' Meg said and took in her breath.

'I do not question what the Master gives,' I told her.

Philip went on stirring the green powder.

'Go now!' I said but she looked stubborn still. 'The Master, need I remind you, is just! He rewards . . . and punishes. When this work is done He will make you Coven Maiden, and will set you above the Captain even.' Her eyes gleamed at that. 'But, if you disobey, though He is your lover and you carry his child—you would do well not to count upon it.'

She grimaced, and swallowed in her throat. 'I will go then. But not for long. My lady will see my burden soon enough. Yes, my chaste lady shall send me away herself.'

She bade us goodbye; but Meg looked away and would not answer."

Chapter Twelve

SAMUEL FLEMING raised his head; his skin was yellow as parchment, stretched across the bones. His lips moved.

"Springtime sleet,
His winding sheet . . .

Francis died in the springtime," he said. "And sleet fell the day we buried him. That was a strange thing; it had been so lovely a spring. The day and the weather—could you foresee it?"

"The day; not the weather. We could hasten his death or delay it. We could take up the glove and prick it again; we could prick many holes or few. As the glove perished, so the child perished. We could, with luck, calculate the day; and, if aught went wrong, we could put it right!" She smiled into his face. "Poison," she said it quite gently.

"May God forgive you!" Samuel Fleming said.

"No need—if you talk of the poison. It was not used. Your true witch will not use it unless she must. To cast the spell, to see it work—that is a witch's joy. Then she knows power; then herself she is a god. But poison! Any fool can give it—if there be a chance. And, if she cannot come at her victim, then the best of witches is hindered; and so it was with Philip. She could not give him the poison; but as for the spell—everything went as we desired. We had set not only the day but the hour. As for the weather, the Master added it for grace."

"For grace!" Samuel Fleming repeated. "Do you talk of grace . . . and the child lying within the dark chamber and none to help him? At the end he was deaf and blind—did you know that? But of course you knew it! And I said to myself, It is spring; and he does not see the primroses, nor will again. And he does not hear the cuckoo call, nor will again."

"And you prayed, no doubt, to your god but he did not

answer you. Well, what matter?" she shrugged. "Had the child died in the summer you would have grieved that he did not see the roses; or, in the autumn, that he did not see the ripening fruits; or, in the winter, that he did not see the snow which is all a child's delight—if," she added drily, "he have stout shoes upon his feet. But—" and she was a little sly, "why break your heart because the child flew straight to heaven?"

"You are right, witch. But so it is. When a child dies—to us untimely so it seems—we, fools that we are, wish for a little longer and still a little longer, seeing no further than the end of our nose." He nodded mournful. "The day I heard the child was dead I went up to the Castle to comfort them; but it was they that comforted me." He spoke as if to himself, remembering Cecilia with her wasted look, Francis his eyes drawn back, dark within the sockets.

"They took it as God's will," he told Joan Flower. "They said they must submit themselves, bearing their grief so that all might see they acknowledged the mercy of God."

She laughed now as she had laughed then.

"But who can help laughing?" She smiled into his sick face. "They should have had the wit to revile their god. And it was our God they should have besought with their prayers. And so the child died!"

"The death of this little one," Samuel Fleming said, "was more bitter than the death of the first. For now there was no heir born of their bodies. Nor—" and he looked at her steadily, "nor was one ever born."

"We willed that also." She held his look with her smiling eyes. "As for the child, you held a service, here, in your church; but they took the body away for burial. Why did they do that?"

"The earl was in attendance upon the King in Whitehall, which is near London. But though he made little show of grief he could not bring himself to part with the child; not yet. So they carried the child with them and they buried him within the great Abbey at Westminster."

"An honour!" She quirked her brows. "Well, honour is balm to staunch the direst wound."

"This wound never healed. But though his heart was broken within him, the earl scanted nothing of his duty towards the King."

"The King, the King!" she broke in, angry. "A black pox upon the King with his hangings and his persecutions of us witches. As if that were not enough, enough! But what must he do now but turn himself about, denying witches and their works. It is better, priest, as you well know, to die for one's faith though the pain be bitter; for martyrs strengthen faith. But to question it, as the King does, to deny it, ridicule it—that is the way to kill it."

"He has never denied the existence of witches," Samuel Fleming said. "He urges care lest the innocent suffer along with the guilty—and that should please you. Martyrs make faith strong; but you were not so ready to proclaim yours when the time came."

"I denied the Master and in the very act was struck down and died. You might say, priest, that denying, still I testified. But for all that you are right. I was not ready. As we grow old, we grow more cowardly, it seems. Yet *you* are no coward . . . and I am ashamed. But if I lacked courage, my daughters spoke the truth, each in her way; Margaret who, like me, was not brave; and Philip in whom passion for the God cast out fear.

So we died; and our name will be remembered as long as Belvoir stands."

"But—*how* will it be remembered?"

"What matter? As long as we are remembered we serve the Master."

Samuel Fleming sighed deeply. "So long we have struggled, we two, pitting word against word; but you have not shifted one hairsbreadth from your wickedness."

"Nor you from your goodness. Surely, one way or another, we must make an end—for until then you cannot die. You would like to die, would you not, priest? The burden of the body is heavy."

"The burden of the soul is heavier," he said and cast about in his mind how he might soften her hard heart.

"So sad a house, Belvoir . . ." he began but she took him up sharply.

138

"Say you so? So gay a house with the King himself avisiting and the fine gentlemen with him. And the music and the dancing and the fine, fat foods. Oh I make no doubt that the lady smiled and often; yes, and the lord, too. And did we not see them hunting and hawking? And there was kissing and wenching and laughter above stairs as well as below—I wager my soul against yours; but it is a bet you would be wise not to take. For human nature does not change for the death of a child; nor yet for the death of a hundred children."

"If witches know pity—and you say they do—then where was yours? For think, think! A house where there were children; and then—no children."

"There was the little lady . . . though she was hardly a child for all her few years. She knew more than many a grown woman. Yes, Philip, even, might have learned of her."

"Let us leave the lady Catharine out of this matter," he told her, stern. "All wickedness in you and yours is to be praised! But let another, however young, take one false step . . ."

"It was no false step the little lady took when she ran from home to creep into the bed of my lord of Buckingham, whose manner of life she knew well. She saw the thing she wanted; and she took it. She had strength and she had courage; and because of it, I desired her for the Master. But I could not win her. It is a strange thing, priest. She was no less wanton than my girls. Yet they were sent away in disgrace but she—the little lady—was hung about with gold; what *she* had done might easily be forgiven . . . gold is your true fuller's earth."

"Every sin may be forgiven," he said. "But first it must be acknowledged and atoned. That you may be forgiven you are here, burdening my heart with a hateful tale."

"And there is more to come!" she told him suddenly spiteful. "And though you have heard it until your soul sickens, still you must hear it again! Very well, then. Let us say it was sad at Belvoir—what then? Turn and turn about! We were merry enough down at the cottage. Philip's hands were full —fine folk make fine work; she could not be spared from the Castle and Meg was left in peace.

Our house was full at nights. Joan Willimott would

come from Goodby and Ellen Greene from Stathorne; and they would bring Ann Baker with them, plucking her from her bed, here in Bottesford, as they went through. Yet that was no witch, priest; she saw us at our sport and looked and longed and took no part. She was a simpleton that knew nothing."

"That was as well," he told her, grim.

"Oh priest, your life has been too snug, too rich in friends to understand. But for us that are poor and hated, what better than the little room fast-shut against the cold—and our friends beside us? False friends; but we did not know it then. And the familiars waiting to do our bidding whatever it might be—to fetch meat and wine; or to strike down the enemy with our curse. Power. That is what the Master gives us; power over life and death. It turns a woman—even the poorest, the stupidest, the ugliest—into a queen."

"Did you truly feel a queen when no-one would willingly pass your door? And when those who met you crossed themselves?"

"Priest, you know how to prick! You can see into the heart of a woman, even though she be a witch. I'd tell myself I didn't care. But there were times I longed for the kind word, the coming and going with one's neighbours—running into a house to borrow this or that; a pinch of salt, maybe, a cup of milk. Or being sent for, when a man lies sick. . . ."

"You could not expect it," he said more gently.

"No, priest. But—" and she wrung her shadowy hands, "must I tell you again? We are only human—we backslide now and then to goodness. And I was wise in curing the sick; my mother taught me long and long ago. She said to throw wide both door and casement to the spirits of sun and wind. She cared not at all for bleeding, except in the way of sacrifice—and then a cock only, or a hen. She did no harm her life long; they called her a white witch."

"There is no such thing," he told her, stern. "All witches traffic with the Devil. When you use the power he gives you, even though you do good and not evil, even when you save a life that had otherwise gone down to the grave, still it is Devil's work and mortal sin."

"There is no pleasing you!" she said petulant.

"Not until you please God—or try to please Him."

"There was one time I might have pleased your god—witch though I was; but I was not let. It was spring, I remember, a month perhaps or less, after the second little lord died. Willows in the hedges, coltsfoot and celandine . . . a golden spring. You'd think, maybe, a witch's eye would not see such things, so common and so sweet. But we that serve the Master rejoice in the beauty of this world because it is the work of his hands."

He shut his eyes against the blasphemy.

"Patchett's child lay sick. A kind and pleasant child; too young to cry out after a witch or cast a stone. I could not rest for thinking of him lying there in the dark room and all springtime shut out."

"You were a strange woman," he said. "You had robbed the grave to make your filthy ointments. You had murdered three children—and one of them your child's child. Yet you hankered to save this child that was nothing to you."

"He smiled at me, priest; he had cast no foul word, no stone."

"And the little boys?" he asked quickly. "And your daughter's child? What foul words had they cast? What stones?"

"The child we kill for vengence—that is not murder but our sacred duty. And the child we kill for sacrifice—that is an act of righteousness. And if we use bodies to make our holy charms, how can it hurt them that are dead? But the child that has not offended, who is too old for the sacrifice and useless for our spells, that is another matter. Why, indeed, should we kill such a one, since he goes straight to your god and is forever lost to the Master?

As for Patchett's child—there were few like him, fearless and friendly. I would have saved him if I could.

I knew I should not be welcome; lucky, indeed, if the dog was not set upon me. But all the same I went.

When I opened the door the stench of sickness came at me and all but drove me back; but still I went inside. And there was the goodwife dragging herself about with a great belly and a peaked face. I knew at once her days were numbered; it was no fruitful belly. When she saw me she opened her mouth to cry out and her eyes were like black holes you might burn in a cheesecloth.

I gave her good day and went over to the child. The mark of death was upon him, too. He lay as though dead already, and his breath so faint I could hardly catch it. If witches could weep I should have wept then; it was a pretty child and had smiled at me.

I turned away—nothing I could do. And there, at my back, stood Patchett himself, looking as though he would kill me . . . as afterwards he did do, witnessing against me with a lying tongue.

'Had you called me in time this child would have lived,' I said. 'Now you may dig his grave.' And I looked across at the woman with the swollen belly that was not great with child and said, 'You may lay his mother beside him.' "

"It was a cruel thing to do," Samuel Fleming said, remembering how, before the may was white in the hedges, they had, indeed, buried mother and child in one grave.

"It was the truth and any leech would have known it. Priest, do you quarrel with the truth?" And when he spread helpless hands and could not answer, she said, bitter, "It is I who should do that, seeing they cried after me that I had killed them both, the goodwife and the child. And they brought it against me complaining to the justices; it was set down in the charges when I was brought before you. Ah well, it matters nothing now!

But for all that I spoke the truth that day in Patchett's cottage. The boy was dying when I saw him. Had they sent for me or for some surgeon in good time, the child would be alive now. It was they that had killed him in their foolishness —his own parents. But I bore the blame. As for the mother, naught could have saved her at any time, for she carried death in her belly. And for that also I bore the blame."

"You were a witch and they were afraid of you. Let any man offend you and—though no harm was meant—your hand was raised to strike. On some you brought ruin; on others death. How should they not turn against you, holding you guilty for every misfortune, great or small?"

"It was unjust," she said. "This one time I would have done good. I had to confess it to the Master and bear the blows." She shook her shoulders as if even now she could feel the strokes. "Surely this one time I should not have borne the blame."

"It is the way of men. As for your master, can you still deceive yourself about him? He lied to you from the beginning; before even you put your mark to a most wicked bond. He brought you to a hateful death; and after that death he shut you out from those delights—delights, God save us, he promised you. Why else do you wander between the worlds? Your master is the Prince of Lies and there is no faithfulness in him." And when she would have spoken he stopped her with uplifted hand. "Can you doubt it? You were promised your heart's desire yet you lived on what you could steal; and men and women hated you."

"We had our fellowship and our Sabbaths," she said, defiant, and stopped. And now she was shaken by so deep a sigh that her body shook. "Oh priest, priest, you are right! The dead when they speak must speak true; it is a compulsion upon us. Our daily life was bitter, indeed. It is hard when men and women hate you; hard to be forever picking and stealing to keep the life within your body. Oh, we could be gay enough at night; when the wine is in the wit is out. But . . . when the feast is over and the guests departed?" She sighed again. "Meg was poor company. She'd sold her wits with her soul, you'd think. A sullen piece of itching flesh.

Philip came down from the Castle, bundle in hand. She was great with her godling; and now that the guests had departed the virtuous lady had cast her out. Philip laughed at the whole matter. She had flaunted her belly before the lady. 'She had a stricken look,' Philip said, laughing still. 'She was like a lamb when you hold the knife to its throat. For all her greatness, for all her virtue she envied me.' Philip patted her belly. 'And I laughed in her face. And now my lady has no child of her own flesh and blood. And what comfort will she get from the proud little lady? But let her find comfort or none, it matters not at all. Now we clear the little lady from the board.'

'No!' Meg cried out, sudden and sharp. 'I have killed my child; I have helped to bring the little boys to their death. It is enough.'

Philip said nothing . . . but her fingers crooked; it was hard for her to keep her hands off Meg.

'You had best tell that to the Master,' she said, cruel. 'Tell Him when you come to the Sabbath. And, if you play the coward, I'll speak for you!'

Meg shrank back against the wall; her face had a blue look—skim-milk blue. She looked a poor thing; but I could not pity her. She had been accepted into our fellowship; power had been put into her hands. Yet she did nothing but mope and make the air sour with her complainings. At our merrymakings she sat forgotten; she spoilt our esbats with sorrowful looks and heavy sighs. Her thoughts, I knew, turned more and more to the lover she had lost and child she had sacrificed. As for the Sabbaths, they had become a terror to her. She was mortally afraid of what Philip might tell.

I made myself gentle. 'Never fear,' I said. 'Philip will not tell—not if you are a good lass and sensible.' But I did not believe what I said. 'Come now, let us forget this nonsense. It is time to deal with the little lady—if we have the means. What have you brought,' I asked Philip, 'that we may cast the spell?'

She smiled and pulled from her bosom a little kerchief stitched about with fine lace. Her smiling face went bitter. 'If this were found upon me I should be whipped and set in the stocks; hanged maybe, since this pretty thing is worth —I know not what! I picked it up in the park as I came through. Well let it be worth what it may—it will serve.' Her hands clawed at the pretty rag.

I brought out the basin and she cast the shreds of linen into the boiling water. 'This is my vengeance,' she said, 'and I take great joy in it. I have stomached enough and enough from my hateful little lady. Oh she says nothing! But let her meet me in the path and her eyes do not see me; and her nose is pinched as at some foul smell. Yet she is no better than the next one, if the truth be known, young though she is!' She drew the knife across her arm; and when the blood spurted she laughed and shook it into the basin. 'But you shall take your part with us!' she told Meg roughly. 'Come, call up your familiar.'

Meg made no answer. She sat deaf and blind and seemed not to know what we did there in the room. So we laid hold of Rutterkin and Philip stirred the brew singing the while.

> Pine and die
> In coffin lie.
> Mistress proud,
> Weave the shroud.
> High heart, saucy tongue,
> Die young.
> On Sathan's sacred Name we call,
> Master, Maker of us all.

There was no sound in the room; only in the basin the reddened water bubbled. Meg went on staring at nothing with her pale eyes. Rutterkin crouched stone-still; there was no purring sound with which he greeted the working of a spell. I knew then that things were wrong; and I was afraid.

Philip said, pale, 'This child is hard to catch; and my sister aids him. Her will is set against ours. It is a strong will but I have something stronger.' She drew from her bosom a green riband knotted still where a careless hand had pulled it from its place; and—caught fast within the knot—a long, dark, curling hair.

'The little lady is not patient,' Philip said and she was smiling again. 'It will be her undoing. This should be strong enough to catch that brave little bird!' She cast the riband still knotted about the hair, into the basin and let fall yet more of her blood. Then, when the steam came up fierce again and the water rose and bubbled, she cast the spell a second time.

Still there was silence. The familiar crouched stone-still. I called his name softly. He would not come, and, when I reached out a hand towards him, he backed into the fire so that I must burn my fingers to lift him out.

'Come,' I said coaxing, 'you shall drink well when this is done. We shall not spare our blood, not one of us.' And still he would not stir.

But for all that I would catch him yet!

I turned my back upon him. 'We must leave spellbinding for today,' I said, my eyes upon Philip. Her eyes just flicked. 'I am hungry,' she said. 'Let us eat.' So I brought out a loaf and some cheese, and we sat down, the two of us, to eat. But still Meg sat in her place and stared at nothing.

As we ate I heard behind Rutterkin's feet sliding and scratching upon the ashes. He was coming for his share.

Philip's eyes glinted between their lids; she went on eating. Suddenly she pounced; and there was Rutterkin held by the neck. He scratched and he clawed but she held on. Then, scratching he drew blood and so sucking, remembered his duties.

He went quiet under her hand; but his eyes glowed red and spiteful; and beneath the fur, I could see him all tight and ready to spring.

With one hand Philip held his legs and the other she plunged into the basin not caring at all that she burnt her arm in the scalding water. She brought out the mess—the rag and the riband and the hair and she rubbed it upon his belly so that he squirmed and mewed; but otherwise he did not move. Then I cried out to him,

> Familiar spirit rise and go,
> In the Devil's name I bid you so.

But he did not stir. We looked at each other across the cat's belly, Philip nursing her scalded arm. There he lay, his four legs still upturned, glaring at us sideways out of his red, red eyes.

Rise and Go. Rise and Go! I said it over and over again. And when he did not stir, still commanding him, I set him upright upon the table. But, instead of rising into the air, he stood mewing like any cat that has been a little misused and not at all like a spirit.

Philip and I stared at each other. 'It is useless,' I said. 'He will not do it, because he cannot do it.'

'Cannot?' she cried out. 'Cannot? He is bound to our command . . . if the spell be cast aright.'

'The spell was right enough!' I said. 'We have cast it twice before; and twice Rutterkin has risen and gone. And twice a child has died.'

'Yes,' she said, thoughtful. 'Yes. The first time was easy. The second time was hard. Rutterkin was not willing—yet he obeyed. Now he refuses utterly.' She stood there, eyes closed, head bent sideways as though she listened. 'There is a will that works against us!' she said. Suddenly, eyes still closed she spun about. '*Your* will!' she cried out and pointed a finger at Meg.

Meg gave a great start. 'What?' she said and it was as though she came back from a long distance. And again, 'What?'

'You have ruined the spell,' Philip said, cold and bitter. 'It is a thing to report to the Master.'

My heart shook at that; but I gave no sign. 'Do not blame your sister,' I told Philip. 'This is the will of the Master; and against it no will can stand. The proud child with her saucy tongue is not to die yet. I think the Master has use for her. Let well alone, my girl.'

Philip looked sulky; yet she could not deny some sense in what I said. And, indeed, that day I spoke truer than I knew. For the child brought stain to the honour of her great name until her father put all right with his gold!"

Samuel Fleming looked at Joan Flower in the gathering dusk. "Did you cast the spell again? For certainly the child was bewitched."

"We did not try again."

"But she was stricken—those fits, those pains, those fears."

"We did not bewitch her—and so I have said before. And so Meg said and Philip also; though they confessed to all else. Believe me, priest, it had been easier for them to lie. They had already confessed enough to bring them to the rope; and this one question was put to them again and again . . . and it was put with torment."

"That, at least, is not true!" he said, stern. "The law does not allow it."

She laughed. Yet had she tears, he could have sworn she wept.

"If you did not know it—then the worse justice, you! And this torment, priest, it is all so useless. For it plays upon pain; and poor human flesh, for the most part, will say anything that it may rest a little from its pain. And, that being so, how shall you know true from false?

Listen, priest! There is more than one sort of people you call witch. There are true witches like Philip and like me; we do our work for the love of the Master. And there is a second sort, like Margaret, who are not witches by nature. They work their evil in fear and without joy because their love has grown cold towards the Master. And there is a third sort; poor wretches who have no dealings with the Master nor ever had; they abhor Him as you do. But because they are old and because they are ugly; and because they have grown a little strange—perhaps with their sorrows—you call them *witch*. And so they come to their hanging."

"No," he said, "no." And covered his face.

"Yes, priest, yes! Nor is it less true when you hide your eyes. Such a poor creature may have a spot upon her body— for it is more often we women that are accused; a natural spot, even so common a thing as a ringworm. But the world cries out, *Here is the Mark*. And so they must hang. It is those you should pity of your Christian charity. You have never been hurt in the flesh, priest; hurt wantonly, hurt cruelly, in the name of righteousness. Till then do not speak of devils; no devil can torment like your righteous man that is afraid."

"It is not true," Samuel Fleming groaned. "In other countries, perhaps. In Scotland and in France, yes; in Italy, maybe; in Switzerland certainly and in Spain. But not here, not in this good land of ours. As my Saviour hears me, if there was torment I did not know it."

"And will your saviour forgive you for not knowing, you that set yourself up as a judge? And if he does? It will not be forgiven you by those poor souls whose bodies you tormented and then hanged."

He held out his hands and looked at them, a little puzzled,

as though he expected to find blood on them; but she went on, implacable. "Yes, you, priest, you! Though your own eyes did not see nor your own hands move—you guard the law; you and the rest of your magistrates and judges. The law of a people is precious and must be guarded—as we witches know, that accept the Law from the Master and cherish it with our lives. For the law is more than any man or any woman or any child. The law is that by which the spirit lives; by which your god himself lives."

He looked at her and there was nothing to say. He was a man reputed wise in words—swift to the reply, cunning in dispute. But she, he thought now, outdid him in cunning.

"Not in cunning," she said gently, "but in the truth. Being out of the body and my soul naked between heaven and hell I can do no other. Priest, I speak the truth."

Chapter Thirteen

SAMUEL FLEMING walked in the August garden; he walked slowly, feeble yet with his sickness. And, as he walked, there came to his ears the purling of the river—a small bright river . . . innocent. Yet he had known it to rise in flood and sweep a man away; he had been all-but drowned himself once! He looked with pleasure at the bridge he had built; the little stone bridge, strong and beautiful. Yes, there it stood—and would stand; he had left money for its upkeep so that ever after men could walk safely when they came to church.

"Yet there were things to do first, priest!" She stood before him, translucent as the water. "Men and women may take the long way to church when the river is in flood—which is not often; or the wooden bridge have served them still. But in this parish of yours there are always some who shiver and shake—yes, even this hot day—because of empty bellies and empty hearths."

And when he would have answered that his sister saw to it that none went cold or hungry, she said quickly, "Mistress Davenport is kind; but her soup, good though it be, is not enough. You cannot keep body and soul together with a sup now and then. A bit of bread and cheese from one's own shelf, every day punctual as the sun and a warm fire, may yet save souls for your god. There are some who make their pact with the Master to save themselves from the slow and bitter death of poverty."

At this moment Hester herself came across the lawn, the white cat at her heels.

"I thought I heard voices," she said looking about her, surprised to find him alone. "I was sure William was with you. I have to speak to him about my new bed of sparrowgrass. He did not trench deep enough for all my talking. Now there is little; and that, poor enough. Oh!" She stopped and shivered. "It is *cold*! Who would believe it is August? And yet—" she looked up puzzled, "the sun is as hot as my kitchen fire. But then," she went on, answering herself as was her way, "the wind blows cold from the river." She looked at it fondly. "Who should suppose so small a river could make so great a difference? Well, Jennet shall bring you a shawl." She turned to go. "Send Will to me, if you see him," she said across her shoulder. "There shall be plain speaking about the sparrowgrass. Francis may come home suddenly—who knows? And certainly there is none fit for Cecilia when she comes to dine."

"Francis is not likely to come for many a long day, more's the pity! As for Cecilia—there's enough and to spare at Belvoir."

"That is not at all the same thing," she said, obstinate as some gentle women can be. "It is my pleasure to give my guests the thing they like whether they have it already or not. Besides, there is no sparrowgrass at Belvoir so sweet and juicy as mine. I had best go and find Will. Come, puss!"

The cat did not stir. She put out a hand and it backed and spat. There it stood, four feet planted, back arched, spitting and glaring.

"What ails the creature?" Hester said. "What does he see? A ghost, perhaps? And who could blame any ghost for wandering abroad this sweet summer day?"

Behind him he heard Joan Flower laugh. Hester stared past him beneath her shielding hand.

"Yes, certainly puss has seen a ghost!" she said and her laugh was uncertain. "Come, puss."

And when the creature stood, unmoving, like a cat in snow, save for the quiver of its anger and the glowing of its eyes, he heard a voice behind him whisper, *Go, cat, go!*

Hester's head turned sharply from right to left. "I could believe in daylight ghosts—all but." She laughed; but again her laugh had an edge to it. "Come, puss."

She turned towards the house and the cat followed.

"If you must come," he told Joan Flower, "then come where you can frighten no-one."

"I have frightened no-one," she said. "As for her—" she nodded in Hester's direction, "she is more likely to frighten me. She is one of God's fighters; for all her gentleness she gives no quarter. As to how I come or when or where—I take my chance as I may; we cannot go on like this for ever. And so, priest, to the battle!"

He sighed, reluctant to leave the bright flowing water, and the garden with its roses nodding and blowing and the lilies pouring richness upon the warm air, and the heartsease and love-lies-bleeding, all enclosed in neat clipped box.

His study had a greenish underwater look after the bright garden. The sky lifts a man's soul heavenward, he thought, and threw the casement wide so that the sunlight rushed in. He could hardly see her now in the strong light; but he heard her, felt her, knew her to be there. He wished he had not refused Hester's offer of a shawl; even indoors, with the sun streaming through the open window, he felt the piercing cold that came from her.

"Well?" she asked. "Have you considered the things we spoke of yesterday?"

He nodded. "That some poor souls are annoyed in prison . . ."

"Tormented was the word, priest."

It was a word he could not take as yet; he went on,

". . . I believe. And I am ashamed; I am bitterly ashamed. And I believe also you did not bewitch the lady Catharine. And yet—" he leaned chin upon palm, "cold as ice and stiff as iron; frothing at the mouth as her brothers had done; like them crying out all wild with terror; staring with blind eyes; passing out of the body and returning not knowing what had passed. Strange, strange. . . ."

She shrugged. "Who can understand the heart of a child?"

"*Suffer the little children to come unto Me,*" Samuel Fleming said softly. "Certainly He understood. They ran and clasped Him about the knees."

"You can draw any child with honey," she said, "but understanding is a different thing."

"And your Master—is he more understanding than the Son of God?"

"Why yes! The Master loves little children; and He is more honest than your god. For you take the new-born babe and offer him to God; you baptize him with your holy water and with the mark of the cross. And he is too little to understand and he is too weak to refuse . . . but often he cries aloud when it is done. And that is a thing you know well.

But my Master. When we offer our children, He makes the Mark, it is true. But He does not accept them; not one does He accept. He waits until they are old enough to know what it is they do. Then He asks them, *Are you willing?* And, *Do you understand?* And again, *Are you willing?* Then and only then does He accept them. And He is very kind to children and they have no fear of Him. They run to his knees and they embrace Him about the neck and they kiss his cheeks. And He calls them sweet names—bird and lamb and little hare. But He allows no child to fool Him. That child who is not true is beaten until he comes weeping and cringing to the Master's grace.

Oh He would have understood the little lady well enough! Sweet, He would have said, deceive whom you will—your god, if you can—and I shall praise you. But try to cheat Me, and it will be a sorry day for you; your last, perhaps! Oh He would have seen through her saucy ladyship! When she knew all hearts heavy with grief, heard the prayers, saw the tears; and when she saw these hearts lift a little when the sickness lifted, drop again when the sickness dropped down again, why then she felt herself left out. Little lady in the cold. Yes, the Master would have understood her very well."

"But," Samuel Fleming said, unwilling even to glance at the truth, "she grieved; she truly grieved. More than once I wiped her tears and we prayed together; I felt my own prayers stronger for a child's tears."

"Of course she grieved; of course she prayed; of course she wept. But do you not imagine that some of it—and not a little—was for the neglected little lady? No, she was not sick; though sometimes she feared she might be stricken. To envy the sick is not to desire the sickness. And when she found she did not sicken, why, then she feigned the matter."

"So young . . . and so cunning? It is not possible."

"You are over-trusting, priest. All children are cunning. Yet, it could be that, in a while, the thing she feigned became real. In the end, maybe, she did not fully understand the game she played.

The spell had failed; the little lady went free of us. My

daughters took failure each in her way. To Meg—child of John Flower—it meant try no more. But Philip—begotten when the blood was hot—failure pricked on. She wore a keen and spiteful look; and I would watch her wondering what she meant to do. Oh I knew well enough what she had threatened; but I could not believe it anything but threat. Margaret was, after all, her sister; and the thing was too horrible."

Samuel Fleming saw the long shudder that shook her body so that it moved and flickered like water.

"But if I did not believe it, Meg did. Fear had sharpened those dull wits of hers. She knew.

And so time dragged on to the next Sabbath. Candlemas, and the cold winter wind blowing and the cold stars pricking; and I riding cold as a corpse with my fears; and as heavy. Lagging behind, Margaret rode. There was a lost look about her as though she carried a dead thing within her. And, indeed, I think she carried her dead child in her heart. It is not given to every woman, priest, to be a witch, any more than every man can be a saint. Philip flew, spurring on her mount, all impatience to be there. She had neither stick nor familiar to carry her; but her mount bore the tormented face of Tom Simpson—a poor creature abused and bedevilled. She had bewitched him so that he must carry her wherever she commanded. And when he did not carry her fast enough, she struck him in the eye with her naked heel and beat upon his back with a wand so that the stripes showed bloody.

She was lit with her malice and I thought, Small wonder the Master loves her above us all. I did not know then that already He was angered by her folly and wearied of her presumption. For she set herself above all others, even the oldest and the wisest. I did not know that already the Captain had been at the Master's ear . . . though I might have guessed it. For I had heard her declare—and not once neither—that soon the Master would set the Captain aside and name her Coven Maiden in his place. So I did not know that already the days of her life were numbered; and with them Margaret's days; and my days, also.

And so we came to the place of the Sabbath. For the first time I was not eager; neither for the rites, nor for the feast.

For myself I was not afraid. I had done those tasks that fell to my hand. No great evils, certainly; and not continual evil. It was not to be expected. The soul can no more bear the weight of continual evil than the weight of continual good. Good and bad is the natural lot of us all—saint and sinner alike.

We began, as always, with the Adoration of the Master. When we had saluted Him in a ring with uplifted foot, the circle broke and the long line moved before Him . . . and all the time my heart was sick with fear. I saw Philip, at the head, rise on tiptoe to reach the light between his horns; her grave thin face bent downwards to her own candle, her long fingers shielded its flame. I tried to tell myself that there was no malice here, but it was no comfort. Philip would perform the rites with due solemnity whatever should come later; behind that quiet face her anger burned.

I moved in my turn and stood before Him seeking to pluck some message from his face. Through the black mask the eyes stared blank as stone. I moved on.

And now it was Meg's turn to stand before the God. And, as she stood, I saw the hand holding the candle tremble so that she could not light it. The line, slow-moving, dropped to a halt; and we stood, watching. The hand holding the candle jerked from left to right. Not one had pity for my wretched child; and, in my own heart, greater than pity, was fear; and, priest, the fear was for myself.

So in the silence we waited. And He, with us; a God in stone.

How long she stood there trying to kindle the light I do not know. But at last the thing was done. It was done and we made as though to move again. She took a half-step forward; and then the shudder took her; her whole body shook, all rigid, like that of the dying; I half-expected to hear the rattle in her throat. The lighted candle fell from her hand.

We stood, not daring to believe the thing we saw—the blue flame drop and disappear in the black earth. Such a thing, within the knowledge of the oldest witch, had never happened. A groan went up; one long groan like the voice of all despair.

But still the Master said nothing. I caught sight of my

younger daughter. There was the faintest smile about her half-open mouth.

I saw the Master sign to Margaret to drop out; and the worshippers moved on.

But it was not the end; for having performed the lighting of the lights, we must move again to give the Homage of the Kiss.

And all the time Margaret sat apart on the ground, her face in her hands, hidden by the long fall of her hair. And so she continued and did not offer the Kiss nor did He ask it. And that, too, had never been known.

Then He gave us the signal that we might sit; and we sat silent facing his throne. Now it was the time for us to tell of the work we had done to his glory; and my fear mounted as, one by one, we stood to speak.

Ellen Greene had robbed the grave of two infants and would have robbed more had she not been disturbed. She had brought a great pot of fat; we should not go short of our ointment for many a day. The man Randall had bespelled the sheep of Sir George Manners so that they sickened and died, they and their lambs with them. And for this an innocent man—William Berry of Langhorne—went to the gallows. Joan Willimott had bewitched the pigs of one who had given her stale bread instead of fresh; and for the same reason she had cursed the wife of Anthony Gill over at Frisby, so that the goodwife and her child died together. As for myself, do you remember, priest, when your orchard failed? The fruit hung full and sound; yet overnight it crawled with maggots and had to be burnt."

He nodded.

"'That was my work. Mistress Davenport, meeting me in the village, had taken it upon herself to scold me that I came to church no more; and that the lights of my house shone till daylight and the noise of our junketing disturbed the quiet night. Nor did she care who heard her words. And I put the curse upon her black pig so that it ran this way and that and swelled and died.

And so it went on, each one standing with his tale."

"And always the same tale," Samuel Fleming sighed. "The fields of the good man blasted, the fruits of the bad man prospered; a cow, a sheep, an ox or a pig betwitched to its death."

"And a child here and there, also," she remInded him, smiling. "Do not forget the children!"

"I am not likely to forget them."

"A fair calendar. I should have rejoiced. And yet, sitting there, I began to wonder if this were all to life—the working of small evils and the trembling of the soul that we had not found sufficient for our hands to do! And, when this life was done, would it be as the Master promised—eating and drinking and the satisfying of desire? And if that were so, what did He promise that we had not already here upon earth? Surely eternal life should promise something better than the life we know. For the first time I began to doubt."

"God was working in you," Samuel Fleming said.

She shook her head. "Why should he? I had renounced my baptism and all hope of part in him."

"He is more merciful than human soul can conceive."

"It was a pity he did not show it that night. For still it went on and on—one after another offering his evil at the feet of the Master. And once again it was Margaret's turn.

She made no move. She sat there in the midst of us; yet she sat alone—abandoned, cast-off. And my fear grew; the fear that was both for her and for me. Hers was a soul not worth the bargain. I had cheated the Master. And the girl, too, I had cheated. I had promised her eternal joys; but it was a path too fearful for her feet to tread. I had brought her along that path; and there was neither going forward nor backward.

Now in the awful silence, the eye of the Master turned upon her. But still she sat, fingers clasped so that the shining bone glistened through the skin like ivory; and her fair hair falling about her face and about her neck and about her bosom. And all the time she neither spoke nor heard nor knew what happened.

And, in the silence the Master spoke. It was not the roaring of the thunder, not the bellowing of a great beast; but a little voice, a still small voice . . ."

"That is an old trick," Samuel Fleming said. "The God of the Jews used it in the dawn of time; but the Son of Man spoke always man-to-man. Can your Master do nothing better than copy so stale a trick?"

"It is his own trick, older by far than the God of the Jews. And it works; it works yet. Priest, my heart stood still.

'Stand up,' the small voice said, 'stand up, my servant, and speak.'

And when she did not move the Captain went to her and took her roughly by the shoulder and dragged her to her feet. She stood there and every limb shook so that it was a marvel she did not fall. I could not look at her. I was her mother; and I had brought her to this.

She stood staring out of blind, blue eyes.

'What deeds have you performed for love of Me?' the Master asked.

I saw her swallow in her throat; I saw her tongue move across her lips. Her mouth began to move but it was hard to catch the words. 'Lord . . . Lord . . .' she said. And then, 'We worked the spell . . . but it failed . . . it failed . . .'

Her voice died away; and, all about her, the silence waited.

'It failed,' she said again. 'The familiar refused.'

'The familiar . . . refused?' And the small, quiet voice, the little gentle voice stiffened the blood in my veins. 'We shall deal with the familiar.'

Her lips just moved but no sound came. Oh, priest, then was the time for your god to speak; but he did not speak, and she stood there with her empty eyes and her dropped jaw and her mouth fallen like the mouth of the dead.

Philip sprang up in the moonlight; she was tight as a bowstring when the arrow is fitted. And I knew that thing I had feared was upon us.

But I was no longer afraid. I looked at her all wild and cruel; and I felt my soul move towards her, as yours, priest, might move towards a saint. There was no pity in me now, but only a hateful joy because of the pain to fall upon the daughter that had brought shame upon me. I looked upon the daughter who covered my shame with her own glory.

'Lord,' she said and came forward and knelt. 'Let your servant speak.' And when He nodded, she said, 'It is right that there be punishment for failure; but punishment should fall where it belongs. It belongs not to the poor familiar but to the one that blighted the spell in the binding.'

He said nothing; nor did He move.

'Lord,' she said and there was no fear in her, 'we had agreed, the three of us, to cast the spells to bring all the children to their death; and afterwards to blast the seed of the father and the womb of the mother. And we bound ourselves in full meeting in your name. So it was, Lord.'

He stood up in his place. 'Was it not so?' He asked of us.

'Lord, it was so,' we answered Him and nodded our heads.

Philip turned her wild head upon her shoulder and stretched a finger towards Margaret. 'It was she blasted the spell in the making. For we cast it watchful that nothing go wrong; but she sat there and set her will against us. But we did not know it, my mother and I, until we rubbed the kerchief upon the belly of the familiar. For, when we commanded him, *Go upward*, he crouched with eyes of fire and could not stir against her will. Then my mother said, The spell is spoilt. But my sister said nothing. She stood up and went away. And after that we dared not cast the spell again until we had consulted with our Lord and confessed and bowed ourselves to his command. Lord, what must we do?'

'We must strengthen the will of our servant towards Ourselves,' he said, still in that small, quiet voice. And then He spoke not at all, but sat, masked face upon his hand. And we crouched still as any stone and watched lest our breathing sound too loud.

And so sitting, the excitement died out of me; and I wondered what punishment He would inflict upon my girl. His lightest punishment—whipping—I had suffered myself, over Patchett's child; and I had not found it so light." She moved her shoulders, as though, even now, out of the body, she felt the pain of the blows. "As for the hardest punishment —it might be stoning. And, though Margaret was worthy of death, I did not want to see her die cruelly before my eyes.

He raised his head at last; his voice was cold as well water. 'This backsliding servant of mine does not know Me. She has forgotten the night she offered herself to my service. When my servant forgets the embraces of the God, then it is time for her to die the death. But because she sacrificed her new-born child I will show mercy. That she may hereafter remember the God, my choice tonight falls upon her. Witches, to the feast.'

The sweet savours of roast and broiled came up to our nostrils, but Margaret going to her place, the least place of all, cried out that it was the flesh of infants. I rallied her that she was fanciful as a breeding woman; it was nothing but pork and mutton.

Margaret had been chosen of the Master; but tonight there was not one that would willingly lie in her place. There she sat, lower than the youngest child in a lost and lonely world.

The Master did not look at her. He played with Philip; and they ate and laughed and kissed together, she lying upon his breast. But Margaret sat upright and looked before her and no crumb passed her lips.

At last, when we had eaten, the Captain stood up and cried out, *Witches, to the dance!* So we ran to make our ring about the God and the Dance of the Adoration began. I looked about for Margaret; she had not taken her place but sat upon the ground. No-one called to her; and if he had I doubt she would have heard. There was nothing to do but throw my head back with the others and move in the measure of the dance, singing the hymn that never before failed to waken desire in me. It is a desire, priest, more than the common delight of women; for singing, I would feel within myself the quickening of the fertile earth and be at one with it.

But tonight I felt nothing only fear and sorrow; and the anger of the God. The whole company felt it too; in spite of the flute, forever quickening, our feet slowed and we came to a halt.

Nor was it better when we came to the dances of our delight, which are not to praise the God but to warm us for our sport. At a nod from the Master, the Captain flung his flute upon the ground and cried out, *Witches, to the sport!*

So we stood still while our partners came to fetch us—to every woman her incubus, to every man his succubus; but still Margaret sat unmoving on the ground. Philip left her place by the Captain and stood over against Margaret. 'Stand up, fool!' she said and the noise of her hissing came clear. 'If you show yourself a coward the Master will tear you in pieces. Show some pleasure, if you cannot show ardour. It is the only way to save yourself.'

But still Margaret sat in her place. And still the Master waited. He was black as coal and his horns jigged this way and that as the wind blew the flame of the candle that was set between them. And, as He stood, the muscles beneath the shining skin rippled sleek with the power and the cruelty that was in Him.

And so we stood waiting until it pleased Him to move.

Margaret stood up on her place. And all the time He stood there and gave no sign. So, inch by inch, moving against her will she came towards Him.

And then it began—the thin sweet sound of pipes that stir the blood; and the pounding of tabors that beat their rhythm within the womb. But, still as I lay with my incubus, my mind was less upon my delight than upon my girl. And once I heard a wild scream and I raised myself to listen. 'Lie still, sweetheart, till our business is done,' he said and pulled me down again.

Dawn was coming up faint in the east. The pipes and tabors slackened and stopped and we came yawning from our embraces.

I saw Philip, sleepy as a cat, mount her tormented steed; she cut at him with a sharp switch and turned his head towards home. But weary as I was, and all longing for my bed, I could not leave the place until I had seen Margaret—that scream rang still in my ears. So there in the empty place, all churned with our feet, its bushes broken by our bodies, and the stink of spent candles in the air, I waited.

And then I saw her.

She was covered with blood—mouth and arms and white body abloom with scarlet. And her face was stiff as stone and her eyes were no longer blank. They were quick with horror; quick and sick. If she could have wept then—though her heart dissolved in its flood and her spirit took flight to the nethermost pit—then she would have wept. For the thing we miss sorest and agonize to win again, but cannot win again, is the power to weep."

Chapter Fourteen

"I WANTED to comfort my poor girl, to wipe away the blood; but I dared not. This terrible mating was her punishment. The Master had judged; who was I to deny his justice? Neither then nor afterwards did I throw her a word of comfort for fear of Philip. Philip would not hesitate to denounce me, any more than she had hesitated to denounce her sister.

It was sad these days in the cottage; yes, and bitter too. Meg went about with a vacant look. I wondered, sometimes, whether she was losing what wits she had. Philip would stand over her, flinging her taunts; asking whether she had conceived yet of the Master. And she would pat her own full belly. Meg would flush or she would pale; sometimes she would lift a hand to her face as though there were tears she must wipe away; and she would stare, surprised, when the hand came away dry. Grief and horror festered in her heart—grief for the slain child; horror of the Master.

Yes, I was sorry for Margaret; but I feared Philip.

Once I came upon Meg when I was gathering faggots in the wood; it was in a dark place and she was kneeling; and she was trying to pray. It was your lord's prayer. But she could not say it. *Lead us into temptation*, she kept saying. *Lead us, lead us into temptation*. She knew it was wrong, you could tell it by the way she shook her puzzled head. She did not know how to set it right. For it is not permitted to us to take your lord's prayer upon our tongue; and, if we should try to pray, the Master confuses the mind and we cannot find the words. We may use them only in the casting of spells . . . and in the order which He permits.

So there she went on kneeling and her empty eyes lifted to the sky. If your god is as merciful as you say, priest, why did he not help her that day?"

"The further we run from God, the longer it takes to run to Him again," Samuel Fleming said.

"That is only commonsense." Joan Flower sighed.

"Ah well! My home had grown strange and sad; I was frightened lest my fool had not yet learnt her lesson. There were days I could bear it no longer. I would leave home in the early morning and wander the countryside asking myself why everything that had started so fair had turned to ashes in my mouth. Sometimes when I had forgotten to put a piece of bread in my pocket I would stop at a house where no-one knew me; but they would not give me so much as a crust; and sometimes they would threaten to set the dogs on me."

"The Devil's Mark was plain in your face."

"But it was the mark on my body brought me to my death."

"It was yourself that set them searching for it. You had justice."

"Your god offers more than justice—if we are to believe you, priest. What mercy did I ever get?"

"More than you could ever dare to hope. That is why you are here."

"You are quick enough with your answers, priest; but while I was on earth I had mercy neither from your god, nor from my God; nor yet from men and women."

"When heaven and hell and earth all fail, it is time to look into one's heart. How many curses did you cast, how much evil did you do?"

"Not enough, priest. Sometimes I failed in my duty; did you never fail in yours? When you are struck upon one cheek, you should turn the other—so you are commanded. When I am offended, the curse must follow—so I am commanded. Yet, sometimes you were content to forget the other cheek; and I to forego the curse. I knew it was a weakness; and a danger, too. For at home and abroad Philip's eye was on me. She would send one of her familiars so that, as I wandered, a hare would leap from beneath my feet, or a spotted rat or a great toad. Wherever I went, eyes went with me.

As for Rutterkin, there was another trouble. So long instant to my bidding, he was no more eager. From that day he had refused his part in bewitching the little lady, my power over him had waned. Now to buy his obedience, before he would do my slightest errand, I must give him blood; more and more blood. I knew that I was getting old and yellow and wasted. I put away my fine mirror. I did not need it to know that my eyes were hollow in their sockets, that every day saw new lines upon my face; as for my hands, they were beginning to look like the claws of an ancient hen. I was tired in my body; I was tired in my heart."

"Forever young, forever fair! So much for the Devil's promises."

"He kept his promise. At the Sabbath the blood ran hot and I was young. But earth's clocks strike a different rhythm; and I was old . . . old. There were times when the Sabbaths seemed far away, a dream; and our daily life hard and full of fear. And I would ask myself, sometimes, whether the Master had not forsaken me. But though it was not always easy, I would manage to thrust the doubt aside. If I had done nothing else I had, at least, brought Philip to Him, Philip in whom He delighted . . . or so I thought. And I had served Him well, doing many small evils as well as some great ones. Surely the two dead boys must count to my credit and count greatly; and if we had failed with the sister, that was not my doing. The fault was Meg's and she had been punished.

But it was all poor comfort; there were times I knew not which way to turn.

Philip came upon me one day when I walked in the woods. 'The God give me patience,' she cried out all sharp with her anger. 'He has set us work to do and we have not done it. My sister moons within, groaning and moaning; and you wander here in little better state. Soon the Sabbath will be upon us and we have not done his bidding.'

'There is time and time enough,' I said, trying to make light of the matter, but she would not be pacified.

'There are no more merry meetings in our house; and you come to the esbats no more. You know not what they say of us, those we call our friends. But *I* know—though they are silent when they see me; for they fear me still. I need no words. A glance of the eye, the back a little turned—it is enough. I tell you there's little love amongst them for any of us. They are afraid because of my sister's disgrace; afraid to be too friendly lest they share it. And there's jealousy in plenty because of me. And any one of them—even Willimott and Greene, your loving friends—would betray you to the Master if they got the chance.'

'There is no chance. They know nothing.'

'Do they not? What of Meg forever kneeling and trying and trying to catch the ear of the Christian god? And what of you? How long since you have set your hand to work for the sake of the Master? A true Christian example!' And she spat. 'Oh,' she said, 'I could work the spell myself. And then? What then? At the Sabbath I must say I worked alone. And the Master will know, and all the covens will know, that you are faithless; not only my sister, which is shame enough; but you that sponsored me.'

'And should you mind our disgrace, except that you might share it?' I asked, unwise—it is not clever to stir the adder with one's foot.

'I am not afraid of pain,' she said quickly; and that was true. I saw her once when a spark flew from the fire and singed her flesh in the thick of the arm. I could smell the burning; but she shook it off and, without a word, set about her work. And once a splinter ran into her thumb under the nail. She bent her head and bit it free—and no wincing. She was one to thrust her right hand in the fire, if need be, without a whimper.

'There is worse than pain,' she said. 'There is shame; and that is a thing to fear; and it is a thing I will not endure.' And that was true, too. She would not endure our shame to dim her glory; to drag her, perhaps, from her high place.

'Come!' she said and put out a hand, fragile as a wren's claw to the eye but strong as an eagle's when it came to the test. 'It is time to cast the last spell; to bewitch the lord and lady. I will wait no longer.'

I went along with her but I could not hide my unwillingness. I was afraid to meddle in so strong a thing, so long a thing we could not see to its end. To kill this one or that—I would do it; to bespell the source of life itself was another matter. It frightened me.

'And your sister?' I asked, making Meg as an excuse for delay.

'That fool!' Philip said. 'The Master is too patient. He should have made an end of her long ago.' She felt my feet drag as we walked and she said, 'Once you were foremost among witches. You might have been the right-hand of the Master and his love. But now . . .'

'I am old and the blood runs thin. Honours and love drop away—especially love. So it is; and so it will always be. Yes, you will come to it, even you!'

'No!' and her voice came out in a whisper. She raised her clasped hands above her head; her voice went ringing through the wood. 'Master, listen, I beseech You!'

I touched her arm; someone might hear us—and I had no desire to come to the rope. She was in an ecstasy—we call it the witch's ecstasy—for she cried out still in that high clear voice. 'Master, let the time not come when my blood runs thin. Keep my fire alight for ever.'

'Not even the Master can do that,' I warned her. 'Not while we walk the earth. At the Sabbath, yes; but only if you are strong enough to fight old age. I am not strong enough; nor will you be, perhaps, when the time comes.'

'Then put out the flame of life before it begins to die!' she cried out. 'Master, put it out for ever and let me dwell with You in the joys of Hell as You have promised.'

And, priest, standing there, we heard it, both of us—the sound among the trees. To me it seemed like laughter, sly, and ugly. But Philip took it as her answer and dropped to her knees, nodding and smiling her thanks.

As we went there came a sound of voices, good human voices, homely; and there, in a clearing, where in summer we would hold our esbats, we came upon Joan Willimott and Ellen Greene—and their familiars frisking about them. One was a rat, and the other an owl; but Pretty was not there.

I was glad of my gossips after the laughter in the woods; and we sat down all four, and talked. We chatted of this and that—how Patchett had lost his wife and child and might have saved them both; and Anthony Gill, also. And we talked about the death of the little lords; and how Tom Simpson

166

went about vacant, the wits gone from him; and how he would go to bed at night and wake up full of bruises; and a mark upon his back the shape of a saddle. And we laughed and we joked, all of us; and Philip laughed loudest.

And, as we sat gossiping and joking, we heard the sound of footsteps, very slow; and a sound of bushes being put back.

We hushed our laughing; the familiars scrambled and scrabbled into hiding; we waited.

It was Margaret—Margaret walking, you might think, in her sleep, her white face all criss-crossed with briar scratches, and her arms also and her bare feet. She came to us and sat down and she said nothing; and then she lifted her head and she said—and it was still as though she slept, for there was neither tone nor colour to her voice—'We have done enough. This thing I will not do.'

Philip turned her head quick as an adder to warn Meg to silence; but Ellen said, all coaxing, 'What is it, child, you will not do?' And took Meg by the hand.

'Bewitch the lord and lady,' she answered simple as a child. 'They are to have no more children . . . ever. Ever,' she said again. 'That's a long time.'

'Time's longer when you're dead, hanged by the neck,' Philip said.

Meg shook her head to left and right; her face swung white as a dead-nettle within the pale gold of her hair. 'Oh no! I shall never come to the rope. I serve the Master.'

'But *how* do you serve Him?' Philip said, very sharp. 'There are two sides to every bargain. And if you break your pact, why then it is broken! You were meant for the gallows, faithless and foolish as you are. And when one is meant for the gallows there is no escape. It is the rope; the rope—no other way! Oh, you may sit staring out of your fool's eyes which shall stare wider when the rope drops! For what I say is true. Do you remember the great picture that is all little pictures and a wise word to each? There is one says, *Born to be hanged you'll never be drowned*. And there is the little gallows in the corner to prove it.'

Meg's hand went to her throat as if already she felt the

167

rope and Philip laughed. 'Come,' she said, 'we must go. There is work to be done. Good-day to you, friends,' and her face was all smiles. But when we had gone a little way she stopped short and her face was dark. 'Fool,' she said to Meg, in that hissing way she had. 'Fool! That's a precious couple!' And she jerked her head backwards. 'And you must needs go blabbing. They would run to destroy you for the mere joy of it.'

Meg lifted her bewildered eyes. 'But they are friends,' she said. 'Friends!'

Philip's eyes met mine over Margaret's head. 'This fool has done more mischief than she knows! Well, we must get the work done while we may; then let them blab if they must. I trust—' and she thrust her dark face into Meg's, 'that you will still call them *friend* when it comes to your hanging.'

Meg shrank a little and Philip said no more. It was only as we reached our house that she spoke again. 'Spoil the spell we are about to cast—and I will kill you. If I have to confess once more to failure I will even it with the tale of your death.' And she lifted her hands all crooked and stiff and brought them to Meg's neck.

Meg said, shrinking against me, 'You wrong me, sister. I had no hand in spoiling any spell.'

'You are such a fool,' Philip said, scornful. 'You do not know the strength of your own power. When you sit there saying nothing, doing nothing, but *willing* the spell to fail— then it will fail. A spell is a strong thing; but the will is stronger.'

I pushed open the door; and, as we went inside, Philip gave Meg a sudden shove. 'Get out—and stay out!' she said. 'Leave this to your betters.' And she shut the door in Meg's face.

'You are not over-kind to your sister,' I said.

'Kinder than she deserves. If she confesses to the Master that she had no hand in this, she will escape with a whipping. But if she spoils this spell, also, why then, at the very least it is death; death by stoning. It is not a pretty sight.'

It was true and I said no more.

'You talk of bewitching the lord and the lady,' I said

when I had barred the door and thrown a cloth upon the window, 'but we have nothing—neither of hers nor his. How shall we bind the spell?'

She laughed at that. 'Truly you grow old!' she said. 'When my lady, of her goodness—' and she spat upon the word, 'sent my sister away, she thought to sweeten the sour deed with a sweet gift. Have you forgotten the pillow, so soft? And the mattress my sister sleeps upon—' she nodded towards the corner, 'was my lady's; and my lord's also. What better could we have to bind them both?'

So I took the basin and blew up the fire; and she took a little knife and let out a handful of feathers from the pillow and a handful of wool from the mattress. And, with the same knife, I drew blood from my arm.

'More,' Philip cried, impatient at the thin trickle. She snatched the knife and drew it deeply across her own arm and laughed to see the blood gush.

Then we stirred the brew; and, priest, it was queer to see her standing there great with her godling, and bewitching another woman that she should conceive no more.

And, as we stirred, we said the Words of Power and then we sang; and these are the words.

> Blast seed, curse womb,
> Sink, sink into the tomb.
> Weep, weep for daughters fair,
> Weep yet more for son and heir.
> Empty heart and empty hand,
> Master, hear me where I stand.
> Sink, sink into the tomb,
> Blast seed, curse womb."

Samuel Fleming, lifting a white face, sighed as though his heart must break.

"Why sigh now, priest?" she asked impatient. "The thing is done; and for the doing we have paid—all three of us."

"But all your paying cannot undo it!" He shook his head, lifting empty hands and letting them fall again.

"I could not wish it undone, since it was paid for—and the price high enough. The price . . . we didn't know it then;

169

not Philip standing there in my darkened room, belly outthrust and smiling as she stirred; nor I, watching her. And yet, I was warned; but I didn't know that, either. For, suddenly, fear fell upon me that what we asked was too heavy, too long, to be contained within the compass of a human spell. Witches may not usurp the power of Devil or God.

'It is too much, too much,' I told Philip; and it was as though someone else used my mouth. And then . . ." Joan Flower's voice lifted thin and sweet,

> "Blast seed, curse womb,
> But not, Lord, unto the tomb.
> In seven year, in seven year,
> Give the lord his son and heir,
> Let her see a daughter fair.
> No longer empty heart and hand,
> Master, hear me where I stand.
> Ere they pass into the tomb,
> Bless seed, ripen womb."

She nodded brightly at the old man. "I found myself changing the spell before I knew what I was about. I was surprised . . . but not so surprised as Philip. She took a step towards me and lifted her hands above the steam of the basin threatening me as she had threatened Meg. Her face and her hands were smeared with blood and her narrow eyes, full open now, blazed with anger. There was a feather, I remember, stuck crazily to her cheek. I was afraid of her; but I would not show it, not I. The girl was my daughter.

'You are a fool and for this you deserve to die, Joan Flower!' she said. It was the first time she had not called me mother. I knew—as she meant me to know—that if I crossed her in any way, she would show no more mercy to me than to Meg.

'God!' she cried out. But it was upon the Old God she called, the oldest of all gods. 'That I must be compassed about with fools.'

'You will use that word once too often!' I told her. 'This time it is you that are the fool. No spell can last for ever. Whether the time be long or whether it be short, there is always a limit; and that limit must be set. You should know that by now, my clever witch! Seven is a number of power; it binds the spell more closely. In seven years we shall cast it again.'

'Not you!' she cried out. 'Not you! In seven years where will you be?' And it was as though she cursed me to my death.

We whistled up Rutterkin and this time he was instant to our bidding. When he had risen and gone, Philip turned about and regarded me curiously. 'It will not help you to backslide into goodness,' she said. 'Between two stools a man may fall and break his neck as surely as by the rope. And if you fall between heaven and hell—where are you then?' It was a strange thing to say and she said it strangely. For come the seven years—and I am a ghost wandering between two worlds; and there was never a child of my lady. That day she saw my future clear; but her own future she did not see."

"Nor yours," Samuel Fleming said. "Not to its end. For the end is not yet. I think it will be remembered to you that you set a bound to a most wicked spell. But—" and he looked at her curiously, "why did you stop at seven years?"

"Was it not enough, priest?"

"It was enough. But the years are almost passed; and there is hope again. Why did you give them that hope?"

"I told you, priest; I was afraid."

"I think it was pity stirring in your heart; I think it was, God, perhaps, whispering in your ear."

"Then, priest, he whispered too late."

"I wonder?" he said softly.

Chapter Fifteen

It was October now and the harvest safely gathered in. Samuel Fleming standing at the west door looked back towards the chancel where he had been kneeling to thank God for the good yield. This year no-one in Bottesford should go short of bread.

And, so standing, he fancied something moved down there before the altar. But the church was empty. He had found it empty. Yet, maybe, someone had slipped in while he prayed.

He screwed up his eyes to focus more clearly.

Yes, there was a woman down there. He knew whose head was lifted defying the high altar. He did not need she should turn her face. He knew her for what she was.

He made a step towards her. "Are you not afraid to set foot in God's holy church?" he asked.

"Why should I be—since he allows it?"

He felt the stirring of hope that he might yet save her soul; he said nothing.

She came softly up the aisle, flitting pale between the dark pews; at the last row, near the door, she stopped, bent and touched a seat with her finger-tip. It was here she had sat, a humble worshipper, before she had sold herself; and here, after she had made her most wicked bargain, she had sat in ugly mockery, the wafer slyly hidden beneath her tongue. And now, now she was here again within his very church. How could a priest not hope to save her?

She sat down in her place; he could see the polished wood shining through the transparency of her body. She was dead . . . but she was more alive than some who came to worship in this place. He had the strongest desire to talk to her, in this holy place. Surely God's spirit, he argued, must be strongest here. But God's spirit is everywhere—and equal everywhere; He needs no especial net for the catching of souls. And Hester expected him; she fretted if he were delayed these days. And, besides, Cecilia would be riding down—

with news, maybe, of Francis. Not for Hester nor for Cecilia would he abandon this lost soul. But Goody Fellowes would be waiting too; a poor sad creature and talking to him her only comfort. To show discourtesy to her was a thing he could not do.

"One might take your courtesy for softness," Joan Flower said, at her old trick of reading his thought. "But it is a cold courtesy. For all your fine manners you would have sent me to the gallows. Well," and she rose, shaking out her skirts as so often she had done in life, "if you will not stay here with me, then let us go together."

Cecilia smiled her welcome when he came into the room; and, as always, at her sick and wasted look, his heart turned to water, remembering the pretty thing she had been a few short weeks ago. And, even while he bent to kiss her cheek, Hester said sharply for so gentle a creature and one zealous for his dignity, "Shut the door, Samuel. You have made the room cold as death."

The little cat stretched out by the fire rose and arched his back and made as though to spit.

"Now that is a strange thing," Hester said and she did not laugh. "You might almost think the little cat saw something. But I suppose the truth is that cold makes her vicious. I have seen it again and again. A sudden draught and she will attack anyone; myself, even. Come, puss, come." She held out an inviting hand. But the cat stood arched and spitting still.

"Go, Cat, go!" He heard Joan Flower's voice beside him; or imagined it, perhaps in the silence of his mind—for certainly no-one else had heard it.

The cat moved inch by unwilling inch towards Hester. Samuel shut the door; he came over to the fire and stood, hands behind his back, trying to warm his fingers at the blaze. Hester saw with alarm how thin the hand; the firelight seemed to shine through it.

He refused the canary since time pressed and anyhow it was over-sweet for his taste, staying for a moment to hear Cecilia's news. And, indeed, a moment was sufficient since there was no word of Francis.

And all the time the thought of Joan Flower dogged at

173

his heels. Until today he had not seen her for several weeks. He had been at Cottenham near Cambridge, which living he held also; and he had ridden more than once into Cambridge that he might refresh his eyes with the fine buildings and his mind with the fine talk. Yet all the time, delighting though he did in the company of old friends and through all the scholars' talk of which he had starved, he had thought of Joan Flower and of the struggle between them.

The air of Cottenham had done him good, Cecilia said. But when he had made his excuses and gone, she looked sadly at Hester; and though she would not put the ugly thought into words, she said in her heart that the Rector was not long for this world.

He stepped along to the study and Joan Flower went with him. He could feel her cold at his back.

In the study the old woman waited. She rose and bobbed her curtsey and plunged into the long tale of her woes. They were slight enough and of her own making; but he listened with kindliness and sent her away comforted.

"I was wrong, perhaps," Joan Flower said where she stood at the window. "Maybe your heart is gentler for my dying. But—" and she laughed a little, "you cannot expect that same miracle of me. It was I, after all, that died."

He said nothing but went across and stood beside her at the casement. The trees held out black branches sharp and precise as though etched in acid. Only the great cedar still kept her summer gown; but she, too, stood dark and heavy against the evening sky.

"It is autumn already," he said and sighed.

"Soon it will be winter," she said.

He nodded. "By winter everything will be settled between us."

"Who knows?" She shrugged. "You are a stiff-necked old man." She came from the window and sat in the chair by his desk. "There is something about this chair draws me," she said. And he remembered how, when she had stood before the justices, he had pitied her wild and haggard look and had bade her sit . . . this very chair; and it had stood exactly so, the light from the window shining into her face.

"So much misery up at the Castle!" She clasped her hands loosely upon her skirts. "The two little boys dead and buried; the little lady with her feigned fits; my lady sick and my lord also. And though they were loving and kind together so that he never lay one night from her bed, yet she did not conceive. But no-one thought to consider how all these evils had come about, and no-one suspected us. Oh, they had long called us *witch* down in the village, blaming us for this and for that; but that we dare lift our hands against so great a lord and lady never entered their heads. Strange . . . strange. And yet, after all, not so strange. The Master protected us . . . until his work was done."

"You are wrong," he told her. "Tongues wagged in plenty. But no-one dared, as yet, carry tales to my lord. He would not listen without proof, nor the lady, neither. And more; talebearers might well be punished for their pains. And I? I heard the tales, too; and I, too, could not believe them. Idle and licentious I knew you to be; but witches—never!"

She sat there white and smiling her wicked smile.

"And so were let to do our work in peace," she said. "The days passed; day after quiet day. My lord went to London to attend the King, and my lady also; and, with them the young lady.

My lord and lady came home again; but the young lady was not with them. She thought no more of drawing all eyes with feigned sickness; she had drawn the eye of the one she desired—my lord Duke of Buckingham; drawn it in a way no honest woman could desire."

Samuel Fleming sighed deeply. This, too, had been added to their burden. It was the first time he had seen Francis enraged or Cecilia bitter. Affliction they had taken from the hand of God; affliction from the hand of man they were not minded to take. *If you do not repair my daughter's honour*, Francis had written to Buckingham, *no greatness shall protect you from my justice.*

Justice! It was Francis himself that, in the end, repaired his daughter's honour—to the tune of twenty thousand pounds down and eight thousand a year, together with lands and titles—and more to come.

175

"There are spots upon the honour of my lady the Duchess of Buckingham but they are well gilt!" Joan Flower nodded. "Well, and why not? Her father has the money—he needs it no longer for his sons. The death of the brothers brings this much good—it gilds the sister's honour. My girls, being humble and poor, were sent away in disgrace; but the little lady, the little saucy lady is hung about with gold. *My lady the Duchess!* Who dare whisper she's no better than the next one —she with her fine gowns all laced with gold and each gown enough to keep a family for a year; and her ropes of pearls big as peas looped about her neck and falling to the waist; and each pearl enough to buy salvation!"

"Tears, not pearls, buy salvation," he said.

"Gold buys honour; why not pearls salvation?" she asked mocking. "I remember when she came home again; it was before she got her wedding-ring—they were chaffering still like hucksters over the price of her honour. She saw me standing in the dirt of the road—she in her fine habit of green velvet and the feather buckled into her great hat—and she all-but rode me down. For I would not curtsey to her, not I. Aha, I thought, my fine little lady, you have not yet got your grand crown—the price is not high enough! And I hated her with her proud spirit and the cleanness of her body that hid the dirt within. And I wished it were she that lay in her grave instead of her brothers."

"Then you are unjuster than my lady countess against whose justice you cry out. She did but send your girls home again; you would have sent hers to the grave."

"And still would! My girls did no worse than her girl; yet they were brought to shame and thence to their hanging; for poverty and disgrace and witchcraft are spun upon one thread. But that girl, bred soft, her every wish granted before uttered, was laden with honours to cover her dishonours; yes, and a handsome husband to boot. But she shall have little joy of him. No, priest, I do not curse—that day is long past. But, alive or dead, it needs no witchcraft to know that man's heart."

She saw the grief in his face and said gently, "The little lady will wed again and there will be happiness . . . but you will not see it."

"Shall her father see it?"

She nodded.

"I am glad of that," he said, thinking of Francis with his stricken face sailing lonely down some mythical river in faraway lands. Why did he not come home again? He was not yet too old to beget an heir!

"Soon the curse will be lifted," Joan Flower said. "It was for seven year; for seven year only and they are all-but run."

"In seven years," he said, "the heart grows weary." And he remembered how month after month had gone by; month after hopeless month. Cecilia's physician, Master John Atkins, coming down to the Rectory to smoke a pipeful of tobacco had said more than once, They are still torn with grief for the boys and with anxiety for the girl; and they are weak, also, from their own sickness. But things are on the mend, you will see!

Well, he had seen; seen again the procession of empty months! But still he had thought, There will be children. Why not?

"We could have told them why not!" Joan Flower answered his thoughts. "Margaret, indeed, was so driven by remorse that had we not kept her fast beneath our eye, in spite of her fear of the Master, I think she would have gone to the Castle and told all.

But if the months were barren for my lady, Philip's months came to a fruitful end. She was delivered of her godling; a thin, dark brat with eyes like her own, slitted and dark-shining. He was a strong child but she did not care for him overmuch; for she found no sign of the God upon him—neither budded horns, nor tiny tail nor little cloven feet. She had hoped to give birth to an undoubted godling; yet this seemed nothing but a common child. I would watch her dark unloving face bent to the child that stared up to her, dark and unloving as herself. But we tended him as though he were indeed a godling; for we planned to carry him to the next Sabbath and offer him to the Master.

It was the Roodmas meeting—Mayday; the best of all our meetings. Springtime, when the sap rises in man and beast and trees alike. But now we did not welcome it; not even Philip sour with disappointment over her godling. Margaret had done no service since our Candlemas festival, not even though the Master had punished her then with his terrible lovemaking. What would happen to her this time? I dared not think of it; and the girl, herself, went about cowed and dumb. I think she had lost her senses."

"Perhaps she had found them again."

"Not she, priest. She was always weak in the wits; and fear had turned what little she had. A fool!"

"God has mercy on fools."

"But not the Master," she said, grim.

"And so God gains."

"He is welcome to his fools!"

"You have a hard heart." He sighed. "As for this Sabbath of yours—you do not speak of yourself. What had you to offer?"

"The best I could; but it was not much." She shook a rueful head. "Having dealt with the family at the Castle, what was left in a village like ours? The same small bewitchings —a pig in fits; beer sour in the vat or milk in the pail; the well run dry, or a child fallen sick. Little things . . ."

"Little things are the things by which we live . . . or die. When you make hard lives harder, then you snuff the breath in the old and in the very young and in those that are sick. Your little things are hard enough, witch!"

"They added up!" she agreed, careless. "And Philip's list was long enough. And she had the child. But we did not know how the Master would accept it. If He declared it his own son, then Philip was certain of his favour and I should share it—the Devil has his own honour, priest. But if He accepted it for sacrifice, only, then she must reckon with favour withdrawn; and she and I must walk warily. But, whichever way it went, it could not help Margaret. Each witch must do her part . . . and she had done nothing.

I remember how we set off—Meg stupid with misery; Philip, the child in the crook of her arm, silent and guarded; myself troubled—all three of us oppressed with foreboding of danger.

Even the journey could not raise my spirits. The neighing of horses, the howls of bewitched creatures driven through the sky, the wild cries of witches urging their mounts in frenzy to reach the sacred place—none of these things could make me forget what might be awaiting us. And, priest, this time it was not so much for myself I feared, nor yet for Philip. It was for my fool I was afraid.

And, as we went, I looked sideways at her, wondering where she would find courage to endure the thing the Master must lay upon her. She had, poor wretch, suffered more than one death already, fearing this Sabbath and weighed down with her sorrows. Reins slack in her hands so that I must catch them lest she fall, she looked already dying.

And so we came at last to the field of the Sabbath, that place to which I could never hasten fast enough . . . but this time I thought myself there too soon. Frost had fallen, frost in May! The ground was hard beneath our feet and, in the cold spring night, stars sparkled like the jewels in my lady's rings. We should have to dance hard, I thought, to keep the blood flowing in our veins.

We greeted our friends, Philip and I; but Meg stood aloof, her lips locked in misery. I fancied we were not greeted as warmly as heretofore. I caught the look Joan Willimott sent to Ellen Greene; I saw the sly way they took Ann Baker, each by a shoulder, and turned their backs on us; nor were they the only ones. But I saw little Ann Baker steal back and touch the infant's cheek with her finger-tip; and though the others called sharply, bidding her come, she would not listen but stayed guarding the child.

For all she pretended to notice nothing, Philip whispered very bitter that they should be punished, every one! But even she could not suppose the Master would punish the whole coven for her sake.

And now it was time to take our places. Philip lifted the child that was all naked beneath the cloth and set him beneath a tree; and Ann sat beside him and would not leave him for all Joan Willimott's urging.

So there we stood alone. Priest, there is no lonelier thing than to be forsaken by the coven; for there is no mercy from the Master; and there is no hope anywhere, for we have turned our back upon God.

I sat down in my place and I dared not raise my eyes; but I knew by the chilling of my blood before ever the silence fell and the great trumpet sang, that the Master was amongst us. And when I lifted my head at last, there He stood upon the altar stone.

We rose then and linked hands for the Adoration. It was a comfort to stand again in the accustomed ring, as though the very rites must protect us. And I was glad to feel another's hand in mine, even though it was an unwilling hand put there not in friendship but in ritual only.

The Adoration done, came the Kindling of the Lights. I lit my candle with a steady hand though the heart fainted within me. And now the line moved forward again for the Kiss. It was this above all that I feared; nor was my fear less when He turned about to take the homage with the high honour of his mouth. I knew that, at times, He would condescend to one here and there He desired to honour; but to the assembly of covens—never.

But now it seemed that the whole assembly was, indeed, to be saluted with honour. One by one the witches knelt and He bent his head. Philip stepped forward, still linked as is our way, and knelt, eyes closed in worship. She took the Kiss and rose and stepped to the left.

And now my own turn had come. But, even as I knelt, He turned about and presented his buttocks. It was the usual form of salute and every part of the God is sweet and sacred; but, kneeling there, I felt my humiliation.

I gave the Kiss and stepped aside; and once more He turned Himself about to take homage from my neighbour upon the mouth. And so the linked line passed before Him; and every witch, down to the youngest child, kissed Him upon the mouth. And so it came to Margaret, standing in the lowest place. And, as she knelt, her hand, as if it had not strength, dropped from that of the neighbour.

She knelt unlinked before the Master.

The power that ran through our linked hands broke. I heard, as though it were one breath, the breath of all indrawn with fear. For all must stand linked when the Kiss is given, that is our custom, priest, unless the Master Himself break it.

He made no sign.

She raised both arms upwards in supplication. The God stared unseeing; an image in stone.

He had refused the Kiss.

She fell forward upon the ground; and the others wheeling about to come again to their places, trod upon her where she lay. For so it is with witches. Whom the Master loves, we love; and whom He hates, we hate. So there she lay until each one sat in his place again . . . and no hand outstretched to help her, not even mine, priest; least of all mine.

We sat unspeaking and we sat unmoving. Then the Captain blew with his trumpet and commanded us to put out our lights. So we sat there in the darkness and no man could see his neighbour. But all could see the God sitting there in the light that streamed between the sacred horns.

And now it was time for each one to proclaim his work in the Master's service. But, as the first of us made a movement to stand, He rose; and, in the silence, He spoke.

'There is a sickness amongst us.' And his head moved to where Margaret lay face hidden, upon the ground. 'Such a sickness is infectious.' And his eyes came to rest upon me, so that I trembled afresh. 'And it is a sickness that ends in death. Not only the death of the body—for that should bring your soul to Me; but in the rejection of the soul itself. And, if you are damned of God and rejected by Me, where then shall you turn?'

He stopped speaking; and we sat crouched in upon ourselves for fear of this Sabbath where the old established order was broken and no man knew what would happen next.

And in the silence He spoke again.

'I will hear no more tonight. Nor shall there be singing nor the dances of our sacred rites; nor feasting nor coupling, nor any holy joy. Go, all of you in fear; and chasten well your souls, lest I chasten you more grievously. I say unto you this only thing. I am the old God, of all gods the oldest. In that moment of time when I created the world, I set therein both evil and good, that every living soul might make its choice.

Servants, choose well. Let no evil pass from my world lest you throw away your portion in Me and in the life to come where the delights of the flesh never fail and my faithful feast with Me to all eternity.

Eternity. It stretches above and below, and to right and left of this little earth of yours; and the earth is lost within it. Eternity is so vast that your little human mind cannot compass its meaning. Yet it is in the little moment of time you call life that you must choose. And so I say, Look how you choose; you choose for eternity.'

And when He had finished speaking we bowed our heads to the ground; then the Captain blew upon the trumpet once more; and when we raised our eyes again the God was gone; and there was nothing in the place where He had stood but the burnt earth whereon his feet had rested. So we stood up, all of us, and without any word, turned our faces towards home. Only, as we went, we three together, there followed after us bitter words, because we had broken up the fellowship of sweet sinning and the great revels of the Sabbath."

Joan Flower's voice dropped into silence; and, in the quiet room, Samuel Fleming said softly, "And was that all?"

"Was it not enough, priest?"

He shook his head. "There is a thing you have forgotten. The babe you had left naked beneath the shawl upon the cold ground."

She shrugged. "We forgot it. How should we remember so slight a thing in the fear of that Sabbath?"

"Did not your Master stoop to the child?"

"No, priest. He left the Sabbath and it lay still upon the ground. Maybe the Captain took it up . . . maybe not. As for us we did not enquire; nor did we see it ever again."

"And this is your Master that cherishes little ones!"

"Everything in season, priest."

"My Master had not done so," he said. "With Him the least of these little ones is first."

Chapter Sixteen

SAMUEL FLEMING had not slept all night for thinking of
Joan Flower. Once he had believed that, being certain of her
guilt, he would be content—a man can do no more than his
duty. Now, in the dark of the morning and sleepless still, he
knew that to do one's duty is not enough; or that he had
failed to do it fully. He had sought to destroy her body; but
wickedness is not destroyed with the body, it harbours still
with the soul . . . and her soul he had not saved.

In his bedgown, he paced the study.

A soul to be saved. Did it matter whether he spoke face-
to-face with her unquiet ghost; or whether she was a dream
born of his own doubts, his own remorse?

"Ghost or dream, does it matter, priest?" And she was
there, picking the thoughts out of his brain and smiling her
sly smile.

He came back to his chair and regarded her, thoughtful.
She was subtle and she was swift; and she had the wisdom
of the dead. It behoved him, whatever she was, to be wary.
So now he left her question unanswered. "Yes, the Devil
does, indeed, cite holy Scripture for his own purposes!" he
said as once before.

"Meaning?" But his mind held no secret from her.

"It is God," he reminded her, "who demands that we do
not throw away our portion in Him nor let god perish from
the face of the earth."

"I think, priest, that your god cites the Devil for *his*
purposes."

Quite suddenly, forgetting the need for wariness, he lost
his temper.

"Beware how you blaspheme, lost as you are between
heaven and hell." And then, ashamed of his quick tongue,
said gently, "If God withdraw his pity, what will become
of you then?"

She did not answer; but in the early light that crept through the greenish glass of his casement, he saw her translucent body tremble like water. "Nearly two years since I died," she said, "but I know it only because of the calendar upon your table. Season follows season; but the sun does not warm my unhouselled spirit, nor winter blow cold in the coldness where I wander. Two little years; but already they have spelt out the great word the Master named; already I have tasted of eternity where time is timeless. I am weary and frightened of eternity."

"Yet you were promised eternal joy."

She made a gesture of impatience. "We were to *choose*. We were to choose between the delights of hell and the cold spaces of heaven."

"But you did choose! You chose hell. Why then does your Master shut you out? Why do you wander lost in eternity?"

"I did not choose. I drifted on the tide; and the tide rose and carried me away. It swept us apart, all three—me and the daughters born of my body who had lived together, worshipped together, sinned together. Me it swept into empty space; Philip it swept into hell where she desired to be . . ."

"I doubt she desires it now!" he said, very dry. "And Margaret?" And now he was gentle again; gentle but insistent. "What of Margaret?"

"You know that already," she said, sullen. "In heaven, as I think. Where else? She does not wander with me; nor, since she repented with a full heart, could the Master receive her. Where then but in heaven?"

His grave face crumpled to a sudden smile, and the smile broke into a chuckle so that she lifted her astonished head. "Oh," he said and wiped the tears of laughter from his eyes. "It is clear you believe in the mercy of God. We shall catch that soul of yours yet."

"I pray someone may catch it!" And there was no smiling in her. "But I would rather it was the Devil."

"You must give up all hope from him—if hope be the word. He has forsaken you. Do not keep God waiting too long. You would do well to come to Him before it is too late."

"Though his mercy endures for ever?" she asked quick and sly.

"You have scored a point," he told her. "But be not puffed up about it. With God points do not always add up. He has his own divine arithmetic. And your spirit, your proud spirit, shall yet be broken."

There was silence between them. Then, "How dark it is!" he said and felt in the pocket of his bedgown for his spectacles and polished them and settled them upon his nose. "These November days!"

"I think there is a storm to come," she said.

For all the broadening day it grew darker in the room, and he reached up to light the candles in their sconces. The clear flames stretched upward; light began to spread in the room so that her pale face floated misty; and when the light was bright and steady he could hardly see her. She drifted into a niche between his book-shelves which the light could not quite illumine and the shadow gave her once more the illusion of substance.

"You doubt Philip's desire to be in hell?" she said suddenly. "Why should she not desire it? Hell is a fine place—fair women and lusty men—very different from your cold heaven where there is neither marriage nor any sweet joy of the flesh. And the table is forever set and the wine forever poured, they say. And the soft bed forever waiting, they say that, too; and there . . ."

"They say, they say!" He interrupted, impatient. "Who are they that *say*, tempting your sick soul with vain imaginings? Listen now to what *I* say! I'll tell you what it is, this hell you so ardently desire. It is the black pit of torment; it is forever dark night, for no sun ever shines. Yet there is a sort of light, also; and from such a light may God protect us! For it is a place of burning—of smoking brimstone and raging coals, where the soul fries to all eternity. And what eternity may mean you have already an inkling. And there you may turn in the flames, turn and burn. And the devils will prod you with their toasting forks and push you back, all writhing, into the fire."

"You may know about heaven, priest—that is your

province. But—hell? Why should I believe you rather than the Master?" She shook her dark head. "Yours is a tale to win timid souls; to catch them for your cold heaven where they will freeze to the end of time." And she shivered in the warm room. "No, priest, if one way or another there is to be everlasting torment, let me, at least, be warm."

He found himself smiling at this; indeed, he was hard put to it not to laugh outright. She said, very grave, "To be tormented by bitter cold is no laughing matter; the poor know that well."

He recovered himself, saying gravely enough, "Who told you your tale of hell? It was the one you call Master . . . a Master that has broken faith with you. He is not to be believed, seeing that he is the arch-deceiver, the Prince of Lies."

He saw the anger flame in her eyes. "It was I that broke the faith—how many times must I tell you? I denied Him, breaking the bond."

And now they were silent in the quiet of the room with the steady-burning candles, remembering, both of them, that denial and the manner of her dying. She stood now so motionless in her shadowed place that, save for the coldness that streamed from her, it was hard to believe her there at all.

He sat head bowed on hand, remembering the day they took Joan Flower and her daughters. Never, as long as he had breath within him, could he forget it.

He had gone up to the Castle to bid his friends Godspeed; it was drawing towards Christmas and they were going, according to their custom, to wait upon the King at Whitehall.

"I have no joy in this journey," Francis had said, "save to pray at the grave of my little son. But then—I leave my other son behind."

"Do you not know," he had asked Francis then, "that I pray for the children when I rise up in the morning and when I lie down at night?"

"I know," Francis said.

"And if it will comfort you I will pray doubly for Henry while you are away."

"Dear friend, do so," Francis said. "It is a big grave for so little a child to lie alone."

It was then that he noticed how ill Francis looked. He had known, of course, that they had suffered, both Francis and Cecilia, from those same fits that had killed the children. Yet he had not feared for Francis—Francis was a man and strong. He saw now how the sickness had wasted his friend's strength. And even while his heart stood still with fear, Cecilia came in. And, eyes opened, he saw that she did not walk like the young woman she was, but with the slow care of old age.

"Should you not consult a physician when you are in London?" he asked gently, his heart shaken with fear for these dear friends.

"Master John is good enough!" Francis said. "We have been ill; but thanks be to God, we have shaken off the fits. Soon, by his mercy, we shall be strong again." He took his wife's hand and held it.

But soon he let it slip and stood up and wandered restless about the great room. Suddenly he stopped short and said, a little bitter, "We have taken our afflictions as from the hand of God. Our souls were glad to bear the burden—though the flesh was not always so willing—for why are we here if not to testify to his goodness? But now . . ." His thin hand went to his forehead, "I don't know . . . I don't know. There are tales; and I begin to ask myself whether our afflictions are truly from God or . . . from the Devil. It is a shocking thing to have to ask. But the time has come to ask it."

"The tales," Cecilia said, "oh, they are horrible!" and she covered her face with her hands.

"Do you believe them?" he asked, grieving that they who had borne their afflictions christianly should be driven to question them now.

She spread frail hands. "It is hard to know what to believe; yet I cannot, cannot believe them true. They are not good women, the Flowers; they are idle and very dissolute, but it is a long way thence to witchcraft. Drunkards and thieves and strumpets may yet have human hearts. And the children . . . so good, so sweet, so dear and so patient! It is hard to believe any human creature should torment them so." Her voice broke. She recovered herself, spoke in a firmer tone.

"These are, after all, women we know; women who have eaten our food, taken our wages, worked for us with their hands. How can such women be witches?"

"You may find a witch anywhere," Francis said, "even in God's holy church, wearing the robes of his sacred office."

Still he himself had not answered. Rector of this dear parish, he wanted to believe with Cecilia that the known person—the member of one's flock, of one's own household—cannot be entirely strange, entirely evil. But he could not rest upon his desire. For, "Do *you* believe these terrible tales?" Cecilia asked him.

He said, very slow, "I have not believed them, because, God forgive me, I have not wanted to believe them. But now . . ."

"Now," Francis said, "it is time to consider them."

"But," Cecilia said again with that sad, uncertain movement of the hands, "women who came to pray with us, to weep with us! It goes beyond reason; the mind refuses."

"God will reveal all in his good time," Francis told her gently.

After that, they had bidden each other Goodbye. "We shall be sad, missing you," he had told them, standing by the carriage, his hand in that of Francis. "Come back soon."

"As soon as maybe," Francis promised, grim. "Nothing but duty would carry me hence now. But we shall think much of the matter, as you may believe. And do you, Samuel, consider it, also."

"It is well that we have time before us," Cecilia said, lifting her worn face. "This concerns the lives of three women; it must not be dealt with in haste."

"By the time the lord and the lady were home, I lay in my grave." Joan Flower spoke softly from her shadowed place so that he started, forgetting she was there.

"Yes, I lay in a dishonoured grave and my daughters lay in prison. You could have spared them much anguish, priest, by stringing them up without waiting for a trial. There was enough against them; why were they tormented to make them speak?"

"It was not torment but Christian charity. They were questioned that they might confess and save their souls."

Her mocking laugh made nonsense of his answer.

"That morning!" she said. "Just before Christmas. And the snow deep; and the holly all green and red; and the children running about and screaming for joy in the crisp cold weather, their cheeks redder than any berry. But we sat indoors, we three; and we were silent. The tales that had been slow-gathering were fast-gathering now; and the words that had been whispered were shouted; and though the lord and lady had gone away meaning to leave all till their return, I knew in my heart that our time had come.

Meg trembled too; but whatever Philip thought in her heart she went about singing; yet it needed no quick ear to know her voice was flat without true tone.

As we sat there we heard the voices of mothers calling their children within. And now it was quieter than natural at such a time when the goodwife is busy within doors and the goodman without; and the children gathering green branches feel the festival in their blood.

It was well I had brought a stock of wood within, for this day I would not open the door to bring in wood, nor water, no, nor even to relieve myself. In the quiet house there was no sound from without or within, except Philip's dreary singing that seemed the music of our fears. And my house seemed no longer strong enough to protect us; but a small thing—like a beehive, perhaps—that a man could lift and carry away. Then the bees will be shaken from it; and, if it be the wrong season, they must die. It seemed to me then that there was no safety within our house from the hands of men. And I was right . . . I was right.

Time dragged. Hour after hour. Endless. Nothing to do but sit and wait; listen and wait. And though I have never taken kindly to household tasks, liking better to gad about or sit within and dream, this day, dreaming was a terror and I would have welcomed any task.

And then, in the quiet, I heard a low murmur, like the humming of wasps, angry wasps . . . but there are no wasps in midwinter. I looked across at Meg. Lost in her own dark and fearful world, the outside world passed her by. Philip sat, looking neither to right nor left, her whole being set to listen. I wondered whether in that moment she, too, was afraid.

I did not know. We were lost, each one, in her own lonely world; and I thought, We worship together, sin together, feast together . . . but each must bear the judgment alone.

And now it was no longer a murmuring but a loud crying out—curses and threats and foul names. And out of the mess of ugly sound, one word rising clear.

Witch.

It fell upon my heart like a stone. And now, stones, too, began to fall. They ripped across my window; but horn is tougher than glass and the stones fell harmless. We heard feet tramp about the house . . . the little house that a man might lift with his hand. And all the time we heard the screaming of one word; that word I had once thought so proud a name; but now I knew it to be accursed.

Meg lifted her head. At the sight of her face I did then what I had thought never to do again—for she was a full woman. But she was frightened; and she was my child. I held out my arms and she came to me and put her head on my breast; and she slipped upon her knees and knelt, clipping me about the middle, her face hidden by the pale fall of her hair. Philip stood a little apart; her head was up but there was neither smile nor fear in her face.

Which of my girls to pity more, priest, I did not know— Margaret scared as an animal is scared, knife at throat; or Philip stiff with her pride, denying all fear.

Suddenly I heard battering at the back of the house; now they were attacking front and back alike. Billhooks and scythes were thrust through my windows; and stones followed them. I heard my door strain and groan against the weight of their bodies; I heard the crash as it gave way; and the room, the little room that was home and that I was never to see again— and I think I knew it even then—was full of faces; and each face hated us and wished us ill."

"How many times had you wished others ill?" he asked, grave.

"But we were three—three only against three hundred."

"You had set yourself against those with whom you dwelt. You should have known that one day they would set themselves against you; you should have known you must face their anger."

"Yes, we faced it!" She nodded and sighed. "There they were, hate and violence blazing out of their eyes . . . the eyes of your good folk, priest.

They took us and they dragged us to the pond; and all the time they screamed out, *Swim, Swim them!* And we planted our feet and we would not budge; but all the same they dragged us inch by inch. Meg they had caught by the hair, the long fine hair; it was Peate's wife that had it wound about her wrist. And Philip's arm they twisted against her back; and they had torn her bodice so that her breast was bare; and me they pricked on with a goad. So they got us at last to the pond and the noise of their screaming filled the air.

It was Philip that saved us for that time, priest. She saved us with the sound of your name. They had already thrown Meg upon the ground and they were tying the ropes about her crosswise, thumb to great toe. She lay there and did not offer to struggle; she was like one already dead. And a pity it was she did not die."

"Even though God saved her in the end?"

"*Because* God saved her in the end. What does a witch want with God?"

"You will be very glad of Him long before the end," he told her.

She hunched an impatient shoulder.

"They put their hands upon Philip and upon me. The strength was out of me and I could not stand . . . I was no longer young, priest. But Philip. There was a different story! For she made no movement to resist but stood out-staring them; and they fell back and no man dared touch her.

'The first one that lays a finger upon me shall die!' she cried out and a woman laughed; and it was Peate's wife. She came forward and lifted a hand to strike Philip in the face. And—we all saw it—it stayed there stiff in the air and she could not move it; she could not move it forward to strike; nor yet

191

could she return it. Nor did she have the use of that arm, and has not, even today; and that is a thing you know well. So she stood there and she was afraid; she was very much afraid. And Philip turned a dark look full upon her and she fell to the ground and her face was twisted.

Then the others fell back a pace further. And Philip cried out, 'Lead us to the priest and let him judge. He is a good man and he hates witches as much as you do. If you carry us to him we will not struggle against you nor work you any harm.'

Mother Simpson cried out, 'God is the greater judge. Swim them!'

Philip said nothing. She pointed to the ground where Peate's wife lay stiff with her blind and twisted face. They were afraid then, each man for himself; and they agreed to do as Philip said. So we struggled no longer—for what could we do among so many? And Philip whispered in my ear, 'Have no fear. The Master will save us all.' But she was wrong; wrong. It was her own quick wit that saved us for that one time; and the Master lifted no finger then . . . or afterwards."

"And even then you did not stop to consider what sort of Master you served?" Samuel Fleming asked.

"Priest, you question like a child! I was in no state to consider anything. For the moment we were saved and I thanked my God with all my heart.

And what happened next you know well enough. For they brought us to you where you sat quiet within your room . . . this room," she said as though in wonder. "And I thought, To be so *safe*! A man can seek no greater happiness."

"Yet I was not happy," he told her, gentle. "I had returned from bidding those I loved, Farewell; and so sick they looked I thought it might be farewell indeed. And I returned to face the tales I had heard against you. The time was come for judgment. Judging is a lonely thing."

"Being judged is lonelier. And how nearly we were not judged at all!" She put up a hand as though, even now, she felt blood upon her face. "I tell you, priest . . ."

A tap fell on the door. Hester in bedgown and nightcap came into the room.

"I saw your light," she said. "You are early awake, Samuel; you would be the better for an hour or two in your bed. Well, now we are both wide awake I will go fetch you a hot drink. Yes, and you should have a fire, too." Hand upon the door she stopped. "I could have sworn I heard voices. It is a habit that grows upon me. I had best beware."

"Poor Mistress Davenport," Joan Flower mocked.

"It is a shame to bewilder her so," Samuel Fleming said.

"It will not be for long," she promised, indifferent. "Let us be silent until she has brought you her hot drink and then we will consider more of the matter."

Chapter Seventeen

HESTER knelt by the grate; she raked the ashes and riddled them; picked out some small dry twigs and felt in her pocket for her tinderbox.

"I am ashamed to give you so much trouble," her brother said.

"Trouble?" she was brisk. "I should have more trouble if you were laid up with a chill." The dry wood was catching nicely and she picked up the bellows. "Besides, it will be a full hour before even Jennet is astir and she is always the first to rise."

She picked up small pieces of sea-coal and laid them delicately, adjusting them a little so that they lay correctly and picked up the bellows again. The growing flames sent her nightcapped head bobbing upon wall and ceiling.

She watched him as, both hands about the silver tankard, he sipped at the mulled wine. Already there was more colour in his cheeks and his head nodded.

"Try to sleep a little," Hester said, "if only in your chair!" She put a shawl about his knees and went out shutting the door behind her.

Joan Flower said, amused yet sharp, "Sleep or wake—it is all one! When I speak you must listen; and I care not which way it is."

"I prefer to listen awake," he said. "But let us have a little light!" He held a spill to the fire and lit the candles upon his table. But the light flickered and danced before his eyes and he was forced to shut them; so after all he could not have said, afterwards, whether she had spoken to him out of a dream and out of a dream he had answered.

"It was a good thing," Joan Flower said, "that you were at home the day they took us."

"I was just back from the Castle," he told her. "I had tied up the nag and come into my study—this very room, as you say." He covered his face with his hand, remembering the women driven before the mob. How wild and fierce they had looked, all three; and how afraid, even the thin, brown girl, for all she carried her head high. In that first moment his heart was broken for them.

And then, suddenly he had thought, They are guilty. They carry their guilt in their faces. He had tried to put the thought from him—they were yet to be judged.

He searched their faces as they stood before him.

The girl Margaret had the look of a sullen child, a lost abandoned child—a child that knows its own guilt. The younger girl had a wicked look; wicked and vicious—he could believe anything of her. As for the mother—he knew guilt when he saw it. There she stood, the blood dripping from the cut above her eye, clotting the tangle of her grey and ragged hair; and more blood upon her trembling, sunken mouth. He had a sudden unwelcome memory of a dark and merry eye, a gay riband threaded through dark curls . . . and a priest turning to smile as she went by; a priest that was also a man.

But though guilt proclaimed itself louder than words, it must yet be proved and the words spoken. Meanwhile they had been cruelly mishandled. They could hardly stand upon their feet, even the girl Philip for all her pride.

He had motioned them to sit and then the mob had broken into an uproar. He had stilled them with uplifted hand, waiting for the women to sit.

"Oh you were courteous to us, priest," Joan Flower said. "But you were not kind. When you looked at us I knew that though you would not allow yourself to judge us till the hour came, still you had already judged us.

But Meg, the simpleton, did not know it. She was even smiling a little. Seeing your gentleness and your courtesy, she took heart, thinking, poor fool, that all would turn to mercy and forgiveness."

"As it did . . . for her," he reminded her.

"But not in the way she fancied in her poor, dim mind. She did not know then that the way to mercy—if so you can call it—lay through prison and torment and the grave. But I was not deceived; and Philip was not deceived. We knew that justice tempered with gentleness is more to be feared than the desire for justice alone. For your merciful man is not to be deceived. Always he will remember that mercy belongs first to those that have been sinned against.

Before ever you asked a question or we had answered it, I knew we were doomed; judged and condemned.

I sat down upon your chair—this chair where I sit now. Poor folk use stools and no back to them; in fear of death I sat upon your chair and my body took comfort from it.

But those that dragged us here were not pleased to see us sitting, as it might be, at our ease. They crowded about your table; and those that could not get within stood in the doorway. The room was full of them; and their eyes were cruel; and they could not leave staring at us, as though, if they took their eyes away, we should vanish into thin air.

Then, priest, you told them to go. But at that, the noise of their anger broke out again—the air was full of ugly sound; but all I could make out was one word, one word only. And it was enough . . .

You held out your hand for silence; and when they would not at once be quietened you cried out quick and loud—for you are not at all a patient man, nor will be until the day you die—'You have brought these women to me for judgment, why then do you take it upon yourself to judge?'

Tom Simpson stood rubbing his back as though he felt the saddle gall; he looked at Philip and could not take his frightened eyes away. Even then she had but to crook her little finger; she could still play stoat to his rabbit.

'Witch!' Mother Simpson cried out sharp and sudden.

'They are yet to be judged,' you said, priest. But you forgot that already you had judged us.

'We shall judge them!' she screamed out, 'we whose farms they have ruined, whose children they have bewitched. They shall be judged in the good old way!'

Swim, swim! At the sound I felt myself shake and your chair with me.

Swim, swim! A glass upon your table sang and broke."

"It was a glass of Venice," Samuel Fleming said. "Beautiful and costly. Francis brought it for me and I treasured it for his sake. We tried to put it together again, Hester and I; but—" he spread his hands.

"Now I am sorry for your glass," she said sweetly. "But then I was glad. I took it for a sign from the Master. I did not know then that we should be broken as your glass was broken.

At the noise of the breaking I looked at Philip, but her eyes were fixed upon Tom's face; they pierced him as though they were splinters of glass. He put out a hand and trembled and leaned against his mother and so stood drooping as though he were a figure of wax set by the fire. He could not look away.

As for Meg, she gave no sign at all. She lay stiff against her chair and her eyes were half-open and no sight to them, like the eyes of the dead.

And now since no black man appeared, horns and hoof, to carry us away, and no smell of brimstone neither, they took courage again. *Swim, swim!* My flesh crept at the sound. Already I felt the water bearing me upward, my body straining and pressing downward, forcing myself to sink; and still I floated, spinning round light as a feather. And I could see the hands stretched towards me, waiting to tear my flesh. For, priest, when the hunt is up your good people are wild beasts."

He nodded, sighing; and she smiled at this so small agreement between them.

"*Swim, swim!* The sound beat upon us like stones.

'They shall be judged by the law of the land and in no other way,' you said.

'To swim a witch is lawful; and more—it is the judgment of God. Let God judge!' Mother Simpson cried out and made a step towards Philip. And the crowd moved with her.

You said nothing, priest. But you stood up and came from behind the table—this table . . ." Her shadowy hand went out and moved gently along the table's edge. "You stood before us; between us and the mob . . . a man not young nor strong; but your will was strong enough to hold them back.

'You have brought these women to me,' you said. 'And

they shall be judged. But not by me alone. I will summon the justices.'

Patchett stepped forward. 'Sir,' he said, 'give us the witches. We are not willing to leave them here.'

'Do you fear the Devil will carry them off—and me with them?' you asked. And then I heard you laugh." And even now her voice held wonder. "A strange sound in all that beastliness and fear."

"Yes, I laughed," Samuel Fleming said. "But I did not feel like laughing. They were—as you say—wild beasts. But worse, worse. Creatures made in the likeness of God, desecrating that likeness with evil passions. Had I not laughed, I must have wept."

"The sound of your laughing cooled them suddenly—like a dish of cold water full in the face. Then Patchett whose child they said I had bewitched . . ."

"And did you bewitch him, Joan Flower?"

"I have answered that charge already; yet I will answer it yet again. I did not bewitch the child. Patchett said, 'Sir, we are not willing; yet we leave them in your hands.'

'Good hands, I hope, friends,' you said. And, 'They had better be!' a woman cried out but who it was I could not see. And so they went; but had you not held them with your will they would have turned, even then, and taken us."

Joan Flower shivered though her body had nothing more to fear.

"And when they were gone," she said, "you turned to us and you were courteous; but it was a cold courtesy. We were already judged; and rightly judged. And, because of that, I wanted the comfort of a friendly word, a friendly smile . . . a little human warmth. 'Sir,' I said; but you held up your hand forbidding me as you had forbidden them.

'You must say nothing until you speak to the justices—all of us together. And, indeed, it is wise to say nothing now but to consider among yourselves the danger in which stand.'

It was good advice, priest. Yet had you looked on us with a little kindness, it would have helped us more; but you did not mean to help us. You looked at us as though it sickened you to breathe the air we breathed."

"I remember," he said. "And I am ashamed. It was as though a dog besought my pity. But you were a human soul that had destroyed others."

"We had not yet been judged," she reminded him again.

"The guilt of all three was clear to be seen. Those very things that had pleaded your innocence, now cried out your guilt. There was that air about you. Fear—yes; but no surprise nor any anger. You, Joan Flower, knew your sins and accepted them. And Margaret knew hers; she fainted beneath the burden of her conscience. And, most of all, Philippa. She not only accepted her sins, she gloried in them; she filled the air with wickedness. How could I look upon you with kindness? I said, 'I shall lock this door and no-one shall come at you to do you hurt. When the justices come you shall be told.'"

"You went out," Joan Flower said, "and we heard the key turn in the lock. Philip laughed out at the sound."

"I heard her," he said. "I thought she might be a little mad."

" 'Now we are trapped indeed,' Philip said and she laughed again. Margaret did not even raise her head at the sound; her eyes stared upon the floor.

'You have not much faith,' Philip told her and could not, it seemed, stop laughing. 'Well, what happens to you is your own concern. As for me—the Master will stand by my side.'

'I should not be too sure of that!' I said, very slow. 'He did not accept your godling.'

'He did not deny it!' she said very quick and her eyes were green as poison.

'He did not accept it,' I said again. 'The child was left to die and its body given for our common purposes.'

'It is not true,' she said . . . but she left her laughing.

'It is true. I would not tell you before, but now we are in mortal danger and it behoves us to face facts.' And then I said, 'I think there is no help except in ourselves. There is but one thing to do. Deny. Deny. Deny; or it is the rope and the noose for us, all three.' And I looked full at Philip.

'I deny nothing,' she said. 'It is the truth we must tell,

199

even if your tale of my godling be true—which I much doubt, seeing your eagerness to lie and lie again!'

'But if it should be true?' I asked. 'If I can prove it true?'

'I should not listen. The Master knows best. He does but try us now; and we must walk carefully lest we anger Him. Happen what will, we must never deny Him!'

She stood there stiff and hard with the strength of her will, and the weight of my years fell heavy upon me though they were not so many as years go. Meg took in her breath; a queer sound, as though she wept without tears. 'I am afraid,' she said. 'I am afraid. The Master will betray us. I cannot believe on Him any more. Our mother is right. We must deny everything. There is no help except in ourselves. Why should anyone help us, least of all God? We have sinned against Him and against men; and I have sinned most of all—for I killed my child.' And her body shook with harsh, tearless sobs.

I tried to hush her then, for who knew but someone listened? But Philip said, 'Let her speak!' She turned to Meg. 'If you do not believe in the Master any more, why then He will certainly abandon you. And God will not help you; nor, as you say, could you expect it, since you have renounced your part in him. Between the Devil and God you will fall between stools . . . and the stools are heaven and hell. But courage, sister, trust in the Master to whose glory you have sacrificed your child; and He will save you.'

Margaret said nothing; she went on staring out of her empty eyes.

'He will never let them hang us,' Philip said. 'I know it. I am his love and shall be his Coven Maiden also. I shall never hang; no, nor anyone that is strong in his faith.'

'Daughter,' I told her, 'I think we have made our first step towards death. And, when we are near our death, many things become plain. In the Master's promise of eternal happiness I no longer believe; nor that we shall ever dance again upon our sacred ground. But that we shall dance upon air—if we do not deny Him—of that I am very sure.'

I heard Meg's breath go grating through her chest; she dragged herself along the floor and knelt at Philip's feet. 'Deny, deny!' and the words were a whisper in her throat.

'Sister, have mercy!' and she caught at Philip's skirt. Philip pulled herself away, and, even before she spoke, I knew it was all useless. 'I am neither judge nor god to show mercy. I am my Master's faithful servant; and—let the time be far or near—shall be till I die.'

'*Until I die . . . I die . . . I die,*' Margaret repeated and there was no sound to her voice. 'I am afraid to die . . . and all my sins upon me.'

Philip turned her back upon us both and went over to the window and stood looking out upon the garden—this window, priest, this garden. Meg lay crouched upon the floor and whispered her fears to it. Once I went over and touched her upon the shoulder; she jumped at that and began to tremble afresh and could not stop herself. I would have helped her to her feet that she might rest again in the comfort of her chair, but she was cold as the dead and as heavy and I was forced to leave her.

Hour after hour dragged itself away. How long? I do not know. There was a ringing in my head and my thoughts were not clear. Once I thought I heard the church bell. Time to pray! And even while I thought to guess the time from that, it changed its tune and tolled instead. And so I listened to think who might be dead—young or old; but it stopped and there was no sound, no sound at all, except the wild ringing in my own head and the sound of tick, tick, ticking, like the lantern clock at Belvoir. But there was no clock, priest; it was the sound of my own sick heart ticking my life away.

Nothing moved in the room, except once when Philip dropped to her knees by the window; and still she stared out upon your garden. Once I went across and stood by her; there was nothing but a robin bobbing about in the snow. And I had thought to see her familiar or mine come with help, or at the least, some message of hope. But nothing; nothing."

Joan Flower drifted over to the window. "It all looked so pretty, much as it does now—bare branches and that great dark tree; yes, and a robin bobbing about in the snow. And yet it was different; hollow and empty; shut away from time, shut away from life . . . because of our fear.

I came back from the window," she moved again and

stood in the old place facing him at the desk, "but my feet dragged like lead; there was a weariness upon me like the weariness of death. I sat upon your chair—yes, priest, the chair where you sit now. There were papers on your table; your sermon, maybe—a Christmas sermon of peace and good-will. But I could not read it; and if I had been able, it would have brought me no comfort. For, in spite of all your fine talk, there was neither goodwill nor forgiveness for us; nor any peace save in the grave . . . and not even there for me.

I put my head down on your papers and so remained. I would have wept then had I been let; but I had no tears. And it seemed to me—eyes all dry and straining to weep—that all the tears I should have shed over the years, gathered themselves together in a cloud; and the cloud pressed upon my head and upon my heart; and I thought I must die of the pain.

But the pain was not without its use. Pain dulls the mind, priest, so that you are no longer so very afraid; and, it wearies you, so that you sleep awhile . . . but the dreams are not pleasant.

I think I must have slept among the papers of your desk, for I started, presently, at the turning of a key.

It was your gardener stood there, the same gardener that, even now, sweeps the snow from the path." She waved a translucent hand towards the window.

"He carried three bowls of soup, one above the other; but there was no bread.

'Does your master fear we shall choke ourselves with bread and cheat the gallows?' Philip asked, bitter, though still she smiled with her mouth. But he made no answer; no doubt he had been so commanded."

Samuel Fleming nodded.

"I drank my soup; it was good soup—the soup Mistress Davenport sends to those who are sick and likely to die. I remembered it; and it took my pleasure from the soup. Philip drank hers greedily; but though Meg lifted the bowl to her lips she could not swallow; she was forced to set it down and the soup slid and slopped with the trembling of her hands.

I felt stronger for my soup; but the fear that had lifted a little, and the pain, came back stronger, too. I went over and stood again by Philip at the window. The snow lay white and untouched. It was pure as heaven . . . cold as heaven. And, as I stood there, your door locked upon us, it came upon me that soon we should be shut within the dark and narrow cell; and I wondered how it would feel when they put the rope about my neck. My hand went up to my throat; and I remembered that a man about to be hanged will feel now and again at his throat. I took it as an omen of death; and terror fell upon me there in your pleasant room . . . with the door locked fast as any prison cell. I forgot my weariness then; and I ran over and beat upon the door until my hands bled; but no-one answered.

Philip said, scornful and smiling, 'The Master is well-served. Of all three, I, alone, am faithful.'

'And you are still sure,' I asked her, 'that He will keep faith with us?'

'Only if you keep faith with Him,' she said.

'And if we keep faith; and if prison and the rope come first, what taste shall we have for pleasure afterwards?'

'Let not that concern you,' she said. 'You will not keep faith—neither you nor my sister.' And then she said very bitter, 'When the cart draws away and the rope drops and you with it; when the breath strangles in your broken neck and the eyes start from your head—then remember as your dying eyes turn upon Meg, that it was you with your fine speeches that brought her to the same death. As for me I shall not be there to remind you. I shall be sitting at the right hand of the Master.'

For a while we said nothing. I sat, sick with my fear, beaten down with my fear; and when I looked at Meg stretched upon the floor and the long shudders taking her from head to feet, I felt already some of the anguish of which Philip had spoken—when I should hang upon the rope remembering I had brought my daughter to this same pass. For what Philip had said about Meg and about me was true and I knew it; though I marvelled that she could bring her tongue to utter it.

Philip stood smiling upon us both; at me huddled in the

chair, at Meg stretched along the floor. 'It is a pity,' she said all soft and smiling, 'that you forswore the god whose son you adore for hanging upon the cross like any felon; though to my mind that is little worse than hanging upon a rope. Can you believe that one who lifted no finger to save his own son —and that son innocent—would stoop to save you who are not at all innocent? Can you be such a fool as to trust in him . . .'

'. . . in whom the greater part of mankind trusts,' I reminded her.

'Whom the silly sheep follow—for he calls them sheep,' she said, scornful. 'The god of silly sheep will not save you, for you have taken yourself out of his hand. And if you deny the Master, He will not save you neither—for you will have taken yourself out of his hand, also.'

Her smiling eyes passed from me to where Meg lay asleep, her hand upon your cassock that hung upon a peg . . . where now it hangs. It was as though, in her sleep, she leant upon you for help. But you did not help her, priest. I sent my thanks that she should have this so small respite; but to whom I prayed I did not know."

"Perhaps . . . to God?"

She shook her head. "Witches cannot pray to God; they have forgotten the way."

Down the stone passage they heard the sound of feet; the door opened and Hester thrust in her head. She had put off her nightcap; and beneath fresh frills her still-dark hair fell in curls. "Have you slept a little?" she asked. "I see you have. But—Samuel! My candles!" And the rest of her followed. She wore her secondbest silk and was trim as becomes a gentlewoman in the morning, from the ribands on her cap to the silver buckles on her shoes. "My best candles!" she said.

She stood on tip-toe and reached the lamp from its hook and lit it. She bent over and puffed out the candles, pinching the wick between finger and thumb lest they fill the room with their stink . . . and she did not see Joan Flower standing and watching in her dark corner.

Chapter Eighteen

HESTER stayed while the flame lengthened and burned steady. And Samuel watched her, smiling.

"You are too careful," he said. "I should think you a little miser if I did not know you better. There is no need to pinch and pare. We have enough to last us; yes, and a little to leave behind also."

"The more we put by, the more there will be to leave. I think sometimes I should like to build a little school here, by the church. And I should like to teach in it, had I the time . . . and the gift; but since I have neither, why then I will save what I may so that others may build my little school. Or, if not a school, then a little house; or two houses maybe, or three, where old people—men or women, I care not which, since we are all God's creatures—may sit in the doorway and sun themselves in the warm summer; and comfort old bones by their own hearth when winter comes."

"Certainly we are all God's creatures," he said. "And though life is hard for those who are both poor and old, yet in general it presses harder upon women. And, besides, we have our charities for old men. So let your hospital be for the old women." And he could not but wonder at the love between them so that, of her own accord, she had come so near his own thought on the matter.

"Well, I must think of it," she said teasing. "I may alter my mind. Perhaps, after all, I should prefer . . ."

"A fine tomb?" he teased her in turn. "Like the one Francis has planned?"

"It is right Francis should have a very grand tomb," she said gravely, pretending she had not noticed his teasing, "Francis is a very grand person. Besides, he is very rich; and certainly he will not be backward in his charities. But us it behoves to be careful, that when we are gone we may give back to God as much as we may."

"You are right," he said. "We will save the fine candles

for fine company; and I will use the lamp when I sit alone. And indeed," he wrinkled his nose, "the smell is company enough."

"Thank you, Samuel," Hester said. And then she said, a little anxious, "We should be careful; but not too careful. You keep the room too cold."

"It is a very good fire," he said, nodding towards the bright blaze.

"Why so it is!" she said. "And yet the room strikes chill. I must be getting old."

"Nonsense!" he said. "You are nothing but a girl!"

She shook a reproving head; but she was pleased with his compliment all the same.

When she had gone, Joan Flower came from her corner and seated herself in the great carved chair. In the bright light she was almost transparent and he turned down the wick that he might see her better.

"You love her very much," Joan Flower said.

He nodded. "She is my young sister."

"Young? Why, she is brindled!"

"Still she is my young sister."

"It must be good to be loved so," Joan Flower said. "Not with the itching of the flesh but kindly, quietly, cherishing. No-one cared for me like that, ever."

"John Flower?" he asked.

"According to his nature. Simple . . . as a beast." She shuddered a little. "Had a man loved me ever, quietly, gently, I think I had not turned to base passions; nor away from God."

"We lead the good life," he said gently, "not because of the goodness of others but because of goodness within ourselves."

"That may be," she said, very drily, "but what others do to us may increase that goodness or lessen it."

"But not kill it. There is always something that remains; a core of goodness, however small, that nothing can destroy."

"You are right," she said, suddenly humble. "Mistress Davenport has it; there goes a good woman. Had I that goodness—the smallest core—I had not ended thus, unhouselled."

"I think there is some goodness left; or it would not be laid upon me to save your soul. So small a core—a speck; nothing more. Yet it will serve."

"You are too persistent, priest. I do not want to be saved. I hanker still after the Master. Only in the sweet delights of hell shall I forget that day—the day they took my daughters and me.

How long we stayed imprisoned in this room I do not know. I had lost count of time. On the floor, holding still to your cassock, Margaret slept; but Philip wandered restless, touching a book with her finger-tip, or a picture or a chair.

At last we heard the sound of feet—quiet feet; but it shattered the silence as though all the weapons in the armoury at the Castle had fallen to the ground together. I turned about to face the door; it was ever my way to face trouble. Margaret opened her eyes; fearful as I was for my own skin, I could yet pity the terror that leaped in her. She got to her feet and, like me, stood watching the door. But Philip went on looking at the book she held—and you would have sworn she read it; and she sang a little beneath her breath.

You came in then, priest, and two gentlemen with you, and a clerk also. One gentleman I did not know; but the other I knew well enough. It was Sir George Manners—and my heart all-but stopped its beat. I had taken him for his brother. They are much alike, except that the earl is sickly."

"Thanks to you!" Samuel Fleming said.

She nodded, smiling.

"When I saw him I thought to myself, He at least should show us some mercy; he has good cause. Now there are no children to stand between him and a great inheritance—nor ever will be. Surely he will protect us.

He raised his head and looked at me; and there was loathing in his eyes. Loathing is worse than hatred, priest. Hatred is a human thing; but loathing is sick, unnatural. Whatever advantage he might draw out of this business, there would be no advantage for us."

"And did you expect it, woman? The children—his brother's children—bewitched to a cruel death; and that brother brought low in sickness?"

"You are too simple, priest, and blinded by your own goodness. Yes, I did expect it. Others in his place have paid great sums to do what we, unasked, unpaid, did for him. Nor would it have been at all strange if some pleasure did not lie deep hidden within his heart. And perhaps it did. For all of us—good and bad alike—are compounded of good and evil."

"But the proportion is different," he said, "and therein lies the difference between the man we call good and the man we call evil."

She nodded, careless. "Sir George took his place in the middle of the table; you sat at his left and the other gentleman on the right. Meg stood there staring and unsteady on her feet; Philip laid down the book as though, any moment, she would take it up again; and still she smiled. As for myself, I stood, head low, lest they read my fear and my guilt.

Sir George opened his mouth; but he could not speak because of the loathing that was in him. We waited, all of us, while he took hold of himself and began again. It was to us he spoke; and the words he said were different from the words that simple people use; very hard to understand. And, harder still, because we were very much afraid. Even Philip, for all her smiling, was afraid."

Samuel Fleming nodded, remembering that voice devoid of human warmth repeating the legal phrases; and how he himself had wondered what these women, ignorant and afraid, made of them.

Now he put his hand within the drawer that held his will and pulled out a copy of the charge, though he knew it well. God knows he had pored over it long and long enough!

"Joan Flower, widow of this parish of Bottesford in the county of Leicester, together with Margaret Flower and Philippa Flower your daughters, spinsters of this same parish, information has been laid against you and complaint made that in the year of grace sixteen hundred and twelve, by witchcraft and enchantments, by sorceries and devilish spells, you did all together contrive the death of Henry, Lord Roos, at Belvoir Castle in the county of Leicester; he being five years old and son and heir to the Earl of

Rutland, so that after you had tormented him with divers fits and sicknesses, the said Lord Roos sickened and in the September of that same year, he died.

And it is also complained of you that he, being some six months dead, you did likewise torment Francis, Lord Roos, aged two years, son and heir to the Earl of Rutland of Belvoir Castle; so that in the March of the year of grace sixteen hundred and sixteen, he being five years old, too, sickened and died.

And you are further charged that during this time you did likewise torment with these same fits and sicknesses, their sister the Lady Catharine Manners, she being fourteen years of age.

And it has also been laid against you that even then you did not cease from your wickedness but tormented the noble lady their mother, the Countess of Rutland, together with the Earl her husband, so that they, too, fell sick of these same fits and for a long while continued.

And lastly you are charged that you cast abominable and filthy spells that this same Earl of Rutland and the lady his wife should have no more issue; and to this day they have had none.

Joan Flower, Margaret Flower and Philippa Flower, have you anything to say to all or any of these charges?

We did not answer," Joan Flower nodded, her eye on the document. "Indeed, we could not; not even Philip. For the charge was very long and many words hard to understand. And while we stood turning them about in our mind, you, priest, spoke, using the words simple folk can understand.

'You are accused all three of you of witchcraft. And that by wicked spells you brought about the death of Henry, Lord Roos and Francis his brother; and you are further accused of bewitching the Lady Catharine—although by God's Grace not to her death. Also you are accused of bewitching my lord the Earl and the lady his wife so that they fell into a sickness from which they are not yet recovered. And, lastly, you are accused of bewitching them still further, that they may have no more children.

Now tell us, each of you, whether you are guilty or innocent of these charges—all, or any one of them.'

You looked at me, priest, and you waited for me to speak. I lifted my head and would have looked you full in the face but I could not. 'We are not guilty,' I said and my eyes were on the ground.

'Speak for yourself alone,' you said quite gently; but Sir George from his place in the great chair cried out, 'You had best speak the truth at the beginning. For, if not, we have the means to make you!'

'I am not guilty,' I said.

'Margaret Flower,' he said next, 'consider well of your answer. You have heard the charges. Are you guilty or not?'

Margaret, her face white and crumpled like cheesecloth, could not speak. Sir George waited as though he would wait till Doomsday. At last, a hand to her throat, she whispered, 'I am not guilty of the charges.'

But Philip hardly waited for him to have done with Meg. She said, very bold, 'I serve the Master whom I adore. I am now and forever his servant.'

'Woman,' Sir George said, 'we ask you a plain question. Do you answer as plain. Philippa Flower, are you guilty of all—or any—of the charges?'

'I acknowledge no guilt,' she said. 'I serve my Master as a good servant should.'

'Who is your master?' he asked her then.

'My Master is the God,' she told him.

'And what is his name?'

'Do you not know the name of God?' she mocked him.

'I ask you the name of your god, which is, I fancy, a very different thing from mine. And I ask you also—Are you a witch?'

She said, very steady, 'My God is the Devil; and I am his witch.'

You groaned then, priest; but Sir George leaped in his seat, his hand upraised as though to strike; and the other gentleman touched him upon the arm. Sir George stood looking from left to right as though he knew not what he did standing there, and his arm fell and he sank down again. Then you spoke, priest, and you looked sick to death. 'It has happened before that a man has confessed to crimes he never committed, being driven by a most wicked pride. So it may be with this woman.'

'Why do we shilly-shally?' Sir George cried out. 'We have the testimony of the witnesses.'

'Witnesses have sworn false before now,' you said. 'It is our duty to examine these women—whether to send them forward to the Assize or no; and it is a matter of life and death.' Sir George made a movement of anger and the other gentleman spoke; and I remember his name now, it was Lord Willoughby from over at Eresby. 'We are met to serve the cause of justice. Joan Flower,' and he nodded at me, 'we begin with you. Here is the Bible; take it in your right hand . . .'

'Bible?' Sir George cried out very bitter, 'what is the Bible to such as these?'

'Still, it is the custom,' Lord Willoughby said.

And, as I took the book in my hand, I knew quite certainly, that though the Master should save Philip, He had forsaken Margaret as He had forsaken me. And I knew that I must save myself—if I could. So I repeated the oath in the name of your god and since nothing happened—no fire either from heaven or hell to strike me down—I was resolved to lie myself into safety if it could be done; lie and lie and lie again.

'I am innocent of every charge. I am no witch, worshipful lords, nor never was.' I saw Meg's face turn to me in sudden hope; I saw the face of Philip all twisted with her anger. I went steadily on.

'I never in my whole life bespelled any living creature, neither for good nor evil; for witchcraft, be it white or black, is an abomination to God. Nor, indeed, could I have cast any spell seeing I know not the way, nor have I the power.

'As for the little lords, how should I harm them that were such sweet little lords? No, sirs; I loved them; and I loved also the lady their mother that was a good lady to me and to my daughters. As for my lord Earl, I have not worked ill against him, nor yet thought ill against him, my life long; but as God hears me, have blessed him always for his goodness and . . .'

'Woman,' Sir George cut me off, very sharp, 'beware how you forswear yourself. We have witnesses against you; and against your familiars, and against all your works.'

'Sir,' I said bold enough but my heart shook, 'there is nothing any man can charge against us.'

'Yet they have charged you,' Sir George said and read out from the paper before him, 'Ann Baker of Bottesford, Ellen Greene of Stathorne, Joan Willimott of Goodby; and there are other witnesses also.'

I almost died in my place. It was a thing I had not dreamed of. For, if they betrayed us, we should betray them—and they knew it. And why should they put their heads into the noose? Surely it was a trick to make us betray ourselves!

And all the time his voice went on sharp and clear but I missed the beginning of the testimony being all confused in my mind.

'. . . and Joan Willimott declares that when she went into your house she saw your familiar spirit; and it was in the shape of a white cat. And when it had sucked you beneath the right ear it made as though to suck upon her but she beat it off.

'And Ellen Greene says that you told her the Earl had dealt badly with you; and though at this time you could not have your will of him, you had espied his elder son and had stricken him to the heart and that you had sent a white spirit to do it, which spirit was in the shape of a cat which you call Rutterkin; and this spirit, Ellen Greene also saw.

'And the witness Ann Baker says that meeting with you in the wood, you raked up some earth and spat upon it and worked it with your finger and put the stuff into your pocket. And you said since you could not hurt the Earl himself, you would speed his second son who is now dead.

'And these testimonies are not of enemies but of your known friends.'

'Sir,' I said, 'Ann Baker is simple, being short in the wits and this all Bottesford knows; and the Reverend Rector knows it also. As for Joan Willimott and Ellen Greene, those are good ones to believe! They are witches if ever there was one! For Joan Willimott, she has a familiar called Pretty and it is very swift and cunning. And it was she that coaxed Ellen Greene to the Devil, as many a time she has boasted. And it was Joan Willimott that bewitched the wife of Anthony Gill over at Stathorne after she had quarrelled with him; and the goodwife vomitted pins and needles and so died. And she bewitched their child also and . . .'

'It is not Joan Willimott we consider now,' Lord Willoughby said, 'it is you we are questioning; you, Joan Flower.' But I saw how the clerk that sat by wrote down my words against Joan Willimott and I was glad. For, if I must come by my death, she that had informed against me should come with me.

'You say that Joan Willimott lies,' Sir George said sudden and sharp. 'Why should she testify against you, being innocent and her friend?'

'Sir, it was because when the tales went about her—that she was a witch, I would no longer be friends.'

He frowned down upon his papers. 'She was with you in your house, it is but a week ago.'

'No, lord,' I said. And why should my word not stand against hers?

'If she was a witch and you knew it; and if you were none,' Sir George said, 'why did you not name her to the justices as is your duty, laid down in the acts of our lord the King?'

'Sir, what do I know of the law? And, besides, I did not know at that time whether the tales were false or true.'

Then, priest, you spoke; and though you were gentle, it was you I feared most. For your heart was not set on revenge but on declaring the name of your god and rooting out wickedness for his sake. 'Joan Flower, you did not know the tales to be true; and now you do know it. When did you discover the truth? And how?'

It was a question I did not expect and I could not answer it. 'Joan Willimott . . .' I began.

'Joan Flower,' you interrupted, 'must we warn you again

that it is you, not Joan Willimott, that are the business of this court.'

'Sir,' I said, 'I am a simple woman and not quick to answer. But I am innocent and so I declare to my last breath. You have known me, priest, for many years and you have baptized my daughters—which is a sign that we are Christian folk. And, though, to my shame, I come not often into church, it is a fault I share with many. For if all those who come not into church be named *witch*, why then you must hang the greater part of this country—gentle and simple alike.'

I saw Lord Willoughby's hand go up to hide a smile and I went on boldly, 'As for the tales that go about me—who knows what will kindle hatred in a wicked heart?'

'But God knows,' I said, and now I had grown bold, indeed. 'And He will make it plain. You know—all of your worships know—that bread, which is the blessed body of our Lord, will not pass into the body of a witch but will stick within the gullet; nor can it by any means be dislodged. And so it will choke her. Bring me the blessed wafer and let God judge.' "

"Were you not afraid of your blasphemy?" Samuel Fleming asked her now.

"I was afraid of nothing but the rope. And, besides, I had held the blessed wafer upon my tongue more than once. Witches prize such holy things; for when they have been desecrated we use them for our deadliest spells. And once, priest, I had come to church to steal a wafer; and feeling your eye upon me I swallowed it . . . and no harm befell me. The saying was an old nonsense and I knew it. But you did not know it; and the others did not know it.

But you, priest, cried out, 'I will not have the holy wafer upon her tongue. If she be a witch then it is desecration. I will be no party to it.'

Then I said, 'Sirs, try me with bread; for bread and holy wafer are one. Bread, also—save it has been first blessed to the Devil's service—will not pass through the bowels of a witch; and this all Christians know. Try me then and see.'

'I will have no tricks,' Sir George Manners said. 'There

214

are other ways to discover a witch. There are . . .' and he fixed me with cruel eyes, 'witchmarks. Let her be searched.'

I saw your eyes, priest, and you were not willing—you were ever delicate in your dealings. You leaned across and asked the others to consider my request. At first they would not listen; then you said, 'If God settles this thing here and now, then we are spared much misery.'

'But the children were not spared,' Sir George said.

'Shall we leave that to God?' you asked, priest. 'Now we seek out justice and not revenge.' And Lord Willoughby agreed; and you were two to one. So you went to the door that no-one should come in and you called for bread; and, since you are a merciful man, you commanded it should be well-buttered.

So there you sat; and there I and my daughters stood. And we waited—all of us—while they brought the bread. And, so standing, I asked myself what I could hope to gain from this. For though I swallowed the bread without choking, Sir George certainly, and Lord Willoughby, perhaps, would not accept it—a sign of innocence. Still it was a chance. What did you hope from it, priest?"

"A sign from God, perhaps. Or perhaps a little respite —time to consider this horrible thing. I am as good a justice as any man, I hope; and my heart as strong to search out evil to punish it. That is the duty of any man; especially if he be a Justice of the Peace and a priest of God, likewise. I knew in my heart that you were guilty; yet how gladly would I have been proved wrong. You, Joan Flower, that I had known as a young woman . . ."

"A pretty young woman," she reminded him, smiling out of sly eyes.

"You cannot forget that, though your body lies in the grave," he said.

"Nor can you, priest; or so it seems."

"As for your daughters, I had—as you reminded us—baptized them both. You had done much amiss, all three. You had lived lewdly; you had stolen; you had been a grievous vexation to your neighbours. And for those things you deserved punishment. But witchcraft. That was a thing I desired to leave with God. So when you offered to prove your innocence with bread—with bread that is so common and so sacred—I was glad. It would take, perhaps, the hateful burden from me."

"As it did, priest. And so we waited. And yet, I suppose the time was not long. Behind your table you justices sat very still. You, priest, I remember, held your head between your hands.

Philip stared at me with her wicked smile. It was as though she cried aloud, *Do you hope to save yourself by so cheap a trick? You have betrayed the Master. Now He will betray you.* But there was still hope in Meg's pale eyes. She knew how often we two had eaten our daily bread and it had gone down smooth as butter for all we had forgotten to bless it in the Devil's name . . ."

At his puzzled look she laughed aloud. "Do you not say your Grace before Meat, priest? So with us—or should be. And, especially it is so with water—which you use for baptism; and for bread—which you use for sacrament. These two things we are commanded to bless in the Devil's name lest they choke us. Yet at times I had both eaten and drunk and forgot the blessing . . . and no harm done. So to ask for bread there in your room seemed no great risk.

I stood there and I was very tired. I was not young and I was very frightened and my body craved for rest. My legs began to shake under me. But not one of you fine gentlemen thought to let me sit down."

"There is no sitting for a prisoner in any court," Samuel Fleming said. "Yet . . . I wish we had given you a chair."

"I thought it must be growing towards dusk; I couldn't see very well. I could just make out you three justices dark and unmoving behind the table; and the figures of Meg and Philip; but I was not sure which was which. That troubled me a little . . . not seeing; because outside the sky was white; the sort of low, white sky you get on a winter afternoon. The white sky hurt my eyes; it was like a sharp knife running round my head. And then, suddenly, I felt it *in* my head, *inside* my head. I bit on my lips to keep myself crying out with pain. But worse than the pain, even, was the worry because of the two lights. I knew it was daylight because of the white sky. I knew it was night because of the darkness . . . night without candles. I said to myself, I am frightened and I am hungry. Soon the bread-and-butter will come; and it will go down into my empty belly and I shall be well again. And then they will let me go home.

It was dusk in the room and it was dusk in the garden; I couldn't see the white sky any longer. It was dark everywhere. And, in the darkness, I heard a voice say—and I think it was your voice, priest, *Here is the bread.*

And I reached out my hand."

Chapter Nineteen

"I REACHED out my hand. I felt the smooth scrubbed edge of the wooden platter. I took up the bread. And all the time I wondered that you had not lit the candles and I must find my way in the darkness."

"It was full daylight," he told her gently.

"I know that . . . now. You were standing by me and I could just make out the whiteness of your face. I think you were praying. Were you praying?"

"Yes, I was praying."

"For . . . me, priest?"

"For you and for all lost souls."

"My legs were shaking so that I could scarcely stand. My head felt as though it had been cut to the bone; and I knew what the dumb beast feels when they slaughter him. I caught hold of the table to steady myself and I heard the voice of Sir George Manners come through my darkness, 'Stand up straight, woman. For now you stand face-to-face with God.'

But I dared not leave the safety of the table. With my left hand I held on still; and with the right I lifted the bread-and-butter and I put it between my lips.

And suddenly there was a roaring in my ears; and, in the blackness, wheels of fire went turning; and lightning zigzagged and darted. And I heard a voice speaking—a strange voice, thick and strangled and slow. *Master!* the voice said; and I did not know it for my own. And after the voice—a whimper; like a little dog when it is whipped; not human. And that voice, too, I did not know for my own. I put out my two hands—whether to the Master or to the little whipped dog I do not know; to the dog, perhaps, since I have always loved small creatures. I put out my hands and I fell down into the darkness. . . ."

She looked at Samuel Fleming's face in the lamplight; there were tears in the old man's eyes.

"You fell into the darkness," he said. "And your face was

twisted and your eyes were blind and your mouth dropped. Sir George leaped to his feet and stood looking down at you. 'God has spoken,' he said; but there was no triumph in him. 'The matter is out of our hands. There is a case to answer.'

And even while he spoke I looked down at your body, and I thought, A stroke . . . natural, perhaps. An old woman, tired and frightened. And then I thought, Even so, still God has answered; He does not need to speak in miracles.

'They had best go to Lincoln,' Willoughby said. 'If we grant them bail the people will tear them to pieces.'

'Or their Master the Devil carry them away, which God forbid!' George Manners said. 'They shall hang. When I think of the children—Henry and little Francis—I could string the creatures up with my own hands. Dear God, we are too merciful in this country of ours. We should do as they do elsewhere . . . burn.' And then, priest, you said a strange thing," Joan Flower said softly. " 'Does that prevent witchcraft elsewhere? And does it save souls?' 'But it hurts the body,' Sir George said. Priest, I heard it all; not with my earthly ears, for I was deaf as well as blind. But I heard with the ears of my soul that had slipped a little way from my body.

My body lay twitching and whimpering; my soul, half-released as though upon a chain, might a little wander. I stood beside you, priest, and looked down at the ugly thing that was yet myself . . . the blue face, the starting eyes, the twisted jaw; and I prayed the Master that I might never return into it.

You said, priest, 'If they are for Lincoln I will have the cart made ready. Take the two young women; but not this one. She would die on the way. I think she is dying already.'

'No cheating of the gallows,' Sir George Manners said; and there was no pity in him.

'Leave her or take her,' you told him, priest, 'still she will cheat the gallows.'

'I am with Manners in this,' Lord Willoughby said. 'This may well be a trick of the Devil to cheat us all. I have heard of such things.' Then, priest, since it was two to your one, you nodded and you all went out, together with the clerk that was with you. And the door closed and the key turned in the lock. And you left the silence behind you.

Philip on the one side and Margaret on the other stared down at me where I lay twitching and whimpering; yet my body felt nothing; nothing at all. Nor was there any fear in me for what might come; nor any joy because I had cheated the gallows. Nor was there any hope of being forgiven by the Master nor any thought of God; nor any pity for my daughters who, through me, must come to the rope. My soul, priest, was too-new free to feel anything. It hung like a sickly bud upon a frail stalk; and that stalk was joined to my body like a new-born child to its mother.

Meg's face stared with horror; she could not take her eyes from me. Philip stared, too; though she no longer smiled I knew the satisfaction in her. 'You see,' she told Meg, 'what comes of denying the Master?' And she stirred me with her foot. 'And death by the rope is yet more horrible. But that need not concern you. You will never come to it—if you are faithful. But, if you deny Him, nothing can save you. So you see you must cry out the truth in a loud voice.'

'Yes,' Meg said, 'yes . . . but they will make me speak and I shall betray Him. I am not brave like you . . . I am not brave at all.'

'You will need to be brave and brave, indeed, to deny the Master,' Philip said. 'You know well what they will do to you. You will suffer at the hands of the searchers, and at the hands of the tormentors, and at the hands of the hangman. And when all these have done with you—you will suffer at the hands of the Master. In case you have forgotten, let me remind you what will happen.

First the searchers. They will search your body for the Devil's Mark; and they will search also for the place where you suckle your spirit. They will part every hair. No crack or crevice will be free of their eyes. And when they have found the marks, they will be at you to make you speak. They will torment you in a hundred ways—starve you, walk you, keep you from sleep—until you can bear it no more and you will tell them the truth. So you see, it is best to tell it at the first.'

Margaret went on staring down at me. You would have thought she did not hear . . . save that her hands crept up to her ears. The voice of Philip went on steady, unhurrying as water forcing its way through a crack.

'Of the hangman and what he will do to you, I need not speak. You have heard for yourself how the breath strangles and the throat chokes and the lungs burst; you have seen the burst eyeballs swim in blood and the blue face and the broken neck. You have seen a hanged man before, yes and smelt him, too!

And then, your earthly torment being over at last—and it will seem eternity until you face eternity itself—you will crawl at the feet of the Master but He will not look at you. He knows better how to punish than any earthly man . . . and it is a punishment that will go on for ever. What you may suffer here will be a feast and a brief one, by the side of it.'

I lay there, my blind eyes staring and seeing nothing; but the eyes of my soul, my soul that was all-but free, saw all. The cord between my soul and my body was growing thinner, growing longer, stretching itself out; soon it must snap and I be free.

Free to what? I didn't know. Had I known I might have agonized to keep within the body, preferring human shame and human torment to the loneliness of the void between heaven and hell.

The fire had burnt low. In the hearth a log crumbled and fell. A small noise, priest, and my body did not heed it. But the cord that held the soul quivered like a bowstring and all-but snapped; for the almost naked soul was not accustomed as yet to the noises of the world.

The wood turned to ash; the winter twilight crept into the room. My soul began to shiver. But it was not with cold; I had done with human warmth, human cold for ever. And it was not with fear of the body; I had done with that, also. Nor did I pity as yet those two that stood on either side. Yet I felt fear—their fear—striking against the naked soul.

And still it went on . . . the room dark and growing darker; and the room cold and growing colder. And those two, their faces colourless as the snow outside; even Philip had lost some of her courage now. Cold and hungry and frightened and alone; prison in front of them and death ahead of them. And on the floor, for company, the dying, twisted thing that had been their mother.

You may well say, priest, that innocent or guilty, their punishment had begun.

There came up to them at last the sound of a cart being made ready—the crunch of wheels in the snow, and jingle of trappings.

Philip stood up and stretched herself and went over to the window; she turned again, and in the gloom, her pale face swung towards that other pale face. 'Sister,' she said and there was kindness in her voice, 'soon they will come for us. Listen to me—it may be the last time we shall be alone together. I shall speak the truth because I glory in the truth; and because the Master will save me both in this world and in the world hereafter. As for you, it will be useless to lie; and that is a thing you must plainly understand. For those things we did—and especially the spells we cast—we did together. And when I speak I must tell your part also; it cannot be otherwise. If you deny what I shall say they will not let you rest till they have got the truth out of you also. Their ways are many and not one of them is pleasant. You will be forced to confess. But mark me well. There is more than one way to confess. If you speak out freely, not at all penitent but glorying in what you have done, then all will be well for you—both in this world and the next. But if you confess only because truth has been wrung from you by torment, and if you admit to sorrow for what you have done, then you betray the Master with the truth as surely as with lies. And you will come to the rope. Do not think their god will save you. Be very sure he will not; for you have denied him and all his works. Denying both Devil and God, how shall you fare?'

Margaret said nothing; she stared into the darkness with her vacant eyes. Presently her shoulders began to twitch and her whole body to shake. Philip said, and now there was no more kindness in her, 'Deny as you may, you will suffer both here and hereafter; my testimony will betray you. Be warned.'

And now there were steps along the passage. The door opened and two men came in carrying a rough coffin. The horror deepened in Margaret's face; she had not truly understood, as yet, that I was dying. She made a step forward as though to thrust them away but Philip held her back; and they lifted my still-living body and thrust it into the coffin . . . and the loathing in their faces was something one should never see.

My soul all gentle in its new condition, hardened again. The body pulled strongly upon the cord and brought it near again. With this last flaming of earthly fire I desired more passionately than I had desired anything ever before, that I might this once have the use of my body, or of my mouth, only, that I might spit into their cruel faces, hurl my last curse."

"God forgive you such a dying!" Samuel Fleming said.

"We die as we live, priest." And when he would have spoken said, "Do not talk to me of death-bed repentings. There is an old saw about the Devil being sick. It is an insult to the Master; but there is truth in it all the same.

The cold air of the stableyard blew upon my dying body but I did not feel it. They lifted me into the cart and Meg and Philip were thrust in after me. Philip tried not to shiver in the cold night air; but she and Meg shook as with an ague. Above us the evening star stared down like the eye of God . . . a cold and heartless eye.

And so we were all set for our journey, the journey from which not one of us would return. The driver climbed into his seat, and, as he took up the reins, a voice called out, *Halt!*

It was you, priest. You climbed up into the cart. You said nothing; but you knelt down and you prayed for me; and though my soul knew it was all useless, yet it thanked you."

"You are very sure it was useless?" he asked her gently.

"I thought so, priest."

"And now?"

"Now I am not so sure. You catch the new-born body with your prayers, you might well work that same trick with the new-born soul. But, if because you prayed, I wander unhouselled, I do not thank you, now, priest."

"You will in the end," he said.

"The cart jingled out of the stable and into the street. There were lights in every house though at this hour folk were usually abed. But now they were in the street; and some carried torches and some carried . . . other things. By the pillory yet more were waiting; not only Bottesford folk, but folk from Frisby and from Goodby and from Stathorne. All waiting to let fly their filthy rubbish, their ugly stones.

But before any man could lift an arm, you stood up in the cart and you held your arms before us like a cross; and you called out, 'These women are not yet judged; neither are you their judges.' And their arms dropped; and though still they cried out their filthy words, their hands they kept at their sides.

I lay there at the bottom of the cart. Why did you permit them to thrust me, still living, in my coffin, priest?"

"It was all the coffin you were likely to have. I was not minded to have them thrust you naked in the earth. But I did not know what they had done until I saw for myself, there in the cart . . . and then it was too late."

"You take some of my bitterness away," she said.

"I lay there in my coffin and I felt the pull upon the cord grow heavier and with each pull I felt it must snap. I prepared myself for the last agony. My body that had lain still began to twitch and to shake; it shook as though it were made of one piece. The rattle began in my throat. Terror fell upon me at this last abandonment of the body.

Then, priest, you knelt in the cart and the quiet night was broken by the sound of your praying and by Meg's sobbing and by the death-rattle in my throat. And, rising above it all, the clip-clop of the horses carrying us upon our dark journey.

And then, still upon your knees, you signed to the cart to stop. There was a last agonized pull; my body arched and twisted. Strange the strength in an old dying body. The rattle stopped; the body jerked forward and lay still. The soul was free.

You put out a hand and closed the eyes."

He was silent, remembering that he had not gone without censure because he had prayed at the passing of a witch. Francis, even, had been displeased. Had she made her peace with God, Francis would have tried to forgive her. But she had died unconfessed and no good man should pity her.

"Because of those prayers, maybe, I am lost between two worlds," she said, sighing.

"Because of those prayers you will yet find your way to God."

She gave her mocking shrug. "Who knows?" she said; and after that nothing, but moved back into the shadow, and so stood swaying like a translucent flower.

Presently she said, very low, "They speak much of your cleverness but of your wisdom they do not speak enough; no, nor yet of your goodness. But I think God will say it all one day."

He looked up surprised. *God*, she had said; not *your god*; but *God*, simply; and she had said it without mockery. And even while he looked she was gone, leaving within his soul a light brighter than that of his lamp. It shone through the thinness of the flesh, so that Hester coming in, the cat at her heels, to see whether he had put out the lamp—since the night had passed and the sun shone—bit back the cry that he was not long for this world.

Chapter Twenty

IN THE springtime garden Samuel Fleming walked slowly leaning upon his stick. He had been ailing since Harvest, speaking little and eating less. For, turn where he would, do what he would, it went forever with him—the memory of the witches and their death; and especially the memory of Joan Flower and her strange dying.

Disquieted and weary, self-questioning and old, he had thought, through the long winter, never to see the spring again. Now, as he walked, drawing the arrowy scents into his nostrils, a pale primrose nodded at him. It was an invitation he could not resist. He bent, rose again a little clumsy, and slipped it within the lapel of his coat and so stood, dizzy from stooping.

"Priest, have a care!" It was the light and mocking voice he had not heard for some time. "Or you will go out as I did. God's servant and the Devil's, departing this life the same way. That would be odd, indeed!"

"Not so odd," he said. "There are not many ways for old folk to die; and a stroke is one of them."

"It is not so bad a death—it looks worse than it is. There is no pain; and, it is strange, priest, no fear."

"God was merciful to you. When my time comes may He be as merciful."

She shrugged. "It happened . . . as it happened. No-one was ever merciful to me. Not your god. And certainly not mine."

"And did you expect mercy from the Devil?" he asked. "God shows mercy always; human creatures, sometimes; the Devil, never."

"If one might believe that . . . about your god, I mean!" She took a step towards him so that he saw the primroses clear through the transparency of her feet.

"It is true," he told her. "And I think you know it is true."

"How should I know? I was a witch and I escaped the

rope—that much is true; but the greater anguish I did not escape. I saw my daughters fastbound in the filth of your prison and the pains that were put upon them. I besought the Master that He would put out a hand to save them; yet my naked soul knew that Margaret, at least, must come to the gallows. From my place between heaven and hell I cried out to the Master to let me, of his mercy, take upon me some of their suffering."

"I think, perhaps, God was beginning to work in you."

"How, priest?" She was all amazed.

"You desired to take the suffering of others upon yourself."

"They were not . . . others. They were the children I had borne; that I had set upon the path that led to their end."

"Every path leads to its end," he said; "but we forget that, often enough, when first we set foot upon it."

"That sounds a simple thing when it is said; but it is the hard truth." She sighed. "Though I was free to come and go; to seek my way to heaven or to hell as I might, still I could not depart from that place. I dwelt within the cell with those two; I went with them before the judge. I could no more leave the place than they. It was as though the chains hung upon my feet also."

"Compassion is no light weight," Samuel Fleming said. "And however it is felt—for whom and by whom—it is of the nature of God. Woman, I shall win you yet."

"There will not be time . . ." She looked into his thin face with something of the compassion of which he spoke, "unless you go within doors and sit by the warm fire and drink wine."

"Go within doors!" he said. "And this . . ." he held out his hands as though to clasp all spring to his sober jacket.

"There is no heat to the sun as yet," she said, gentle still, "and the wind cuts like a knife . . . and you have been ill. Certainly you must go within." She bent and plucked some violets he had smelt but not seen, for his eyes were growing dim; she bound them about with a blade of grass and put them into his hand. "Come!" she said and went before him. And, as they went, he saw that the white cat had sprung from nowhere and went with her.

Hester, inspecting the young shoots of the new sparrowgrass bed, came from the kitchen garden, softly calling. "Puss," she cried, "puss!" He saw how the little cat stood undecided between the woman and the ghost of the woman. The ghost bent downward. "Go," she whispered. "And no wickedness. Be a good little cat, I command you."

Hester cast a puzzled look about the lawn empty except for her brother and herself. "I thought," she said, "I thought . . . Never mind what I thought!" She laughed. "Come, Master Puss." She picked him up though he struggled and scratched and drew blood. "Naughty little thing," Hester said. The cat put out a little red tongue towards the scratch—and fell to the ground as though someone had struck it from the living woman's arms.

"Those games are over!" the ghost of Joan Flower said and again Hester lifted a puzzled face.

"Let the creature go!" Samuel told his sister. "It is a little wild thing and may do you a mischief."

"It is wild," Hester said, "but still it is a good little cat. I could not drive it away since I have coaxed it to stay. Come, puss." She spoke as to a child. "Be good and you shall have your warm, sweet milk."

He said, smiling, seeing her coax the creature, "Have a care, or they may take you for a witch!" And when he saw offence in her gentle eyes, said quickly, "Forgive an old man his foolish joke."

She smiled back at him; but for all that she was not best pleased. She left the cat there upon the ground and walked into the house.

They stared at each other, he and the cat; then he said, and he was not smiling now, "Perhaps it was no more than this with a many a one they call *witch*. A lonely old woman and a little cat she loved; or a little dog, or a bird maybe . . . some small, soft creature . . ."

He looked at the cat as though asking an answer; but the creature lifted a disdainful head and arched itself. Quite deliberately it turned its back and minced into the house.

He smiled ruefully, his eyes following the cat.

And they took the old woman, the thought nagged and nattered and would not let him be, *the harmless old woman* . . .

"*. . . and they hanged her.*" Joan Flower finished the thought for him. "So it was with some. But not with us, priest; not with us. When you dealt with me and my daughters, you judged rightly."

"Then I thank God." He saw her clear outline blur; and when he lifted a hand to his eyes it came away wet.

"It is the wind," he said, "the sharp wind."

"Yes," she said, "it is the wind. Come within doors."

Her hand lay transparent upon his black sleeve so that the neat darn Hester had made showed through. They went together into the study and stood by that table where once she had called God to be her witness, and still calling, had fallen stricken to the floor. When he had seated himself in his own chair she took the one that stood opposite and made a gesture towards the jar that held his pipes.

"Here we sit like man and wife." She smiled a little sadly. "And so it might have been had I been a lady and good . . . with a little learning perhaps. I was quick to learn; but the things I learned were the wrong things."

He looked at her then; and it was the face of a girl untouched, wilful, a rose thrust through the dark of her curls. So she must have looked before she had wed John Flower.

"My heart is all for God's service," he told her gently. "It was never large enough to hold a woman, too. But you were comely; and, priest though I was, my blood stirred as you passed."

"Passed," she said and it was as though she wept upon the word. "All, all is past."

He shook his head. "You have still a choice to make. That is not yet past."

His voice dropped at the sound of Hester's heels tapping along the stone passage; she came in carrying a tray.

"It is cold in here," she said and the tray rattled in her hands. "But it is a good fire!" she said surprised. "I cannot, it seems, warm this room."

"What have you here?" he asked, sniffing with pleasure.

"Guess! But here's a clue. It comes all the way from the great Amazon River; a package from Francis. Cecilia sent it down this morning."

He sniffed again, puzzled. "It is chocolate . . . and yet, not chocolate."

She laughed. "Yes, it *is* chocolate. But Francis wrote to serve it a new way; hot and very sweet," and she set down a dish of sugar chips.

He watched her pour the rich, frothy liquid from the silver jug. "How goodly are His gifts!" he said. "This same chocolate that makes a cold and savoury soup for hot days, now makes a hot, sweet drink for cold days." He picked up some sugar chips and dropped them into the aromatic brew. "How fortunate I am to taste so rare a drink! When Columbus took the first chocolate home to Spain, they threw it away. Useless, they thought. Useless—this! How good of Francis to tell me about the sugar." He sipped. "How good everyone is to an old man," he said softly. "You, my dear. And Cecilia; and Francis. And, most of all . . . God."

It is not hard to be good to you, Hester thought and smiled down into his face; she brought over a rug and tucked him about as though he were a baby, telling herself that John Atkins must come down from Belvoir again. Surely he could prescribe some strengthening physic. Yes, she would send up a message at once.

She shut the door gently behind her and he sat back, a tired old man wrapped in a shawl and stirring the rich chocolate in a fine Delft bowl.

"We long for heaven," he said, "but there are times when this world is very good." And he sipped contented, his fingers caressing the gay tulip border of his dish.

"Have a care, priest," Joan Flower warned him, her eye on the picture beneath the flowered edge. "See how Eve lusts for the apple! And if you turn your dish about, there she is—and her spouse with her—driven from the garden. Through the senses the Master will catch you yet!"

"God likes us to enjoy his good things . . . if we do not enjoy them too much. I am a weak and sinful old man; but my Master is not like your master. God does not betray the heart that loves Him."

"Do you know," she said with one of her sudden changes, "I never in my life tasted that!" And her eyes were on the sparkling whiteness of the sugar-cone chips. "Honey is for common folk—and not too much of it. My girls were light-fingered but they never brought me sugar, maybe they ate it themselves—and who can blame them? Here I am, lost between heaven and hell; and, had I tears, I would weep because I have never tasted sugar."

"It is a pity." He looked at her over the blue and flowered edge of his cup, "but . . . there are worse pities."

"Yes, there are worse pities," she agreed and for a while was silent. Then she said, very grave, "Did you ever see the inside of a prison, priest?"

"It did not come within my duties."

"Did it not, Sir Magistrate?"

He flinched. "I understand well enough that it is not a pretty place, and you could not expect it."

She laughed; and he did not like the sound of her laughter. "Oh priest, priest, you hunt poor witches because you fancy we have bewitched some creature here and there . . . and maybe we have. But consider this. The creature we have bewitched dies in his own familiar bed; and about him are those who love him; and a surgeon perhaps; and certainly a priest. And there is weeping and there is praying to speed him on his way. But you, the righteous ones! You thrust us still living into the grave. For what are your prisons but an open grave where the flesh rots from bodies that are not yet cold? And that is no lie, priest, as you may see for yourself.

Your prisons are sinks of corruption and of foul cruelty. How could it be otherwise? Without a heart of stone your gaolers could not endure; their cruelty is armour against your cruelty. And, if they were not beasts, they themselves could not endure the filth. Before you condemn human flesh to such filth of body and spirit, you should know, priest, what it is you do. We were vile some of us; vile enough to die . . . but not vile enough to deserve your prisons; and some of us were not vile at all. Consider Ann Baker, her only sin a lack of wits. Your god cherishes fools—so we are told; but that was a fool he did not cherish.

But I run ahead of my tale. And in a measure, I am un-grateful, too. For it was through you that my daughters reached the gaol unhurt. Many a witch has had the skull laid bare, or an eye lost through a sharp stone, yes, and many an innocent, too. That, at least, you saved them. But, having brought them to the gaol and seen them handed over—your job was done."

"I could not over-step my duty," he said mildly.

"Had you no duty to those you had baptized?"

"They had put themselves beyond my ministry. There were prison chaplains, were there not?"

She laughed again, the same bitter laugh. "Yes, there were chaplains! My girls that were prisoners now, passed through the great gate and the porter locked it behind them; and even as they were driven across the courtyard, the filthy prison smell tainted the sweet air of heaven. But you, no doubt, found a warm fire in the house of a friend, or at the White Hart Inn; and there you sat warming your bones and drinking good wine until it was time to go to your good bed.

But what of them, priest? Did you ask yourself that?

They were hustled along, down a dark and filthy passage. They knew it was filthy in spite of the darkness because their bare feet slithered in the muck; and because of the stink. And now and again a rat would push its sharp nose beneath their skirts.

Philip went, steady enough; but Meg, poor wretch, could hardly put one foot before the other; and when she fell, and could not rise at once, the turnkey cried out, It is darker in hell, witch, and fetched her a blow across the head. And remember this, Sir Priest-Magistrate, they had not yet been judged.

The dreadful journey came to its dreadful end. He unlocked a door with a great key and he thrust them within; and I passed in with them.

Priest, I have lived poor all my life. I know the smell of a room where every crack is sealed against the cold; and I, like many another, have lain shivering in my bed for lack of covering. But that room! It was cold as death. And for the stench, there are no words; that is the plain truth—there are no words. The smell of dirty bodies shut in without air—that is no new thing. But, consider it, priest. Human bodies unable to relieve themselves save upon the filthy ground; bodies stinking with running sores, the smell of living flesh rotting in corruption."

"And the human soul rotting in corruption?" he interrupted, his face all drawn in horror.

"There is no stench from the soul."

"Is there not? To God? And should we not cleanse it at the expense of the body?"

"You should leave God out of this," she said, surprising him. "For I doubt—even if it could be done—he would care for such a manner of cleansing. Priest, you tell us that hell is a place of terror; and I have seen you search for words that shall enough describe its pains. No need to look further than your nearest gaol; for crueller than God or Devil, is man to man.

There was one small grating high up and through it the cold wind whistled; but it could not drive away the stink. There was a rush candle burning in a dish upon a ledge; and I tell you, priest, there had better been no light at all to look upon the misery that crept and crawled and twisted upon the floor. Even you, priest, would be hard put to it to name it human."

She closed her eyes as if she would, even now, shut out the sight.

"Grey faces . . . greyish-white . . . like maggots; or else scabbed red and blue. And hair matted and moulting like the pelt of a sick animal. And eyes raw and red, too weak to stand even the light of your farthing dip. And naked for the most part; greasy rags not covering enough for decency."

Her voice dropped into silence. He had long forgotten his chocolate which stood now cold beneath its wrinkled skin. He looked at her, helpless, not knowing what to say. But still she waited, forcing him to speak, to make some defence of the justice he served, and of those who outraged the god whose servant he was. And when still he found no words, she said, smooth, "You will tell me again, no doubt, that prison is not meant to be a sweet place, seeing it is meant for punishment . . .

Punishment!" she cried in a dreadful voice. "Then be careful who it is you punish. What of those that are innocent, forced by fear and by pain to 'confession'? And all the time those prison-priests of whom you spoke, winking at the torment and pressing with their questions, until the words are said that shall bring these innocents to a cruel death. Priest, the god you worship—did he see what I saw in the place— would go again upon the cross in despair of human cruelty . . . the cruelty of your good men."

And now when he would have spoken she went steadily on.

"There they were, thrown one upon the other in the stinking cell—virgins and harlots, lewd men and children whose flesh had once been sweet and clean—rotting upon the filthy ground. And some were innocent and some were guilty but none of them—not one, priest—had been brought to trial. Is this your justice? Even the guilty—should he not know the charge against him and hear the judgment; and make his peace with whatever master he serves before he goes to his death?

And yet I tell you, priest, that some of these never came to trial at all but died first, rotting by inches—human flesh made, so you tell us, in the image of your god. Reconcile that with your conscience if you can! I doubt he will forgive you.

When the turnkey had thrust Meg and Philip into the stinking darkness, he waited to see if they had any money. But they had none; nor, if they had, would they have offered it, not knowing that money can buy sweeter air, sweeter company, even in such a place. And there's your justice, priest! The innocent may rot in misery; but your guilty man with a guinea in his pocket may make himself comfortable enough, putting off his hanging from day to day. He may even—if he have sufficient guineas—escape the rope altogether. There is nothing like the rattle of guineas to deafen your turnkey's ears; no, nor nothing so blinding as their glitter to make him wink his eye. And that, too, is your justice!

Philip stepped delicately, her head high. Filthy hands crooked as she passed. I heard the rending of her skirt; but she gave no sign. Margaret followed. Meg I think had the best of it—if best is a word to use of such a place. For she walked as in her sleep. When you looked through the window of her eye the soul was not within.

The walls were wet; and filthy like the floor; and creatures hung in webs or swung upon threads or crawled. I heard the crack of a beetle as Philip put out a foot; she ground it beneath her naked heel, glad to punish the creature for her misery.

So they stood together those two; and then, nature being too much for them, they slid upon the ground and rested one against the other as they had not done since childhood. Their god had deserted them."

"*Their* god?" Samuel Fleming said quickly. "Is he no longer *your* god?"

"A slip of the tongue—and you need not smile, priest! Sometimes they dozed a little; but more often they were awake with hunger and with cold. And—if this offends you, priest, then shut your ears; but they had to endure it, as others still endure it—when they had to relieve themselves they did so then and there and shivered in the filth of their clothes.

It was a long time till morning. The dirty light stole through the bars; it picked out a face here and there. And they all looked evil; for put innocence among filth and you must expect it to take the stain.

Some faces I knew—and they were faces I had not expected to see so soon—but you justices do not waste time! Joan Willimott lay asleep against the wall and her face grey as the wall. And though she had turned traitor against us, I pitied her. And I saw Ellen Greene but I did not know her at first. In those few days she had fallen from a stout and cheerful body into a withered hag. Good fellowship we had known together, until that last gathering when she would not take my hand and had turned her back crying curses upon us because we had spoilt the Sabbath. And her I pitied also.

But most of all I pitied Ann Baker that was, as I have told you, no witch but a simpleton who believed in fairies, confusing them with the prophets of old—seeing a hand reach down from heaven, and a flash of fire; and not knowing whether these signs came from Jehovah or from your Christ or from the Devil."

"She was at your unclean Sabbath," he reminded her, grave.

"They carried her there. But she understood nothing. When she lit her candle she did not know why, copying the others; and so it was with the Kiss and with the dancing. But she, too, they forced to confession, sparing no secret of her child's body. She was one they handled so cruelly that she said whatever they put into her mouth and went obedient to her death . . . and knew not why she died."

She saw him pale at that.

"It hits you hard," she said. "And so it should! A little girl yourself had baptized . . . and simple as you well know. But for all that they took her and they hanged her. Oh priest, priest, is it not time that the wickedness of man towards man should cease?"

"That comes well from you!" he said; but he could not cover the sickness in his eyes.

"I am a witch; but you are a man of God. Would you not expect a difference between us?"

"God forgive us all," he said.

"You may well say that! It was just before Christmas when they took my girls away—the season of goodwill. But there was nothing of goodwill in the gaol, no, nor of common decency neither. And there they stayed until it was mid-March; March when the wind blows clean and the air is clear as your fine Venice glass. But they languished in the dark amongst the stink of rotting flesh.

It was late January when they came again before the magistrates. Gaol delivery was not till March. *Delivery*—a word to make saints laugh or devils weep. But though they had not come before their judges, their judges had not forgotten them. Your fellows were forever at them seeking to ferret out the secret places of their souls as already they had desecrated the secret places of their women's bodies. Never shake your head at me, priest. You cannot be a justice and take no blame.

If you could see what I saw, priest. Day after day, hour after hour, midnight till morning, morning till midnight! And the questioners taking their turn, coming to their work fresh and rested, picking up where their fellows had stopped. But the prisoner . . . always the same prisoner. Eyes closing, head nodding; no rest; no rest at all. And always the questions—the questions to entrap; never the question to release.

Think of it, priest. You, and your like! Gentlemen, well-fed and warm, full with learning as with food. And those poor souls ignorant and frightened, helpless and hopeless. Is it any wonder they said, in the end, the thing that was death to say?"

"That was life to say; eternal life," he said quickly; but for all that his face was puckered like a child about to weep. "For they confessed; and heaven received their souls."

"There is no comfort for you that way—heaven may come too soon. You, priest, hope for heaven; yet still you find joy in a primrose and pleasure in your fine chocolate drink. And they; might not they, too, find joy in a primrose and pleasure in rough ale? But they were hustled brutally from this life to a shameful, cruel death. And some of them were young; and some of them—must I tell you again?—were innocent."

He lifted his hands and let them fall again. "You do wrong to break my heart with your tale of innocence. Those that were hanged that March were guilty; all of them guilty, as you yourself admit and the evidence shows. For it was the same tale they told—your Margaret and Joan Willimott and Ellen Greene; yes and Ann Baker—all of them who feared to die. And more. Philippa, who did not fear the rope since she thought she would never come to it, she too told the same tale. All of them—the frightened and the fearless—telling the same tale, implicating each one the other, and everything fitting together like a mosaic. Let us have no more talk of innocence."

"Let us leave it then, since it is a thing you cannot face. But, did you never ask yourself why they all told the same tale word for word, even little Ann? They told the same tale because they could tell no other. For the questions were always the same. And to them there were but two answers—the answers you wanted and the answers you did not want. When it was the answer you wanted, then you were satisfied. But when it was not the answer you wanted, though they spoke the truth, then they must recant with lies to stop the torment, so that they might go back again to the filthy cell and close their eyes in peace."

Chapter Twenty-one

GAOL delivery! From such deliverance good Lord deliver us! Samuel Fleming said and laughed; and, still laughing, woke to the safety of his bed. He sat up shivering in spite of the warm spring. This last week he had not been well again, sleeping little; and that sleep forever haunted by Joan Flower and her tale.

It was not the hangings that distressed him; for so the wicked, repentant, come clean into heaven. It was the prisons that haunted him—the stinking holes where human creatures rot to their death, innocent and guilty alike, dying of gaol fever, of gangrene, of a consumption of the lungs before ever they come to trial.

He was a Justice of the Peace; Joan Flower had fastened that responsibility fair and square upon his shoulders, so that at night he lay remembering her words and seeing it all clear as a picture before him. Or else, fallen into uneasy sleep, he would awake laughing as now; or weeping perhaps, and his old heart pounding as though it must burst the frail envelope of flesh.

He had no more desire to sleep again. Bedgown about him, he stirred the ash into flame and put on fresh logs. He moved quietly lest Hester, a light sleeper, too, and worried about him, should come from her bed. He knelt for a moment warming his chilled hands, then went to the window and opened the curtains.

Dawn was warming the grey sky and he knelt in prayer; then, absorbed in thought, he forgot to rise again but remained staring out into the garden. Yet it was not the garden he saw; it was the stinking cell and the floor foul with the filth of the prisoners' relieving.

No wonder they died off like flies—not only in Lincoln Gaol but in every prison in this sweet England. And, in his heart, he had known it this long while, though he had preferred not to know. Now, with Master John Stowe's report under his hand, he could pretend no longer. In the last few years thousands of prisoners had died in their cells.

Yet he had hardly given the prisons a thought; he had kept his eye on the duty before him, judging to the best of his ability between innocence and guilt and shutting all else out. And, afterwards, he had dismissed the matter from his mind, never thinking to ask what became of the wretches he and his fellow justices had sentenced, or had sent forward to the Assize.

And here he knelt in his clean warm room looking out upon his garden—upon the noble cedar and the lilacs in tight bud and the pale new shoots of roses. Every moment the light came stronger, warmer; but for them in the dark cell, the darkness, the dirt, the filth . . .

He turned from the window as though he could no longer bear the sweetness of the garden.

"Time runs out, priest!" And there she was standing by the hearth and lifting her hands to the blaze. Her own showed thin against the morning light. There was not much between his translucency and her own.

"I spoke of your prisons, priest—the cold and the wet, the dark and the filth, the vermin and the disease. And it is the lot of every prisoner, tried or untried—if he have no money— let his guilt be great or little; yes, even though he be thrust within for default of a small sum . . . or if he be innocent, priest.

But for witches there is contrived even greater cruelties. Do you know, priest, how one may tell a witch?"

He nodded. "By many ways. First and foremost by the Devil's Mark; the spot where your master drew blood to sign the bond. And there are other marks; two perhaps or three, where you suckle your familiars. All these marks cannot be mistaken."

"Can they not?" Her voice had its sorrowing sound as though since she could not weep with her eyes, she must weep with her voice. "Well, priest, since you are so wise, describe me these marks that cannot be mistaken."

"A red mark," he said thoughtful. "Or a raised mark; or a mark as big as a shilling . . ."

"Or a blue mark, or a sunken mark, or a mark no bigger than a pin's head. Or a pimple or a ringworm or a fleabite," she interrupted him. "Or any mark at all! It is easy enough to find some sort of mark anywhere—on your own body, maybe; or on Mistress Hester's; or on my virtuous lady the countess. Shall we call the whole world witches and dangle them at the rope's end?"

He shook his head. "The marks cannot be mistaken . . . and you know it. Where you suckle the familiar the place is wet still with blood. As for the place where the Devil has nipped you, it will not bleed, prick or cut it as you may. The place is dead."

"And where do you find such a mark?" And now she was grave indeed.

"Anywhere, anywhere at all. Upon the left eye or the left ear or upon the neck—the left side; or upon the left breast, or . . ."

". . . or in those parts you are too nice to mention! Or not at all! Priest, consider this. Though a woman be old, still it is hurtful to have strange hands rifling the secrets of her body. And if they are cruel hands, and if they are lustful hands then the thing is an offence to my God and to your god alike. But how if the witch is no witch at all? And how if she be a virgin like Ann Baker? Oh priest, I have stood by and I have seen; yes, and I have heard, too!

There was that man from Scotland, that righteous man, so zealous to discover witches; not for the sake of righteousness but for the jingle of the fee in his pocket. A witch—a guinea. It is handsome payment, you must own. The tale I will tell you now, I had from my mother; she was there when the thing happened. It was in a town named for a saint, St. Peter, I think; but I cannot rightly remember."

"Peterborough?" he asked.

She nodded. "Maybe you have heard the tale?"

He shook his head.

"In this town there was a young maid that had never made a bond with the Master, nor practised witchcraft, nor known a man. A virgin and virtuous.

Now this maid was informed against for witchcraft. And

who should inform against her but my fine gentleman from Scotland smelling yet another guinea for his pocket. So they thrust her into prison—just such a prison of which we have been speaking—along with those that would have taught her any sin in the calendar had she been minded to learn; but she was not minded. And though they would not let her sleep and were forever tormenting her with their questions, she confessed nothing. And though they searched the secrets of her virgin body, they found nothing. And there she lay until she came to trial.

And at this trial still she would confess to nothing; nor was there man, woman or child to testify against her. So this fine gentleman, afraid for his shining guinea, cried out, 'Let us search her before all the people; they shall stand for witness.' And he seized her petticoats and threw them above her head. And there she stood, naked from the waist downwards—a young maid, modest and virtuous.

Then he drew a pin from his lappet and drove it into her flesh and flung down her petticoats and cried out, 'Witch, you have something within you that belongs to me!'

But she in her shame and her anguish had felt nothing. So he cried out—this man, this virtuous snatcher of guineas, 'The place is dead where the Devil nipped her. Good people, she is a witch!'

Now, priest, this maid was not only innocent, she was comely, too. And a captain that was in the court—or the judge himself, maybe; my mother being ignorant would not know—taken by her face rather than by her virtue, cried out, 'This is no witch. Sir Witchfinder, you must try again.'

And so this grabber of guineas was forced to try again. He drove his pin into the same place; and the blood welled and she cried out. And so she was cleared of the charge and went free. But, priest, mark this! Had she not been so fair a maid, she would have hanged. So much for your witchmark, and so much for your justice!"

"Yet justice is done . . . for the most part." And it was as though he pleaded with her.

"That is not enough when it comes to hanging! You may be sure, priest, that for every true witch that is hanged, one innocent goes to his death. Well, then, since your witchmark is not always a true test, what are your other signs?"

"The familiars," he said.

"Oh priest, priest!" And again there was a wailing in her voice. "Do you talk of familiars? Have you forgot the question that troubled you not long since—the forlorn women and the creatures they cherish in their loneliness? And have you forgot your own sister and her cat—a little white cat not very different from Rutterkin that helped to hang me? And your sister, having no child, feeds her little cat with sweet milk and she talks to it as though it were a child; and she takes it to her bed and grieves that it will not stay curled against her pillow but chooses to wander the dark night. And, but the other day, it scratched, impatient as young cats are, and it would have sucked her blood. And if it had dug deep enough, or if it had bitten with its sharp teeth, why then, she, too, might have borne the witch's mark!

Priest, there are true Devil's Marks and we witches carry them. But there are other marks the innocent carry and for these they may well be hanged. So much for your familiars, and so much for witchmark! On what then will you hang witches?"

"On their own confession," he said, more shaken than he cared to admit.

She made a gesture of impatience. "Some of us will confess to anything . . . if you hurt us enough. Ann Baker was one. I saw her arms; and her back, too, where they had torn away the clothes. You would have been hard put to it, priest, to find the Devil's Mark—had there been one to find—in that mess of prison scabs and bruises and open places clotted with dark blood.

The wounds she bore as best she might—quiet for the most part; but whimpering now and then very softly. What she could not endure was lack of sleep. For when their blows could no longer keep her awake, two women came—good women, priest, very virtuous. And they took this child beneath the arm —one each side—and they walked her. *Walking the prisoner.* Have you heard the words before, Sir Magistrate? Witches know them well. Though the eyes close with weariness and the limbs move no more, still we must walk . . . walk. And, if we sleep even as we walk, why then we are awakened—and not gently, neither.

And so it was with this young child.

On the third night of the *walking* she burst out wailing like an infant; so they told her to listen and then she should sleep. So she listened; and when they wanted her to nod, then she nodded like a mad thing; and when they wanted her to deny, then her sick face flew from side to side. And they brought her a pen and she made her mark; and she went off to sleep the pen still in her hand—the pen that had signed her life away and the lives of others.

And when they brought her to trial, they read over her 'confession' and still she nodded. Any right man could see that she nodded with sleep and not with understanding. Priest, think upon it! This young, poor thing, simple and friendless; and set against her—the law; all its strength and its power, from your brutish turnkey to your fine gentlemen, your Eresbys and your Manners, yes and you and your earl thrown in for good weight. Priest, are you not ashamed?

I think she was not full awake until they walked her to the gallows; and then, the fresh air blowing upon her face awakened her . . . yes, then she awakened fast enough.

Priest, I run ahead of my tale. But it was to tell you what you should know yourself—what those places are like to which you condemn those that offend you. And now I go back to my daughters and their first night in the gaol.

That night they were left in peace—if peace you can call it, with the weeping and the crying out in nightmare dreaming, and the stinks and the bitter cold. There was no sleep for either of them. They sat leaning one against the other like sisters, for the first time in years taking comfort each in the other.

Meg was for denying everything. But Philip would have none of it. 'Our mother denied the Master,' she said, 'and she died horribly.'

'If I could weep,' Meg said, very bitter, 'I would weep for her. But I have no tears, so I curse her instead because she has brought us down to the pit.'

There is anguish of the naked ghost, priest, that no man can understand until he be out of the body. And such anguish I knew then. It is an anguish sharper than the anguish of dying; than the desolation of being lost between heaven and hell."

"Greater than that?"

"Greater than that. For it falls without warning upon the naked soul; and the soul takes at once the full measure, the full pain. And it is an anguish that grows never less but burns like poison within the soul.

Philip said, 'You blame our mother now, in this fearful place; but you will not blame her when we stand before the Master and He takes us by the hand.'

'You He will take.' Meg's body shook with the strain of weeping denied. 'But not me; never me.'

'He will welcome all the faithful,' Philip said and there was a warning in her voice.

'But I am not faithful,' Meg's voice came in a wail so that those who had a little forgotten their troubles, woke to the sound and hissed out in anger. 'I am faithful neither to my God in hell, nor to the god in heaven.'

'You cannot be faithful to the god in heaven since you have abjured him,' Philip told her, scornful. 'Be faithful then to the God of hell.'

'Faithfulness is not in me,' Meg said very sorrowful, 'and it is too late. It was already too late when the Master made his Mark and drew my blood. It was too late, I think, even at that moment the priest held me at the font. All my life I have not hated good nor loved evil with a whole heart. What must I do now?' She clutched at Philip's skirt. 'What must I do?'

'You no longer have any choice,' Philip said quick and sharp. 'You made it long ago; to that the Master's Mark bears witness. Do not think to win the god of heaven, you have sinned against him beyond his pardon—not only by witchcraft and by murder; but most of all by renouncing the sacrifice of his blood.'

'His mercy endures for ever,' Meg said very low.

'*For ever* is a long time—and you have little or none. Your glass is almost run, unless the Master save you. And, if you are not faithful, why should He?'

Meg said nothing to that. She sat there upon the filthy floor and her pale hair fell about her face.

'I have been thinking,' she said at last, 'that the priest held me at the font and put the holy mark . . .'

'It is not *that* mark will count!' Philip said, and her smile was cruel.

'. . . and put the holy mark here,' Meg repeated obstinate and slow, and touched her forehead, 'then he gave my soul to God. I gave my soul to the Master; but it was not mine to give. Christ had already redeemed it with his blood.'

At that name, at that thought, anger shook Philip; and fear, also. If this soul slipped through the Master's fingers, then she, herself, grovelling at his feet must acknowledge failure and bear the pains—she that was the Master's paramour. She showed neither anger nor fear. 'That is a great nonsense,' she said and laughed so loud that once more the sleepers wakened from their pitiful, needed sleeping.

'Yet still what I say is true.' Meg nodded. 'I know it. It is as though someone stood by my side and whispered in my ear . . . the priest, maybe, who baptized me.' "

"I had been praying for you all," Samuel Fleming said, and there was a sweetness in his eyes, a hope. "And most of all I prayed for Margaret that looked a lost soul. I do not mean lost to the Devil; that, of course; but adrift . . . no compass."

"As I am," Joan Flower said.

"I pray for you, also," he told her. "If you will, you shall come to the same place as Margaret at the last."

"I care not which place it may be as long as I may find rest at last," she said petulant.

"You shall never rest until you do care . . . and greatly care," he told her, very grave.

She shrugged and took up her tale.

"Philip said, 'Do not deceive yourself! Your soul is firmly lodged with the Master, never doubt it, nor rob yourself of those joys that shall yet be yours. It is the Master that is merciful and no other. Do not believe that you will ever win to heaven; or, if you could, that you would be satisfied with its cold, chaste joys.'

Meg did not answer. Too long she had turned like a

245

weathercock from this side to that; now she had set her lost soul on heaven. She would endure such pains as your god thought fit to lay upon her, so she could win there at the last.

After that they sat in silence, and, from my corner, I watched them and knew the thoughts of their minds.

At last Philip whispered in the stinking darkness, 'Do not hope to save yourself by denial. They will torment you to make you speak. And should your body stand firm against the pain —which I much doubt—your wits will never stand against the Justices. Something, in spite of yourself, you must admit; and I will tell the rest. And even without me, enough has been said already; Joan Willimott has testified and Ellen Greene; and Ann Baker, here.' And she stirred the child with a cold bare foot, so that Ann awoke and whimpered and went back to her sleeping. 'You cannot escape, never think it. When we go to hell we take you with us.'

Meg said, 'I will not deny my part. I no longer wish to deny it. I will keep nothing back. I will confess all . . . all.'

Philip said, very quick, 'There are two ways of confessing. You may speak the selfsame words, yet the confessions may be different as heaven from hell. For you may confess to the glory of the Master; or you may confess to his shame and the glory of the Christian god. The first way brings you life both here and in the world to come, together with all that heart can desire or flesh enjoy, according to the promise of the Master. The second brings you bitter death and shuts you from the forgiveness of both the Master and the god of heaven.'

Meg's cold hand went to her forehead as though to smooth out her troubled thoughts.

'Sister,' Philip said. 'We are bound to confess the Master; to confess Him with pride and with adoration. So we enlarge his kingdom here upon earth. It was the bond. If you confess his glory, then, for all you are a fool and a coward, He will forgive you and receive you into the mercy of his everlasting joy.'

And when Meg made no answer but went on staring into the darkness, Philip went on, pitiless, 'If you confess, abjuring the Master's service and repenting those things you have done in his name, He will never forgive you. He will cast you upon living coal; or else He will throw you into the uttermost freezing space of hell.'

And still Meg made no answer. She let her head drop upon her breast and pretended that she slept. But I could see how her thoughts ran. If she testified against the Master, crying out in repentance for the things she had done in his name, then, perhaps, at long last, the god in whose name she had been baptized would forgive her.

I went over and stood by her and sent out my ghostly will towards her. *God will not forgive; he will reject you. And the Master will not forgive; He will reject you. You will wander to all eternity in the cold white loneliness of the lost. It is a loneliness beyond all enduring. It is worse, believe me, oh believe me, than any torment you can imagine. Will you throw away for this the sweet companionship of hell?*

And the sweet companionship of heaven? her poor bewildered spirit answered mine.

You will never attain to it, my soul answered hers."

Samuel Fleming sighed so that his frail body shook. "Had I known. Had I but known!"

"What then?" she mocked. "Would you have trusted yourself among the stinks and fevers of a prison cell? Not you, priest, not you! You left it to the ordinary who tormented her with false hope of pardon—both King and God; and when he had got what he wanted, took away the hope he had given. Had it been left to him—or to you, priest—she had gone hopeless to her hanging."

"And I might have strengthened her!" Samuel Fleming said very low.

"God Himself strengthened her," Joan Flower told him. "As for yourself, you could not play priest as well as magistrate. Here is a thing I have thought in my wanderings. Your god is capable of winning his own. He needs no man's help—not even his priest's."

"It is true," he said. "Therefore no net is strong enough to hold the soul that would escape to Him. Remember your thought. Remember it."

He lifted shining eyes. The spring sunshine fell about his head as it might be a halo; the ghost stood staring. Up from the wide staircase came the jingle of pots and pans; the cheerful smell of bacon; and a pleasant aromatic smell she could not name

"Coffee," he said. "One of God's little miracles. Francis sent it from the Amazon." He sniffed delightedly. "How wide the world grows."

"Or small," she said quickly.

"That is a profound thought," he told her. "For here is the Amazon upon my doorstep; or its gifts, at least, upon my table. You would have made a philosopher," he said and threw back his head and laughed so that the halo shivered and broke.

"Why, you are only a man after all," she said, peevish at his laughing at her.

"And what did you think I was?"

"I had begun to think you a saint . . . almost."

Chapter Twenty-two

"I HAD begun to think you a saint . . . almost." She sighed.

"How you were mistaken!" He echoed her sigh.

"I wonder?" She spread her hands. "One is wrong about so many things. A lifetime is not enough to learn."

"We are given another life that we may go on learning."

"After death one learns most of all!" She nodded, sombre. "When I was alive I thought it was your good man that is steadfast; I know now it is not so. It is your wicked man that does not waver; your good man trembles like a compass before it finds the north."

"But the compass points true; and, in the end, good men return to God who is their Home. But, good or bad, we are but human. There is not one that does not waver before the course is set. And afterwards; afterwards also."

"Philip did not waver," Joan Flower said. "But Meg shifted to this side and that and did not know what to do. It is folk like Meg that suffer most. For when the day comes there is no compass to tell them which way to turn."

"Yet Margaret was told; and she was saved," he reminded her.

"But first she suffered a thousand torments, died a thousand deaths. It was Philip that had the best of it!"

"And did she have the best of it in the end? Not to be shaken from wickedness . . . and death waiting a few steps away. Is that so enviable?" Samuel Fleming sighed, remembering the girl and her boldness and her defiance and her mockery.

"When one has chosen, one should stick by the bargain."

"Even though one was deceived in the bargain? Now that Philippa lies roasting upon coals till the end of time, does she find herself so fortunate, do you think?"

"You suppose hell to be a burning pit for those that deny your god. Why should not heaven be such a place for those that deny the Master?"

"There is no *why*," he said, stern. "The thing *is*—as your unhappy girl must find. If ever a creature deserved the pains of hell, it is Philippa. When she was brought to us for examination we could feel, every justice there, the evil that came forth from her."

"It is not for the King's Justices to feel, nor yet to fancy," she said, tart. "It is for them to use what wits your god—or the Devil—gave them, and come to a true judgment."

"Her examination was just; every question fair, every answer weighed, every word sifted and compared with the testimony of those that had witnessed against her."

"Yes," she admitted grudging, "it was fair . . . as it turned out. But how easily it might not have been! For Philip was branded guilty and the rope set about her neck before ever she set foot in your court."

"From her own mouth she was condemned," he reminded her gently.

"She was steadfast always; her compass never wavered. But with Meg your task was not so easy. When they tormented her she confessed; and then, a little rested, denied it all. But my fine magistrates must have their evidence! They spared her no torment. But then you knew nothing of that—if we are to believe you!"

"Still I did not know; and you may believe me."

"I believe you; but I do not forgive you. A justice should know what is done in the name of the law. Well, since you do not know, I will tell you.

They took my poor girl all bewildered with lack of sleep and with hunger and with fear, and they forced her cross-legged upon a narrow beam very high up. No need now to watch her lest she sleep. Should she nod she would fall and break her back. Now she must keep herself awake. And there she sat, trembling like a sick bird on her high and narrow perch."

Samuel Fleming flung out bewildered hands. "Why did they do that?"

"You are too innocent, priest. It was to catch the familiar. It would come when all was still to suck upon her—so they thought. Eighteen hours perched high; and no relief from the cramps of her body and no sleep and no food. A wonder, indeed, she did not fall and break her neck upon the stone floor. And, once, priest, she stirred and stretched a foot; and they cried out, *Do you stir, witch?* And they took a thin cord and they bound it about her arms and about her breasts and about her feet; and they drew it so tight that the flesh rose either side of the cord. They had made a little hole in the floor so that her familiar might come at her. And they watched the long night through. And all the while she sat high up, bound hand and foot and no rest from the torment.

But you knew nothing of this, Sir Priest-Magistrate— under whose authority it was done. Yet you questioned her there in the courthouse of the prison when she had suffered a month of torment. You examined her twice—you and your friends. Any man's eyes should tell him when a woman has been tormented. But, being a priest—and an old one—maybe you look no more upon women!"

He said, sorrowful, "I have failed as a priest as well as a justice; yes, and as a man, too. It was a wicked and cruel thing; and I accept the blame. And yet," he raised his troubled head, "we are bound by our office to punish witchcraft. And we are bound, equally, to acquit those that are wrongfully accused. How are we to come at the truth?"

He fell to silence, head upon his breast, thinking upon the dilemma. He raised his head at last. "And did the familiar come?"

"It did not come. Did you expect it? Some kind soul suckled it for love of the Master. So there was no peace for my poor girl, not even when she had confessed all. Nor was there any peace for Joan and Ellen and the child. For cruelty is a madness in the heart; and neither rhyme nor reason can set its bounds. Only Philip they left alone. There was a power about her and they were afraid.

And so it went on. Day after day; night after night—the walking and the binding on the narrow beam. And always the questions. And when they had been answered once, twice, thrice, still it was not enough. For answers must be twisted and turned so that they form a net to ensnare others. Think of it, Sir Priest-Magistrate! Wise men, learned in the law, setting their wits against poor and simple women."

"It is for justices and priests to look to the safety of the people. If witches suffer it is a thing they must accept."

"You did not know then whether these were witches or no—they had not been judged. But, if they were, you had them safe enough! You had sent them forward to trial, was it not enough? No! You must still ferret out with your cruelty, doing the judge's business for him, handing in your writings before-hand, moving his mind against them that could not write. Questions and answers, answers and questions . . . and the little persuasions to make them speak. Oh priest, there is none so cruel as your good man at his duty.

And so time dragged on until the great judges should come from London.

In the stinking prison my girls were enemies once more one to the other; the little kindness Philip had shown at first was turned to bitterness. They were near their death; and Meg knew it; she knew it as an animal knows, within the blood. But Philip feared nothing. Had your god himself appeared in all his glory and his angels about him, she would have spat in his face.

And still Meg wavered between God and the Devil. Surely she must trust the Master still! How could her life come to an end in this filthy place? But . . . how did those that served the Master come to his place at all? Suppose that for all his promises He was faithless? Then, much as she feared to die, she must fear what comes after, still more . . . the undying pains of hell.

And every day increased her fear. She would crouch there brooding, eyes dry and stony as an empty river-bed. Without sleep and without tears no man can live. For the one comforts the body, the other the soul.

It was late February now. Two months in the dark and stinking cell. Outside the air was sharp and clean; in sheltered places pale leaves of celandine were pushing through and buds of bright and naked coltsfoot which is a kindly herb. But the prisoners knew nothing of it. Within the cell they dozed in uneasy sleep; yet, even then, they could not forget their fears but would start and moan so that the place was full of the sound of their pain and the smell of their pain.

The watchers had stopped their torment. The great judges were already come from London; before them the confessions of the tormented lay written in a neat and clerkly hand.

From the narrow barred window, if you could climb to it, you could look out upon the courtyard. Snow had fallen thick and soft, covering the ugliness and the muck so that the world, for all its cruelty, was like a soul new-born to heaven.

In the dark cell the prisoners lay tossing and moaning in sleep. Only Philip lay quiet, smiling in her dreams.

Meg lay watching the high barred window and the little patch of night sky, pale and heavy with snow; she tried to fall into the uneasy dreaming that was all the sleep she knew. But still her eyes stared up at the pale sky. I could see how her thoughts twisted and turned; how fear beat upon her heart in hammerstrokes.

. . . Time passing, passing. Soon it will be tomorrow . . . I think it is already tomorrow and I must face the judges.

Deny? Confess? Deny? Confess? Deny? Confess?

Deny. Deny everything. Useless . . . useless. They have betrayed me —Joan and Ellen and little Ann; and, above all Philip. They have betrayed me all four and the judge will hang me, hang me, hang me . . . and I can hope for nothing from the Master nor yet from God. Deny; and I betray the Master. Lie; and I take myself still further, if that be possible, from God.

Confess. All that's left. There, perhaps a chance of God's mercy —the last, the littlest chance. But . . . how mercy? I have put myself outside his forgiveness. Yet, pin my dying hope upon the Master? What promise has He ever kept?

Like a rat you may see driven between this pitchfork and that, so was she driven backwards and forwards between God and the Devil.

And as she lay there, she saw a spirit come forth out of the darkness and stand at her feet. Black against the blackness; yet she could see Him clear by the light that streamed from those terrible eyes. He wore an ape's head to cover his glory; but she knew Him . . . she knew Him.

She cried out lifting her arms, 'Master, take me from this place!'

'Why, yes,' He said.

'Shall I move in the air and dance again in the place of the Sabbath?'

'Yes,' he said again and nodded his ape's head. 'You shall be taken from this place; you shall dance in the air. You shall dance; how you will dance!'

She dragged herself along the ground and lay, her lips upon his feet. 'I am ready,' she said.

'I do not doubt it,' He said smiling. 'But the time is not now . . . it is not now.'

'Tomorrow will be too late!' She stared upwards with parched eyes. 'Already the judges are here; the great judges from London—the King's lord Judges.'

'You fear these judges that are but men—and some of them my own servants. Do you not fear Me still more?'

She knelt staring and dumb. She shook before Him to the depths of her soul; yet He had promised to save her . . . and there was no-one else.

'You are not worth saving—and only a fool would expect it,' He said. 'Witch, you have not been faithful. Even now you would make your peace with my Enemy—if you knew how! Why should I keep faith with you—except I am merciful. But *my* mercy does not endure for ever. Remember it. When you have proclaimed your love of Me, then I will save you—in my own way and in my own time. And it will not be now.'

She said, and her breath came out in a long sigh, 'Then I am to hang?'

And still He said nothing; and still He smiled.

She cried out then, 'Save me from the rope!' and fell upon her face in the straw.

She lay there awhile and when she looked up He was gone.

She dragged herself to her knees and tried to pray; but her heart could not restore the lost words. When she would have besought the kindness of your god, offering herself to death as willingly as she could, if in the end she might be forgiven, one thought rose up, *I have made my life a filthy thing*. And against that thought all other thoughts stumbled and broke. There was no release for her soul's torment."

"I think there was," Samuel Fleming said. "She had no words; yet she prayed and God heard her."

Joan Flower nodded. "Even then, standing and watching, I knew God would save her—if she were constant. But constancy; it was a thing I had never known in her. And how would she fare rejected alike by God and the Devil? Yet that night, at least, she knelt till morning on the cold and filthy stone.

The dirty light crept through the high grating, picking out the poor wretches that lay upon the floor. Philip had slept well; but those others awoke weary, stretching cramped and twisted limbs, throwing back the unclean tangle of their hair. You could see how they opened puzzled eyes, not knowing, at first, what they did in this place . . . and then remembering . . . remembering.

You are a holy man, priest; and these had sold themselves to evil. Yet even you must have pitied them crawling like vermin in the straw, crawling back to the bitterness of living and the fear of dying.

But Meg did not stir; she went on kneeling. Nor did she stir when the key sounded in the lock and the door swung open.

The turnkey came in with his jug of dirty water and his basket of mouldy bread. 'The judges are come!' he cried out. 'The Governor has presented the Calendar and your names stand first. The witnesses are ready; but what need of them since those things you confessed to the magistrates are witness enough against you? You would save us all time and trouble to plead your guilt. For, let things go as they may, you will sup with the Devil ere long.'

'He will feed us better than you do!' Philip said quick and impudent. 'If we are to stand our trial today then let our bellies be full and our looks seemly.'

'Hold your saucy tongue,' he said and set down his burden.

'It might be saucier . . . if I choose to wag it,' she told him. 'Gaoler, there is a tree stands upon a heath no great distance from this place—a stricken tree, naked summer and winter alike. And about it there is a ring where the grass is worn by dancing feet. I fancy you could tell my lords the judges something about that ring . . . and those that dance there.'

He turned green and did not speak; but his eyes shifted this way and that.

'Men and women dance about that tree,' she said thoughtful. 'The judges might be glad to know the names of all that dance.'

If he had been green before, now he was pale as death; I saw how he tried to moisten his dry tongue. And she cried out, 'Bring clean water and towels; and good food to comfort our bellies. Remember, in a little while, we face the judges.'

He turned and went without a word carrying his jug and his basket with him. Ellen Greene said, 'I have not clapped eyes on him in my life. Does he dance at the Sabbath?'

Philip shrugged. 'I know not and I care less; but he has a look of guilt upon him. Let him do as I bid and I will hold my tongue. If not he shall suffer, let him be guilty or not!'

Presently the fellow came back and there was fresh bread in the basket and beer and meat. 'I will bring you the water when it is heated,' he said and he dared not look Philip in the face. 'And the food I have paid for out of my own pocket.'

She nodded without thanking him and he went humbly away.

Then the others came crowding about the food like flies, all except Meg who knelt apart. 'You see,' Philip said, 'all we ask—the Master gives. His word stands sure.'

'Not always,' Joan Willimott said beneath her breath.

Philip sent her a look of contempt. 'He gives us what we ask; and more. But He gives it in his own way. He expects us to help ourselves a little.'

'Then why,' Ellen Greene grumbled and mumbled over the food, 'did you not ask for meat and drink before?'

'The time was not ripe. The first turnkey was not one to frighten with threats. This is a new fellow, did you not notice? We have to watch men and women to get from them—under the Master—what we desire.' Philip fell again to eating with good appetite, her sharp teeth tore into the bread and meat. She turned suddenly upon Joan Willimott. 'Eat up the good food while you may,' she said scornful. 'No need to shiver and shake. The judges are but men when all is said; but our Master is the God.'

The gaoler returned with a jug of warm water and a clean cloth; he trembled still. Again she did not thank him, nor so much as look at him. He said, very humble now, 'My lord judge has commanded the sheriff to open the court; to prepare a sufficient jury of life and death; and to present the prisoners. You will be called any moment now.' Again she did not thank him nor so much as look at him. She pushed away the broken food and began to set herself to rights. I could see how her eyes closed in delight over so simple a thing, so dear a thing as clean water. She took a comb from her bosom and fell to straightening the tangles of her hair; and all the while she hummed to herself, and now and again she cast a look towards her sister. Meg, though she had come from her knees, did not eat but she drank thirstily of the water. Now she lay back, eyes closed in her stained and swollen face, hair hanging dusty and tangled, and cared not at all how she looked . . . my pretty Meg!

Philip put back her comb and stood up fresh as though she had this moment come from the crisp air, so that the others stared with their dim eyes.

'Listen,' she cried, 'all that be witches, whether of my coven or no. I have the Master's orders for us all.'

Ellen Greene came forward dragging Ann by the hand; and Joan Willimott came also. And here and there, this one and that one pushed forward, some of them against their will, muttering as they came. And she waited until all were seated there at her feet. But Meg stayed still in her place and Philip made no sign towards her.

'Listen well,' she said and there was power all about her. 'When you come before the judges you shall testify, each one of you, to the power of the Master and to his glory. You must remember every evil you have done in his name. And, when you have spoken of yourselves, then you must search in your mind for those you know to be witches—though they have not as yet been named. You must not keep one name back— not though it be your mother or your lover, or your child, even. And if there are not enough names for his glory, then you must find more, naming this one or that you know to be guiltless—and let their own god save them if he can! And this you shall do neither in hope to save your own skins, nor to spite any that has ill-used you, but only to magnify his name. For, do what we will, we are already judged and condemned of men; and there is no hope save in the Master. If we speak out for Him, then He will save us.'

Ellen Greene said very low, 'I think we shall come to the rope,' and she covered her eyes with her hand. 'Had He meant to save us we had not ever been taken.'

'Here is a fool that understands nothing,' Philip said with rough good-humour. 'This is his way to make his name a trumpet in the ears of men. If we had not been taken how could we testify to our faith? Testify. It is his command; and in the end He will save you.'

'The end. What end? The rope's end!' Ellen began to sob the tearless, racking sobs of witches.

All this while Ann Baker had sat silent; and now, though she neither moved nor spoke, the salt tears poured down her face. That was enough to show she was no witch had anyone the desire to save her. But no-one had the desire.

'Stop your whining,' Philip said, and her eyes did not soften though Ann was but a child. 'I have this message for you all. *You shall come to the rope but the rope shall not come to you. All who believe on Him shall live.*'

Ann raised her wet face, and like the child she was, smiled through her tears.

'We shall be condemned,' Philip said, 'each one of us.' Her eyes turned towards Ann. 'Even you, for all your tears. And, afterwards, in two days or three we shall be carried to the gallows piece. But we shall not hang; not one of us that keeps faith. We shall be carried away and images hang in our place. But we shall be riding through the sky to the everlasting Sabbath.'

'Why does the Master leave images in our place?' Ann asked with the terrible simplicity of the simpleton that, in spite of himself, has hit upon the truth. 'Why does He not take us away in the sight of all the people and leave the gallows empty? That would be a greater sign of his glory.'

'Do you seek to teach the Master?' Philip said and made a step towards the child. But Meg came suddenly from her thoughts and stood up quickly and put herself before Ann. Philip fixed bitter eyes upon Meg; Meg, very steady, stared back. So they faced each other, those two. Then, arm about the child, Meg spoke.

'We shall die, all of us. And we deserve to die—except this child who does not deserve it. But God, I think, is too far away to wipe her tears. Ellen is right; our end is the rope. Had the one we have called Master meant to save us, we had never come to this place. But He has left us to shame and to fear; to filth and to cruelty. There is neither truth nor kindness in him . . .'

It was then that Philip struck her full upon the mouth and Meg fell forward upon the straw.

The others sat crouched in their places for fear of Philip; but Ann bent down and put her thin arms about Meg and helped her to rise, saying in that simple way of hers, echoing perhaps what she had heard and not understanding fully what she said, 'God will see our tears and He will wipe them away. There is no kindness anywhere but in God; there is no hope anywhere but in God.'

And so they knelt, those two, to pray together."

Chapter Twenty-three

"Out of the mouths of babes and sucklings, yes and of the simple, too, hath He ordained truth," Samuel Fleming said.

"Yet they took her, this simpleton, and they hanged her," Joan Flower reminded him.

He leaned his face against his hand and groaned. And so leaning, remembered. . . . The courtroom of Lincoln Gaol and the judge in his great robes, Sir Henry Hobert, the great Chief Justice himself, come to see with his own eyes this nest of vipers the quiet countryside had so shockingly produced.

"Witches were two-a-penny, you might say," Joan Flower spoke, mocking. "Yet here was the great judge himself! But then this was no bewitching of common folk. Would you not say his anger was the hotter because the prisoners had dared to lift their hand against the great?"

"There is always anger in decent folk against those that have dealings with the Devil." He parried the question.

"You have not answered me, priest."

And, since she still waited, he said, "Certainly the anger was more because those that were murdered were little and good, yes and noble, too. Yes," he said again, very firm, "and because their father matched the greatness of his name. He had done nothing but good to the whole countryside. Do you pretend," he asked suddenly sharp, "that justice was not done?"

"Justice was done."

There was silence now—he white in his chair, the untasted coffee pushed to one side; she translucent, mocking.

"Justice was done," she said again. "But how easily it might not have been done! Had my girls not been witches, had they been innocent like Ann Baker, still they would have hanged . . . as she did. The court was set upon their death; you cannot deny it."

He could not deny it. Behind closed eyes, he could see it now, see the small dark courtroom; the guttering candles drawing up what little air there was, and sending it in waves of stinking tallow up to the low roof. Only before the canopied seat wax candles burned steady and sweet, lighting the dark face of the judge and the sick face of Francis sitting by him—Francis come in his two-fold capacity—Lord Lieutenant of the county, and father of the dead children. Yes, Francis had a two-fold responsibility to see justice done.

And then the voice of the Clerk of Assize. *Bring forth the prisoner*; and then a silence; and, in the silence, Margaret Flower leaning upon the bar.

In that first moment he had not known her. He had thought, at first, there was some mistake. And yet it was but two months since she had stood before him at her questioning. She'd been a little grey in the face; thin, perhaps. But for all that she'd appeared to be well enough. He had not concerned himself unduly with her looks. His concern had been all for justice—the way she had taken the questions, the way she had answered them.

Two short months. Now, it was hard to guess at her age—dirty, dishevelled, peering about her, the poor light of the courtroom too bright for her dim eyes. The pretty young thing she had been! *Suppose she is innocent—and we have done this to her!* He sickened at the thought; almost he prayed she might be guilty, remembered with relief her own confessions and was ashamed that he had pitied the blemish to her body rather than the blemish to her soul. But, curiously, even that was little comfort.

When they read the charge against her, she seemed not to understand clinging there upon the bar as if without it she must fall and peering out of her dim and troubled eyes.

If she were guilty, though he hated her crimes, he must pity her still. For what had she got from her wicked bargain? Nothing. Nothing but misery and fear and a most hateful death.

But the children. Their death had been even more hateful. And what of the curse she had put upon Francis and Cecilia? And what of the whole countryside in terror because of her and her mother and her sister? And looking at her spoiled and broken youth, he was able to thrust down pity in his heart. Let her stand where all might see the reward of them that make their Devil's Pact.

Again he found himself wishing they could use simpler language; for though she knew well enough the charges against her she was ignorant and forgetful and she looked sick.

"Margaret Flower, spinster of the parish of Bottesford in the county of Leicester, you stand here charged with murder by witchcraft, whereby you, together with your mother Joan Flower now deceased, and with Philippa Flower your sister, spinster, both of this same parish of Bottesford did, at divers times in the year of grace . . ."

The indictment thundered on, the damning damnable indictment, beating about her head; her poor wits must long be scattered beneath the impact.

"And lastly you are charged that you, together with your mother and sister, did, with abominable and devilish practices, bewitch the noble Earl of Rutland and the lady his wife, that they should have no more issue; since which time they have had no more issue. . . ."

At that he saw the poor creature, almost imperceptibly, shake her head. So she had understood!

"All these things, according to the indictment, you maliciously and feloniously did against the peace of our sovereign lord the King, his crown and dignity . . ."

And what, he had found himself wondering, did she make of that? . . . *the King, his crown and dignity* . . . What had it to do with her?

"Margaret Flower, how say you, are you guilty or not guilty of all or any of these charges?"

Sitting now in the warm safety of his room, his familiar things about him, he was taken again with pity for the lost creature standing there, her lips moving . . . and no sound.

"My poor Meg," Joan Flower said softly. "She was not one of your great sinners, for all her pact with the Devil. Nor was she one of the company of martyrs. There in the cell she had meant to confess, had longed unspeakably to confess, to cry aloud her sins against God and to throw herself upon his mercy. Now she was afraid. The strange language she could not understand and which was so terribly important for her to understand; the room, over-bright to her poor eyes, crowded with those that wished her ill—ill she knew well she had deserved; the terrible figure of the lord judge of life and death. All these things made yet more fearful the danger in which she stood.

She did not know what to do nor whom to beseech—the Master or your god. She turned blindly to God—your god, priest—the god she had forsaken. If these terrible people would only believe her lies and let her go free, she would serve him— if he would let her—for ever and ever."

"That is no way," Samuel Fleming told her gently, "to bargain with God, to ask Him to condone our wickedness and lies."

"What did she know of God?" Joan Flower asked.

His lips moved. *Mea culpa*, he said and knocked against his breast.

"Priest," she said, "never blame yourself! You tried to teach her but she would not learn. And, besides, at this moment she was not capable of reason. She was like an animal mad to be free . . . and no way to freedom save by lying. And all the time the court waited; and again the clerk asked her, *Are you guilty or not guilty?*

No, she whispered. *No.* And they asked her to speak louder since they could not hear. And she shook her head from side to side; and the hair that was gold so short a time ago was white . . . it was white. And *No*, she cried out, *No, no, no!*

And then, do you remember, priest, a gentleman stood up in the court and it was one of the magistrates; and he said, 'My lord, she has confessed already. And it is written down and a copy lies even now under your hand. She has confessed before us all that examined her; before Master Samuel Fleming and before Sir George Manners and before Lord Willoughby of Eresby and Sir William Pelham; and they are in this court to say so.'

But still she shook her pitiful head; and she put up a hand to her throat but no words came.

Then the judge said, 'Yet now she pleads not guilty to the indictment. Master Sheriff, you must return a jury of worthy gentlemen of understanding, to pass between our sovereign lord the King's Majesty and the prisoner at the Bar that stands upon her life and death.'

And so the jury was sworn. And as she stood, her head moved from side to side and she shook so that she must have fallen had not the officer laid hold of her. Then, since you cannot force the dumb to speak nor hang a witch until she be found guilty, my lord judge ordered them to take her away and bring her again later; and to call the next prisoner.

And so they brought Philip into the court. Two daughters, priest, to come to the rope! Even the heart of a ghost might break at that! Sisters born of the same womb and in the same place—but how different! Meg; the blood in her body was thin and flat as vinegar; but in Philip it ran rich and bright as good wine.

She showed no fear; her look was gay and wanton, so that men stared at such a fashion of witch; and I saw Tom Simpson cover his eyes with his hands.

When they had finished reading the charges, she standing and smiling the while, she turned towards my lord judge and fixed him with a wicked eye, so that strong as he was, and wise as he was, and safe in his high seat, he could not look at her but must turn away his head.

And when the clerk asked, 'Are you guilty or not guilty?' she threw back her head and cried out, 'I am a witch. And all you have heard is true.'

Then the lord judge said, 'Do you know, woman, what you say? For if you plead guilty I must find you so. And I must pronounce the sentence of which you know.'

She nodded. 'I know. And I know this, too. Were I to deny my Master, still you would hang me So I should lose not only my life here but life in the world to come. Therefore I trust in the Master and glorify his name.'

Then my lord judge said, 'Prisoner at the Bar, consider well. Do you plead guilty or not guilty?' And again she smiled and she said, 'The things with which I am charged are true. If that is to be guilty, why then I am guilty!' So my lord sent away

264

the jury and he said, 'It now remains for me to pass sentence against you.'

Then they brought the black scarf and they laid it upon his head and he said the words that are uglier than any witch's curse and which, you would think, might blister a man's tongue. And he said it as though it were too heavy for him so that when he had finished his voice came out in a great sigh. But Philip did not sigh."

They were silent both of them, remembering the girl standing there and smiling her wicked smile. Joan Flower said —and her voice came out in echo of that long-ago sigh—"The officer touched her arm to take her away but my lord judge spoke again.

'Do not think to escape the consequences of your crimes, for that is beyond any man to alter . . .'

'But not beyond the Master,' she told him.

He took no notice but went on speaking. 'If you will help the court by witnessing against the others, so that we may come at the truth, you may gain remission from God.'

'I desire no remission from your god. But I will speak that I may magnify the Master.'

And, do you remember, priest, how, when they would have put the Book into her hands she pushed it away, crying out, 'I would swear, rather, in the name of the Master. He will not fail to punish if I do aught amiss.'

The judge told her that without the Book her testimony would not stand; so she took the Book and she repeated the oath; and there were many that wondered the Book did not burst into flame and she shrivel to a cinder.

Then the judge said, 'Bearing in mind the oath you have sworn, you may speak freely.'

She folded her hands together as though she were a child and innocent—she that was neither.

'We are witches, my sister and I; and my mother was a witch also and she brought us into the coven. We made the pact and we bear the Mark. We went to the Sabbaths and we worshipped the Master. As for my sister, they said the Black Mass, and her naked body was the altar.'

At that there was a hush throughout the court, do you

remember, priest? And in the quiet Philip's voice rang true as a bell. 'My sister and I know very well how to cast spells; and she took her part in every spell we put upon the Earl and his family. Indeed, it was for her sake we moved in the matter at all.' "

Samuel Fleming nodded, remembering the girl standing there proud with her evil; and the stern face of the judge; and the sick face of Francis within his shadowing hand. And he remembered the judge had tried to speak and could not speak, so hard it was for him to look upon her without disgust—Sir Henry Hobert, the Chief Justice of England, well-inured to the wickedness of men.

Joan Flower said softly, "Yet it was not for spitefulness Philip testified. It was that Margaret must be condemned so that she might be snatched from the gallows and her soul not escape the hands of the Master. There was a great stillness in the room and into the stillness the judge spoke. 'We have heard enough. For what this prisoner testified before us, Margaret Flower has already confessed—except only that she took her part in bewitching the Earl of Rutland and the lady his wife. And though, like every prisoner that smells the rope, she now recants, yet the confession was signed with her mark.' And again he tapped upon the paper beneath his hand.

Philip said, very quick, 'There is a thing you have not heard. My sister made human sacrifice before the Master. Sir, she slew her own child.'

There was a hissing then went about the court but the judge only said, 'It is not in the indictment.'

'Then you may add it now,' she said, impudent. 'My sister was big with child; she had it out of Peate or Master Vavasour —or another, maybe; who knows? It was for that reason my lady turned her away. It was a child she did not want; she was glad to sacrifice it to the Master.'

'By what means?'

'She held it out and my mother drove a silver pin through to the brain. I was not there but my mother told me. And Ellen Greene will tell you and Joan Willimott, also. They were both at the Sabbath when it was done.'

Then the judge said slow and thoughtful, 'It is right that

every wickedness witches do should be brought out into the daylight. For there are still folk here and there who because they would be merciful do not inform against witches. But if these same folk understood the evil these creatures do, they would save their mercy for those innocents that have been bewitched and destroyed.' He turned to the clerk and said, 'Let the murder of the infant stand a while. If there are witnesses as the prisoner says, then you must add that, also, to the indictment.' "

Joan Flower looked full at Samuel Fleming. "Suppose the charges against Meg had not been hanging matters! Is it just that a crime which is a hanging matter be added to the charge and the prisoner not know of it until he come into the court?"

"It is not just," he said slow and troubled. "I have not considered it before, for it is the law. It is the law; but it is not just."

Joan Flower nodded. "My lord judge turned again to Philip. 'What did they do with the child they had murdered?'

'Sacrifice is not murder, lord; you must strike that word from the page. But all the same I will tell you what they did with the child. They let the blood flow into a basin; and they boiled the flesh that the fat might run; and when that was done they ground the bones. From the fat we make our ointments, and from the powder our charms.'

I could see how the judge swallowed in his throat and could not speak for disgust. Such niceness, priest, seeing how many he himself had sent to an ugly death!

'Poison?' he asked her at last.

She shook her head; the dark tails of her hair flew from left to right. 'Not from the fat and not from the bones. Our poisons we distil from herbs.'

'What do you do with your accursed ointments?'

'We anoint ourselves that we may fly.'

'Do you take upon your sinful bodies the glory of the angels?'

'Yes, lord. The angels of darkness.'

'How do you concoct your foul grease?'

'The fat of the stillborn is best, for that is the purest; and we can also use the fat of the new-born. But when we have not enough of one or the other, then we make do with what we may. We prefer infants unsoiled by baptism; but beggars cannot be choosers and we take them from the churchyard.'

There was a shudder ran through the room at that; do you remember, priest?"

"I remember." He would not ever forget it—the girl standing upright at the Bar where so many poor creatures had trembled . . . and the air of triumph all about her.

"And so she stood there, priest, smiling out of her slanted eyes 'and out of her slanted mouth and telling . . . but not telling all.

'This fat we mix with henbane and with cinquefoil; and we thicken it with white fine flour. Then we drop into it aconite and deadly nightshade and after that, batsblood. But do not think, lord, to make this ointment for yourself!' She sent him a mocking glance. 'You would fall to the ground and you would break your neck; and what would good folk do lacking so righteous a judge? For there are things we use but I will not tell them; nor how they must be gathered nor when.'

'You have told us enough,' he said again, and he shuddered. 'The fat of the unborn; the fat of murdered babes; the fat of little children clawed from a Christian grave.'

She stood there smiling and nodding.

'You have told us,' the judge said, 'that you distil deadly poisons. Have you ever given poison through the mouth?'

'Why yes,' she said. 'But not often. Poisons are hard to make—ingredients difficult to come by. But we gave some to the second child—to little Francis. A pinch; a pinch, that was all. It was to finish matters. He had to die. It was a pity to let him suffer. He was a nice child.'

Then, priest, there was a hubbub if you like! Men and women leaping to their feet and crying out and shaking their fists and the judge sitting there and his mouth moving and not a word to be heard."

"I remember," Samuel Fleming said and looked her in the eyes. "I remember the face of Francis, my friend . . . and how I dared not look at him again."

"Then, priest, the officer knocked with his staff upon the

floor; knocked again and again but they would not be still until the judge lifted his hand for silence."

And there, in the quiet of the Rector's bedchamber, it was as though they heard him speak.

I can take the prisoner no further at this time. Take her away. She shall be sent for again.

Joan Flower chuckled. "Old as he was and seasoned as he was, my girl was too much for him. And when they would have laid hands upon her she stiffened herself and they could not move her until she had finished speaking.

'I serve the Master who is the old God; I honour and glorify Him. And, Judge, know this! All over this country—as over all countries of Christendom—in castle and in cottage, there are witches who hate your Christ and work the will of the old God. And day by day our number grows. For ours is a joyous faith, with music and dancing and the rites of love. And your sad faith can never stand against it. Kill me if you can! For every witch you kill, ten others will start up in her place.' "

They looked at each other, Joan Flower and Samuel Fleming, remembering how the judge had raised his hand more than once to stop her; and how he had let it fall, listening as though she had bewitched him too. And when she had made an end of speaking, 'Are you not afraid to die in your wickedness?' the judge had asked.

And they remembered how she had laughed aloud at that; and her laughter had rung true. 'For all your fine speeches and for all your fine laws, for all your gaolers and your gallows, you cannot harm me—save by the will of the Master. And that you should hang me is not his will. He has allowed you to cast me into prison, that He may the more show his power—your stinking prison, where men and women rot in the name of your righteous laws and your righteous god. It is no clean death they come to but a filthy one. And they do not come to trial, many of them, but rot in the darkness until they are dead—Christian folk, good folk some of them, made in the image of your god . . . and your god allows it. As for me, my Master will not suffer you to touch a hair of my head that am his paramour and have borne his child.'

And, sitting there in the comfort of his room, Samuel

Fleming remembered one more thing, a thing so shocking, that even now the memory turned him sick. 'The woman is mad,' the judge had whispered bending towards Francis; and she, hearing the breath of his whisper in the stillness of the court, had turned at the door and cried out, 'Not I, lord. But you. You and all good men who condemned your god to the agony of the cross.'

"Would you say she was wrong?" Joan Flower asked, sly.

"I despair," he said and covered his eyes. "I shall never win your soul."

"Do not be too sure," she said. And when he lifted his surprised head the room was empty. He rose, a little stiff, and went to the window. It was full morning now; and from the budding plum tree a starling mocked him with what might have been the sound of her laughter.

Chapter Twenty-four

AND, standing there, he heard in the quiet house the clack of Hester's pattens down the stone passage. Her head turbanned in a flowered kerchief came round the door. In the afternoon she would be as fine as my lady countess herself; but in the morning she was satisfied to turn her hand to any small thing. The rest of her person followed, looped petticoats, wooden pattens and all.

"Why!" And she looked with reproach at the untouched cup. "Did you not care for the coffee? Well, well, it is cold and you cannot drink it now. Besides it is time to set your chamber to rights; the study has been ready this long while."

"I will walk in the garden," he said.

"Do not walk too long," she advised. "I shall have a posset for you at ten."

He nodded his thanks.

"Do not forget your hat and cloak. You grow forgetful . . . a little." And then, lest she had seemed to criticize, said gently, "Dear Samuel, do not wander too far." He promised to remember and dropped a light kiss upon her cheek.

He came out into the spring sunshine and felt his sluggish blood run livelier for it. He stepped out with something of his old briskness and walked without thinking, so it seemed, for his feet led him out of the garden and down the little street and along to the patch of trees where the empty house stood.

The blind windows gaped and grass grew among the thatch. The door stood ajar as though inviting him. He pushed it open; and the sunlight came in with him.

It was neat and clean within; and he was not surprised to see Joan Flower sitting there by the hearth. He went over and sat down on the rough stool no-one had thought worthwhile to carry away.

"Both my girls were born in this place," she said when they were sitting one each side of the empty hearth. "In one place they were born; and in one place they died.

They had carried Meg back to the dark cell and there she lay and did not know that even now, Philip was standing her trial. She knew nothing, not even whether it was night or day. For now that she had denied everything the tormentors were at her again. Her poor body, you would have thought, could take no more punishment. Even you, priest, had you seen her, must have said she had suffered enough."

"There is no suffering too great to save a soul," he said; but his answer came slowly.

"Might not great suffering break a soul?" she asked.

He sent her a startled look. How had she known his innermost thought, a thought so hesitant he had hardly recognized it himself?

"It might well be so!" she said and nodded. "You have a good heart and would hurt neither man nor beast for wantonness; yet you think it right to torment these poor creatures. Surely you Christians are over-fond of suffering!"

"But she was saved," and it was almost as though he comforted himself. "God showed his mercy."

"That does not excuse the cruelty of men," she said and again he started; she had uttered his own secret, scarce-realized thought. "When a man is given licence to hurt his fellows, even the good man becomes corrupt; and the desire to save souls becomes the desire to hurt bodies."

"It is true and it is hateful," he said. "But who shall question the ways of God? She called to Him and He saved her."

"Priest," she cried out very sharp, "had my girl been innocent, still she would have suffered those same torments. Must I tell you again and again?"

"Still you must leave it to God. For you cannot leave it to the Devil."

She shrugged and took up her tale.

"Meg lay there deaf and blind when Philip came back to the cell. She stared, impudent, at your officers that still stood about Meg, ready with fresh torments to make her speak. 'You had best leave her in peace,' she said, insolent. 'And you would do well to wash her face and comb her hair. At any moment she will be called; and how will it look for you?'

The turnkey nodded at that; and he and your tormentors went out together.

Philip made a dancing step in the dark cell and only the crowded bodies stopped her short. She was gay as a thrush. She had been condemned to die but it did not touch her at all —she did not believe she would ever hang by the neck. She had enjoyed her trial. She had stood there, all eyes upon her; she had spoken freely to the judge and he had let her speak. And she had drawn the rope so tight about her sister's neck that Meg must call upon the Master to unloose it.

The excitement in her blood would not let her rest. She was to be asked yet more questions; and she could not wait for the moment to return to the court. But the judge was at his mutton; and, you, too, no doubt, priest, with the other magistrates; all of you sitting very comfortable together in *The White Hart*.

Philip cheerfully munched at the mouldy bread and drank the stale water—for the first turnkey was back again, and all the time she kept going over and over within herself the things she would say. Her eyes were bright and the blood was in her cheeks; and the others, seeing this, began to hope a little . . . all except Meg who slept in the dirt of the floor.

Within the hour the turnkey came again and bade her go with him into the court. You would have thought her bound for the Sabbath the way she followed all eager to be there.

'Philippa Flower,' the clerk cautioned her, 'you must be sworn again. My lord is about to ask you some questions.' She took the Book in her hand and again the judge warned her, 'The answers you shall give cannot help you in any way; for you have been judged and sentenced according to the law; and soon you must face your Maker. But upon the words you shall speak may hang the life of others—and hang, indeed; this you know. Therefore consider well before you speak. Was your sister Margaret concerned in the death of the children of the Earl of Rutland?'

'Lord,' she said, 'we were concerned equally.'

'Was she concerned to bewitch the Earl and his lady so that they should have no more children?'

'We were concerned equally,' she said again. 'All three.'

273

'Would you like to consider again of your answer?' he asked, very grave.

'I am sworn to the truth,' she reminded him. 'My sister was as hot about the business as I was. And what could you expect? We were two poor girls that had lost their sweethearts.' She turned about and fixed Tom Simpson with a wicked eye so that he trembled white as any bone and all-but slid to the floor. 'He was a poor thing,' she said smiling, 'and not worth grieving for.'

There was a titter ran through the room at that. But the judge did not smile.

'This is no playhouse,' he said, 'but a court of life and death. Therefore search your mind well before you let your tongue wag. Do not doubt that I am set to uncover the truth about the bewitching of the lord and his lady. Tell us what you did when you cast the spell that they should have no more issue. Neither add nor take away but tell it step by step, word for word.' Priest, what did it matter? There was enough against Meg already to hang her three times over."

"It was that wise men might consider the spell—whether it might be broken while yet there was time."

She nodded. "That is plain commonsense. 'When you cast a spell,' Philip began; but he interrupted her very stern. 'Speak only for yourself.'

She sent him a smile—the wicked smile poor Tom knew too well. She began again. 'When we cast a spell we must have something belonging to the one we are to bewitch. We had such a thing; my lady gave it when she cast off my sister. It was the mattress upon which my lady countess had lain together with my lord. It belonged to them both . . . we could not have done better. We unripped the mattress and we took out the wool . . .'

'Whom do you mean by *we*?' the judge asked.

'My mother, my sister and myself; all three, as I have said.' "

"So she lied!" Samuel Fleming said.

"Of course! Philip was not there to save Meg's body but to save her soul for the Master—if it could be done."

"It could not be done," he said.

"No," she sighed, "no!" She brightened again. "Do you remember, priest, how every face was turned towards my girl?"

"I remember one face . . . one face, only."

She nodded. "The face of my lord earl. His hand sheltered it; but for all that I saw it clear. Cankered . . . withered. And do you remember the quiet in the court—silence as for a queen? And, into the silence, Philip's voice clear as a sharp little knife telling them everything. How we had set the kettle upon the fire and cast into it the feathers and the wool together with our own blood; and how we had stirred the mixture turn and turn about and how we had recited the words.

'Repeat the words, witch!' the judge commanded. And she, hands folded as though to pray, began,

Blast seed, curse womb . . .

There was a sudden, sharp, noise; a chair went screaming backwards. My lord earl could endure it no more.

Philip gave no sign; she stood still as though in prayer; only her voice rose a little that it might go with him,

> Blast seed, curse womb,
> Sink, sink into the tomb.
> Weep, weep for daughters fair,
> Weep yet more for son and heir.
> Empty heart and empty hand,
> Master, hear me where I stand.
> Sink, sink into the tomb,
> Blast seed, curse womb.

She finished and there was no sound in the room. It was, priest, as though she had cast a spell to bewitch you all.

At last the judge spoke and his voice came out like that of a sick man. 'Such evil. The mind cannot take in the half of it.'

'What your hand finds to do, do it with your might,' Philip said in no way abashed. 'So it stands in your scriptures. And it is a true saying. My mother was half-hearted in this business and so she came to an evil end. She would have set a term of years to the lady's barrenness. Seven years. Seven years!' she said again and she laughed.

'And do you not consider seven years sufficient?' the judge asked, very drily.

'Why, no!' she said at once. 'The lady had robbed us of our sweethearts for ever!'

'In seven years will the curse be lifted?' the judge asked her then.

'No, lord,' she said and laughed. 'We held fast, my sister and I, against our mother and we prevailed!' "

Samuel Fleming covered his face with his hands.

"Priest," Joan Flower said, gently, "she lied. The term was set. I have told you before. Seven years. Not more. Not less."

"But we believed her," he said and groaned. "Francis and Cecilia believed her . . . I think there will be no more children."

"That was why she lied."

"She deserved to die," he said, remembering the stricken faces turned towards the smiling girl. It was as though they, not she, had been condemned to die.

"I thought the judge would never speak," Joan Flower said. "But he spoke . . . he spoke."

And sitting there one each side of the empty hearth they remembered both of them the waiting stillness of the court and the judge speaking at last, his voice coming out on the breath of his sighing.

'Such wickedness in the course of a long life, I have never, by God's Grace, heard before; and, by that same Grace, trust never to hear again. I am amazed not only at your wickedness and at your cruelty; but that you have willingly given your soul to the Devil to damn it for everlasting.

The noble Earl of Rutland has suffered grievous loss at your hands. But he has borne it with a most Christian patience, believing that it had pleased God to inflict on him such a fashion of visitation. But now it has pleased God to disclose the matter in his own good time.

You stand here, a witch by your own confession; and you have been sentenced to the only punishment I can inflict—death by hanging. Alas, that I cannot send you to the fire as they do in countries more zealous than our own. If it were in my power to add to your punishment by burning I would do it. For, if in your own flesh you might feel a little of that agony you have inflicted upon others—and those others innocent of all malice towards you or anyone—then you might at the last

276

repent; though I much doubt it, seeing how you have borne yourself here in this court with lewdness and with laughter. Your sentence I have already pronounced; and nothing remains for me to say but *God have mercy upon your soul.*'

And Samuel Fleming remembered how the girl had answered impudent as ever, 'You do me good service seeing that you send me to join Him who is my Master and my paramour.' And then the voice of the judge, very sharp, 'I trust you will think so when you join him.' And she, quick upon his words, 'Be very sure I shall!'

Quite suddenly her face had changed. 'You shall never hang me,' she had cried out all anger and spite. 'He will not suffer my foot to be moved, no, nor one hair of my head to be plucked.'

Yes, he remembered her eyes and her mouth . . . the tongue flicking like a snake, a little red snake. And how they had sat, all of them, staring at her. There were some that had expected the Devil himself to appear and carry her off then and there . . .

"And so He would have done had He been honest!" Joan Flower's voice chimed with his thoughts. "Priest, it was then I knew He would lift no finger. Had He meant to save her that was the time. What better moment to declare his power, to snatch her from beneath the noses of priests and magistrates; from beneath the great nose of my Lord Justice himself? Such a tale would have rung the length and breadth of Christendom, to confound scholar and simple alike. But she left the court like any other prisoner that is condemned to die —she that had been the Master's love.

And so, priest, I saw one daughter bound for the gallows; and I knew that in a little while, the other must follow.

It was growing towards evening when they brought Meg again into the court—but morning or evening, it was all one in that dark place lit by the flickering candles.

Now there was a new charge against her—the murder of her own child. I need not tell you, priest, they had lost no time! Already the evidence was set down against her—signed and sealed; but she knew nothing of it."

"Yet it was true," Samuel Fleming reminded her.

"Yes, it was true. But it might have been false; that is a thing to remember. So there she stood, a poor ignorant creature, feeble with lack of sleep and with ill-treatment. I tell you, priest, she was scarce able to follow the charges, let alone reply to them . . . and there was no-one to help her.

Yet she who was never brave showed courage now. Cast off by God and by the Devil, yet she would speak the truth. She stood leaning against the bar and listened to the Clerk of Assize.

'Margaret Flower, this morning, in this court, you heard the charges against you to which charges you pleaded not guilty. Those charges I will now repeat.'

She stood there, her eyes closed and the words passed over her head. Then he said, 'There is now a further charge against you . . .'

She opened her eyes at that and I saw how she listened that she might understand.

'. . . that you, not having the fear of God before your eyes . . .'

At that she nodded gently.

'. . . and being seduced by the instigation of the Devil . . .' and she nodded again, 'did in the year of grace, sixteen hundred and twelve, against the peace of our sovereign lord the King, his crown and dignity, murder . . .'

She looked up at that, priest, she was puzzled by the word. Her hand went to her breast; she leaned more heavily against the bar.

'. . . your new-born child. How say you, Margaret Flower, are you guilty or not of this most wicked crime?'

For a little space she stood silent and her eyes were closed. Then she lifted her head and spoke. And, priest, let me go to heaven or to hell, I shall remember the way she looked and the words she spoke. I shall never be free of them.

278

'Being seduced by the Devil and forgetting God which is in heaven, I am guilty of all the charges save one. Of bewitching my lord earl and his lady I am innocent. I was not willing; and therefore my mother and my sister put me without the door; and they took the mattress and the pillow to work the spell, but I did not give it them.' "

Joan Flower's voice trembled and dropped into silence. They sat there remembering, both of them, how there was no sound at all in the court; and then the small rustle of robes as the judge turned towards the jury.

'The prisoner has pleaded guilty to every charge in the indictment against her but one. And though she is already condemned out of her own mouth, you must now consider that one charge she denies—that is the charge of bewitching the noble Earl of Rutland and the lady his wife that they may have no more children—and return the verdict that no man hereafter may question the justice of this court.'

And sitting together in this very room where Margaret had first opened her eyes to the light, they remembered both of them—the mother that bore her, and the priest that baptized her—how the jurors did not leave their places but looked and nodded one to the other; and how it needed no man to ask the verdict . . . and how all the time the prisoner stood there watching them. She did not tremble when the clerk asked the verdict; and at the word *guilty* she did not tremble.

It was only when the judge raised his head and looked at her to pronounce sentence, that she began to shake as with an ague.

'Margaret Flower, you have pleaded guilty to all the charges in the indictment against you, except one; and on that charge, also, you have been found guilty. And I am amazed not only at your wickedness but at your foolishness, that you gave yourself to the Devil, body and soul, whereby you are damned to all eternity.'

And they remembered how she had nodded, gentle and patient, so that when the judge—the black square upon his head—pronounced the sentence, he spoke the ugly words quietly and, as it seemed, gently also. And when he had finished, he asked, 'Have you anything to say why this sentence against you should not be carried out?' And *No*, she had whispered, and again, *No*.

And then, her eyes upon the judge and trembling still she had spoken.

'Lord, when a man comes to his hanging, then he is allowed to speak a few last words. Do me the grace to let me speak them now, for when I come to my death, fear will dry up my tongue.'

And those two, remembering together, could see it all as in a picture—small and faraway and very clear—she waiting and the judge nodding and the prisoner speaking.

'It is just that I should die the death. For though I had no hand in bewitching the lord earl and his lady, yet I took my part in the death of the little boys on whose sweet souls may God have mercy; and, also, of bewitching the lady Catharine. But she was a sturdy child and we could not harm her.

All these things which I denied before, I now confess. And I confess, also, to the charge that, I am told, now stands against me. I agreed to the death of my little child. But we did not speak of murder; we spoke only of sacrifice. I was not clear at that time as to the difference.'

'And you are clear upon the matter now?' the judge asked.

'Lord, I am clear.'

She stood silent for a little space and then she spoke again.

'The Devil is a hateful and deceitful master. There is no end to his lying nor to his cruelty. And I do implore you, all Christian souls, not to throw away your part in God, but to take example by me that stand before you here, where the Devil has brought me and lifts no hand to save me. Nor would I receive my life at his hands, if I could, knowing what manner of spirit he is. Good people, if by my dying, I have saved one Christian soul from the net of the Devil, then my wicked life and my shameful death will not have been in vain.'

"And so, priest," Joan Flower said and sighed, "she ran straight to the gallows."

"To salvation," he said.

"But the gallows came first. And . . . do you remember, priest, when they would have taken her away?"

He remembered; and it was a thing he would never forget

his life long. For the gaoler had laid a hand upon her arm and she had turned to go, stumbling a little upon her feet. Then, she had stopped suddenly and turned herself about; and she had looked not at the judge, but at Francis who sat by him.

'My lord earl,' she had said, 'you and your lady were ever good to me; and when she turned me from the Castle she had good cause. I have done you both so much evil I doubt you can forgive me, ever. But you are a merciful man and walk in the fear of God. So, if you cannot forgive me now before I am taken hence, if you could of your charity *try* to forgive me, then nod your head and I shall go to my death with a lighter heart.'

And Samuel Fleming remembered how, sitting in the court, he had prayed that Francis would show her this sign of grace. Yet, even while he prayed, he had doubted that any man could have enough of Christ within him to do as she asked.

Francis had made no sign; he had sat there like a man in stone. It was, Samuel knew, lest he break down and weep before them all, weep for his young children; and for the ruin of Cecilia's life and his own.

The gaoler had touched her again but not unkindly now; and she had begun to follow with slow step. Then she had stopped again; and for the last time held out her hands—her chained hands—towards Francis. Perhaps it was the chains; or perhaps Francis remembered then that for all her bent body and her white hair, she was young. Maybe the punishment that had withered her youth, and the certain death to which she must go, had moved him. Francis had tried to speak and could not speak. And then, at the last, he had managed to nod and his lips had moved in token of forgiveness. She had bowed her head then, and curtseyed to him with her stiff and twisted limbs and had gone stumbling from the room.

Chapter Twenty-five

SAMUEL FLEMING lifted his head. It was dark now in the deserted cottage and very cold. How had he come here? He remembered only walking along the road in the spring sunshine. Had he, indeed, followed that unquiet ghost, sat facing her through the lengthening hours? Or had he wandered in, unthinking, and fallen asleep? Whichever way it was, Hester would be troubled at his long absence.

He rose stretching his cramped limbs and shivering more than a little.

When he stepped out-of-doors he saw that the stars rode high and clear in the night sky; the budded branches of the elms were bespangled with jewels. It quieted his soul so that, for a moment, he forgot Joan Flower and her ugly tale.

But only for a moment.

"And so, priest, I saw both my children condemned to die." Her voice wailed like the wind in the quiet night; he felt his cloak move as in a light breeze.

"Hanging is no pretty matter, priest, as you would know, if ever you saw one. But you are liker to keep your nose in a book than lift your eyes to a hanging. Yet you should go. And, if you have no stomach to see them turned off—those you have helped to their death—why then you may look upon the gallows later where still they twitch and dance upon air. And I would recommend you to look upon the face . . . and especially upon the eyes.

Oh priest, could I have cried to your god, why then I had cried; for in our anguish we cry for mercy where we must least expect it. And could I have cried to my god, why then I had cried, also; for we cry for mercy where no mercy dwells.

In the dark cell Philip was merry as a starling singing her lewd songs; but Margaret knelt apart, her whole being set upon finding the lost words of prayer. She would send her thoughts back to childhood, remembering her father and the way he had prayed with her; and she would beat upon her forehead with clenched fists as one knocks upon a closed door; and here she would find a word and there she would find a word—words long lost and now found again. She would sit for hours stringing them together now in this order, now in that, mouthing to hear how they might sound . . . *lead* . . . *lead* . . . *lead us into temptation.* Surely that was right! But—*Lead us into temptation* . . .? She would shake her piteous head. One little word escaped her."

Above its dark walls, the windows of the Rectory shone with light and he quickened his step. The garden gate stood open, and he saw the front door a rectangle of light; and, dark against it, the lamp high above her head—Hester.

"Samuel," she called softly anxious. And again, "Samuel."

"You must go," Joan Flower said, "and I must come with you. For the thing between us must be finished one way or the other." She put her hand upon him; it was the first time she had touched him and he trembled with cold so that he all-but fell.

Hester came running to meet him. "Where have you been?" she asked sharp; and yet tender, too. "I have called you this long time; yes, and we have searched for you as well. Come!"

He went obedient and followed her in.

    ·   ·   ·   ·   ·

He sat up in the warmth of his bed and he was trembling still; his hand about the tankard of hot ale shook and he was forced to set it down. His eyes went this way and that. Joan Flower was not there as she had promised. He was glad of it. He could not endure, at this moment, to go back over the whole thing—to the very end, until his heart broke. Still less did he desire to sleep; in sleep we are defenceless against our dreams.

His head nodded. He jerked himself awake. He was in his own room, thank God; his own bed. And yet, he was on the Bench along with Eresby and Pelham; and before them Joan Willimott kneeling. The bedroom and the courtroom were both there, like two drawings, superimposed the one above the other. And it was not strange but natural.

Willimott was kneeling and they could not get her to stand; and she was talking and they could not get her to stop.

Yes, sirs, I have a spirit and it is called Pretty. And it was breathed into my mouth by William Berry over at Langhorne . . .

"That was an ill thing she did!" And there was Joan Flower standing by his bed and whispering his own doubts. "She named one that was never mentioned in the matter before and she brought him to the gallows."

He turned to Joan Flower; and all the time Joan Willimott knelt there and her lips moved.

"He was innocent." Joan Flower nodded. "Such a spirit she had but he did not give it to her. When you hurt prisoners to make them speak or promise them favour, then you will always get false witness. It is not hard to understand. So she brought a good man to his death."

Joan Willimott kneeling before them reached up and plucked him by the sleeve. He struggled to come back again to the warm room, the familiar room; but the fear in her eyes held him back.

I did no harm, sir. I never harmed anyone my life long. I did good, sir . . . I cured sick folk . . . not harm but good.

He turned and moaned in the bed.

"She was guilty." Joan Flower's voice quieted him. "I have seen her raise a storm by writing in the dust. She was a dirty soul; not worthy of your god or of mine. It was well you hanged her when you did, before she thought of more innocents to drag to the gallows along with her."

He did not hear her. His eyes were on the wretched old woman with her palsied hands lifted towards him. She was still talking when they dragged her away on her knees.

Joan Flower bent to him in the bed. "She had no pity for anyone; not even for Ann—the child she brought to the rope."

"The other one," and his voice came out in a wail. "Ellen Greene, she is coming . . . she is coming. We must judge her; and I am broken with my doubts."

"That is another for whom you need waste no tears," Joan Flower said. "She was guilty. She betrayed those that served the Master; and she brought to their death innocent souls that served your god."

284

"But for all that I wish the thing undone. Look at her where she weeps."

"Those are not tears. She has a sickness of the eyes; she is all-but blind."

"They are tears," he said.

"Witches cannot weep." Joan Flower's voice came to him as he sat among the justices, the bright quilt crumpled still beneath his hand. "And she is a witch if ever there was one. Listen where she stands betraying her friends."

The evil came from the Flowers; from the one that is dead, and from those that are to die. But most of all it came from Joan Willimott. She had other spirits, Master, besides the little lady. One was like to a kitten that could work no harm; but it was no kitten and it worked harm aplenty. And the other was like a mole but it was no mole. And they would jump upon her shoulders, the one black and the other white, and they would suck upon her ears. And she sent them forth to injure a man and his wife; and it was Anthony Gill and his wife; and they died both of them within the fortnight. But I never worked ill in all my life and I have no familiar and I am no witch . . . and . . .

And now they were taking her away; and though her place was empty, he could still hear her high, thin screaming and the retching of her sobs.

And now they were bringing in the child, the simple child. He could not look. Dear Christ, let him not look!

He turned and twisted from side to side. Joan Flower put out a hand and he was back again in his bed.

"It was Ann that suffered most," Joan Flower said. "Ann that knew nothing and had no wit to lie. They would not let her alone; they were forever working upon this simple child that should have been one of your god's lambs. I saw them at their cruel tricks. Let us hope your god keeps his account of what is done in his name. Once I saw her head pulled back sudden and sharp by the hair, so that I thought it must crack. But they were too clever for that! Break the neck! There was a time and a place for it. And once I saw a woman bring a sly coal between the tongs and drop it within the childish breasts. Here is one devilmark the more, the woman said and laughed . . . one of your good women, priest.

Oh priest, priest, could you not see when they brought her before you that this was a child and a simple one? And the things she testified were so foolish, it might have made an angel weep. Could you not see that this child was God's fool rather than the Devil's?"

"She consorted with witches," Samuel Fleming said, sighing. "And her testimony though childish was damning. I am a priest. I could not save the body and so damn the soul."

"Was it as simple as all that? Was there no anger in your heart, no loathing? Do not blind yourself with talk of compassion; there was little of it in your heart then."

She was silent awhile; then she said, "You knew her well; a child given to dreaming and not knowing dream from truth. Her testimonies were not such as witches give but rather as a sick child might fancy; or one of your saints, perhaps, with their strange notions. She saw a hand reach down from the sky; a flash of fire leap from the ground. Is this stuff on which to hang a human soul?"

He said—and his body shook with sighing, "She confessed to a spirit; a good spirit, she said, in the shape of a white dog."

"Oh priest, did you not know better? The girl wandered in her wits; she would stand or sit or come or go; and not know where she might be. And the dog her father gave her; and it was white. And it appeared good to her; and it *was* good to her, seeing it led her home. As for a spirit, I doubt she knew what such a thing might be. She had heard the word—Joan and Ellen often used it. And so she used it, also, thinking perhaps it was a word for animal. I think your God, for all his enduring mercy, will remember it against you."

He lay there shivering with cold. She bent and picked up the quilt where it had fallen upon the floor. "You lack your quilt," she said and put it about him. "Yet, lacking it you have still good bedcovers; yes, and a warm fire, likewise. Think then of them that lay shivering in your cold cells."

A tear burst from under his closed lids, and then another; lay in dark spots upon the quilt's brightness.

"You weep," she said, "though all is past and we are dead —all, all dead. Think, instead, of them that lie even now in your cruel prisons waiting for what is yet to come."

"I do not weep for justice done," he told her. "I weep because I did justice without compassion."

"It is something to weep for," she conceded, "yes and to tremble at likewise. But—" she shrugged, "those that wait for death in your stinking cells have more cause to tremble and to weep.

For Meg and for Philip time was nigh spent. The day of their hanging was fixed. Mid-march; the eleventh day. It is a pity to die in March, priest. For March is the month of growing; and the air is sharp with the smell of life. New buds break; and there is the scent of violets; the earth shines purple through the wet green and the birds are singing fit to break your heart . . . and you going to your death. But then it is never a good time to die—especially by the rope—unless you are sure of your joy hereafter, as martyrs are. One might call Philip a martyr."

"You blaspheme," Samuel Fleming said; but he said it gently.

"I think not, priest. For Philip was steadfast in her faith and certain of her joys. It needs a martyr's faith to be steadfast in your prisons.

I tell you, priest, once you are within—be you innocent or guilty—you had best say *ay* when the justices want *ay*, and *no* when they want *no*. For it is better to die quickly by the rope than to rot in the filth or to go crazy with the pains they put upon you.

You are a priest and you are a justice. You serve God and the King. But what do you know of the things that are done in the name of both? The King cares nothing; he is like any fine gentleman. But your god? Will not he enquire it of you one day?"

He said, "You are right, I am not fit to be a priest or a justice."

"Yet," she said, gentle in the face of his humility, "I think you will not find the way to heaven too hard. But time grows short." She looked with something like compassion upon his thin body that scarcely lifted the bedcovers. "Soon the tale will be told and I shall come here no more."

"Then I shall miss my friend," he said and smiled a little.

287

"If priests were merry as well as good," she told him, "there would not be, perhaps, so many witches. Philip was right, maybe, when she said ours is a joyous faith; and your crucified god cannot stand against it."

"Did Margaret find it joyous? Or Philippa herself in the end? And you; how did you find it?"

Her eyes fell before his. "There were times I asked myself if there was nothing beyond junketing and coupling. There were times I thought upon the cleanness of heaven. But it was too late."

"It is never too late."

"Not though I have sold my soul?"

"It was not yours to sell. It was ransomed long and long ago. Margaret was right."

"Do you not promise eternal damnation to those that traffic with the Devil?"

"There is always hope of repentance. I think you have always known it."

"How should I know it? I had to die before we could talk face-to-face. Oh priest, you were too grand for me, hobnobbing with the gentry up at the Castle and not caring overmuch for the ignorant and the poor."

He wanted to tell her that it was not true; that he loved all men alike—his brothers. But how should she believe him? She was wrong about the ignorant and the poor. He did love them, down to the poorest, the most ignorant. Yet it had never been easy for him to show them his heart. His scholarship, his tastes, his very priesthood, God forgive him, had stood between them.

"I am a bad priest," he told her, humble.

"Not bad; but too fine. Had you been less fine you might have helped us more. Nor can I forgive you, quite, that you did not visit my girls in the prison. Certainly there were priests, but not you. Some of them were good men, maybe; but I never saw them. They carried themselves not like priests but like lickspittle servants of the law. They would not ask mercy on any man's soul until that soul was shrivelled to a parched pea with their questions and their threats. Yes, even at the gallows, there they would stand; and though some poor soul might thirst for prayer as a sick man for water, still these gentry would be at their games. And once I have heard the hangman himself cry out, *Away and torment them no more. Think shame to yourself! For these poor souls buy mercy with their death.*"

Samuel Fleming groaned at that and she said, "It was just such a one that came to Margaret in the cell; a surly dog that yapped at her heels even to the gallows. Oh, why were you so fine, priest? It does not become a priest to be a fine gentleman and a great scholar but only to serve his God and to be merciful and gentle with rich and poor . . . and especially with the poor since the burden of life is heavy upon us.

And so the last night came. You are a good man, priest, a friend to your god. But if you knew you must die tomorrow —even though it were in the comfort of your bed and those you love about you and prayers for your passing—would you be so eager for the morning? And, would you not be a little afraid? Think then of them in the dark and stinking cell . . . a few small hours between them and a cruel death.

I stood always within my corner; and the smell of their pain struck upwards to my naked soul. All they suffered, I suffered. And more . . . more. I suffered with Margaret that must come to her death—and no hope of your god or of mine. And with Philip I suffered yet more—knowing what she did not know—that in the last agony she must find herself betrayed; and the betrayal for eternity. For the face that had kissed her face would be turned away as she struggled and span upon the rope.

But most of all I pitied Ann that suffered and knew not why. She would kneel by Meg until her frail bones ached, praying that God—your god, priest, remember that—would take away the black fear that hung all about her and that it would be bright morning again. And having prayed, she would take Meg by the hand and whisper how they two would go back to the cottage together and the white dog with them. And maybe, if they served Him well, God would give them a little baby to care for; and they would live happy for the rest of their lives.

But you hanged her instead, priest."

Chapter Twenty-six

"You hanged her instead," Joan Flower said and her ghost's eyes stared into his. "I wish you had seen her, priest, the simple child, walking to the gallows between the two old women that had brought her there . . . walking; and puzzled a little, and not knowing truly what was to come, but smelling trouble as the simple do; and all the time fear growing

I think she was not full awake until she came to the gallows-piece and there the sight of the gallows awakened her fast enough! Oh priest, I wish you had been there to see how she stared and the eyes starting from her head; and how she looked this way and that and began to cry—which showed she was no witch; but the madness of your good folk blinded their eyes. And she would have turned to run but they put their hands upon her and lifted her into the cart. And she turned and twisted under their hands and she began to scream—the thin, high scream of a rabbit in the trap. And she called upon your god . . . and the sound of her crying might have made him weep; but he let them do it. And she cried upon her mother that was dead; and she would have leaped over the side of the cart but they held her fast; and they put the rope about her neck. She was, you may believe it, full awake there in the cart beneath the gallows and the rope about her neck.

And so she died, little Ann Baker with her nonsense about a great hand reaching from heaven—from heaven, mark you! She was innocent; but your law murdered her as surely as any witch by any spell. I think, priest, your god will remember it against those that did it."

He covered his face with his hands. "We may not suffer a witch to live. So we are commanded."

"She was no witch. And—*who* commands? Is it to be found in the sayings of your Lord Jesus? I think not. You will find it in the older Scriptures. When you hang a witch you obey the old God and not the new. Your god commanded you to mercy.

I deserved to die; and Margaret and Philip; and Joan and Ellen. But what we deserve, and what mercy is prepared to grant, are two different things. The plain truth, priest, is this. You are not worthy of your god any more than I was worthy of mine. You cannot reach to infinite good, nor I to infinite evil. For between these two, the poor human soul faints and loses its way.

But it is not of ourselves we should be thinking now but of those that were to die. They lay upon the filthy straw that no man had changed since they were thrust within; and upon it for nearly three months they had slept and eaten and relieved themselves. And this night, this last night, their bowels ran with their fear; and the stink of their fear—be not so nice, priest, since it was they, not you, that must endure it—was enough to make a man retch. You say, you good Christians, that a man should go clean before his Maker and therefore you pray at his passing. But, if the body be stained with filth, does the soul take no stain, no stain at all?

So there they lay sleepless throughout the long night hours that were all too short. Joan Willimott and Ellen Greene lay without hope and full of fears; though they had not as yet come before the judges the smell of death was in their nostrils. In the foul straw Meg knelt, and Ann knelt with her. Now and again, Ann—her simple thoughts running still upon the cottage and the dog and the baby—would smile and nod.

But nothing could quench the spirit of Philip. She sang her lewd songs and curled her hair with the little comb she kept within her bosom. And when Joan and Ellen nodded towards sleep, she would wake them, crying out one thing or the other.

And once she cried out, 'You who are yet to face the judges know well what your end must be. You are as much condemned, and the rope about your neck, as we who must die in the morning. Do not think to count upon the mercy of men—even if it is promised you; no, not though the priest nor the great judge himself should promise it. For what that mercy is you already know. We have suffered as no woman should suffer. May those hands wither and rot!

You have but to stand strong through the short days to your trial; and after it, through the shorter hours before the walk to the gallows. And there the Master Himself will be waiting. And the rope shall fall from your necks; and He will carry you away in the sight of all your enemies; and they shall be confounded. Yes, you Joan Willimott and Ellen Greene that have denied Him. He will forgive your lies and your denials. You shall cast off your old tormented bodies and be forever lusty, taking your delight in love; and desire shall never fail. Yes, even you . . .' Philip twirled about and stretched her finger towards the kneeling child so that Ann started and came from her prayers and stared with wide eyes. 'You are stupid as a sick sheep; and what good He can get out of you I do not know. Yet He will save you also. So stands his word.'

Ann made no answer; the words that Philip spoke held no meaning for her; her eyes closed again above her folded hands. Her poor wits could never remember the words of prayer; but still she knelt. She was simple and she was innocent; and your god did not help her. Was he so merciful then that this one small thing he denied her?"

"Prayer is no small thing," Samuel Fleming said; "especially when we are near our death."

"You have all the answers, priest. This child stood at death's open door and your god did not hold out his hand."

"I believe He did . . . in his own way."

"Let us hope so," she said, very drily, "seeing how she died.

And so they knelt, those two, prayerless; and Ellen and Joan stared out of reddened, rheumy eyes. They themselves had knelt once; and I could see sweet memories flooding back to withered hearts . . . Churchgoing; clean, folded kerchief, clean, pressed gown. Easter and Harvest and Christmastide. Choir; words of the priest . . . and the sacrament. All these things they had thrown away; and what had they been given in return? Nothing. Nothing but fear and pain and the hatred of men; and, if not tomorrow, then the next day or the next, they must die a hideous death.

And they looked from Meg to Philip and back again.

'Take your choice—if you can,' Philip cried out. 'But what choice have you? Do not think their righteous god will receive you; no, never think it! For you do not repent but are

292

shaken with your coward's fears. As for these—' and she cast her spiteful glance at Ann and Meg, 'they do not pray; they have no words; and though they wear their knees to the bone, the Christian god will not hear them. You would do well, poor fools, to take what rest you may. As for me, I am for my bed. It is the last time—thanks be to the Master!—I lie upon filth.' And she curled up in the straw and was suddenly asleep.

Joan and Ellen stared down at her as though even in sleep she followed to spy upon them; then, saying no word one to the other, they crept towards Meg and knelt at her side like dumb beasts in that Manger—though not so innocent.

Pray they could not; yet the bent knees, the folded hands, the closed eyes brought a little comfort. Ann nodded where she knelt and Meg laid her gently in the straw; then they lay down all four, and slept.

Philip slept smiling; she lay upon her back, her arms clasped as though she embraced not her own breasts but a lover. Sometimes her body moved and trembled as in the act of love; and I heard her whisper, *How should You let me hang. You that so love my body?* And I understood how we may deceive ourselves with our longing and our dreaming.

The bitter March dawn stole in on the darkness. Philip sat up, stretching and throwing out her arms. And, now awake, she had no compassion upon them that snatched their moments of sleep but must wake them to their misery before need."

"Before need? Was there nothing needed?" Samuel Fleming asked. "No prayer?"

"The question does not come well from you! Meg asked for a priest and Philip laughed out sharp and bitter. 'You think their god will forgive you now you see fit to whine and crawl?' she asked.

'Their God is my God and Ann's God,' Meg said and held the child fast by the hand. 'And who can measure the mercy of God?'

'It is not the mercy of your god you will measure, but the length of the rope!' Philip turned her back upon her sister and spoke to Joan and Ellen; their peaked, pale faces looked towards her in the dirty light.

'Listen,' she said, 'for I have this last message for you. Last

night the Master came and lay with me; and He promised me
once more that you should not suffer the death. You have but
to magnify his name. But if you do not spit upon the name of
the Christian god, then certainly you will hang by the neck and
your tongue swell in your throat and your eyes grow upon
stalks for the crows to pick. And before the breath is out of
your carcasses the servants of the Master will tear your souls
from the flesh and shovel them into the Fire.'

Ann began to tremble so that the teeth rattled in her head.
Meg put an arm about her and spoke to Philip.

'You have given the message of your Master; now I give
you the message of mine. You are hard and you are stubborn;
but if you will repent now, even at this last moment, He will
listen and He will save.'

'Fool!' Philip cried out, 'lying, dying fool! For me the
glory and the bliss; for you the burning and the Pit.' And she
twisted on her heel. There was no doubt in her, nor any fear;
only bitterness and anger that they had betrayed the Master.

And now there came the jingle of keys and the door swung
open. The turnkey came in carrying a jug of crawling water
and a basket of green bread. For though a prisoner must die
for his sins, and though God may care for him, yet men do
not. So he goes hungry and thirsty to his death."

"Not hungry nor thirsty in the soul," Samuel Fleming
said.

"Meg went comforted to her death; but not by any
kindness of man. 'Sir,' she said to the turnkey, 'we are to die
today. And since there is no hope but in God, I pray you,
send us a priest.' "

Joan Flower was silent; then she said, "They brought her
a priest. But it was not you. You had baptized her, but it
was not you." Her voice came out in a wail. "It was not you,
Samuel Fleming, not you."

He bowed his head at that.

"The priest that came . . ." she said and choked upon
her anger.

"The priest that came?" he prompted gently.

"A gallows-bird."

"Yet he had been a priest," Samuel Fleming said, very

gentle, "and yet he was able to pray with her. Do you not think, daughter—" and it was the first time he had called her that, "it might have been God's way to show mercy to them both; to Margaret that saved her soul; and to the priest that, saving it, saved, perhaps, his own?"

"I could wish God less sparing of his tools."

"The stone that the builders rejected; we have considered it before," he reminded her. "And this priest whom men rejected, whom the Church even rejected, became the means of her salvation and his own."

"It might be so. For certainly she was comforted when they took the priest away. And comfort was still in her when she went to her death. For, very soon, the turnkey was back again and bade my daughters follow him.

Margaret stood up, very quiet; but flinching as human flesh must do. Philip, for all her rags and dirt, carried herself like a queen.

'Sister, Goodbye,' Margaret said and stretched out her hand but Philip struck it aside. 'It is indeed, Goodbye!' she said. 'I shall never see your white fool's face again . . . until I see it frying upon coals.'

Margaret stood there and her hand was outstretched still. And then, priest, I saw it. I saw the thing that fell shining upon the upturned palm. She felt it drop and looked. And looked again. I saw the smile that trembled on her bloodless lips. For her a miracle had been worked. A tear. Her own tear. She was weeping; she who had not wept for six long years. God had forgiven her. He had sent her this sign.

Weeping her tears of joy she went across to Ellen and to Joan and to Ann; and, finger in the blessed dew, marked each one upon the forehead. It was as though she baptized them afresh.

'That will not save you!' Philip laughed; but laughter was choked by the storm of her fury. She moved to the door, turned and spat towards the pale faces that swam in the dark of the cell. 'I look upon your coward's faces for the last time . . . until I come to fetch you—all three—for your last journey.' She laughed again and the turnkey laughed, too. 'That will not be long,' he said. 'The gallows are wide.'

And now, Ann, seeing that they were taking Meg away, ran forward but the fellow thrust her back, saying, 'No need of haste. Your turn will come soon enough.' Meg looked at Joan and Ellen—a last, long look. 'Take care of this little one,' she said. 'Let her not be too frightened. Pray, all three of you, Oh, pray. And, if you truly seek his mercy He will not turn away his face. Let us forgive each other now, that we may meet in heaven.' And she reached up and kissed them, all three.

So they went out those two, together. Together . . . and all the space of heaven and hell between them.

I followed them down the narrow passage where there was no light save from the lantern the fellow carried—and that was little enough. They slithered and slipped and water slopped upwards upon their bare feet. And all about them were the terrible prison noises, and all about them the terrible prison smell . . . the smell of dirt and pain.

They came at last into the prison yard; and their feet though blue with cold yet stood firm upon clean cobbles. And the March wind stirred their hair and their rags; and the spring sun was sharp as a sword so that they were forced to close their eyes and walk like blind things after the dark prison.

And they reached the courthouse where they had faced the great judge and heard the sentence that was now to be fulfilled. And there they halted; for at the door stood my lord sheriff in his warm scarlet robes and his furs and his great gold chain —and his officers with him; snug men also in their good coats. And there was a priest with them but he made no sign of greeting to them that were to die, nor offered any word of prayer; and if he spoke of forgiveness, I did not hear it. And, before them all went a man with a great sword lifted high before his eyes; and beside him a man bearing a stout stick that he might help them if they faltered by the way.

But neither in Margaret nor in Philip was there any faltering. They took their places in the sad procession. Margaret walked with downcast head but Philip carried hers high. And, as they began to move, the priest began to chant; but he might have saved his breath since the words brought neither comfort nor any hope to them that were to die. But they carried within them their own comfort. For, low against the chanting, I heard Philip whispering. You might have thought she prayed; and, indeed, she did pray. *Har Sathan, Sathan, come. Hail Master, Master save. Devil come, Devil save . . . come and save . . . save, save.* There was no sign of fear. That was to come. I knew it must come and my naked soul trembled.

Margaret walked beside her. She was saved. And joy blunted her fear. God would receive her. It was a mercy she had not dared expect. Her dim eyes were dark with tears, but they were tears of gratitude. She, too, murmured beneath her breath. She was repeating the Lord's Prayer; and when it was ended she started again. It was a treasure new-restored; she could not put it by.

And now the prison gate swung open. Their feet trod the world again where men and women go free about their business. But those two were not free; they were passing through this sweet world, they were going to their death.

And so the procession went its slow way; past the good comfortable houses of the good comfortable churchmen of the cathedral; where ladies peeped behind curtains to see the witches go by. But there was no need for the servants to peep; they were waiting with the rest down by the gallows-piece. And, as the procession passed the great minster that soars to the sky, Margaret halted and the procession with her.

She lifted her eyes all blinded with her tears—her blessed tears—and she crossed herself; and so stood and could not take her eyes away from this great symbol of God's strength and his glory. But the man with the stick would have no more delay and thrust her on.

In the street where the shops are, there was no buying and selling this morning—every shop was shut; and the booths facing them, where the gaol ditch runs, was shut, too. For when a man hangs, why then your good folk make holiday. There they stood waiting in the dirt of the road, to go with the prisoners and miss nothing of the fun.

And fun there was! It was muddy, priest, for rain had fallen overnight; and when there is mud, the prisoners, like as not, will stumble and fall. And that is a sight that can never be relished too often! So there they waited, the good

297

folk, ready with their lewd jests to those about to die. And who can blame them? Not you, Sir Priest-Magistrate, nor yet your judges. For is it not a rejoicing to see one's fellows done to death—and your own hands clean?"

"Is it not a holiday and a rejoicing to know that when the agony is over the soul returns, forgiven, to God?"

"Was it so with them that shouted? As for forgiving—do you think God forgave Philip?"

"Not then. How could He forgive her when she hankered still after the Devil and his filthy lust?"

"And so in the noise and the shouting, in the whistling and the vile insults, the procession turned the corner and came upon the gallowspiece.

Philip walked as though she did not see what waited there; but Margaret lifted her head that had been bent low, and when she saw the high crosspiece and the uprights; and the tall, tall ladder and the dangling rope, she, being weak with fasting and with prayer, and her eyes all blinded with tears, stumbled and fell. Then the fellow with his stick pulled her roughly to her feet and she stood there stained with mud. And the people laughed; your good people, priest. And Philip laughed also. That was the worst thing of all . . . Philip laughed, also.

But Margaret gave no sign. She had seen the gallows and she had seen the cart and the eyes darkened in her head. But God gave her strength. She climbed into the cart—the death-cart, priest—and stood there patient. She put her hands together to pray but the men seized them and tied them with a cord. She made no offer to struggle; not even when they put the cloth about her eyes—and that is when the poor soul that is to hang struggles most. Nor did she stir when she felt the rope about her neck.

And when all was done and the fellow stood back satisfied, she spoke and her voice though low was clear. 'May God forgive me and,' she turned her bandaged eyes towards the executioner, 'you, also. The Lord is my shepherd, I shall not want.' Then she stood very quiet—save for the great shaking of her body which was a thing she could not help—while the man on the high ladder tested the knot on the crossbeam.

But with Philip it was not so. Hers was a hard death. She ran lightly from her place and leaped within the cart; and, standing there, her head moved from right to left and back again. When they would have put the cloth about her head she stared so fierce and proud that they fell back. She let them put the rope about her neck—her little neck, and still her eyes went searching. Then one of the wags in your crowd of righteous folk cried out, *She looks for her lover. She looks for the Devil to save her!*

The crowd laughed. And she laughed, too—but not for long . . . not for long.

She lifted her head and saw the hangman testing the length of the rope and looking to the knot. Her laughter wavered and died. And I saw her face; the way the blood drained away, and how her eyes widened and darkened with horror. I have seen death, priest, and I have seen horror—this was not my first hanging. But such fear, such horror, I had never seen before. She cried out; but there were no words. Only the first shocking cry and then the long and fearful wailing.

And then I saw Margaret—Margaret, the despised, the coward, the fool. She turned her bandaged head and she lifted her pinioned hands, and, as best she might, made the sign of the cross towards her sister.

And the cart began to move . . . and I could look no more.

For though I was a witch, priest, that had delighted in evil, yet these were my daughters I had carried within the womb and brought forth in pain . . . and they were dying the death to which I had brought them. And though one had come to the end of her wanderings and was gathered to God's mercy, still, hanging is no sweet matter. And for the other—what a death was that! Cast-off and betrayed; and the power of the Master nothing. For either He could not or He would not.

In those last moments of her agony she knew the worth of the Master's words. She was indeed bound for Hell; but it was not the Hell of the Master's promise, it was the Christian Hell . . . eternal Pit, eternal pain."

Joan Flower's voice broke sharply; the quiet room was

full of sorrow, full of pain. He dared not stir the sorrow with his words; he could not assuage the pain. And then, into the silence she spoke at last.

"There was a thing you said before, priest. I asked, Could God forgive Philip? And you said, Not then.

Not then. And her voice held wonder. "Do you think even such as she shall come to Him at the last?"

"Who shall understand the Mystery of God or measure his compassion? Not I. Not you. But this I believe—there is no end to his mercy."

"Then there is hope for her, even for her; and for me, also . . . if you are right. And I pray you may be right. For I weary of wandering the eternal loneliness. And this house may receive me no more, nor any place where we have met and spoken one with the other. The tale is finished."

"Why did you come at all, Joan Flower? And who was it gave you leave?"

"Priest, do we end as we began—the same question, the same answer? I came because you called me, because you would not let me rest with your eternal questioning. Yet the answer is no longer so simple; I know that, now we have talked together. I know now I came also that you might understand the cruelty you have done, you and your good men with you. And that you now understand very well. For with all your faults and with all your blindness, you are certainly God's priest. And you, who believe in the everlasting mercy of God, know that man must show mercy also.

And for one more thing—and that I did not tell you before.

I think you loved me . . . once . . . a little. And because of that God let me come since he is a God of love. He knows well that where there is love, be it never so little, the Devil's way must turn in the end to God's way. And there are your questions answered.

And since all is finished now, and this is the last time I shall come, will you, priest, answer one last question for me. If God is as merciful as you say, shall we, in the end, meet before his throne?"

"I doubt I shall get so far," he said, humble.

"You will get there; and you will get there soon. But you will wait long and long enough for me. For you purposed much good and did a little evil; and I purposed much evil and did a little good. And God, I think, is not only merciful; He is just. I am the stone the builders rejected—for my Master will have none of me. And, though I cannot hope to be a cornerstone in heaven, yet in the end God may make use of me . . . even of me.

And, priest, I believe we shall meet again and know each other. And however long that time may be, still you will not forget me, not though human time falls broken before the patience of God. For you loved me once, a little; and you might have loved me more . . . had things been different. But you are a gentleman and I was not a lady and did not know the ways of gentlefolk. Yet, even then, I might have been your wife, for I was quick to learn. Ah well, that is all guessing, since you were a priest and I was a witch. But, because you might have loved me—did, indeed, love me that little—let us say Goodbye as lovers use."

He felt a touch upon his lips cold as death. It was a coldness that set him shivering so that he thought he must die of it. He saw the outline of her body begin to thin, to melt. He was touched with an acute sense of loss and put out a hand as though to hold her back; but she shook her sorrowful head.

And now, the door opened; and through the thinning mist of her body, he looked across at Hester. She turned her head this way and that, calling softly. "I cannot find the cat," she said, "I have searched and searched but I cannot find her anywhere."

"I think you will not find her ever again," he said, gently, and saw the all-but vanished spirit nod. "Well, it was a little wild thing and we must find you another."

She shook her head. "But still I must look. He is a clever little cat and good company. Puss, puss . . ." She went out of the door; he heard her voice grow faint along the passage.

It is cold, he thought, cold. But, *Poor folk are always cold in winter . . . sometimes they die of the cold.* She had said that—Joan Flower. And now, her kiss upon his lips, he thought, It is coldest of all when you are dead . . . and remembered the unfinished will. He was reluctant to rise, all cold as he was; but the unfinished will reproached him.

He climbed stiffly from the bed, and, bedgown about him, made the careful descent of the stairs. Now he stood in the dark study and his hands were so cold they scarcely obeyed him; yet he managed to light the candles upon the table. The wicks caught and the flames lengthened. He thought, surprised, It should be lighter in the room; and put out a hand to the drawer. It was so heavy in his hand, he could hardly move it and that surprised him, too. But for all that he managed to pull it open. He took out the will and spread it upon the table.

Dim eyes screwed against the candleflame, he made out what he had written.

> . . . and maintaining of a hospice for four poor women of this parish . . .

He lifted the pen and driving stiff fingers to their task, slowly and with difficulty, wrote,

> . . . together with such allowances of coal . . .

He stopped and considered . . . Coals to warm old bones in the pious evening of their lives. Or—he smiled a little—the not so pious evening. All human flesh, good and bad alike, is subject to wind and to cold.

His fingers tightened about the pen, drove on to the end. *Samuel Fleming,* he wrote; and laid down the pen.

SOME BOOKS CONSULTED

ANDREWS, W. . . *Bygone Lincolnshire*, Vol. II. 1891.

BERNARD, R. . . *Guide to Grand Jurymen.* 1627.

Bottesford Church records.

CONWAY, Moncure D. *Demonology and Devil Lore.* 1879.

DALTON, M. . . *The Countrey Justice.* 1618.

DARE, M. P. . . *The Church of St. Mary the Virgin, Bottesford, Leics., and its monuments.* 5th ed. Gloucester: British Pub. Co. 1955.

DAVENPORT, J. . . *The Witches of Huntingdon.* 1646.

DAVIES, R. T. . . *Four Centuries of Witch Beliefs.* Methuen. 1947.

ELLER, I. . . . *The History of Belvoir Castle.* 1841.

EWEN, C. L'Estrange . *Witch Hunting and Witch Trials.* Routledge. 1929.
Witchcraft and Demonianism. Heath. 1933.

HARLAND, J., *and*
  WILKINSON, T. T. *Lancashire Legends.* 1882.

HUEFFER, O. M. . *The Book of Witches.* Nash. 1908.

HUTCHINSON, F. . *An Historical Essay Concerning Witchcraft.* 1718.

JAMES I . . . *Daemonologie.* 1597.

KITTREDGE, G. L. . *English Witchcraft and James I.* 1912.

LANGTON, E. . . *Essentials of Demonology.* Epworth. 1949.

MacCULLOCH, J. A. . *Witchcraft.* (*In* Chambers' Encyclopaedia. Vol. XIV. Newnes. 1950.)

MATHER, Cotton, *ed.* . *Wonders of the Invisible World.* 1862.

MURRAY, Margaret . *The Witch-cult in Western Europe.* O.U.P. 1921.

NICHOLS, John . *The History and Antiquities of the County of Leicestershire.* Vol. II. Pt. 1. 1795.

NOTESTEIN, Wallace . *History of Witchcraft in England.* 1558–1718. O.U.P. 1911.

POTTS, T. . .	*Discovery of Witches in the County of Lancaster.* Edited by J. Crossley. 1845. (Chetham Soc. 6.)
RUTLAND PAPERS (Vols. I and IV)	*Royal Commission on Historical Manuscripts,* 1888. 1905.
SUMMERS, Montague .	*History of Witchcraft and Demonology.* Kegan Paul. 1927. *A Popular History of Witchcraft.* Kegan Paul. 1937. *Witchcraft and Black Magic.* Rider. 1946.
WHITE, William .	*History, Gazeteer and Directory of Leicestershire and . . . Rutland.* 1846.
WRIGHT, T. . .	*Narratives of Sorcery and Magic.* 2 vols. 1851.

AND THE FOLLOWING TRACTS AND PAMPHLETS

Collection of rare and curious tracts relating to witchcraft. 1838.

A Discourse on witchcraft as it was acted in the family of Mr. Edward Fairfax . . . in the year 1621. 1858–59. (Philobiblon Soc. Misc. 5.)

The Examination and confession of certain witches at Chelmsford . . . before the Queen's Majestie's judges, xxvi daie of July, anno 1566. 1864–65. (Philobiblon Soc. Misc. 8.)

The examination and confession of a notorious witch named Mother Arnold . . . at the Assise of Burntwood, in July, 1574. 1575.

A Tryall of witches at the Assizes held at Bury St. Edmunds . . . on the 10th day of March, 1664. 1716.

Tryalls of four notorious witches at . . . Worcester. [n.d.].

The Wonderful discoverie of the witchcrafts of MARGARET and PHILLIP FLOWER, daughters of JOAN FLOWER neere BEVER CASTLE. 1619.